AF568058

# AMICUS CURIAE

## Khaitan & Co is 100

Aditi Roy Ghatak

RUPA

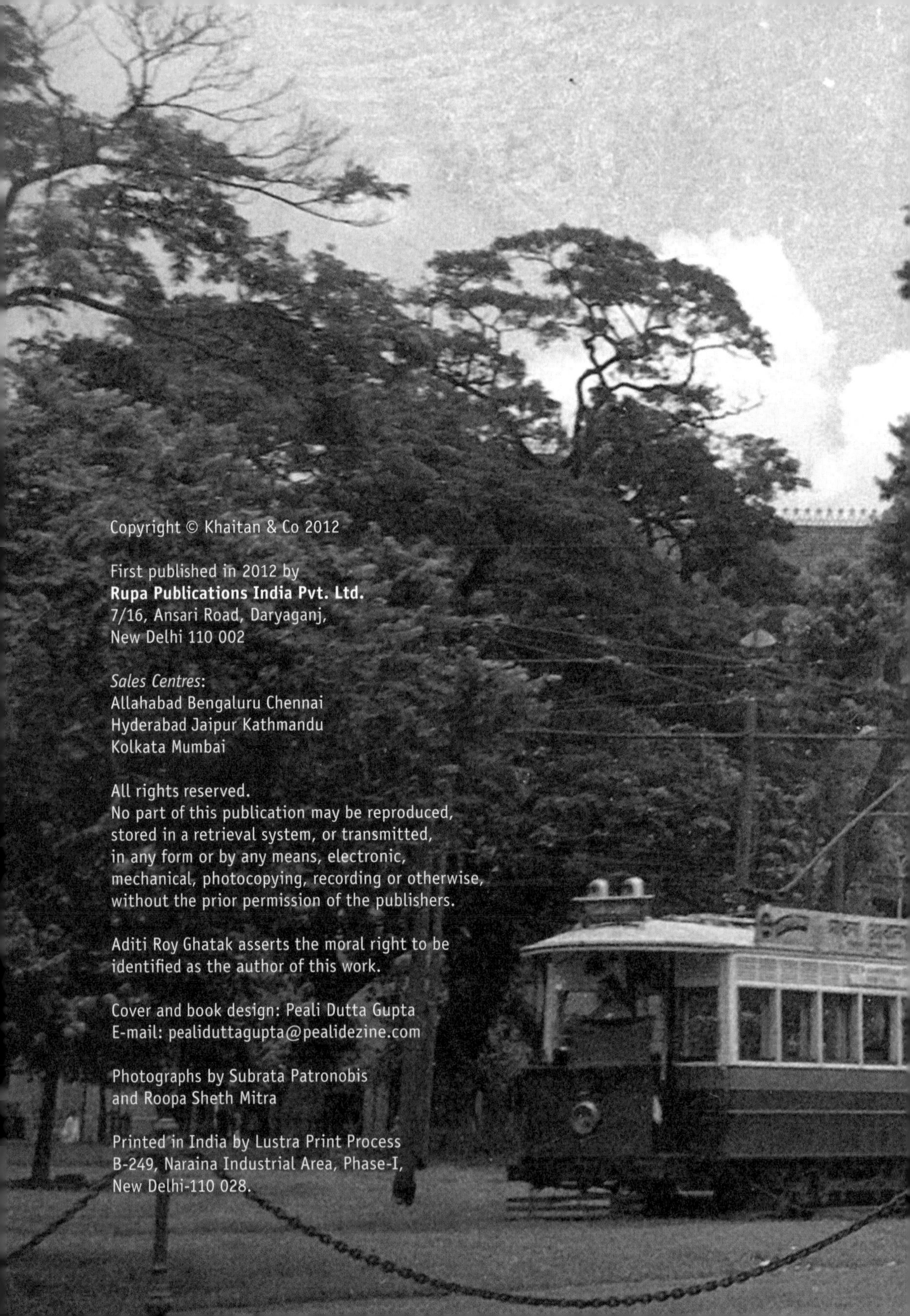



First published in 2012 by
**Rupa Publications India Pvt. Ltd.**
7/16, Ansari Road, Daryaganj,
New Delhi 110 002

*Sales Centres*:
Allahabad Bengaluru Chennai
Hyderabad Jaipur Kathmandu
Kolkata Mumbai



Cover and book design: Peali Dutta Gupta
E-mail: pealiduttagupta@pealidezine.com

Photographs by Subrata Patronobis
and Roopa Sheth Mitra

Printed in India by Lustra Print Process
B-249, Naraina Industrial Area, Phase-I,
New Delhi-110 028.

# Contents

| Plaintiff | | Defendant | Rs. | As. | P. |
|---|---|---|---|---|---|
| Kessurdeo Chamaria | -vs- | Rampratap Chamaria | 2,860 | 1 | . |
| Ramprasad Sukla | -vs- | Sewnarain Gulabray | 306 | 12 | 9 |
| Ramkrishna Mohta | -vs- | Ramchandra Saraogy | 1,998 | 1 | 6 |
| Cl. Sewnarain Gulabrai | Re | Kalikaprasad Sukla | 117 | 12 | . |
| Jokurmall Boid | -vs- | Labhchand Boid | 258 | 13 | 6 |
| Issurdas Deora | -vs- | Rampratap Chamaria | 833 | 1 | . |
| Gopikisen | -vs- | Raghunathprasad Jalan | 22 | . | . |
| Bhagatram Sheopratap | -vs- | Jayantilal Amritlal | 221 | 8 | . |
| Bhagatram Sheopratap | -vs- | M. C. Sethia Co. | 15 | 1 | . |
| Harakchand Bansali | -vs- | Ramkumar Poddar | 98 | 2 | . |
| Nawratanlal Burma | -vs- | Kantaprasad Chowdhury | 893 | 9 | 6 |
| Tarachand Ghanshyamdas | -vs- | Sreekisen Khannah & Son | 166 | 14 | . |
| Sures Chandra Roy | -vs- | Krishnalal Roy | 5 | 12 | . |
| Tarachand Ghanshyamdas | -vs- | Amarnath Khannah | 228 | 6 | . |
| Nikaram Parmanand | -vs- | Amiruddin Md. Amin | 36 | 3 | . |
| Srikisen Khannah | -vs- | Tarachand Ghanshyamdas | 523 | 2 | . |
| Surajmal Nemani | -vs- | Bajranglal Nemani | 73 | 14 | 6 |
| Udaychand Pannalal | -vs- | Taisho Marine & Fire Ins. Co. | 220 | 4 | . |
| In the goods of Sewratan | | Mahto ... | 30 | 4 | . |
| Behar Rice Mills Ld. | -vs- | Amoluck Chand Dawar | 76 | 8 | . |
| Bridge & Roof Co. (India) Ld. | -vs- | Seksaria Sugar Mills. | 249 | 11 | . |
| Sewdeji | -vs- | Johurmal Khemka | 158 | 12 | . |
| Kabir Hosiery Factory Ld. | -vs- | S. Mohamed Saymed Co. | 134 | 7 | . |
| Surendra Nath Banerjee | -vs- | Calcutta Stock Exchange Assn. Ld. | 186 | 3 | . |
| Jhumarmal Sethi | -vs- | Dudhmull Bagaz | 56 | 8 | 6 |
| Udaychand Pannalal | Re | Hanumanmull Kedarmal | 38 | 5 | . |
| Fazal Hossain Khaja | -vs- | Bata Shoe Co Ld. | 114 | 4 | . |
| K. Kasturchand Co | -vs- | H. L. Sandford | | | |
| Ganpatrai Saraogi | -vs- | Gulabchand Ganeshilal | 223 | 6 | . |
| Pratapmal Agarwala | -vs- | Dhanbati Bibi | 611 | 1 | . |
| Tarachand Ghanshyamdas | -vs- | Ramgopal Ramrick Pandey | 413 | 10 | . |

# Foreword

## A Solicitor's Story: The Essence of Law

The easiest thing to do around a century is to applaud it from the sidelines. Accomplishing a century in any walk of life is a matter for the truly outstanding. For a law firm to have done so, navigating the tumultuous waters of pre-independence India and negotiating the even choppier oceans of post-independent India is truly a herculean feat. To have accomplished it all without sacrificing any of the founding fathers' entrepreneurial spirit or zealous commitment to justice and to the client is what makes Khaitan & Co's history over a century quite outstanding.

Capturing this magnificent history, through the memories of those who have been associated with it – tapping into the recollections of even nonagerians – could not have been easy either. Nor could have been the task of delving into judgments, reported or otherwise – in which the firm features – and presenting them in a story-telling mode have been simple. *Amicus Curiae* accomplishes all this and more; indeed seeking to inform the legal fraternity about the value systems that today seem to belong to eras bygone; where society was more important than the firm's self-interest and client satisfaction was more important than anything else.

There is thus a great deal that goes into the making of a truly great institution, particularly knowledge and hard work. Had it not been for the exemplary scholarship, commitment to truth and justice of the founding fathers of Khaitan & Co, who were not only brilliant in their own right but who also instilled in others the importance of hard work and the urge to serve the client to the best of one's ability in the organizational set-up, the firm would not have been where it is today. The other great quality about the early leadership of the firm, which I have had the privilege of knowing since I was a junior lawyer, was its impressive scholastic approach and the humility with which the early Khaitans went about addressing their often impossibly difficult assignments for intransigent clients, tapping the best legal minds of the time that Bengal could boast of. My father, N.C. Chatterjee, was one amongst them and it was courtesy his chamber that my first interaction with the firm took place.

Aditi Roy Ghatak, amongst the most exciting business writers of our times, uses the felicity of her pen and knowledge of the corporate and legal world not only to capture the spirit of the legal goings on when the firm was born but also takes the reader through an informed and often entertaining journey into the evolving legal system in India through most of Khaitan & Co's path-breaking cases.

*Amicus Curiae* is the story of a group of solicitors, who trained themselves to be complete business managers – not only mastering law but mastering finance and corporate systems as well – and fortifying this wholesome ability with an understanding of human emotions and the workings of judicial minds. The numerous cases presented in the book are a testimony to this extraordinary attribute. Indeed, *Amicus Curiae* pauses to focus on those cases in which the firm helped to change the course of Indian law: helped make new laws and the system of legal administration of the country.

Yet, *Amicus Curiae* is not exclusively about law. It is about people, situations and thought processes; it is about nationalism and globalization; about tradition, heritage and modernism. It is a fascinating tale of using the law to mould a society; to help India march into the 21st century and beyond; to evolve cautiously and yet with a sense of palpable dynamism. It is the story of an intrepid law firm that has steadfastly climbed the echelons of the legal firmament but has captured the hearts and minds of its clients in the process. Indeed, it has become an institution by itself.

I recall with a great sense of nostalgia my association with some of the stalwarts of the firm, who, to my mind, adorned the legal profession by following its best traditions. Lawyers like B.P. Khaitan, whose affability was endearing to all, Kishan Khaitan, Sitaram Jhunjhunwala, Ram Kishore Choudhury, Pradip (Pinto) Khaitan and many others, not only showed exemplary acumen as lawyers but also displayed great expertise in discharging their duties to their clients and to the courts as well. These are attributes, which have made Khaitan & Co, what it is today and the title of the book, *Amicus Curiae*, is truly justified – 'a friend of the court'.

*Amicus Curiae* is, more than anything else, about a firm that literally seizes the client's loyalty and, in the world of 21st century modern management, there is nothing more precious than that. It provides a peek into the Khaitan strategy of winning and retaining clients: clients are not retained by the thoroughness of the legal strategy only – critical though that is – they are retained by the comprehensive management of the complex issue facing the clients, to deliver the bottom line that it desires. *Amicus Curiae* is a case study in comprehensive modern management in which law is one important element, and I am sure that it will be read not only by lawyers but also by all discerning people.

Somnath Chatterjee
Kolkata
November 2011

# Preface

## The Prosecution Rests; it's a Birthday!

**Lawyers' Law**

The law the lawyers know about is property and land;
But why the leaves are on the trees,
And why the waves disturb the seas,
Why honey is the food of bees,
Why horses have such tender knees,
Why winters come when rivers freeze,
Why faith is more than what one sees,
And Hope survives the worse disease,
And Charity is more than these,
They do not understand.

*– H.D.C. Pepler; The Devil's Devices*

There are two legal arguments that one can use to overrule Pepler's severe indictment of the legal fraternity. In India, no lawyer worth his gold mohurs can afford not to understand why the leaves are on the trees or why the waves disturb the seas courtesy the Environment (Protection) Act, 1986, or, for that matter, the Wild Life (Protection) Act, 1972. More money has transferred hands because of these Acts by way of legal fees than the keenest of legal minds would have imagined. It is another matter whether nature is being adequately defended in the courts of India though.

The other argument that one can use against Pepler is about the unkindness that nature has shown to lawyers, in this case the hero of the day; the centurion, KCo. Why else would those ravishing floods of 1978 drown all the documents and photographs that the firm of solicitors had carefully stored in a godown at 52/2, Ballygunge Circular Road, Calcutta?

The upshot has been that much of the story about the century maker has had to be based on oral history gathered assiduously from those associated with the firm, ranging in ages from 21 to 91; and that has been no holiday. It is a story that had its genesis in the twin forces of an independence movement that would, a hundred years later, give rise to a country that would be poised to conquer the 21st century and an entrepreneurial gene that could make a success of anything. Between the two, they had virtually set the scene for a 'street legal': the name was KCo.

Not every lawyer is a satisfying chronicler of legal tales – notwithstanding the oratorical skills on display before the honourable justices. Obtaining the oral history of the firm often meant untangling a complex thought process rendered through a string of what sounded like 'Section 352, IPC read with section 34, ... under section 304, Part

II, IPC read with sections 352 and section 3… to be seen with section 352 of the IPC but not u/s … see judgment Kesavananda Bharati vs State of Kerala and Anr of 24 April, 1973….'. So where was the story and could the honourable counsel add some meat to the legal lexicon? The chronicler would be considered a Shylock seeking his pound of flesh. 'Madam! aur meray paas meat nahi hai; sub ley liya aap nay', would be the hapless plea. In the absence of a Portia to defend them, the current chronicler did obtain a fairly intelligible account of an amazing story of wit and grit; scholarship and court craft and a commitment to a culture where the client is king.

We are the KCo family!

It would be befitting to end this preface with a story featuring some of the most outstanding of the dramatis personae appearing in this account, as told by Ashok Sen to Fali Nariman, who recounted it in his book *Before Memory Fades*: Bhagwati Prasad Khaitan, never known to get flustered, was at the end of his tether: for three weeks he had been pursuing Bhulabhai Desai, whom he had briefed in 'a very important testamentary suit (concerning a will) to come up in Bombay High Court. The client trusted his solicitor implicitly and took BP with him from Calcutta to Bombay to wait on Bhulabhai Desai and to hold conferences with him'.

BP, the stickler for perfection that he was, had gone to Bombay a month ahead of the suit being heard and had been chasing the elusive counsel. For the few minutes that they could get him, they would reiterate old facts while there were 2,000 pages of the brief to be read. After three weeks of such futile dialogue, a hapless BP told his client (in the words of Fali Nariman): 'My dear fellow, the case is tomorrow! We have done all we can but fate is against you. Your counsel has not read your brief and all you can do is to go to the Mahalaxmi Temple and pray that some miracle happens'.

No miracle happened; but Bhulabhai Desai did! He stood in the court and rattled off the facts of the case without any aide de memoire or having to refer to the brief even once. Having presented a masterly summation of the facts, he addressed the points of law with equal elan. Bhagwati Babu had never seen such a consummate performance and must have told this story to his attorneys a hundred times over.

The world of law is not a world of chicanery; it is a world of erudition; intellect, morality, righteousness, ethics, rationality, natural law, fairness, equity... This is what the centenary brand identity exercise for KCo has sought to establish, the interlacing blue ribbon girdling the KCo lozenge emits a kinetic energy that is so palpable in KCo offices; positioning the firm as a benchmark brand in the legal space.

Facing page: KCo's masthead evolving down the century

**K. KHAITAN**
SOLICITOR & ADVOCATE
PHONES { OFF. 28-3197-9
20-7872
GRAM : "KHAITANCO" CAL.
TELEX : CA - 7045
FAX : 20-7857
(91) 033-28-7656
RES. 3, QUEENS PARK
CALCUTTA-700 019
PHONE : 75-9956

1B, OLD POST OFFICE STREET.
*Calcutta-700001.............................19*

---

# KHAITAN & CO.

ADVOCATES AND NOTARIES
1B OLD POST OFFICE STREET
2ND FLOOR
CALCUTTA 700 001

R. K. CHOUDHURY
PRADIP K. KHAITAN
P. L. AGARWAL
R. N. JHUNJHUNWALA
PRAMOD KHAITAN
UMESH KHAITAN
N. G. KHAITAN
G. S. ASOPA
PADAM KHAITAN

TELEPHOPNES
248 3197, 3198, 3199, 8018
220 6411, 7053, 7150, 7442

TELEGRAM
KHAITANCO, CALCUTTA

TELEFAX
(91) (033) 220-7857
(91) (033) 248 7656

IN REPLY PLEASE QUOTE

OUR REF

---

# KHAITAN & CO.

ADVOCATES AND NOTARIES
1B OLD POST OFFICE STREET
2nd FLOOR
CALCUTTA-700 001

K. KHAITAN
R. K. CHOUDHURY
PRADIP K. KHAITAN
P. L. AGARWAL
R. N. JHUNJHUNWALA
PRAMOD KHAITAN
UMESH KHAITAN
N. G. KHAITAN
G. S. ASOPA
PADAM KHAITAN

TELEPHONES :
28-3197, 3198, 3199, 8018
20-6411, 7150, 7053, 7442

TELEGRAMS :
KHAITANCO, CALCUTTA

TELEX :
21-7045 KHTN IN
21-2187 KCL IN

FAX : (91) 033-20-7857
(91) 033-28-7656

IN REPLY PLEASE QUOTE

OUR REF

YOUR REF

---

# KHAITAN & CO.

ADVOCATES, SOLICITORS, NOTARIES, PATENT & TRADEMARK ATTORNEYS

EMERALD HOUSE
1B OLD POST OFFICE STREET
KOLKATA 700 001

PHONE : +91 33 2248 7000/2231 3838

FAX : +91 33 2248 7656/2230 7857

EMAIL : kolkata@khaitanco.com

PRADIP KUMAR KHAITAN
RAM NIRANJAN JHUNJHUNWALA
PURUSHOTTAM LAL AGARWAL
RAVI KULKARNI
NAND GOPAL KHAITAN
GOURI SHANKAR ASOPA
OM PRAKASH AGARWAL
PADAM KUMAR KHAITAN
OM PRAKASH JHUNJHUNWALA
RAJIV KHAITAN
ARVIND KUMAR JHUNJHUNWALA
ANIKET AGARWAL
HAIGREVE KHAITAN
RABINDRA JHUNJHUNWALA

Senior Consultant
RAM KISHORE CHOUDHURY

---

# KHAITAN & CO

Emerald House
1B Old Post Office Street
Kolkata (Calcutta) 700 001, India
T: +91 33 2248 7000 F: +91 33 2248 7656
E: kolkata@khaitanco.com

CELEBRATING
A CENTURY

# KHAITAN & CO

Has the firm found itself wanting on these counts over its hundred years of existence? Possibly, but this is not the occasion to judge the errors of being human. The only certainty is that nothing survives a hundred years without exceptional qualities of character and commitment; certainly not a legal firm. As independent ratings show, those qualities have been the hallmark of the brilliant maiden century completed by KCo.

KHAITAN & CO
Advocates
Estd
1911

The most seasoned batsman, baptized in copybook batting technique, is not averse to learning and perfecting the rather cross-batted reverse sweep because it fetches runs in limited overs cricket. Not even Sachin Tendulkar is averse to going for the slog; or even a switch and a scoop. Runs have to be scored just as the client's interest has to be protected. The practice of law is not cricket but it is – and must be – a gentleman's game; more so when the times are becoming complex and the role of the law is becoming more and more pre-eminent. It is to face this world that KCo is taking fresh guard from the umpires: society at large and, of course, the legal fraternity. Its term sheet with the new century has been signed and one hopes that the logical conclusion will be even more satisfying. The billion-dollar deal that Haigreve Khaitan recently stitched together in Mumbai just marks the dawn of a new era. A very satisfied client says so.

Happy Birthday KCo! May you live in interesting times.

*Aditi Roy Ghatak*
*November 2011*

# Acronyms: Dramatis Personae

The city of Calcutta (Kolkata)
Khaitan & Co (Khaitans, KCo)
Debi Prasad Khaitan (DP)
Kali Prasad Khaitan (K.P. Khaitan; KP)
Bhagwati Prasad Khaitan (BP; Bhagwati Babu)
Pradip Kumar Khaitan (PK; Pinto Khaitan; Pinto Babu)
Lakshmi Narayan Khaitan (Lukkhi Babu)
Krishna Prasad Khaitan (Kishan Khaitan; Kishan Babu)
Ram Kishore Choudhury (RKC)
Nand Gopal Khaitan (NG)
Hari Das Mundhra (HDM)
Siddhartha Shankar Ray (S.S. Ray; Manuda)
R.N. Bajoria (RNB)
Sita Ram Jhunjhunwala (SRJ)
Ram Niranjan Jhunjhunwala (RNJ)
Abhishek Manu Singhvi (AMS)
Samaraditya Pal (Bacchu Pal)
P.C. Sen (Mintu Sen)
P.L. Agarwal (PL)
C.M. Ghorawat (CMG)
Soumendra Nath Mookherjee (Gopal Mookherjee)

# ON A 'FIRM' FOOTING
## a Centurion is Born

*It was the best of times, it was the worst of times, it was the age of wisdom, it was the age of foolishness, it was the epoch of belief, it was the epoch of incredulity, it was the season of Light, it was the season of Darkness, it was the spring of hope, it was the winter of despair, we had everything before us, we had nothing before us, we were all going direct to heaven, we were all going direct the other way – in short, the period was so far like the present period, that some of its noisiest authorities insisted on its being received, for good or for evil, in the superlative degree of comparison only.*

— **Charles Dickens** (1812-1870);
*A Tale of Two Cities*

Charles Dickens may have been talking of a different time and a different place; or he might well have been talking of Calcutta of 1911. The massacre of Jallianwala Bagh was still a disaster waiting to happen but both the British and Bengal had just had a foretaste of the might of a people in a state of revolt against a patently unjust administrative move. The Alipore Bomb trial had given nationalists all over the country a vivid picture of the perverseness of the legal and police system under the Raj and while the awesome defence put up by the firebrand Deshbandhu Chittaranjan Das secured an acquittal for Aurobindo Ghose, other patriots succumbed to the might of the British law.

Calcutta 1911: the best and worst of times. A city in a state of ferment experienced the might of the law; sometimes perverse; but always all-pervasive

'Bengal united is a power; Bengali divided will pull in several different ways': Lord Curzon admitted as much in his private communications but as he bulldozed through with his plans to partition the state, he spoke in a forked tongue. The huge state – bigger than France and the British Isles combined

'Calcutta is the centre from which the Congress Party is manipulated throughout the whole of Bengal and, indeed, the whole of India. Its best wire pullers and its most frothy orators all reside here. The perfection of their machinery and the tyranny which it enables them to exercise are truly remarkable. They dominate public opinion in Calcutta; they affect the High Court; they frighten the local Government and they are sometimes not without serious influence on the Government of India. The whole of their activity is directed to creating an agency so powerful that they may one day be able to force a weak government to give them what they desire. Any measure in consequence that would divide the Bengali-speaking population; that would permit independent centres of activity and influence to grow up; that would dethrone Calcutta from its place as the center of successful intrigue, or that would weaken the influence of the lawyer class, who have the entire organization in their hands, is intensely and hotly resented by them. The outcry will be loud and very fierce, but as a native gentleman said to me – "my countrymen always howl until a thing is settled; then they accept it"'.

*Excerpts from Curzon's letter (February 2, 1905) to St John Brodrick, Secretary of State for India, explaining the need to partition Bengal*

Debi Prasad (DP), the son of Naurangrai

– was greatly under-governed and effective administration demanded its partition was the official argument but no Bengali was buying that cynical story as Calcutta 'came alive with rallies, bonfires of foreign goods, petitions, newspapers and posters', to quote Lord Metcalfe.

Amongst the most impassioned were young Khudiram Bose and Prafulla Chaki who decided to kill Magistrate Kingsford for his harsh sentences against nationalists. That they ended up killing two unintended women, the wife and daughter of barrister Pringle Kennedy, was another tragedy; but their trial was a cause célèbre by all accounts. There were 49 accused; 206 witnesses were called; around 400 documents were filed with the court; and more than 5,000 exhibits, including bombs, revolvers and acids were produced for the trial that continued for a year (1908-1909). The boy Khudiram Bose was found guilty and hanged, but out of the churn evolved an indestructable Swadeshi movement that would fight the imperial design to crush the Bengal-inspired nationalist movement; and fight it did successfully.

In the corridors of the Presidency College, where the cauldron of nationalism was simmering, were the finest young minds of the region debating their future free from the British yoke. There was a bright spark from Chhapra (Bihar) answering to the name of Rajendra Prasad, who stood head and shoulders over the rest, standing first in every subject. There was a 14-year-old from Buxar, Debi Prasad, the son of Naurangrai, an illustrious jailor. In 1902, he passed the entrance examination with a first class first in the Patna division and had come to Presidency on a scholarship. There was Badridas Goenka, younger brother of Hariram Goenka, a Rajasthani vaishya of considerable means and there was J.N. Mazumdar, who would one day become an eminent jurist. It was an interesting, cosmopolitan and spirited group but everyone was clear in his mind that the future lay in an independent India. The court was the hub of activity for matters political or of business. Law was, of course, in the Bengal air.

A bright spark from Chhapra (Bihar) answering to the name of Rajendra Prasad was to be DP's friend and later the first President of Independent India

As early as March 23, 1774, the British Parliament had formed the first Supreme Court at Calcutta with Sir Elijah Impey as the Chief Justice, even before Calcutta had been made the capital of India in August that year. Various legal

## Aurobindo's angst

'On the whole during this trial at every stage I could find, in the British legal system, how easily the innocent could be punished, sent to prison, suffer transportation, even loss of life. Unless one stood in the dock oneself, one cannot realize the delusive untruth of the Western penal code. It is something of a gamble, a gamble with human freedom, with man's joys and sorrows, a life-long agony for him and his family, his friends and relatives, insult, a living death. In this system there is no counting as to how often guilty persons escape and how many innocent persons perish'.

— *Sri Aurobindo; Tales of Prison Life*

Sir Elijah Impey was the Chief Justice of the first Supreme Court at Calcutta

cases of historic significance were decided by the court; beginning with the public hanging of Maharaja Nanda Kumar, at Kuli Bazar on June 15, 1775, following a death sentence pronounced by Chief Justice Elijah Impey, on a case that shook the faith of the people in the fairness of the British justice system. The Maharaja was later found to be innocent and some of the best-educated Indians began to hone their skills at using the law to their advantage. In 1823, Raja Rammohun Roy initiated the first constitutional agitation in India against a press ordinance issued by Governor General Adam. Then came the all-inspiring Alipore Bomb trial that must have possessed the spirited group of friends at Presidency College.

If the group was spirited, it had even more spirited, highly motivating teachers: Acharya Jagadish Chandra Bose, Acharya P. C. Ray and even Sir Jadunath Sarkar for a while. From science to sociology, from enterprise to nationalism, from social work to heated arguments on the position the boys would take vis-à-vis the British, the youthful minds were constantly engaged in a pursuit of a fair and free future. There was room for boyish light-heartedness too. J.N. Mazumdar recalls: 'I came in contact with DP in 1902. We had both passed the entrance examination and joined Presidency. DP, Rajendra Prasad and I joined the col-

## Deshbandhu's defence

Chittaranjan Das concluded his defence of Sri Aurobindo saying: 'My appeal to you is this, that long after the controversy will be hushed in silence, long after this turmoil, the agitation will have ceased, long after he is dead and gone, he will be looked upon as the poet of patriotism, as the prophet of nationalism and the lover of humanity. Long after he is dead and gone, his words will be echoed and re-echoed, not only in India but across distant seas and lands. Therefore, I say that the man in his position is not only standing before the bar of this Court but before the bar of the High Court of History'.

lege on the same day and DP was dressed in his traditional Marwari attire; a round cap on his head and a dhoti and kurta; he looked most handsome. In fact, he looked so handsome that some boys teased him as the college queen'.

DP (L), with friend, philosopher, guide, J.N. Mazumdar

There were English boys too and there were the sons of bureaucrats, many possibly in totally antagonistic positions vis-à-vis the Raj; there were the sons of the wealthy zamindars of Bengal, some immersed in the fight for freedom and others choosing a life of pleasurable abandon. The young Marwari boy was called just that: D.P. Marwari! It was, however, the zeal to rid the country of the Raj that really stirred emotions. Its cynical moves to annihilate the intellectual drive that Bengal was providing to the freedom movement, by literally ripping it apart, infuriated the boys and if Rajendra Prasad's passion for freedom bordered on the violent; Debi Prasad's was the voice of reason.

What was happening around defied reason though: there was the evil arm of the British law on the one hand and the nationalistic fervour on the other that sucked in the entire society. The Nobel laureate set the revolution to mesmerizing music and verse as Lord Curzon announced the partition of Bengal, which was implemented on October 16, 1905. Bankim Chandra's *Bande Mataram* and Rabindranath's *Aamar Shonar Bangla* reverberated in the hearts and minds of people and terrorist groups sprang up in nooks and crannies of the city. For some the motherland was equated to the goddess Kali and it was from from this goddess of power and destruction that they would derive the strength to throw the British out. Anything anti-British would magically unite the country.

It was to this goddess that the 11 footballers of the Mohan Bagan Club turned on the morning of July 29, 1911, for they were attempting the impossible. They were taking on a mighty British football team in the IFA Shield finals; all of Bengal was in a state of rising ferment as the Calcutta team eliminated competition one by one. The first to feel the punch was St Xavier's: three-nil; then out went the Rangers Club: two to one; the third to be shown the door was Rifle Brigade by a solitary goal; and while the first semi-final against the Middlesex Regiment ended in a draw, the replay saw Mohan Bagan make short work of the opposition in a three-nil victory. Bengal had gone wild as 80,000 turned up to witness the final against the East York Regiment.

When a barefooted Mohan Bagan won the IFA Shield, it felt as if the British had been thrown out of India

Aficionados had poured in from Patna, Purnia, Kishanganj, Assam and Dhaka to witness a possible barefooted Indian victory. The East Indian Railway arranged for special trains from Burdwan and Ranaghat and there were special steamers bringing fans from Raiganj and Baranagar. Local transport was overflowing as trams from Shyambazar and Chitpur had people hanging out of the windows, and the streets were teeming with fans. Treetops, telegraph posts, vantage points on high-rises around the field, were all taken, and a black market for tickets had made its advent in Calcutta;

people thronged to see their boys take the field against East York, their foreheads resplendent with the red tilak from Kalighat, even as their feet were bare: Hiralal Mukherjee; Bhuti Sukul, Sudhir Chatterjee, Manmohan Mukherjee, Rajen Sengupta, Nilmadhav Bhattacharya, Kanu Roy, Habul Sarkar, Abhilash Ghosh, Bijoydas Bhaduri and captain, Shibdas Bhaduri. As the blessed warriors of Ma Kali lifted the IFA Shield two to one, it was as if the British had been forced to quit India.

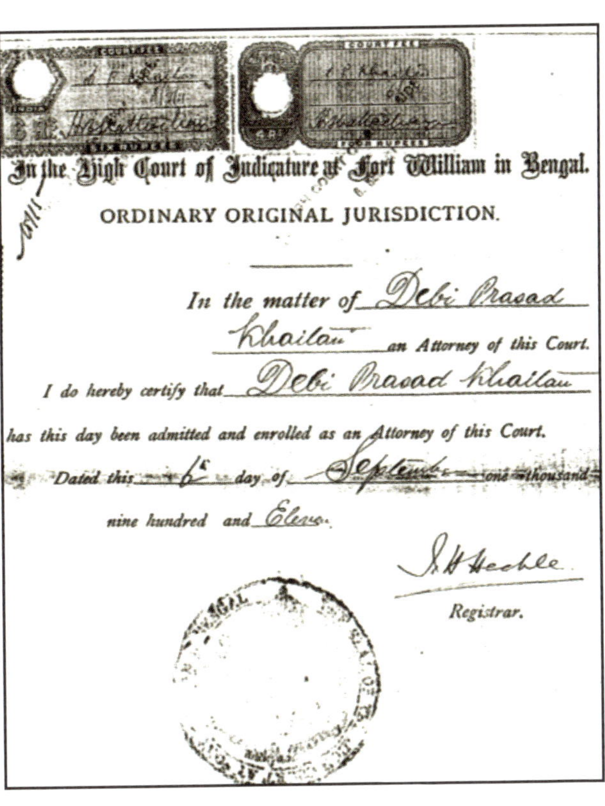

In the High Court of Judicature at Fort William in Bengal.

ORDINARY ORIGINAL JURISDICTION.

*In the matter of* Debi Prasad Khaitan *an Attorney of this Court.*

*I do hereby certify that* Debi Prasad Khaitan *has this day been admitted and enrolled as an Attorney of this Court.*

*Dated this* 6th *day of* September *one thousand nine hundred and* Eleven.

*Registrar.*

Debi Prasad becomes attorney of the High Court

It was again to this powerful deity that two young boys turned around November that year. Debi Prasad Khaitan had just passed the attorneyship examination with a first class – becoming one of the earliest Marwari attorneys; much to his father's pride. The firm he was articled with, Manuel and Agarwalla, would not make him partner and the young attorney wanted to test his own spirit of enterprise. For Dutch courage he took J.N. Mazumdar along to meet a Burrabazar astrologer who promptly assured him that an independent practice was just what the stars foretold. Armed with this prophecy, he went to Kalighat. There the two offered puja, purchased some furniture, a typewriter, and the office of KCo was up and running at 10, Old Post Office Street, as the report of the Incorporated Law Society of Calcutta (1909 to 1929) indicates. The firm shifted to what was then 1&2, Old Post Office Street (Emerald House) in 1928. This plot was later divided; Emerald House becoming 1B, Old Post Office Street.

It was probably Joharmull Khemka, who was instrumental in helping DP earn his first income: a handsome Rs 3. The first earnings in hand, the young attorney once again took J.N. Mazumdar to visit the goddess and spent the entire amount on the prasad. For the rest, he was prepared to work very hard, since the general consensus was that except for the British attorneys and some Bengali firms, others would find the going impossible. The naysayers were not prepared for the legal acumen that the young attorney would unleash on the legal system in Calcutta. The Marwaris loved him and he reciprocated their sentiments by sheer diligence. In due course, he inducted his gifted brothers to help him in the profession.

The business community, of course, had a million issues within itself and with the British administration. As far as the legal system and the community were concerned, DP had already positioned himself at a vantage point, becoming a member of the working committee of the Marwari Association. The Marwaris had enormous business acumen and even larger ambition. Life had not been kind to the vaishyas of Rajasthan, who were forced to sacrifice the security of their homes and travel to every nook and corner of the country to establish themselves as men of business. Over the years, they had mastered trade and, from the early days of the 20th century, they began venturing into industry.

Following in the footsteps... younger brother, Durga Prasad Khaitan becomes an attorney

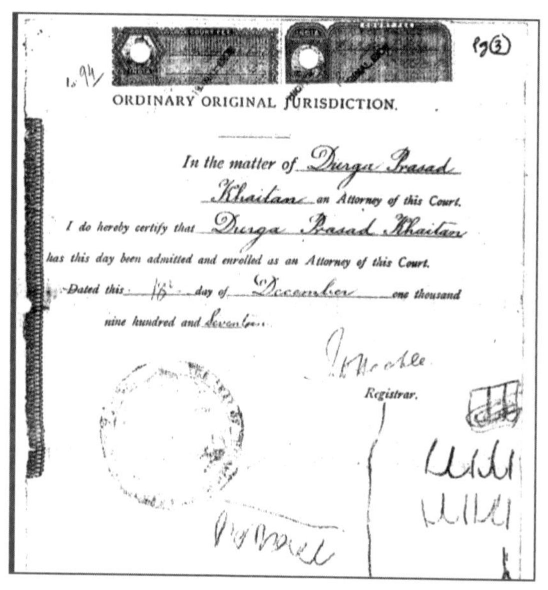
ORDINARY ORIGINAL JURISDICTION.

*In the matter of* Durga Prasad Khaitan *an Attorney of this Court.*

*I do hereby certify that* Durga Prasad Khaitan *has this day been admitted and enrolled as an Attorney of this Court.*

*Dated this* [illegible] *day of* December *one thousand nine hundred and* Seven[illegible]

*Registrar.*

With the spirit of freedom permeating the Calcutta society – that had indicated to the British industry that it was time for it to contemplate returing to home shores – the Marwari man of business found the playfield uniquely suited for him to take over the reins of business. Not too many

At home anywhere in the world. DP with Sir John Anderson, 1st Viscount Waverley, the Governor of Bengal from 1932-1937

Bengalis were keen to consider enterprise as a career, leaving the Marwari man of business a reasonably clear shot at the goal. What was perhaps missing in the community was formal education and even that was soon set right.

Having been made conscious of the need to educate its youth, the Marwari community started its own school, the Vishuddhanand Saraswati Vidyalaya, in 1911. It had become clear to the community leaders that the business potential of the Marwari would flourish many times if complimented by learning. The Vishuddhanand Saraswati Vidyalaya offered education in the Hindi medium up to high school. It was in this school, in class II, that Debi Prasad's youngest sibling would be admitted when he was sent to Calcutta, as a boy of eight.

On the business front, every line of industrial activity was opening up. The managing agency system had founded a firm industrial culture that encompassed shipping, textile, jute, banking, engineering and insurance. There was also merchant trade from grains to jute and broking in shares that the community excelled in. Besides, there was the rather promising real estate. As a natural corollary, there was law: from around 1906, several Marwaris had become honorary magistrates and jurors in the courts; others were accepting leadership roles in society. In 1891, Hariram Goenka became a municipal councillor.

Burrabazar was the hub of trade and the Marwari community controlled it with great gusto. The Khaitan family too had a textile business there

Even as Debi Prasad studied, he actively participated in all community activities, literally soaking up its traits; learning the ins and outs of the business and societal customs, getting insights into the mindsets of his own community. He also sunk his teeth into the British business and legal system. His own community and the British were generally in adversarial positions. Sometimes the relationship was bitter, vindictive and harsh, and the young man was training himself in the art of beating the Englishman at his own game.

The community had already formed a Marwari Chamber of Commerce, which took an active part in setting up the Calcutta Stock Exchange in 1908 with as much flourish as its London counterpart was. The Jute Balers' Association was also established in the same year. Successful institution building of this nature gave the community the credibility to have its voice heard in matters of business and finance and the Marwari Association started receiving invitations from the government to participate in various fora. DP was genetically designed to take advantage of such opportunities: he had business in his blood; he had law in his mind; he had bright and industrious siblings whose talents he would harness to provide muscle for his fledgling organization. When the time came, he would have the faith and conviction that he had trained them well enough to take over the reins of governance and lead the firm to a glorious future - one that even he may not have contemplated in those early years.

The community too was quick to recognize Debi Prasad's exceptional talents and, by 1910, even while he was studying for his attorneyship, he was elected member of the working committee of the Marwari Association. The members were a youthful lot, in the age group of 15 to 25, reasonably educated and zealously ready to move up in society.

CONSTITUENT ASSEMBLY
OF INDIA

DRAFT CONSTITUTION
OF INDIA

PREPARED BY THE DRAFTING COMMITTEE

PRINTED IN INDIA BY THE MANAGER
GOVT OF INDIA PRESS NEW DELHI
1948

CONSTITUENT ASSEMBLY OF INDIA

DRAFTING COMMITTEE

Dr. B. R. Ambedkar—Chairman.
Shri N. Gopalaswami Ayyangar.
Shri Alladi Krishnaswami Ayyar.
Shri K. M. Munshi.
Saiyid Mohd. Saadulla.
Shri N. Madhava Rau.
Shri D. P. Khaitan.

[Sir B. L. Mitter, though originally appointed a member of the Committee, was unable to attend after the first meeting, as he ceased to be a member of the Constituent Assembly.]

Page from the Indian Constitution showing D.P. Khaitan as one of the members of the drafting committee

Yet another important development took place in 1910: a man by the name of Ghanshyam Das Birla was making a serious bid to progress from broking to industry and was just as keen to take an active part in the affairs of the community. Birla Brothers was formed some nine years later, in 1919, but GD and DP had come to be recognized as a formidable team in every walk of life. Debi Prasad himself was destined for far greater glory. An independent career that evolved into becoming a full-time adviser to Bengal's leading family, the Birlas, Debi Prasad Khaitan was made a member of the Constituent Assembly that drafted the Indian constitution. What greater honour could be bestowed on a product of the Indian freedom movement?

As far as the firm was concerned, Debi Prasad had never looked at it as a one-man show. While he had little influence over the academic pursuits of his elder brother, as far as his younger siblings were concerned, he wanted to ensure that they excelled in studies. Indeed, the sons of Naurangrai Khaitan had been well named; after the eldest, Lakshmi Narayan, the boys that followed were named Debi Prasad, Kali Prasad, Durga Prasad, Gauri Prasad, Chandi Prasad and, the youngest, Bhagwati Prasad. The important thing was that the boys were all blessed by the goddess Saraswati. Learning came easy to them. Lakshmi Narayan Khaitan, the eldest, did not become a partner (not having become an attorney) but controlled the office and its finances, which held the key to successful enterprise. It was for his sons and grandsons to contribute to the firm's legal acumen over the years, with great credit to themselves and the firm.

The brilliant Durga Prasad topped every examination that he took: a bachelor's degree, a master's, followed by a

We are seven!
L-R, top row: Durga Prasad, Lakshmi Narayan, Debi Prasad, Kali Prasad. Bottom row: Chandi Prasad, Bhagwati Prasad, Gauri Prasad

Bachelor of Law and Attorneyship before getting enrolled as an attorney in 1917. A hundred years after the firm was established, eminent jurist and former Speaker of the Indian Parliament, Somnath Chatterjee says: 'Kali Prasad Khaitan was the barrister in the family but Bhagwati Babu was an "institution"'. The jurist recalls seeing two gentlemen at his father's house even as a child: Bhagwati Babu and Kishan Khaitan, who would visit the chamber of the illustrious N.C. Chatterjee. Later, he had the privilege to work with them, on becoming a lawyer and starting his career in the chamber of R.C. Deb.

'Kishan Khaitan and my father were particularly close', recalls Mr Somnath Chatterjee in a very significant statement. The Bengali and the Marwari community have always shared a love-hate relationship – the former was considered more blessed by the goddess Saraswati and, therefore, artistically and culturally gifted. The latter blessed by the goddess Lakshmi had material wealth far beyond the average Bengali's range. If the Khaitan brothers seemed to bridge this divide remarkably, it was because of their exceptional academic brilliance and charming manners that both fellow students and society leaders found endearing. Sir Ashutosh Mookerjee loved the boys and exhorted them to excel themselves, not just in the field of law but to contribute in every aspect of the evolving society; providing an ideal foil to the foreign rulers and their laws.

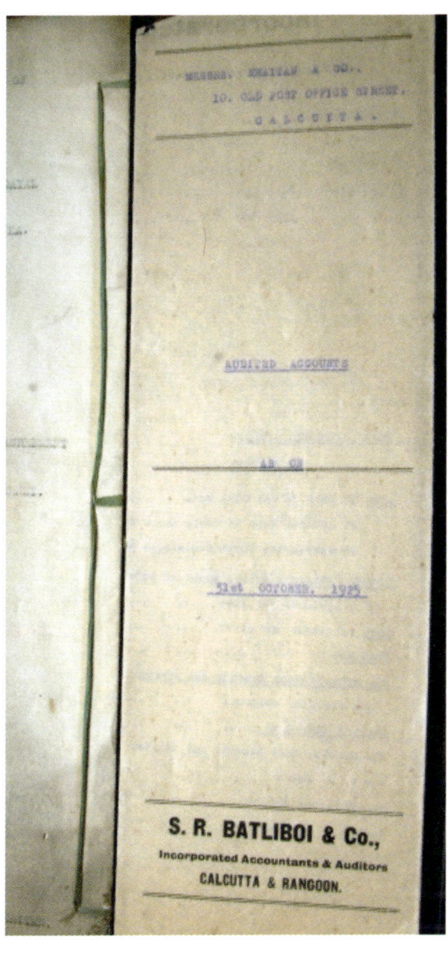

AUDITED ACCOUNTS

AS ON

31st OCTOBER, 1925

S. R. BATLIBOI & Co.,
Incorporated Accountants & Auditors
CALCUTTA & RANGOON.

An S.R. Batliboi 1925 statement of accounts, when the office was at 10 Old Post Office Street

Between themselves, the brothers had developed a near $360^0$ vision as far as the societal perspective was concerned. From Meerut to Agroha (Haryana), DP would attend conferences on the emancipation of the

## Spot on with banking advice

Teaching the sahibs a thing or two: BP's sharp mind and wise counsel saved the day for many a firm in trouble.

When it came to getting foreign accounts, the firm had to prove itself the hard way, as Bhagwati Babu did vis-à-vis Grindlays (whose India headquarters were in Calcutta) in 1969. The bank was then represented by Orr Dignam while KCo was representing a new client, Bank of India. Both the banks were involved in sorting out the affairs of Westinghouse Saxby Farmers, which had run into rough weather, thanks to labour unrest among other reasons and owed the two banks a great deal of money. Grindlays' London headquarters asked the Calcutta general manager to file a suit for enforcement of security and recovery of dues immediately but Westinghouse needed time. It requested the banks to accept additional securities and not file the suit, so that it could sort out its labour problem and reopen the factory. Grindlays' fear was the claim would get time-barred and accepting additional securities would mean waiving its option of exercising the right to go to court immediately. Orr Dignam too advised Grindlays to file the suit, and the bank, in a quandary, asked for a joint meeting with Bank of India that was inclined to give time.

Bhagwati Babu's wise counsel saved the day: he advised Grindlays that there was no need to panic because it could accept additional securities against acknowledgement documents; take a letter from the borrower and guarantors stating that 'in consideration of the bank not enforcing the securities and recovering the dues for the time it was being offered further securities as detailed in the agreement and for which it would execute necessary documents immediately'. Bhagwati Prasad Khaitan explained that under Indian law, keeping enforcement of security in temporary abeyance being would be 'good consideration in law' and constitute an enforceable contract between the parties. The claim would not get prejudiced by deferring the action. In support of his contention, he referred to the Privy Council judgment in which the Punjab National Bank was a party, which was accepted as the valid law in India.

The three senior-most officers, Messrs Bennett, Jackson and Pennyfather, were relieved. Mr Bennett stood up and complimented Bhagwati Babu by saying: 'Wonderful Mr Khaitan, this is exactly what my bank wanted. I am greatly relieved to know that here is a solicitor whom my bank can consult for on-the-spot advice'. Gradually, Grindlays cases started to come KCo and over time the firm became the bank's principal solicitor, says R.N. Jhunjhunwala.

Marwari community. He would enjoy equal prestige in the profession, getting a nomination to the Governing Body of the University Law College by the Incorporated Law Society. In the field of education, he served on the board of the Vishuddhanand Saraswati Vidyalay in 1916 and later joined hands with such stalwarts of Indian society as G.K. Gokhale, Madan Mohan Malaviya and C.F. Andrews to fight for the rights of the Bharatiya Coolies – poor Indians from many parts of the country who would be picked up or lured to go overseas as labour in what was virtually slave trade. He would also work closely with G.D. Birla, who was emerging as the most powerful voice not just of Marwari business but Indian business as a whole. It was for Debi Prasad's outstanding younger brother, Durga Prasad, to focus on the 'firm', which he joined in 1917, while the eldest brother administered it with iron hands. Since Lukkhi Babu (as the name appears on one of the partnership deeds) could not be a partner of a firm of solicitors, the brothers made him one through a special agreement. The only indulgence that 'Lukkhi' Babu permitted himself was the cigarette that he firmly held between two fingers, which his peon fetched for him; the cost debited to petty cash. Grandson Padam, who has very little recollection of his grandfather, remembers his tins of State Express 555. For the rest, he was strict with every penny. The story goes that when his son, Moti Lal joined the firm as a partner and had passed an expense, the chief cashier looked at the voucher and refused to pass it. The voucher went back and forth till an irked Moti Lall went up to his father and reasoned with him that while Lakshmi Narayan was his father, at the place of work, he was the boss!

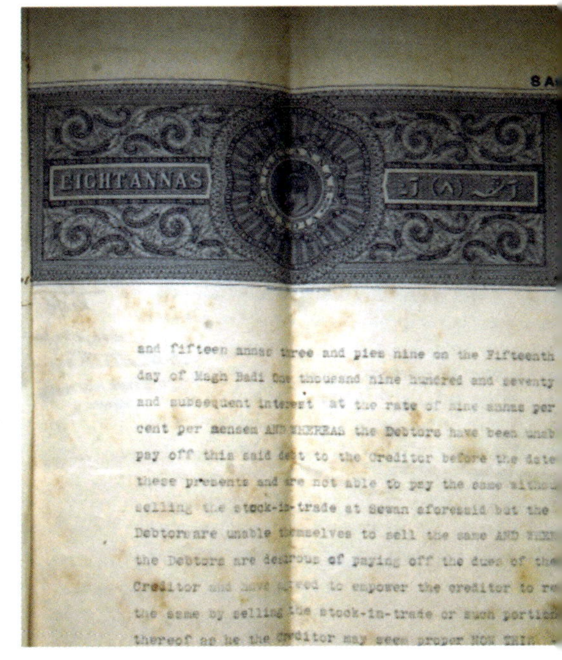

EIGHT ANNAS

and fifteen annas three and pies nine on the Fifteenth
day of Magh Badi One thousand nine hundred and seventy
and subsequent interest at the rate of nine annas per
cent per mensem AND WHEREAS the Debtors have been unab
pay off this said debt to the Creditor before the date
these presents and are not able to pay the same witho
selling the stock-in-trade at Sewan aforesaid but the
Debtors are unable themselves to sell the same AND WHER
the Debtors are desirous of paying off the dues of the
Creditor and have agreed to empower the creditor to re
the same by selling the stock-in-trade or such portion
thereof as he the Creditor may seem proper NOW THIS

Document on stamp paper purchased in the name of D.P. Khaitan, 10, Old Post Office Street, Kolkata

The work was varied and vast. There were property cases, conveyancing, disputes over land, fights between traders and trading partners, over shares and, of course, wills and family settlements. An old 1914 document shows Debi Prasad drafting a deed of settlement between debtor and creditor, for a Sewan (Chhapra, Bihar) based firm of traders and commission agents that had the power of attorney for realization of rents. This deed was drafted, engrossed on a stamp paper, but not executed. The stamp paper was bought in Debi Prasad's name.

The Marwaris, it is said with a great measure of accuracy, can make a success of any enterprise. Was there, however, a non-Marwari business ethic about the firm that would enable it to live to be a hundred and more? Were there management principles that transcended the typical Marwari traits of enterprise and industriousness? Bhagwati Prasad Khaitan believed that the firm succeeded because it was treated as a professional firm and not as a business. The profession of solicitors had established norms of conduct and the Khaitan brothers learnt to respect and imbibe the best practices of the times. Not all solicitors did (See Bhagwati's Gita). Fortunately, as Mrs Justice Manjula Bose informs, the Calcutta High Court of the time (1911) had excellent judges, including

## Bhagwati's Gita:

- Work as a professional company not as a business company: If a case comes to us we fight it to the best of our ability and only charge our fees; we do not try to make money in any other way through the case.
- Stay away from wrong: If we believe that the case has no merit and some one is doing something unethical, we do not take up the case. If we do not believe in the fairness of what we are doing, we will not be able to fight with full heart and soul for the client. That is why we refuse to take up the case and suggest that the client go elsewhere.
- Use judgment even before seeking justice: There are cases where a person who is unable to pay is liable to get arrested and face detention. While we did take such cases, we realized that if the person was basically good but unable to pay it would be unfair to get him arrested and detained and we began to refuse such cases. People realized that such cases were not welcomed by the firm and stopped coming to us with them.
- Arbitrate; do not litigate: Finally, try your best to settle cases through arbitration. We have done more such settlements through arbitration and settlement outside the court than any other solicitor firm.

four Indians of outstanding merit, of whom three were Bengalis: Sir Ashutosh Mookerjee (CSI, DL), Digambar Chatterjee and Nalini Ranjan Chatterjea. The other Indian was Saiyid Sharf-Ud-Din. They were the puisne judges along with H. Harington, C.M.W. Brett (CSI, ICS), H.L. Stephen, J.G. Woodroffe (MA, BCL), C.P. Caspérz (ICS), H. Holmwood (ICS), C.W. Chitty, E.E. Fletcher, H.R.H. Coxe (ICS), H.W.C. Carnduff (CIE, ICS) and W. Teunon (ICS, Offg). The Chief Justice was Sir Lawrence Hugh Jenkins (Kt, KOIC), G.H.B. Kenrick (KC) was the Advocate General and H.K. Mitter, the standing counsel, said the Weekly Notes of the year, printed by Joy Gopal Das of the Weekly Notes Printing Works, which was located right next to the High Court, at No. 3, Hastings Street. The Weekly Notes was to be one of the most important documents on matters of law for times to come.

## Friend to the 'enemy'

The war years of 1939-1945 found the Japanese residing in India being placed in the category of citizens of 'enemy' countries with talk of imprisoning them. The Japanese citizens gave the power of attorney to Bhagwati Babu to negotiate with the British government all points regarding their safety and their rights. This was the faith that even non-Indians had in his sense of client loyalty.

For the Khaitans in the fledgling years, everything Indian had to be supported. The Indian perspective had to find a place in every policy; the voice of the Indian business community had to be heard by the British administration and the law had to work for Indians as much as it did for those with lighter-coloured skins. A hundred years after his uncle had started the firm, Pradip Kumar (Pinto) Khaitan, son of Bhagwati Prasad Khaitan, says: 'KCo was in a unique position to serve the Swadeshi interests and industrialists; it was born out of a felt need for such services to be provided by Indian firms and we were automatically in parallel to multinational interests. It represented the Indian Chamber – which it had helped create – as opposed to the Bengal Chamber that had multinational members. This was in tune with the spirit of the Independence movement where it was felt that Indian enterprise had to stand on its own feet and not survive as a satellite of foreign interests.

'Thus, KCo was always on the Indian side when the British were selling and even if it did get a British client who wanted it to handle a deal, it would decline because it was already representing the Swadeshi side'. Indeed, well after the playing fields had become level, the Khaitans did start accepting British clients but had to prove their class for such custom. Grindlays was among the early birds to have been impressed by the firm.

Nevertheless, the pervading notion of the superiority of everything western continued till the 1990s when the liberalization of the Indian economy promoted the growth of Indian multinationals and globalized India's trade and commerce. The character of the firm, too, had changed dramatically from the days of Lukkhi Babu's control and Bhagwati Babu's genial brilliance. Today, KCo

## Trusting its own

Nearly a hundred years after the firm was set up with its motto of training the young, Mr Parag Tripathi (currently India's Additional Solicitor General), who had once trained with the firm, emphasizes the confidence that the firm had in all those that it had trained: 'Even when I left the company, KCo allowed me to continue with the matters that I was dealing with and also continued to give me briefs. Thus it was that even as a 25-26 year old I was independently working on a very important Kanoria Chemicals arbitration and writ proceedings, with Ashok Desai and G.E. Vahanvati. The firm always encouraged its former employees and briefed them on a regular basis. This is not the practice with some other leading firms that I know of. In fact, most other firms avoid ex-employees thinking that they would run away with their clients. They never brief lawyers who had left them till they had reached a certain stature in the profession. This was not the case with KCo. In fact, lawyers who have left the Khaitans are all successful and well-known names in the legal world today. The credit largely goes to the firm whose unstinting support they have had'.

is a full-service law firm with a very strong management consulting business. While the children and grandchildren of some of the founding partners are still with the firm – 'Sita Ram Jhunjhunwala's brother and their children are still with us', says PK – the character of the human resource has changed. Even after the firm had branched out to Delhi and Bangalore with 40 lawyers, 16 were from the Khaitan family. 'Today, out of the 50 partners, only five are Khaitans; out of 250 associate lawyers only two or three are Khaitans', says P. K. Khaitan. None of this has diminished the professional competence of the firm that has been winning accolades at the client and industry level. Khaitan & Co LLP (LLP Identity No: AAA – 0866) is registered as a limited-liability partnership with effect from March 4, 2010 on conversion of KCo, a partnership firm registered in Delhi. Today, the firm is ranked third in the country.

Over the pages one will come across accounts of how the firm has helped guide the evolution of law and its practice in India by virtue of the individual brilliance of its many outstanding partners and through the collective action of the firm as a whole. One will examine how the company has professionalized its operations and is now managed by an executive committee of lawyers, which comprises members elected by the partners. Says Haigreve Khaitan: 'Some members of the executive committee have dual degrees from India and overseas and bring in their international law practices to our firm. This exercise in professionalizing the management resulted in KCo being recognized as one of the top three firms in India by a group of international rating organizations' in a globalized India, far removed from Calcutta, where Naurangrai's boys set up shop'.

Calcutta began losing its industrial and political eminence from 1911, the year D.P. Khaitan set up the firm, when the capital was transferred to Delhi, to isolate India's political capital from the hotbed of the freedom movement that continued to be centred in the city. KCo, too, spread its wings across the country and while the city continues to inspire and enthuse it with its intellectual stimulation, it is the commercial capital of the country, Mumbai, where the firm receives the largest financial sustenance. It is from Bangalore that it has served some of its most outstanding technology clients and from Delhi, where it has helped shape the destiny of some of India's most important political personalities.

How does the emerging generation of leaders within the firm perceive the rich legacy and the challenging future? How does it envision the next 100 years? Says Haigreve Khaitan, grandson of Bhagwati Prasad: 'It is customary, while articulating the vision for any organization with aspirations, to emphasize one way or the other an ambition to be the very best. This goes without saying for KCo. We see ourselves as a first-choice law firm for our clients; we seek to be known as professionals that contribute genuine value add and an excellent work product. We are a great place to work in for young lawyers and most importantly, we intend to remain uncompromising on quality'. It is this pursuit of quality that has enabled the firm to secure the confidence of a state-of-the-art, $40 billion pure play fund, Apax Partners, even while retaining the continued faith of its oldest clients: the Birlas, the Singhanias, the Kanorias.... 'The important thing is that, while the firm has been running for generations, it is not run like a *lala* company. The attitude of turning a family firm into a professional firm is very impressive as they have built up a strong practice because they recruited strong talent',

Three generations – B.P. Khaitan, Pinto Khaitan and Haigreve Khaitan

## K.K. Birla on the Priyamvada Devi will case in his autobiography, Brushes with History

'...Sometime in early 1983 Madhav Prasad told me that ... in 1982 (he and his wife) had made wills leaving behind all their assets ultimately to charities. I was made one of the executors of the 1982 will. The language of Madhav Prasad's will and his wife Priyamvada Devi's will was identical. Madhav Prasad's assets at that time were valued at approximately Rs 5,000 crores. Today, perhaps their valuation may be anywhere between Rs 20,000 and 25,000 crores... After his death, his wife took up the management of his property... A few days after his demise, Lodha (auditor Rajendra Prasad Lodha) sent word to me to state that he had the latest will of Priyamvada Birla and would like to acquaint me with the same... All the members of the family were stunned when they heard this so-called will allegedly executed on 18 April 1999 as read out by Lodha... They felt that this could not be the genuine will. Members of the family sent for Nand Gopal Khaitan of KCo and entrusted their case to him. Nand Gopal consulted some other lawyers...The case is going on in various courts. As the matter is sub judice, I am not offering any more comments'.

says Shashank Singh, Apax Partners.

Possibly, the headline-grabbing case of the century that KCo has been associated with is the Priyamvada Devi Birla will case that is still sub judice. One can only quote what K. K. Birla had to say about it: 'Nand Gopal Khaitan, who is a bright young solicitor, was entrusted with the responsibility of conducting the litigation'. In 21st century India, where only the fittest survive, the 100-year-old firm not only has professionalism on its side, it has a century of experience supplemented with a century of trust from its oldest clients, a heritage that very few others have.

'Throughout my long association with the firm, I found KCo extremely efficient and organized with multilayered teams dealing with diverse aspects of procedural and substantive lawyering. I realized the strong bond of trust that it developed with the top bosses and owners of the corporations that it represented, Marwaris and non-Marwaris alike. It is a bond developed painstakingly over generations', says

## Neighbours envy; owner's pride: Emerald House

As the administration of the East India Company was transformed into that of the British Raj, so did the courts of Calcutta evolve. First, the Sadar Dewani Adalat and Sadat Nijamat Adalat, which made way for the Mayor's Court in 1728, functioning from the company-owned Ambassador House. That was at the corner of Lalbazar and Mission Row, from where Haridas Mundhra still operates: the Martin Burn House, which has replaced the earlier structure. It then moved to the premises of Charity School in 1732, to a two-storied building where St Andrew's Church now stands, across the road from the Writers' Building. The Mayor's Court then made room for the Supreme Court of Judicature at Fort William on March 26, 1774. The original Supreme Court, one understands, was not much of a building from the outside – the inside was imposing though – but what replaced it at a much later date, was the magnificent building of the High Court of Calcutta. It comprised the area occupied on one side by the Old Supreme Court house, which stood upon the West portion and the houses of three distinguished gentlemen of the law: Longueville Clerk, who founded the Bar Library Club, William Macpherson and William Colville. The neo-Gothic structure, a replica of Belgium's Town Hall at Ypres is as grand as ever but the years have not treated the structures around the High Court well; save the building to its left. Right next to the Calcutta High Court, the Emerald Company constructed a lovely building: green and gracious.

The municipal records have dealt with the plot exhaustively: being premises No. 1B, Old Post Office Street and earlier being a part of No. 1, Old Post Office Street (Calcutta Improvement Scheme No. IX and being Plot No. 1 and Lot No. 1 of the surplus land in Sale No 6, now containing an area of eighteen cottahs and eight and half chittacks, be the same as a little more or less formed out a portion of Old Municipal premises No. 1, 2, and 3 Old Post Office Street and being parts of revenue free holdings Nos. 29, 29/2, 47 and 49 all of Block No. XXIII of the south division in the town of Calcutta and butted and bounded on the north partly by 1A Old Post Office Street and partly by No. 4, Hastings Street, on the south by High Court compound wall, on the east by Old Post Office Street and on the West by premises No. 3, Hastings Street.

This property so elaborately described in the municipal records was to be the centre of celebrations at a time far removed from then. It would house the headquarters of KCo: Emerald House, clearly the best preserved building in the area and probably one that makes many a rival turn the colour that it dons.

The best-maintained building on Old Post Office Street, Emerald House, the home of KCo; the best performing firm as well

Facing page: Antique wooden nameplate that still adorns the Emerald House entrance. Many names have changed over the years. KCo lives on.

Fascinating rise. Rabindra Jhunjhunwala and Ravi Kulkarni at the IFLR Awards (third and fourth from the right)

parliamentarian, Abhishek Manu Singhvi, former Additional Solicitor General of India.

From actor Uttam Kumar to Narsingdas Bangur; from actress Sumitra Sen to Om Dhanuka; from R.K. Dalmia to Leena Chandravarkar; from Indira Gandhi to V. V. Giri; from the Concourse of Princes (Privy Purse) to Sonia Gandhi, from the Ramakrishna Mission to Hari Das Mundhra; from Shri Shikshayatan to St Xavier's; and from Jyoti Basu to the magician Gogia Pasha; the firm has worked with the entire spectrum of Indian citizenry. If the firm demonstrated its strategic magic, Gogia Pasha demonstrated his own brand of wizardry. Having come to Emerald House on business, he was asked to sit in a room to meet Ram Niranjan Jhunjhunwala. RNJ found him sitting in another room and, then, when he looked at the first room, there was Pasha sitting there as well. This was a case of multiple

Pashas that the firm has not been able to solve, though it has achieved several trend-changing legal victories; it has influenced policy on taxes with its erudite representations to various commissions; it has set up institutions and probably single-handedly prevented the nationalization of jute in the country; it has provided a nursery for leading jurists of the day to learn their craft; it has structured charities and specialized in wills and encouraged research in law, especially for traditional families.

In more modern times, it has ushered in the country's first fully foreign-owned retail chain into India, using the existing laws of the land; it has changed the concept of wealth and the way income-tax law is practised in India. There had been a day in the 1970s – when there were no photocopiers – that KCo filed nearly 400 writ applications against the order purporting to control all sugar dealers. With all the clients in court it was almost like a festive atmosphere! Underlying that was the herculean effort put in by the solicitors in preparing all the writs where the only mechanization available was the cyclostyling machine.

There have been heartaches of cases lost and the jubilation of victories achieved. There have been strikes and sports within the KCo family; workplace anger has ended in a massive hug on the field of cricket, where only sportsman spirit survived. There have been bloomers – some unforgiveable – and hilarious situations even with the strictest of judges. Two bloomers bear retelling: One when the Delhi office signed a back-sheet where it called itself 'S'haitan & Company – the typist had got his qwerty wrong, though the firm's oft-battered opposition would have agreed with the slip. No harm was done because the error was detected before the brief left the office. The firm was not so lucky with another matter though and that was quite unpardonable: A petition was addressed to the 'T'hief

Justice of India, another qwerty error that made the Chief Justice, Supreme Court, Mr A.N. Ray's face turn red. He looked at the petition and said: 'Dismissed; Petition wrongly addressed'. Fortunately for the firm, the client was not present in the court and was never told why the petition had been dismissed. It took all of the firm's ingenuity to have the matter readmitted!

Even the normally staid and serious Shanti Bhushan has amusing things to say about his experiences while working with KCo: He was appearing in a matter of a person charged with bribing Doordarshan officials. When the police went to arrest the man, they found that he had fallen sick and had to be hospitalized. The legal point being discussed was why the bribe takers should not go scot-free but Justice Binayak Banerjee's pointed question was how the accused managed to fall sick just when the police turned up to arrest him. That was when Shanti Bhushan told him the story about Justice Vashisht Bhargav of the Allahabad High Court complaining to his brother judge about so many illness slips that he received from his lawyers. The brother judge is believed to have answered: 'When they receive the list in the morning and see that their case is appearing before you, they get a heart attack'. Recalls Shanti Bhushan: 'I told Justice Banerjee the story and the question was settled amidst great hilarity'. With solicitors and barristers of stature, even the judges occasionally shed their sombre demeanour.

At the threshold of success: entrance to Emerald House

The stamp of success

On the top floor of Emerald House is a room under lock and key that holds the secrets to so many family intrigues. Anand Mishra keeps vigil there… just as his elder brother, Ram Kumar Mishra, had done before him; yet another tale of generational commitment. Ram Kumar's son, Jaiprakash, and grandson, Mukesh, have risen in stature, serving as court clerks with the firm. There are wills, testaments, settlements, division of family property, details of sensitive arbitrations, conveyances dating back to 1906, even before the firm was born, which cannot be a part of this centenary history because they are matters of a sacred trust; reposed in the firm a hundred years ago.

Nothing leaves the room without Mishraji's scrutiny and a commitment of being restored to his care after they have been perused. They might have made for interesting and historic reading on the occasion of the firm's 100th year but that is not what the firm is about. It is about treating the client as God and never betraying their trust. If a secret was bequeathed to the firm; it would remain thus. For that is the essence of trust between the firm and the client.

# THE DNA FOR SUCCESS

Knowing where the law is: The ladders in the law library hold the steps to legal success

*It was all in the alphabet 'n'( nuh) in the Devanagari script. The Khaitans did not spell their name with the normal 'nuh' but nrunh, say the knowledgeable who trace the history of the family to the 11th century. The vaishya family, which spelt its name with a nrunh, had special attributes: it was resilient, gutsy, intelligent, persevering and industrious. The character of the vansh (family), founded by Khetsi Das, possibly some 400 years ago has been built over 14 generations. It was character built over years of struggle as the family was forced to flee from the combined exploitation of the Mughals under Aurangzeb, the Pathans and the British simply because they knew the art and craft of business. Adversity was good for the family; it gave it inner strength and external confidence.*

— **Binod Khaitan**

It must have been a strange spectacle. The all powerful deputy commissioner of Purulia, Colonel E.I. Dalton, surveying his territory on horseback – as the burrasahibs did in those days – emanating terror as he did so and seemingly sending everyone around scampering for cover. Save a little boy who stood his ground, watching the commissioner pass by, even when all his friends (and the elders) had fled. Colonel Dalton was, however, not typecast in the hated mould of many commissioners of the times, even though he had played a singularly important role in dealing with the Sepoy Mutiny. A fine human being, he must have been amused at the sight of the slip of a boy observing him and asked him his name.

Naurangrai Khaitan; smart and poised as a child; savvy and professional as a jailor

This was Naurangrai, smart and poised, as he had a chat with Dalton, just as he would with any adult. The commissioner was quite bowled over and decided to accompany the boy to his home. There he met the family: the two uncles, Jaisraj and Rishikesh, who were running a small clothes store in village

Lakri Bakri. Naurangrai's father, Puranmull, a former judge in Ramgarh (Rajasthan), had died fighting the British on behalf of the Nawab of Jhajjar, but that was possibly a tale that they did not share with the commissioner sahib, who complimented them on the fine young man that their nephew was. Naurangrai must go for higher education to the Government Zilla School in Purulia, Dalton Sahib insisted. More importantly, the Englishman kept in touch with the young man who lived up to the promise that Dalton Sahib had seen: five years later, in 1872, he passed the entrance examination, standing first in the Bengali language.

This development was to be of historical import for both the Marwari community and the Khaitan family that had made Bengal its home. How come the Khaitans came to Bengal? How come they had this academic bent of mind? To go back a couple of generations ahead of Naurangrai, the Rajasthan society of those years was feudal and harsh and even a senior government officer in Fatehpura, Kewal Ram, could not escape its exploitative ways. Kewal Ram, the grandfather of Naurangrai, quit Fatehpura to move to Ramgarh, where the Thakurs were not as ruthless. Kewal Ram's son, Puranmull, too turned out to be a good judge and was doing well in Ramgarh. A kind man, he gave shelter to two homeless people one night. It turned out that they were two dacoits of the

Map of the region

Robin Hood mould, Dungji and Joharji. Once it got known that Puranmull had given them shelter, howsoever unwittingly, life became impossible in Ramgarh and Puranmull had to leave in search of safer pastures. It was in Purulia in Bengal that he finally found a home – some members of the community had already travelled to these parts – and this was where he started a small business, selling clothes with his two brothers, the elder brother Jaisraj and the younger, Rishikesh. Their families stayed on in Ramgarh though, where Naurangrai was born on July 27, 1854, three years before the Sepoy Mutiny. Puranmull himself died soon after, in a fight with the British.

Nursery for legal excellence: the home at Chandil, where the first generation of the Khaitan lawyers was nurtured

Naurangrai continued to live in Ramgarh, completing his studies at the local pathshala till the age of 11 with excellent grades. It was now time for him to go to Purulia at the age of 12 in 1866 to join the family business. Fate had other things in store for him: the child, who lost his father to the British armed forces, was to find a mentor in a Briton, whose personal attention to his well-being ensured that Puranmull's son would always be well looked after.

Quite outstanding in academics, Naurangrai continued to impress everyone, winning four special prizes at the district level, then passing the entrance and becoming the most qualified boy in eastern India amongst the Marwari community. His teacher, Banku Behari Sarkar, was a wonderful influence; so was Dalton Sahib, who wanted him to go to Calcutta for further studies. This the family would not allow: with so much Christianity in the Calcutta air, the boy could well become a Christian if let out of sight. So

Naurangrai had to stay put in Purulia.

Over the years the family business was doing reasonably well and the Khaitans had bought a zamindari. Suddenly circumstances were straitened with the clothes business suffering losses, compelling the family to sell the zamindari. Naurangrai had to take up a job in order to bail the family out and redeem its reputation. It was the redoubtable Dalton Sahib who stepped in once again, giving Naurangrai a job of a sub-jailor at the Purulia gaol at Rs 15 a month. If Naurangrai had impressed Dalton with his academic performance, he impressed him even more with his work. Indeed, so happy was the commissioner with the young man that he bought the zamindari of Chandil, comprising 33 villages along with a larger house and gifted it to Naurangrai. No father could have done more for his son.

By then Naurangrai was himself a father. He had married Surya Devi, daughter of Gulabrai Jhunjhunwala of Jhunjhunu (then settled in Calcutta) and the couple had four daughters followed by six sons. The first son was named Lakshmi Narayan; the sixth child, born on August 14, 1888, was named Debi Prasad. An inmate of his jail prepared the horoscope for the newborn that foretold an illustrious life. The children brought good fortune to their father for Naurangrai's income had increased from Rs 15 to Rs 1,700. He had a government house and other perks and did not want his children to lack anything - least of all the best education that he could afford.

Naurangrai becomes Rai Sahib

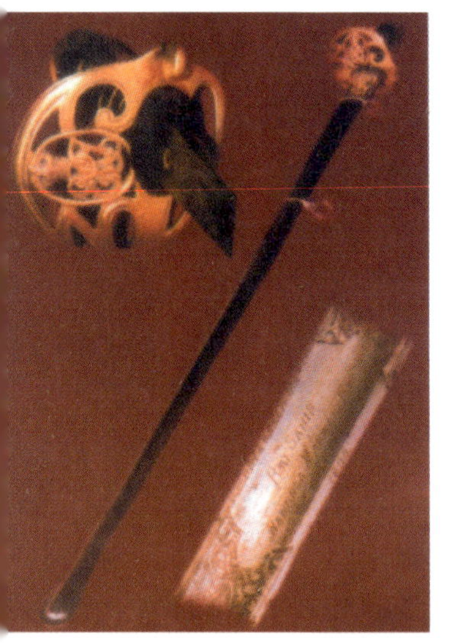

Professionally, Naurangrai enjoyed quite a meteoric rise for an Indian of those times. He became the first Indian jailor and then the first deputy superintendent of jails. In 1862, he took over the region's biggest central jail in Buxar, having successfully administered jails in Ranchi, Cuttack and Medinipur. The improved status in life meant improved finances and Naurangrai could recover the lost family zamindari. His bosses trusted his judgment, and society as

## For he was named after Durga!

Durga Prasad, who was born in 1892, was everything his brother could have dreamt of. He studied in Calcutta at the Hindu School and Presidency College and did not see merit in securing the second position in any examination: he stood first class first in his Bachelor's, Master's and his Bachelor of Law from the Calcutta University along with the final attorneyship examination, before getting enrolled as an attorney in 1917. For a while he ran KCo, when elder brother DP moved over to the Birlas. However, just as law was in his blood, so was enterprise and his life was full of accomplishments in the legal and insurance professions, enriched by the stellar role that he played as councillor of the Calcutta Corporation. As an institution builder, he served as the president of the Indian Sugar Mills Association, president of the Tanners' Federation of India and vice-president of the Indian Chamber of Commerce, apart from being a member of the advisory board of the Calcutta Traffic Advisory Committee of the East Indian Railways. Later, when the opportunity presented itself to provide industrial leadership to the Birla group, he joined Birla Bros and rose to become the vice-chairman of Bharat Insurance Company. Durga Prasad Khaitan passed away on November 19, 1943.

a whole respected the self-made man. Indeed, the British government conferred on him the title of Rai Sahib on January 1, 1906. It was possibly his stature that emboldened him to ensure that his son, Debi Prasad, received an education in the English medium in the Buxar District School; something that was quite abhorrent to most of his community members. One suspects though that there was a sneaking admiration for those who mastered the English language. Debi Prasad picked up the language beautifully and, as a boy studying in class IX, totally impressed Badridas Goenka, who was visiting his father's home.

Modern education was gradually finding respect within the community that began to appreciate that education did not amount to a loss of religion or culture but was the avenue to enlightenment. It came as no surprise when Debi Prasad secured a first class in the Patna division and won a

## Legal eagle

Kali Prasad Khaitan commanded great respect amongst the legal fraternity that gave him the sobriquet of: 'a moving legal encyclopedia'. He was often asked to arbitrate on very important matters. Not very many people who had worked with him are alive but Ram Kishore Choudhury recalls having appeared before him in an arbitration relating to the construction of a bridge over the river Subarnarekha. The client was Hindustan Construction of G.D. Kothari and Bhagwati Babu was handling the matter. Given the compulsions of professional ethics, Bhagwati Babu chose not to appear before his elder brother but entrusted the work to RKC. 'It was well known to all that KP was a very straightforward man and he believed in a systematic handling of all matters. He was also a firm believer in legal decorum. I was, therefore, entrusted with the matter and I appeared and even got the chance of leading evidence and cross-examining the witnesses of the government of India in the matter in which we succeeded eventually', recalls RKC.

scholarship; nor was there much debate that he would study at that hallowed institution in Calcutta: the Presidency College. Before that, Debi Prasad got married, at the age of 13! His child-bride had fragile health and stayed with her parents till she came of age. She never did get acclimatized to any place save Jaipur and succumbed to illness at a very tender age.

Calcutta had meanwhile, become a second home for the Khaitans, who were people of unquestionable stature by then. Their father had been awarded the title of Rai Bahadur for his distinctive services on January 1, 1913. Eminent persons from all over the country congratulated the man whose jails many of them had visited and whose standards of prison administration all of them had admired. Rabindranath Tagore, who visited his jail on December 2, 1914, wrote in the visitors' book: 'I have been greatly impressed with whatever I have seen in this jail. It seems to me quite a model of what this kind of thing should be'.

The family home in Calcutta was another happy place to

be in. The Khaitans then lived at 125, Harrison Road, and later at 92, Harrison Road, only to return to their former home where they lived till 1923, before shifting to 11, Syed Sally Lane. Naurangrai's eldest son, Lakshmi Narayan, was already there when DP arrived. He was assisting his uncle, Anandi Ram, who had a textiles or garment business there. It was assumed that DP would join him after he completed his education. Amidst studies, physical training – DP was a bit of a health freak too – community service and heated political discussions evolved a well-rounded personality that was trained to think about self, service, society and Swadesh.

For such a man destiny had different plans. First the adversity: the family business went under and Naurangrai knew that his sons would have to look for alternative means of livelihood. He also knew that it was his sixth child that would show the path. Yet, like a typical father and despite his own elevated status in life and the zamindari that the family owned, he worried about his children, especially with DP graduating from Presidency.

Naurangrai considered his options and one of them was to return to his home state, from where the maharaja had been tempting him with lucrative offers to run the Jaipur jail. The Governor General of Bengal was not willing to lose his prized prison administrator though. The man had spent three decades handling the Bengal prison system and had to be retained at all costs. He made a counter-offer that Naurangrai could not refuse: he promised to make Naurangrai's son, who had graduated from the Presidency with flying colours, a district magistrate. Naurangrai responded with great joy and requested an English prisoner, Ernest Hardwicke Cowie, to help him write a letter to the Inspector of Prisons that he would continue in Buxar provided his son was secure in a job.

Reference to Cowie is to be found in the India Office Records (Public and Judicial Department Records [L/PJ/6/623 - L/PJ/6/711]) that talks of a 'request from the Calcutta Police for the arrest of Ernest Hardwicke Cowie, a solicitor, wanted for fraud IOR/L/PJ/6/683, File 1516, 24 Jun 1904'. Cowie, who used to be a partner in a firm of solicitors, Synder & Company, considered the rather brilliant curriculum vitae and advised his jailor that it would be a pity to waste the boy as a magistrate. He suggested that Debi Prasad be trained as an attorney instead and predicted that the young man would secure his family's financial future with his sheer brilliance. It is another story that records also show that the Criminal Investigation Department of New Scotland Yard sent a message informing that Ernest H. Cowie had been arrested in Western Australia (IOR/L/PJ/6/689, File 2053, 20 August 1904). The point was that he was doing time at Naurangrai's jail and, when it came to offering his counsel, he was spot on. Cowie, a member of the Incorporated Law Society since June 8, 1903, was involved in a much-reported case of misappropriation. Jailed or free, he thought he could get DP an articleship in his old firm but that was not to be.

No English firm wanted a Marwari articled clerk. Finally, it was left for Naurangrai to place his son with the firm of Manuel and Agarwalla, who accepted DP for what was then a princely fee of Rs 2,500. Manuel probably was a C. N. Manuel (who qualified as an attorney in 1871 and became a member of the Incorporated Law Society in 1889). No one would take DP as an articled clerk for less and it was the generosity of one of the partners, Baboo Dhannu Lall Agarwalla (who passed his attorneyship on January 17, 1895, and became member of the Incorporated Law Society on August 3, 1899) that swung the deal. Naurangrai would happily spend on educating his son for another five years, secure in the knowledge that Debi Prasad would become one of the first Marwari attorneys. He achieved that distinction in 1911, with a first class in the

## Torn papers case

There was the rather interesting 'torn papers case', so named because it was so old that the papers were in tatters. The family involved in the matter wanted to meet Durga Babu, who was not in at that time. His younger brother, Bhagwati, was sitting on a small table in his brother's room. The young man examined the papers and gave his expert opinion: 'there is no merit in the case'. The family that had been advised by leading barristers was surprised to hear the young man say that there was no point pursuing the matter in the court. The matter involved three parties: A had sold the same thing to B and C. C sold it to D. Now A had started the case against D. Bhagwati Babu had heard a lecture on this subject in the Law University and it was fresh in his mind and he had no hesitation in advising that A could start a case against B but not against D. When Durga Babu arrived and examined the papers he was delighted that his younger brother had hit the nail on the head. The family then took the matter for a private settlement that was acceptable to both parties.

attorneyship examination. Interestingly, it was the same firm of Manuel & Agarwalla that also gave an articleship to P.D. Himatsingka in July 1912. PDH served with the Khaitans till he set up his own firm.

Yet that was not enough for any British firm of attorneys to give him a partnership. Not even Manuel & Agarwalla agreed. Not that the young man cared: he would start off on his own. His reputation within the community had already secured for him the support of one of the biggest commercial firms of those days: Taradas Ghanshyamdas, which gave him business from day one. The Marwari vakil attracted the attention of the Bengali law firms too and there were some mighty names: N.C. Ghosh, the knighted Sir Dev Prasad Sarvadhikari and Bhupendra Nath Bose amongst others in those days but the young Marwari attorney soon caught the eye of the court.

The story goes that Debi Prasad was appearing as the legendary C.R. Das's junior in an insolvency case, when his senior was called away. Suddenly, the matter was called and Chief Justice Fletcher found himself being addressed by a young substitute. Debi Prasad Khaitan floored everyone with the fluency of his arguments for the 20 minutes allotted to him and, when his senior arrived and indicated his willingness to take over, the Chief Justice said that he would be happy to have the young man continue. The arguments went on for two-and-a-half hours and the eloquence of the young man won the day: that day and ever after because Debi Prasad started getting flooded with cases. The outstanding Marwari vakil would wear his pugree with pride and carried off his churidar sherwani with great elan.

Not just was DP acquiring an iconic status for the community; he was an inspiration for his younger brothers: Kali Prasad Khaitan secured a first division in his MA and was felicitated by the Marwari Association. In fact, so promising was the young man that he caught the attention of Sir Ashutosh Mookerjee, who insisted that Kali Prasad be sent to do his bar-at-law in London; a move that was wholly supported by such enlightened members of the community as G.D. Birla and Sir Jamnalal Bajaj though it was condemned by the more conservative families.

It was Sir Ashutosh who found a way out for Kali Prasad to go abroad. He suggested that their father, Naurangrai, call

## Kali the renunciator

Amongst Kali Prasad Khaitan's many ardent admirers was the then Chief Justice of India, B.P. Sinha, who was delivering a lecture at a function in Delhi. From the podium he spotted Kali Prasad Khaitan in the audience. The Chief Justice, got off the stage, walked into the audience and escorted the barrister to the stage introducing him as his 'guru'. If that was remarkable, what followed was astounding.

Kali Prasad Khaitan announced then and there: In deference to the sentiments expressed by the venerable Chief Justice of India, he was renouncing the practice of law in view of clients possibly wanting to take advantage of what had just been said about him vis-à-vis the Chief Justice of India.

That was it. Kali Prasad Khaitan never practiced law thereafter, recalls RKC, eyewitness to the Delhi function.

Marwari Students Union, Executive Commitee 1941-1942

a panchayat meeting to get the permission of the society at large. It did so but on three conditions: that he would have to remain a strict vegetarian; that he would have to take his own cook with him to prepare his food; and that he would have to abjure the company of women. He agreed to all these conditions and a cook was sent to prepare his food. The Birlas gave him a warm send-off on the eve of his departure by ship from Mumbai, accompanied by the Marwari cook. He passed the bar in 1914, getting a special cash award for his knowledge of constitutional law. On his return he was felicitated in Mumbai and on his way back at several stations where his train stopped from Mumbai to Howrah. At the Howrah station there were more than 500 Marwaris to welcome him but there were dark clouds in the horizon.

The conservatives raised their vested heads and had KP declared an outcaste and even the Marwari Association with which DP was so actively associated chose to support the move. It needed a promise of a prayaschit (penance) by going on a pilgrimage for KP to cleanse himself of his 'sins' and gain readmission into his community. The cook, however, could not live down the dishonour of having travelled overseas and came to a sorry pass when he returned to his home in Chandil. For Kali Prasad, there were great honours in store. He joined the Calcutta bar in 1914 and quickly established a formidable reputation. After three decades of outstanding practice K.P. Khaitan was appointed advocate general of West Bengal, the highest legal office of the state, upon Sir S.M. Bose demitting office in 1949. For two years prior to that he had served as standing counsel. Congratulating him, the Calcutta Weekly Notes said on May 16 (page 99) that he had risen to this high position 'by sheer self effort … pushed his way through to success. That furnishes the key to the character of the man – his remarkable qualities of head and heart, which, may we say, unmistakably qualify him for the august office to which he is now called. We have complete faith in his personality and have no doubt that he will be the leader of a strong and independent Bar…. We all know that Mr Khaitan has adopted this Province as his home and his appointment must give satisfaction to all concerned. We hope he will be a genuine success as Advocate-General of West Bengal in a Free India'.

DP had acquired an iconic status in society; even the English took him seriously

Meanwhile, KCo was carving out a niche for itself doing special and routine cases. Amongst the earliest reported judgments featuring the firm was a case of Joylal & Co. vs Gopiram Bhotica of 1919. The bench comprising Justices L. Sanderson, A. Mookerjee and E. Fletcher ruled against KCo's clients: the plaintiffs, Gopiram Bhotica. It was a dispute over a contract for sale

## Trusteeship

The concept of Trusteeship was, of course, a gift of the Mahatma, but it was Bhagwati Prasad Khaitan who strongly urged his community to follow the concept that industrialists consider themselves as trustees of society. He even helped them set up trusts, agreeing to become a trustee for some of them to ensure that the Mahatma's ideals were put into practice. BPK helped in the establishment of such trusts as the Raghumal Charity Trust. Raghumal Khandelwal was a man of wealth and a leader of the Arya Samaj. He also helped form the Halwasiya Trust and worked with Bhagirath Kanoria to serve his trust along with many other private trusts set up by industrial and business houses of the time.

He helped many to be converted into public trusts and indeed made his views on the matter public at a meeting of the trustees of the Govindram Bajaj Charity Trust. He insisted that the activities of charitable trusts be made public; their accounts become transparent and subject to audit. Personally, he became an expert in running trusts and guiding their activities. Many important trusts wanted him to join their board of trustees so that they would be run efficiently and ethically. BPK obliged quite a few of them.

of hessian cloth (contract no. 13,700, dated December 6, 1917) wherein there was a clause that any dispute would be referred to arbitration under the rules of the Bengal Chamber of Commerce and resolved. KCo had first obtained a stay on such arbitration from a single-judge bench because it wanted the matter to be settled in court but the order was set aside by Justice L. Sanderson's order: 'I am not able at the present stage of the proceedings to say that the matters in dispute between the parties are such as should not be submitted to and decided by the Arbitration Tribunal…' The not so good went with the good and the better, but one thing was certain: things were moving fast and furiously on the business and political fronts.

On the personal front, Debi Prasad's youngest brother was coming of age, with the Khaitan academic imprimatur all over him. Bhagwati Prasad Khaitan graduated with economics honours from the Presidency

College in 1924, completed law from the Calcutta University in 1927, enrolled as attorney-at-law on April 3, 1930, and was finally enrolled as a notary by the Archbishop of Canterbury on August 30, 1934. Whilst all this was going on, DP and BP got married to two ladies selected by the family. DP married Narayani Devi and BP wed Tija Bai at the family zamindari in Chandil in 1916. Like his elder brother, BP too lost his first spouse to illness and then married Laksha Kumari.

The firm, meanwhile, secured the respect of competing firms too. Dinesh Himatsingka of Himatsingka Siede recalls: 'Our association with KCo went much beyond the legal. Indeed, our own family firm was a legal firm of great stature in those days and almost since my birth I was given the impression that there were just two legal firms: Khaitan and P.D. Himatsingka. Between our families and firms there was a different kind of understanding; for me they were family'.

The fraternal bonds stayed just as strong between the sons of DP and Bhagwati Prasad, even after DP was no more. Indeed, it was after his passing that BP emerged as a source of strength for his late brother's family for reasons personal and professional. People often say that one should not do business with relatives because that spoils the relationship. Not so for Dhruv Khaitan, the grandson of Debi Prasad Khaitan, who is closely associated with the son and grandson of Bhagwati Prasad Khaitan. 'Our family's experience has been the exact opposite. Both our businesses and our relationship have been enhanced by working together'. More so because 'for all times, KCo,

It was DP's youngest sibling, Bhagwati Prasad Khaitan (BP) who was to take the firm to greater glories, dealing with leading business men and counsel with elan. Seen here with G.D. Birla during the golden jubilee celebrations of the firm

headed by Bhagwati Dadaji, acted as our mentor and advisor at both personal and business levels'. Dhruv Khaitan and his brother, Piyush, are liberal in the acknowledgement of their affection for the extended family.

BP and his family have seen them through good times and bad. 'We were closely associated with him, his son Pinto and many other relatives and non-relatives who were part of the firm. Each one went much beyond a purely "dry professional" approach. The approach has always been to get comprehensive results, not just to give advice. I speak for Piyush and myself when I say that Pinto Khaitan has been our mentor all through and our association has continued at personal and business levels even as I moved out to Delhi and then to Mumbai'.

## Trust forever

S.B. Mookerjee, jurist and former Union Minister, India:

'I would like to emphasise that when I began my professional career KCo was a flourishing firm and it continues to grow today. It owes this to a number of leading business houses that were its clients and who have expanded (even though Calcutta has not) and have still retained KCo as their solicitors. Faith and trust of clients account for a great deal in our profession and the firm has retained that trust over the decades. Its clients then were mainly the Birlas and it still has the Birlas as its clients today'.

There is a pearl of wisdom that the Marwaris share with their progeny; one that Sir Badridas Goenka shared with his grandson, Sanjeev: 'never hide anything from your lawyers'. There was an addendum that was Sir Badridas' own: '... particularly if the lawyer is KCo'. This is something that even the third-generation Goenka-Khaitan association respects; something based on total trust on the part of the first party and total commitment on the part of the second. 'My grandfather shared all his problems with Bhagwati Prasad Khaitan, who was someone special to our family, as I learnt even as a boy going to Class X', says Sanjeev Goenka. 'Ours was a very disciplined family and it was a ritual to pay our respects to our elders. I had to see my grandfather at 8.30 every morning. One day, in 1976, he said that he wanted me to meet someone special and there was BP with him. They were discussing some M&A transaction. That was my first meeting with BP and my first exposure to an M&A discussion'.

It was in this milieu of caring and sharing on the one hand and delivering shrewd legal opinion on the other that Bhagwati Prasad matured into a position of professional leadership. For all practical purposes, he had received comprehensive training from watching his brothers at work: from the family's sense of social responsibility – even though it was not labelled thus in those days – to community service, to sheer corporate leadership and an immeasurable thirst for improving the circumstances of everybody that they came in touch with. He had also had the privilege of working with the finest legal minds that the firm engaged as counsel. If these sharpened his mind, there were other aspects of the firm's activity that enhanced the qualities of the heart: enthusing young men who had come to work in the family concern; young lawyers whose services the firm would employ on the one hand and, on the other, being a part of virtually every endeavour of the times to build institutions that would build character and industry, from health to academic institutions.

## Beyond law

Dr Kamal Hossain, vice chair, International Law Association, recalls his meeting with Bhagwati Babu in March 1991, on the eve of the International Law Association Seminar on Right to Sustainable Development and the New International Economic Order. 'Lawyers, judges, jurists, professors and international delegates from all over the world attended the four-day long seminar organized with full support, participation and involvement of KCo, its partners and staff on instructions of Bhagwati Prasad Khaitan', he says. Another day-long seminar was held in 1993, at the West Bengal Assembly Building (Legislative Council Hall). Dr Hossain also recalls the firm's help during the Berlin, 2004, International Law Association's 70th Biennial Conference, which 'had significant support of KCo and the Law Research Institute founded by B.P. Khaitan'.

The home at Ballygunge Circular Road was where big business met the legal minds.
L to R - Mr Pran Prasad, Mr Shankar Das Banerjee, Mr Bhaskar Mitter, Mr Prem Nath Seth, Mr Sachin Chaudhri, Mrs Soni Prasad, Justice Leila Seth, not known, Shri B P Khaitan and Dr Shankar Ghosh

The importance of academics was never lost on Bhagwati Prasad Khaitan, who personally founded the Law Research Institute to encourage juniors and to identify those keen to pursue legal study. He created an institution that had provided yeoman services towards advancing the pursuit of excellence in law beyond law firms and courtrooms. Where did knowledge and legal acumen merge with naivety and occasional exasperation for the rest of the family?

There was, indeed, a rub! Occasionally, one could win BP over with a sob story and extract a fair amount from him. 'My father was generous to a fault and could not be dissuaded from helping others. If he were told that the person he was helping was actually cheating him, he would argue that he was doing things from his heart, while we were assessing it with our heads. If one argued that charity should go to deserving people…he would say that he was probably repaying past dues to the person', says Pinto Khaitan.

People recall the tale of a man from the municipal corporation coming to assess the value of BP's home at Ballygunge Circular Road; offering to bring down the valuation for a price. BP said that he would not pay a bribe but would be happy to pay the fair valuation. The man argued that he was not trying to extract a bribe but that he wanted his son to have a good education, which was expensive: thus the need to raise finances. The argument appealed to Bhagwati Prasad, who offered to pay for the son's education but not a bribe to reduce the valuation. Now it was the turn of the bribe seeker to be in a fix: how could he accept the money without rendering any service? It needed all the persuasion of Calcutta's most powerful vakil to make the man accept help for his son's education but return home empty-handed as far as palm greasing for a reduced valuation was concerned.

What was the takeout for his son? 'The point is that people like B.P. Khaitan recognized human failings and inefficiencies and were selfless as they tried to help, and this won them universal trust even within the Khaitan family'. The influence of propriety and honesty goes beyond exercise of might and authority. Thus, when it came to converting the now derelict Khaitan zamindari at Chandil into a trust, B.P. Khaitan needed some 100 people to affix their signatures on the deed for him to be able to do so.

They all did it without asking a single question. The operative word here was 'trust'.

Facing page: BPK, life was a matter of trust

# JUSTICE MUST BE JUST

*Ghanshyam Das Birla could not believe his ears. There was a matter of arbitration between his family and another from his community. Bhagwati Prasad, whom he trusted like a son, was appointed arbitrator on his behalf and he was sure that justice would be done. Justice was done by Bhagwati Babu's own standards. Having understood the meat of the matter, he decided that the award should go to the other side.*

When it came to fair play, Bhagwati Babu had a lesson or two to teach the world, says Justice Leila Seth, who recalled this story. Justice Seth has worked with KCo quite intimately; actually from its offices in Calcutta and Delhi. Bhagwati Babu had confirmed that incident in an interview: 'Ghanshyam Das Birla got very angry with me because he did not like the settlement that I had arranged and he did not talk to me for several years. Later, when he understood that I was standing by my principles, he came back to me and treated me as a member of his family. Sometimes, he even took me along when he went abroad. I must admit that the help of the Birla family has been a big factor in the success of our firm'. So were the principles that the group adhered to.

The times, as one has seen, were tumultuous, but it was through the tumult that the destiny of the Indian firm of solicitors would have to be guided. Debi Prasad was increasingly getting sucked into the demanding ways of Ghanshyam Das Birla, because the emerging industrialist needed the best possible guidance to manoeuvre his business through the treacherous ways of the British and their laws. Eight years into his firm and DP had realized that he had extremely competent human resources to run the firm and that he could afford to work full-time with Ghanshyam Das. This he did in 1919. It was certain that the Birla business would come to the firm and that the well-oiled machine –

Facing page: Laying down the law. The fabulous archways at the Calcutta High Court

that his office had become – would be able to deliver.

Bhagwati Prasad himself was still a child but Kali Prasad and Durga Prasad were quite on top of things. Helping them as a partner was the equally outstanding Ishwar Das Jalan, the son of a family friend from Muzaffarpur, who had performed brilliantly in his studies in Calcutta. Ishwar Das, who lived next to the Khaitans on Zakaria Street when they had shifted there, had become friends with the Khaitan boys: Debi Prasad, Durga Prasad and Kali Prasad. When he completed his attorneyship, the brothers unhesitatingly invited him to join as a partner.

Later, when Bhagwati Prasad was ready to join the firm around 1927-28, he was asked to work directly under Ishwar Das Jalan though brothers Durga Prasad and Kali Prasad were his teachers too. So was S.N. Banerjee. 'Ishwardasji was invested with the best traits in a solicitor; his legal eloquence was mesmerizing; his knowledge of the intricacies of the law was superb and he would bring it all into his arguments, which were intelligent and impassioned', said B.P. Khaitan about him. Success came to him swiftly and substantially and

Relationship based on trust: at the formal signing over of the control in Pilani Investments in favour of B.K. Birla by transfer of shares. Pinto Khaitan (C) flanked by Mr and Mrs B.K. Birla on his right and Mr and Mrs Sudharshan Birla, Siddhartha Birla and Manjushree Khaitan on his left

## Speaker Ishwar Das

Ishwar Das, a patriot-lawyer and a partner of KCo, was arrested in the course of the final run of the Indian freedom movement. When freedom dawned, he was still behind bars. Meanwhile, the country was set to institute its own governance at the centre and the states. In West Bengal, B.C. Roy was forming the state's first government and could think of no better person as Speaker than Ishwar Das Jalan.

It was the day of the swearing in and RKC, then in his teens, remembers accompanying some members of the community like Devki Poddar and Shyamanand Jalan to fetch their hero from the Alipore Jail. There, they garlanded him after he had changed into his customary khadi dhoti, panjabi (kurta); Gandhi topi and the khadi chaddar and took him straight into the Assembly to be sworn in as Speaker.

Privileged though he felt about the position, there was fear that his earnings would drop and his family would probably suffer. Almost as if he had read ID's mind, Bhagwati Babu told him not to worry because he would offer partnership to his son Krishnanand.

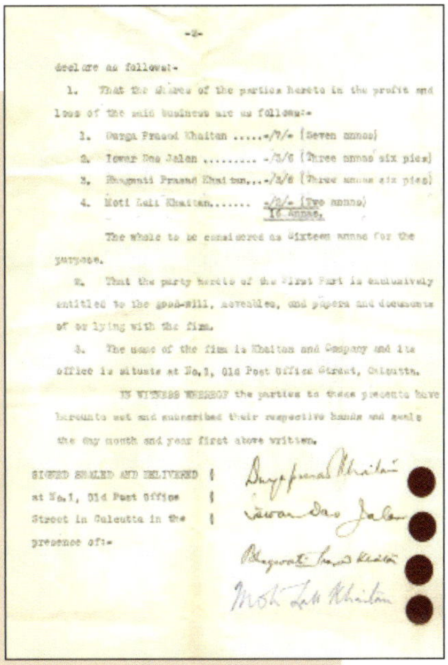

-2-

declare as follows:-

1. That the shares of the parties hereto in the profit and loss of the said business are as follows:-

1. Durga Prasad Khaitan .....-/7/- (Seven annas)
2. Iswar Das Jalan ......... -/3/6 (Three annas six pies)
3. Bhagwati Prasad Khaitan,..-/3/6 (Three annas six pies)
4. Moti Lal Khaitan...... -/2/- (Two annas)
16 Annas.

The whole to be considered as Sixteen annas for the purpose.

2. That the party hereto of the First Part is exclusively entitled to the good-will, receivables, and papers and documents of or lying with the firm.

3. The name of the firm is Khaitan and Company and its office is situate at No.1, Old Post Office Street, Calcutta.

IN WITNESS WHEREOF the parties to these presents have hereunto set and subscribed their respective hands and seals the day month and year first above written.

SIGNED SEALED AND DELIVERED at No.1, Old Post Office Street in Calcutta in the presence of:-

Page from the past: Partnership deed of September 3, 1934, shows Ishwar Das as partner

the young Bhagwati Prasad had the opportunity to work with him 'subhah se shyam tak (from morning till evening)'.

What must have endeared Ishwar Das Jalan to his young protégé was his keen interest in youngsters. He would actively keep in touch with youth organizations; they were inspired by their interactions with him. He would felicitate the young graduates and treat everyone at work or at his numerous charitable and social endeavours with extreme cordiality. He continued to work with the firm till he became the Speaker of the West Bengal Legislative Assembly when B.C. Roy was the Chief Minister. His son, Krishnanand, joined the firm in his place and continued till he started his own firm. The friendship between the two families was cemented with one of Bhagwati Babu's sons marrying Ishwar Das's daughter. For BP, his working days and holidays spent in the company of Ishwar Das were a privilege because, as he acknowledged in public, there could be no better role model: Ishwardas was deeply religious, soft-spoken, kind and charitable on the one hand; and had a razor sharp mind on the other. He was also honest and impartial to a fault. He spoke the English language with great felicity and was an outstanding speaker at an international conference of Speakers organized by the Parliament of Great Britain. It was his oration that made headlines, Bhagwati Babu said.

Dr Bimal Jalan, the grandson of Ishwar Das, might have become a lawyer; indeed he was studying to become one in the UK – where he went for higher studies after graduating from Presidency – but he chose to be an economist and 'no one protested when I did so, because we were brought up in an environment where there was freedom of choice'. One was welcome to choose a vocation that would pay less if one wanted to. 'Thus, if Bidhan Chandra Roy wanted you to become Speaker of his Assembly, giving up a lucrative partnership in a law firm, you did so because serving the country came first. More importantly, the firm encouraged you to do so'.

Leading institutions were its clients. A 1949 letter from KCo client, India Exchange

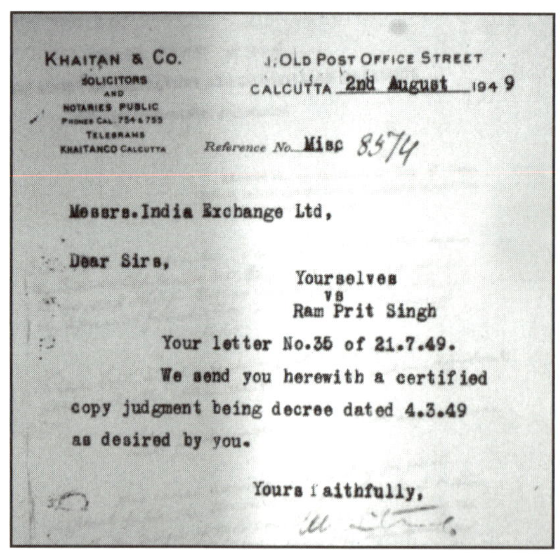

KHAITAN & CO.
SOLICITORS
AND
NOTARIES PUBLIC
PHONES CAL. 754 & 755
TELEGRAMS
KHAITANCO CALCUTTA

1, OLD POST OFFICE STREET
CALCUTTA 2nd August 1949

Reference No. Misc 8574

Messrs. India Exchange Ltd,

Dear Sirs,

Yourselves
vs
Ram Prit Singh

Your letter No.35 of 21.7.49.

We send you herewith a certified copy judgment being decree dated 4.3.49 as desired by you.

Yours faithfully,

Were it not for the free, intellectually invigorating environment that encouraged one to pursue the wider dimensions of professional life at KCo, 'we would not have been where we are; my grandfather may not have been able to pursue his political interests without the support of the firm. It was this nationalistic fervour that was

## Country above self

'I was no more than five or six when my grandfather left KCo to become Speaker in B. C. Roy's government but the important thing was that even as a partner, he was welcome to follow his political instincts because the firm believed in serving the community and in those days there was no question of vested interests in pursuing politics, recalls Dr Bimal Jalan about his grandfather, Ishwar Das. 'He was allowed to fight elections and even after he left there was so much warmth and respect in the relationship with all the Khaitans. I saw B. P. Khaitan visiting and talking with my grandfather and it was so obviously an endearing relationship and showed the high esteem with which the family was regarded'.

'Clearly the Khaitans were a different, path-breaking family. They were all highly educated and followed an open, accommodative approach to professional choices that one made. As you are probably aware, my father was offered a partnership with the firm after my grandfather left. My father was a highly qualified lawyer but liked to step out of line as far as the traditional path was concerned. He chose to start a chain store company – the first in India'. That it did not succeed is another story but Krishnanand Jalan came back to the profession and set up an independent firm, Jalan & Company 'not because of any problem with the Khaitans but because he wanted to work as he felt like', says Dr Jalan.

passed on to us, as was the ability to follow the heart, take chances and not always worry about the money. This was the biggest lesson; the biggest gift'.

Meanwhile, youngsters from the community were welcome to work with the firm and everyone was constantly urged to improve himself. Getting articled with solicitor firms was an expensive proposition in those days. It cost at least Rs 5,000 to get an articleship and not every firm could accept apprentices; a qualifying firm had to be of seven years standing. Ramkumar Bhuwalka recalled how Debi Prasad allowed him to work with the firm anyway, supporting him all the way: making him an apprentice; encouraging him to work his way up and sit for the many qualifying examinations till he became an attorney.

By 1924, the family was well established. The youngest son was shaping up well and it was decided that the brothers should build their own home. Their social circle had become large and national leaders of great eminence were constantly in Calcutta, visiting their home. So the Khaitan house was built on Zakaria Street in 1924 and the family shifted there, making it almost an open house. For Debi Prasad's classmate, Rajendra Prasad – this was his home in Calcutta. So was it for Jamnalal Bajaj, a friend of Naurangrai, who stayed in their house when he came to Calcutta. Also for Mahatma Gandhi, who would drop in for a siesta in the afternoons, whenever he was in the city and working in the Burrabazar area. C.F. Andrews was yet another special friend with whom DP worked on the indentured labour issue. The galaxy of guests was vast and impressive. Calcutta continued to be the fountainhead of the nationalist movement. The high court once again became the centre of attention with the trial of the accused in the Chittagong Armoury case.

Whatever may have been the complexities of law in the world outside, within the Khaitan family even the trickiest of issues was settled amicably. In 1929, it was felt that the family property be divided between the seven brothers. The youngest, Bhagwati Prasad, had to sit for his attorneyship exam and his mother was anxious that they wait till he passed. The brothers assured their mother of two things:

## Dalmia Jain and Vivian Bose

The break-up of Dalmia–Sahu Jain – as the combine of Ram Krishna Dalmia, his brother Jaidayal, and son-in-law Sahu Shanti Prasad Jain, was called – was the first and the most bizarre, to have taken place after Independence. It saw Ram Krishna Dalmia in deep trouble from which his solicitors had to bail him out, especially during the Vivian Bose Inquiry Commission in 1962. Recalls RKC: 'It meant several meetings in Delhi, at 6, Kitchener Lane, now Sardar Patel Marg, between Bhagwati Babu, Ram Krishna Dalmia, K. L. Mishra from Allahabad, Shanti Prasad Jain himself and Hira Lal Sibal. I recall a tea party given by Shanti Prasad Jain, where the entire legal team was called and there were discussions on how R.K. Dalmia's companies could be restructured under the evolving law. It was a very difficult matter to resolve but it was successfully accomplished'.

One, that the youngest sibling would be well cared for till he passed. Two, that she could take it for granted that he had passed. The trust and affection between the brothers continued to be a bonding factor and people got to hear about the division of property only years after the event. The examination was, as foretold, a mere formality and the older brothers knew that the youngest was to accomplish a great deal in life. What he did end up achieving was more than legal success. He became a lawyer-friend to his clients. For many, he became a member of their extended families.

Helping the Sahu Jains acquire the prized Bennett & Coleman

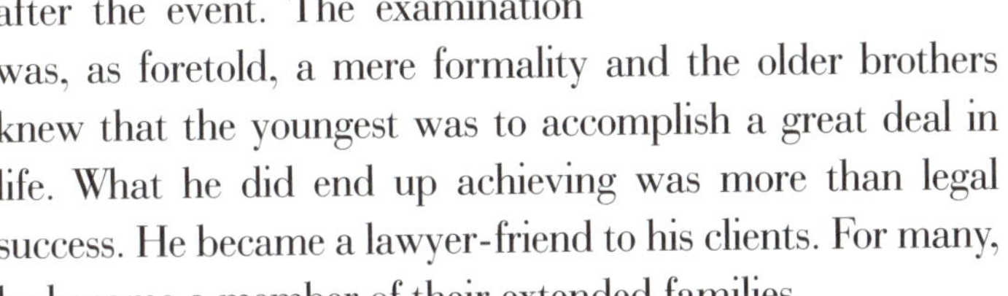

Indeed, amongst the most interesting cases that Bhagwati Prasad Khaitan handled in his life must have been the Dalmia-Jain cases that not only cemented the ties between the families but ensured business for the law firm over the decades. Pinto Khaitan recalls the family's association with the Dalmia-Jains from his childhood. 'We were treated as members of their family. Their contribution to the growth of the firm was immense'. One may dare add, the firm's contribution in helping them navigate the troubled legal waters was not inconsiderable.

It began with the biggest takeover of the times. It was around 1946 that Ram Krishna Dalmia purchased Bennett, Coleman & Company for Rs 2 crore. The company, which owned the *Times of India*, was the cynosure of all eyes because it owned what was then amongst the largest circulated English broadsheets in the world. Following a twist in the tale, Ram Krishna Dalmia finally sold the paper to the Sahu Jains in a deal that was handled by KCo with great finesse. Shanti Prasad Jain, son-in-law of Ram Krishna Dalmia, became the first chairman of the group and it was BP's nephew, Krishna

Prasad Khaitan, who had joined the firm by then, who handled the Sahu Jain affairs. More difficult than handling the complexities of the case was 'dealing with Shital Prasad Jain', who looked after the Sahu Jain matters and it was in handling him that Krishna Prasad showed great maturity, recalls Ram Kishore Choudhury. A young man then, even he would lose his patience, but never Kishan Babu, who would advise patience and fortitude: 'Lose this man and you lose the client', he would tell his young assistant. Kishan Babu had

## Like father, like son

For all his stern ways, Kishan Khaitan had quite a fan following: Says P.C. (Mintu) Sen: 'I have been working with KCo for a pretty long time and first started working with Nandu's father: Kishan Khaitan. One of the most important cases that I worked on was the Lohia family dispute that went in for arbitral proceedings, first under Justice Amiya Mukherjee and, upon his passing, under Anil Sen. The proceedings went on for a very long time and resulted in an award, a Bel Chamber's Gold, but the matter finally went up to the Supreme Court, before good sense prevailed and the matter was brought to a negotiated settlement. Kishan Khaitan was quite a volatile person, a very strong personality, who would control his client. Rarely did a client dare to raise his voice against the position that he was taking or say something that was contrary to Kishan Babu's understanding of the case. Of course, his understanding of the law was very good. He was a clever and capable man; a bit dogmatic at times though being a little dogmatic is important to make a success in life.

'I have had the occasion to work with his son, Nand Gopal, on several occasions. Like his father, he is a clever man, with a fair knowledge of the law and great practical sense. He has been working in the Birla-Lodha matter, in proceedings arising out of the sections 397 and 398 before the Company Law Board that has, on appeal, landed before the high court under Section 10F of the Companies Act'.

A Bel Chamber's Gold for N.G. Khaitan. Chief Justice, Sankar Prasad Mitra, doing the honours

## Figuring out Fera

Mr R.N. Bajoria, who was counsel in this case, says: 'The government's position was that money being held by a foreign shareholder against a possible future claim against a supplier of machinery on the ground of such machinery not being up to the mark amounts to lending of such stake money to the stakeholder and, therefore, a violation of Section 4 of the Fera, 1947. The Supreme Court held that there was no lending vis-à-vis the stakeholder because the amount held by him could not be considered a debt. It would become a debt only on the happening of the contingency for which he was holding the money, which may or may not happen. The law laid down was: a contingent debt is no debt, which means right in praesenti solvendum in futuro... Right is today but payable later. This was the definition of debt as laid down by the Supreme Court, and when the stakeholder is holding the money, there is no such right in praesenti'.

another fan in octogenarian S. Tibrewala, who recalls a very intelligent Krishna Prasad Khaitan with his knack of coming up with exactly what to do when circumstances were tricky. 'It was he who guided senior counsel and had the ability to turn matters around'.

Krishna Prasad Khaitan had other admirers too. Recalls S.K. Kapur: 'I remember working with Kishan Babu. There was a very small matter of an interlocutory application before Justice A.N. Sen and my opponent was the Standing Counsel, Anil Mitra, assisted by Mrs Deb Burman. This was an opportunity for a junior not to be easily lost. I got ready with my case, which was extremely weak, and then I went in and gave them the beans. Mrs Hansa Deb Burman was, of course, furious, and it took some time to placate her. Anil Mitra's response was to invite me to dinner alone to Calcutta Club and, Kishan Khaitan, the solicitor, thereafter, adopted me as a preferred junior. The application had been for the appointment of a receiver in a money suit and the thread that I had to go on was that, in principle, the application was bad even though the merits were wholly with the other side. We got a favourable order. This was followed by a flood

## Moti Lal: the smiling solicitor

Moti Lal Khaitan was the first of the second generation Khaitans to enter the firm. In intellect and demeanour he had all the Khaitan qualities but then he was a man of passion; he loved the niceties of social life. He joined the firm in 1933 and introduced to it some high-profile emerging companies as clients. Eventually, he quit to join one of them as chairman. M.L. Khaitan became chairman of Bata India in 1948. By then the firm was on a very solid footing.

Nephew Padam Khaitan has the fondest memories of his uncle. 'M.L. Khaitan, was a charmer; he was a lawyer but had an air of flamboyance about him. He went around the top social circles and was particularly close to Rai Bahadur M.S. Oberoi, whom he advised during his early phase of hotel acquisition. He was soft spoken and kind-hearted and my only regret was that I got to know him well only towards the later part of his life, when he would come home and play bridge with his brothers, my father included. He was very fond of my wife and would not tolerate anyone being unpleasant with her, particularly me.

'Rai Bahadur M.S. Oberoi was so fond of him that there was a suite reserved for him at the Maidens, where I recall visiting him. I remember the Oberois in Calcutta opening the city's first health club and I was interested in a membership. I asked my uncle what the purpose was of having him there if I did not have a health club membership. The next day there was a complimentary membership waiting for me, which made for a lot of interesting times. Amongst others, I would get to meet the cricketers staying at the Oberoi, whenever there was a match at Eden Gardens, apart from other people. I enjoyed the membership as long as the hotel offered the facility to non-residents.

of work from Kishan Babu both in the Calcutta High Court and in Alipore'.

The important thing was that KCo had successfully defended its clients and that meant more custom. The law became more complex and, towards the 1950s, Krishna Prasad Khaitan, found the Sahu Jains in serious trouble. It was his success in this matter that brought great acclaim to the Khaitans because the person charged with Fera violation was Shanti Prasad Jain himself and the matter was a complicated one. It was June 30, 1958, when Shanti Prasad Jain went on a tour of Europe. On his return to India, on October 1, he was searched at New Delhi's Palam Airport and several 'incriminating documents in relation to transactions in respect of violation of Foreign Exchange' were alleged to have been found in his briefcase. Proceedings commenced under the Foreign Exchange Regulation Act, 1947, and the matter went up to the Supreme Court, before Chief Justice B.P. Sinha, P.B. Gajendragadkar, K.N. Wanchoo, N. Rajagopala Ayyangar and T.L. Venkatarama Aiyar. Significantly, B.P. Khaitan appeared personally in this matter.

Indeed, as Ram Kishore Choudhury, who was entrusted with the case that entailed numerous conferences with the redoubtable Sachin Chaudhuri, recalls: 'Our handling of the case was greatly appreciated by the clients and by Kishan Babu himself'. The facts of the matter were thus: Shanti Prasad Jain had claims for compensation against certain German firms for machinery supplied by them to his concerns, New Central Jute and Rohtas Industries. He went to Germany and settled with the firms that they would deposit certain sums in his account with the Deutsche Bank with the stipulation that the money be used for purchases of new machinery from the same firms after obtaining import licences from the Government of India. When he was searched at Palam, the document stating that the funds from the Germans had been deposited in the account was found in his leather attaché. The problem was that SPJ had not obtained RBI permission, general or special, for opening this account.

Section 4(1) of the Foreign Exchange Regulation Act, 1947,

## A resident is a resident!

'The expression "resident in India" has been held to be in the same sense as that of "resident of India"', explains RKC. 'The judgment also held that "a contingent debt is strictly speaking not a debt at all". In its ordinary as well as its legal sense, a debt is a sum of money payable under an existing obligation. It may be payable forthwith, solvendum in presenti, when it is a debt "due"; or it may be payable at a future date, solvendum futuro, when it is a debt "accruing". In either case, it is a debt but a contingent debt has no present existence because it is payable only when the contingency happens and exhypothesi that may or may not happen'.

prohibits a 'person resident in India', inter alia, from lending to any person outside India foreign exchange without the permission of the Reserve Bank. Section 23 lays down the penalties for contravention of Section (1) on adjudication by the director of enforcement and on conviction by a Court. Section 23D confers upon the director the power to adjudicate whether any person has contravened Section 4 (1) and empowers him – if he is of the opinion that the penalty, which he is empowered to impose, would not be adequate in the circumstances of any particular case – to make a complaint in writing to the court.

KCo contended (i) that Section 23(1) of the Act offended

## Krishna Prasad 'Tiger' Khaitan

Krishna Prasad Khaitan was the 'tiger'; a man whom even Bhagwati Babu feared because of the occasional shortness of his fuse. He was a strict administrator and could work ceaselessly. He demanded hard work and was happy to reward. S.K. Kapur, whose association with the Khaitans goes back to 1967, was amongst his favourites: 'Without my asking, just before the Puja vacations, he would come to me with a memo that he would draw up for me and it would say: "this is what I owe you. I would draw up a bill for the amount and he would pay me on the spot"'.

Says son NG: My father was not just the doyen of the firm but as a litigation lawyer he commanded high respect of judges and clients'. Indeed, all major groups were his clients, including the J.K. Group, McLeod Group and Hari Das Mundhra. 'The Surajmull Nagarmull settlement was handled by him and it was he who instilled the basic values of professional life in me: integrity to client; commitment to hard work; and always to go deep into a matter'. Unfortunately, ill health cut short his active working life.

Truth to tell, Kishan Babu's iron demeanour concealed a velvet touch as the registrar of the Original Side of the Calcutta High Court realized. He had just completed marking the answer papers for the 2nd year Attorneyship examination and had given the highest ever marks to a Nand Gopal in a Transfer of Property Act Paper. Indeed, the registrar was so impressed that he thought it fit to call the candidate's father and inform him that he felt proud to have examined the paper. The father's eyes swelled with tears, for he had just realized that his progeny would not let him down. He did not. The father was Kishan Khaitan and the son was Nand Gopal, who went on to win the Bel Chamber's Gold.

Article 14 of the Constitution as two parallel procedures were provided for the same offence and it was left to the discretion of the executive to choose which was to be applied in a particular case, and (ii) that there was no loan by the appellant to the bank and therefore there was no contravention of section 4(1). Appearing for SPJ was B.P. Khaitan, S.K. Kapur and B.P. Maheshwari (in C.A. No. 319 of 1961). The director inquired into the appellant's Deutsche Bank account, held that the appellant had contravened Section 4(1) and imposed a penalty of Rs 55 lakhs. On appeal, the Foreign Exchange Appellate Tribunal held that the deposits amounted in law to loans by the appellant to the bank and consequently Section 4(1) was contravened but it reduced the penalty to Rs 5 lakhs.

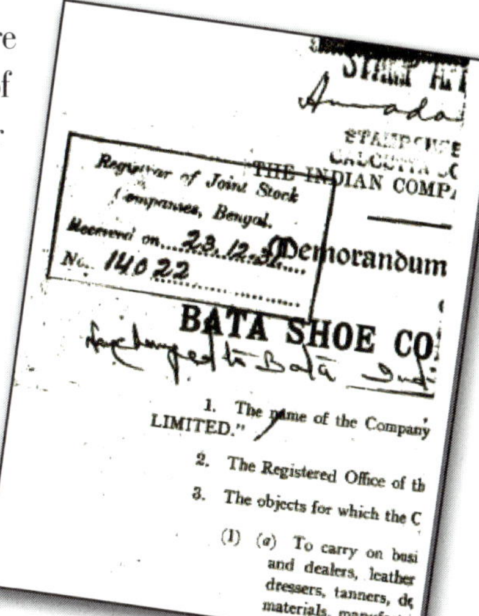

THE INDIAN COMP

Registrar of Joint Stock Companies, Bengal.

Memorandum

BATA SHOE CO

1. The name of the Company ... LIMITED."

2. The Registered Office of th

3. The objects for which the C

(1) (a) To carry on busi and dealers, leather dressers, tanners, de materials, manufactu

Both SPJ and the Union of India preferred appeals under Article136 of the Constitution against this order. Eventually, the court ruled that: 'We have no hesitation in holding that if the appellant did in fact lend monies to the Deutsche Bank while he was in Germany he would, have contravened Section 4(1) of the Act. In view of our conclusion that the appellant has only a contingent right to the amounts standing in credit in account no. 50180 and that the deposits were made in the bank not in the course of normal banking business but under a special arrangement, it must be held that there was no lending of those amounts by the appellant to the bank within Section 4(1) of the Act and the order of the Appellate Board imposing a fine of Rs 5 lakhs on him under Section 23(1)(a) must be held to be illegal and set aside'.

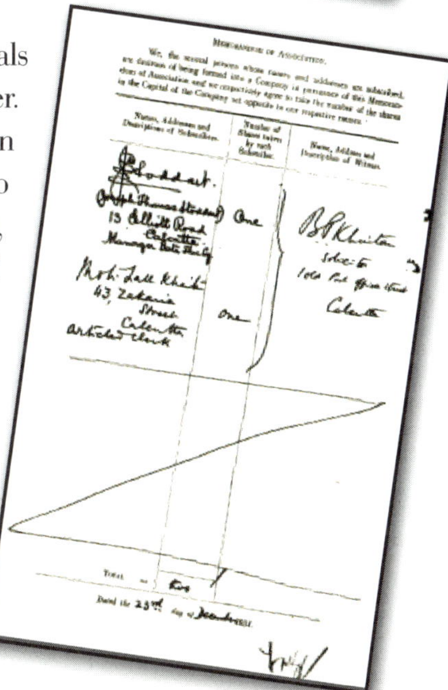

Bata Shoe Company's Memorandum of Association

As cases of great import started coming the firm's way, the firm needed sharper minds. The next-generation Khaitan lawyers had already entered the firm and had their own ideas on how to do business. This generation had the genes and was raised in relative affluence, which showed at times. Moti Lal Khaitan, the eldest son of Lakshmi Narayan, had a fine legal mind but he fancied the finer things in life too. Participation in matters of law apart, his social connections proved immensely useful to the firm for several decades to come; amongst others it brought in the Bata connection. MLK had a way with people and would not fight shy of getting his youngest uncle to share his sense of adventure. Once in London together, he took a bemused BP to a nightclub. Back in Calcutta, BP told his young assistant, Ram Kishore, about his nocturnal adventure and was chastised by the young man: 'How could you go there with your nephew?' The big-ticket solicitor said with his tongue firmly in his cheek: 'I swallowed my uncleship for then'.

KCo had also become the place to which any bright Marwari boy could go in search of a career. Amongst the brightest was Sita Ram Jhunjhunwala. After completing his matriculation at Deoghar, he moved to Calcutta to stay with his uncle Jagannath Jhunjhunwala of 7, Mandeville Gardens. The uncle, who had moved out of Deoghar several years ago and had done well for himself as a share broker, was a friend of Bhagwati Babu. SRJ was studying for his BCom at the Vidyasagar College in 1939, when his uncle introduced

## Silent support: Lath & Kandoi

There were many who served the firm silently. Recalls S.K. Kapur: 'Some people I remember dearly include S.K. Lath, who used to ring up early in the morning and ask: 'How do I solve my conveyancing problem?' He being the conveyancing expert in the Khaitan office, it was flattering to have him seek my guidance on questions of titles that were intricate. S.K. Lath was a hard-working man though not very generous with the pennies'.

'I also dearly remember Kanhaialal Kandoi. He was one of the backroom boys and handled work at the city civil court. He would bring his little cases to me and they were little because they were "city civil" work though grassroots litigation was of the essence of the original side, whether in the high court or the city civil court'.

him to the solicitor. BP loved bright youngsters and was particularly impressed by the sincerity and motivation of the young man; more so by his beautiful handwriting. He asked for Sita Ram's biodata and an application for a job and within a few days SRJ had a job as clerk at KCo at Rs 25 per month. Over the next eight decades, the firm would have a greatly satisfying relationship with this young recruit and his progeny, including his grandson, who now serves at Emerald House. This building has been office to three generations for several families.

It was an early 20th-century structure, architecturally described as one with a 'symmetrical façade. Central entrance bay defined by projected balconies. Deep cornice at the roof level. Rectangular windows defined by architraves in plaster'. This lovely green property, owned by the Bangur-held Emerald Company, first hosted the firm in 1928. In 1979, the entire property was leased out to KCo for five years and then renewed for another five. The lessors and the lessees decided in 1989 that the Khaitans would be the tenants of the premises in its entirety without any need for the five-yearly renewal. Its home secure, the firm today has a plush office on the ground floor; more staid offices on the first and the second floors; and a BPK Centre on the third floor for conferences. Its Bombay office, however, is the showpiece, wowing even the most fastidious of international clients.

India became free and had embarked on its journey to keep its celebrated tryst with destiny. Industry meant contracts; contracts meant law and more and more complicated law. Bhagwati Babu was dealing with the Bombay Naval Dockyard case, around 1953-54, for G.D. Kothari of Hind Construction which had secured a Defence Ministry contract to construct a dockyard in Bombay in front of the Taj. Sir Alexander Gibbs & Partners of London were the consulting engineers for the Defence Ministry for this contract. Its salient features were: Construction of a wharf, so that the first 'dwarf' of the ship could get in and out of the dockyard without any risk of damage. The condition was that the underwater ballast rocks – the hardest stones in India – should not have any pinnacles. Blasting was prohibited and only rock breakers belonging to the Bombay Port Trust could be used. However, this was a very old rock breaker that was unfit for the purpose and correspondence regarding this ran into some 6,000 to 7,000 pages.

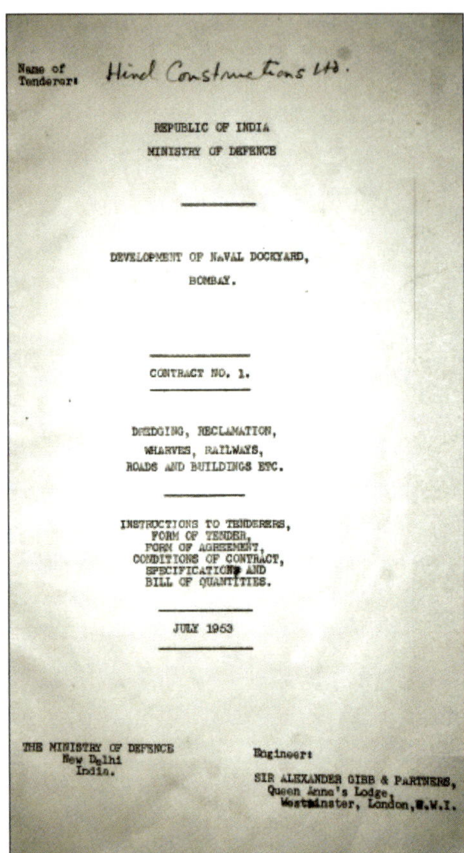
Name of Tenderer: Hind Constructions Ltd.

REPUBLIC OF INDIA
MINISTRY OF DEFENCE

DEVELOPMENT OF NAVAL DOCKYARD,
BOMBAY.

CONTRACT NO. 1.

DREDGING, RECLAMATION,
WHARVES, RAILWAYS,
ROADS AND BUILDINGS ETC.

INSTRUCTIONS TO TENDERERS,
FORM OF TENDER,
FORM OF AGREEMENT,
CONDITIONS OF CONTRACT,
SPECIFICATIONS AND
BILL OF QUANTITIES.

JULY 1953

THE MINISTRY OF DEFENCE
New Delhi
India.

Engineer:
SIR ALEXANDER GIBB & PARTNERS,
Queen Anne's Lodge,
Westminster, London, S.W.1.

Contract Document of Hindustan Construction Limited in 1953, case handled by R.K. Chowdhury

Despite its best efforts, Hind Construction could not break the rocks in the manner specified and chose to abandon the contract and quit the site. The military took over the site overnight (December 4, 1956). The questions before BP were whether the contract was frustrated or whether there was a mutual mistake or there was a 'supervening impossibility'. Also to be ascertained – given that the contractors had left the site – was which of the provisions of the Contract Act would be applicable. BP's precise draft left the client dissatisfied, but in a conference with N.C. Chatterjee and Somnath Chatterjee, it was BP's draft that was amended and used. BP's reputation as an excellent strategist had long been established. Now lawyers who wrote long-winded drafts, because they were ignorant of the art of precise writing, started emulating him.

The dispute went into arbitration and two of the judges appointed passed away in the course of the proceedings. It was finally concluded by Justice Bishen Narain, whose award went partly against the clients. KCo then fought the matter in the Bombay High Court, which upheld the arbitration award with the client having to pay a penalty of between Rs 4 crores and Rs 5 crores. It was a very big case and 19 witnesses had to be cross-examined, including Rear Admiral Nanda. The importance of the case owed to it being a project of national importance and a 'top secret' one. The firm could only draw solace from the fact that even the government could not finally break the rocks with rock breakers and had to resort to blasting using caissons under water.

Recalls RKC: 'Initially, BP would attend all the meetings but later asked me to deal with it along with counsel, Amiya Nath Bose. BP fixed the firm's fee for my attending out of Calcutta at Rs 400 per day. I had objected to such a low fee but he advised me that "work begets work" and that if we worked at a reasonably low cost successfully, we would continue to get more work'. The case may have been a challenging one but the real adventure for RKC lay in being taken in a submarine to check out the underwater conditions and get to appreciate the technical difficulties in breaking the rocks.

There were a lot of takeaways for the firm from this longest ever case that it had handled. There were 14 trunks of documents that had to be carted to Delhi whenever arbitration meetings were held there. Recalls RKC: 'We learnt that it was important to be precise in our representations; we had to argue that our clients had no option but to quit the site; the statement of claims by Mr P.N. Bhagwati, who went on to become the Chief Justice of India, had to be amended. BP taught us that it was far wiser to go for arbitration than to go to courts that were far more expensive. He said: "discourage litigation, pursue arbitration as the alternative remedy".

Chief Justice P.N. Bhagwati recalls his five-decade-old association with the firm, from the time he was practicing as a lawyer. He had been briefed by Khaitans several times as counsel, both in court and in arbitration: 'I particularly remember the arbitration in the naval dockyard case, in which I was engaged as a counsel. I drafted the statement of claim in one case after studying more than 6,000 pages. This was one of the most important arbitrations in which I advised KCo'.

Bhagwati Babu was right and there was much more work coming KCo's way from G.D. Kothari between 1955 and 1960, when BP had several arbitrations to handle. In some he would appear in person and in others as the instructing solicitor. One such matter concerned a Damodar Valley dam construction and the clients were Hind Patel, a consortium of Hind Construction and the Patel Engineering of Bombay. During the course of the arbitration, BP had to go to London and he confidently entrusted the job to his junior, RKC. 'I was given the sole responsibility to conduct the arbitration; it was my first big arbitration assignment'. Matters went the firm's way with Justice Sambhu Banerjee awarding in favour of its clients. On returning from abroad, BP was pleased that RKC had conducted matters well and rewarded him with more work. 'I was given the responsibility of realizing the award money from the Government of India. In the process arose a question of taxation and BP entrusted that job to me as well, giving me an opportunity to learn income tax. Ultimately, I did secure the release of the awarded sum'.

Youngsters were allowed to flourish; Ram Kishore Choudhury welcoming Justice Sabyasachi Mukherjee at Ashoka Hotel, Delhi, to the Khaitan Law Lectures

There were times when the solicitor got sued too. In 1955, a suit was filed against the firm for negligence in terms of ascertaining the marketability of a property by a Sheobhagwan Bubna. The property pertained to a Sonarpur bheri (fishery) owned by the Sarkars (Bidhubhushan Sarkar and others). It turned out that the property was under acquisition when the Bubnas approached BP to conclude the deal quickly. This case dragged on and turned out to be a major on-the-job learning for R.N. Jhunjhunwala, who was brought in to assist BP in this matter in 1968. Bubna had negotiated the purchase of a huge bheri with Bidhubhushan Sarkar. His broker, Hari Bux Singhania, had met BP at his house and requested him to act in the matter; prepare a sale deed and have it done in the shortest possible time. It was Bubna's contention that, as per his understanding with BP, it was the duty of the firm to carry out title searches and all investigations to conclude the deal.

According to the firm, the truth was that BP was specifically asked to have a sale deed prepared for approval by the seller and have it signed and registered at the earliest. He was not required to make any investigation or search of title because Bubna would lose the deal in that delay. Accordingly, the sale deed was prepared, approved, executed and registered. Later, a substantial part of the land was acquired by the government and Bubna filed a case against B.B. Sarkar and others, including KCo and BP, for damages of Rs 1,55,000 from the firm and BP on grounds of negligence.

The suit was filed in 1955 and went on for more than a decade. After 1968 it needed serious efforts to be brought for hearing. BP's evidence before the Alipore sub-judge established that he was specifically asked to go ahead with the sale deed without investigation or search for verification of title. Eminent counsel/barristers from the Calcutta High Court worked on the brief from time to time and at the final stage A.C. Mitra and Bholanath Sen argued the case.

RNJ recalls: 'Those were the days of frequent Bangla bandhs. I would walk all the way from Lake Gardens, papers in hand, on a bandh day, and BP would come walking for the conference at Anil Mitra's house at 18/2, Ballygunge Circular Road. On one occasion, he drove a blue Ambassador himself. I did not mind the strain; the motivation lay in the opportunity to interact with Mr Mitra and place matters before him. That zeal and the motivation instilled resides in me to this day. I was happy to sit in the Alipore sub-judge court's record room, day in and day out. For hours together, I minutely studied the contents of the documents tendered in evidence, marked as exhibit or for identification, copying them by hand, taking due care of marginal notes, the overwriting, corrections. It did not matter whether the document was big or small, even a small visitor's slip. It could turn the case this way or that'.

Senior barrister, Bholanath Sen, while analysing the evidence during conference was impressed with the precision with which BP had deposed from the witness box. On one occasion, he jumped up from his chair to pull out the House of Lords judgment from his rich library at 46, Raja Basanta Ray Road, turned the pages and thumped the table in excitement when he found a 'judgment, pat on the point'. The relevant passage (ratio decidendi) of the judgment read: 'The case alleged in the plaint has not been proved and what has been proved has not been alleged, hence the action brought by the plaintiff must fail'. Eventually, BP's testimony proved to be strong enough to demolish Bubna's case and while the suit was decreed against the Sarkars, it was dismissed against KCo and Bhagwati Prasad Khaitan.

Work begot more work and while 'BP was not particularly money-minded, it was more important for him that lawyers treat their profession with respect', says RKC. He himself worked very hard. Conferences began at his residence from 7.30 a.m. One could see all the top businessmen in the city visiting him then. This was in 1956 when he lived at 52/2, Ballygunge Circular Road. 'We had to keep pace with him though there was no conveyance for us to move around with the briefs; nor any time for ourselves: 7.30 a.m to 9 a.m. at his house; followed by 10 a.m. to 10 p.m. in the office… till I finally asked for my timings to be changed to give me some time with my family'. However, the young ward never failed to realize that the reason BP wanted him at the house was not because he was a slave driver but because that would give the young man an opportunity to meet the clients and their senior executives at close quarters. In a world of legal practice, that meant the world.

BP did not pursue money. He pursued ethics and excellence. Money followed. Eminence would follow from hard work; not fees, he said. The Khaitan supremo on one of his tirth yatras

Thus was Bhagwati Prasad growing in stature in the profession and his competence and sagacity would be tested again in the Jaipuria arbitration matter between the father and son: Mangturam Jaipuria and Sita Ram Jaipuria. The relationship between his junior and himself had become filial by now and RKC asked: 'Chachaji, do you have any idea of the kind of fees that you lost? You should have represented one of the two parties'. Bhagwati Babu's response was to be a lesson for the junior for the rest of his life; especially as the firm celebrates its 100th year: 'Do not always work for fees. This case will make your firm eminent'.

Reasonable fees apart, commitment was a keyword in Bhagwati Babu's lexicon. Years later, a KCo partner would understand the meaning of commitment first-hand. 'By encouraging young lawyers to take charge of their briefs, the firm provided the opportunity to many of contemporary India's pre-eminent lawyers to learn the work, greatly enhance their skills and help them develop on the common foundation of dedication and sincerity. However, the most important lesson of all probably came from one phone conversation with a Calcutta-based partner', says Gauri Rasgotra.

'He was visiting us and was really concerned about his client's case. He sent me a message when I was in the Supreme Court, wanting to speak to me urgently. Mobile phones were not in vogue then and I called him from a public phone in the court. As he made his arguments regarding his case listed for the next day and explained what we needed to tell our counsel, his voice suddenly dropped and I could only hear some noise in the background. I disconnected and asked the operator to re-connect with him He was back on the line as if nothing had happened. Before we finished, however, I could not contain my curiosity and asked him what happened. He paused briefly and then confided that his chair had rolled backwards and he had fallen off! Lesson learnt: no matter what the fall, nothing can dampen the spirit of lawyers and nothing can stop them from making their arguments'.

There was also the effort to create a team spirit at all times that Samaraditya (Bacchu) Pal was to notice when he started working with the firm in the late 1960s.'KCo, like many other firms, was a partnership. The legal work was and still is well shared. Apart from partners, it had articled clerks and some lawyers as employees. Each was assigned a particular class of litigation. He was responsible for conducting the case, which included choosing the counsel who would argue the case before a court and a junior to assist him. The person at the top of the firm, when I joined,

Members of the Incorporated Law Society at their Golden Jubilee. B.P. Khaitan is at the third row from the bottom, sixth from the right

was Bhagwati Prasad Khaitan. He was highly respected. It would not be an overstatement when I say that his clients would unquestionably and unhesitatingly accept his advice'.

Even the opposition accepted BP's commitment to justice. In a matter going on for years, the lawyer of the party opposing Bhagwati Babu got so tired that he asked BP to settle the matter in the manner that he deemed just. BP pointed out that it was unlikely that the client would abide by the advice of the lawyer of the other party. The opposing lawyer said that he had full faith in Bhagwati Prasad's sense of fair play and would ensure that the client accepted the settlement made by BP; whatever it was. He kept his word and the two became close friends thereafter.

That is possibly when KCo arrived at its principle that while settlements outside the court could not satisfy both parties, such settlements had to be fair, even if one party felt aggrieved. Also, once the two parties had agreed to a settlement and put their signatures to it, there could be no going back. This principle of the firm became well known and clients began to realize that there would be no point in coming to the firm to have settlements changed. Bhagwati Prasad Khaitan's personal grace rubbed off on the growing numbers entering the KCo ranks. Even rivals talk of the dignity that has informed relations between two solicitor firms. Says Mr M.L. Bhakta from Kanga & Company, Bombay, about the 75-year-old relationship between the two firms: 'It has been my proud privilege to have interacted with various partners of KCo almost from the late 1950s. BP had a close personal relationship with my senior, Tricumdas Dwarkadas, and in those days the two firms, Khaitan and Kanga, were closely associated and each one freely recommended the other to their standing clients for professional work at their respective locations. In the early part of my career, I had the privilege to visit Calcutta to meet Bhagwati Babu, the senior-most partner of the firm. I will never forget my pleasant experience and the treatment that I got from a person of his seniority and high professional repute'.

Probably the greatest satisfaction that Bhagwati Babu had was in the manner the next generation of the Khaitan family was shaping up. There was Nilratan Khaitan, son of Kali Prasad, who astounded every client with his erudition and meticulous work. There was nephew, Purushottam Lal, son of his eldest brother, Lakshmi Narayan, who was not just a fine lawyer but a fine human being. Son Padam Khaitan talks about his father: 'My father, Purushottam Lal, was a lawyer who joined the firm fairly late in his life though he had represented it earlier. He was a truly cool customer, who never lost his temper and was a contented man, not overly ambitious. He did mainly commercial matters and writ petitions and all matters in the appellate side of the high court were filed through him. However, his real joy lay in an evening game of bridge and playing the doting grandfather to all his grandchildren'.

Krishna Prasad, the second son of Lakshmi Narayan Khaitan, was cut in an entirely different mould and had an imposing personality in his prime but, as his son, Nand Gopal, recalls: 'We became friends when I became a lawyer and he felt confident about me. My son and I would go off on holidays with him to any place that he wanted to see and we would share a room and be close to each other. We could be watching tennis at Roland Garros or cricket somewhere else; it did not matter. We were a group of sports enthusiasts: tennis, cricket, hockey, football and even table tennis, which we often played together. At Roland Garros,

The extra curriculars in legal practice: the Law Research Institute seminars were supported by the firm: NG and PK welcome Justice R.S. Pathak as R.N. Jhunjhunwala looks on

I even had to procure tickets in the black market for him. We did this as long as he was well enough to travel. I even took him to America for treatment and looked after him when he could not take care of himself. That, to me, is the most highly cherished memory of my father'.

Edcuation was forever close to his heart. BP welcomes Governor A.L. Dias to a Shri Shikshayatan School function

There was also this growing faith that clients were placing on the firm. Pratibha Agarwal writes about an interesting case featuring the Indian Sugar Mills Association, which was involved in a dispute with an American firm and the government of India. The ISMA came to Bhagwati Babu to arrange a settlement. The lawyer representing the American firm was his friend and the Americans thought that they would be able to get Bhagwati Babu to swing the deal for them and were even happy to grease palms for the purpose. The then food minister also asked Bhagwati Babu for a particular verdict and BP said: 'If you give me a written order, I will carry it out'. Otherwise he would do what was right.

BP must have known that the minister could not possibly give him written instructions and the minister had to stay satisfied with the belief that Bhagwati Babu would not do something against the country's interest. BP would certainly not do so but he would be fair to the Americans as well. He did not want anyone to get the impression that Indians were cheats. After getting the order, the Americans offered him money – over and above his fees – which BP turned down, saying that if there were occasions in the future for them to brief him, he would accept whatever fees they offered. Apparently, the Americans then gave a donation to the Ballygunge Shiksha Sadan, a school that Bhagwati Babu had set up. This was a 'thank you' that BP could not refuse.

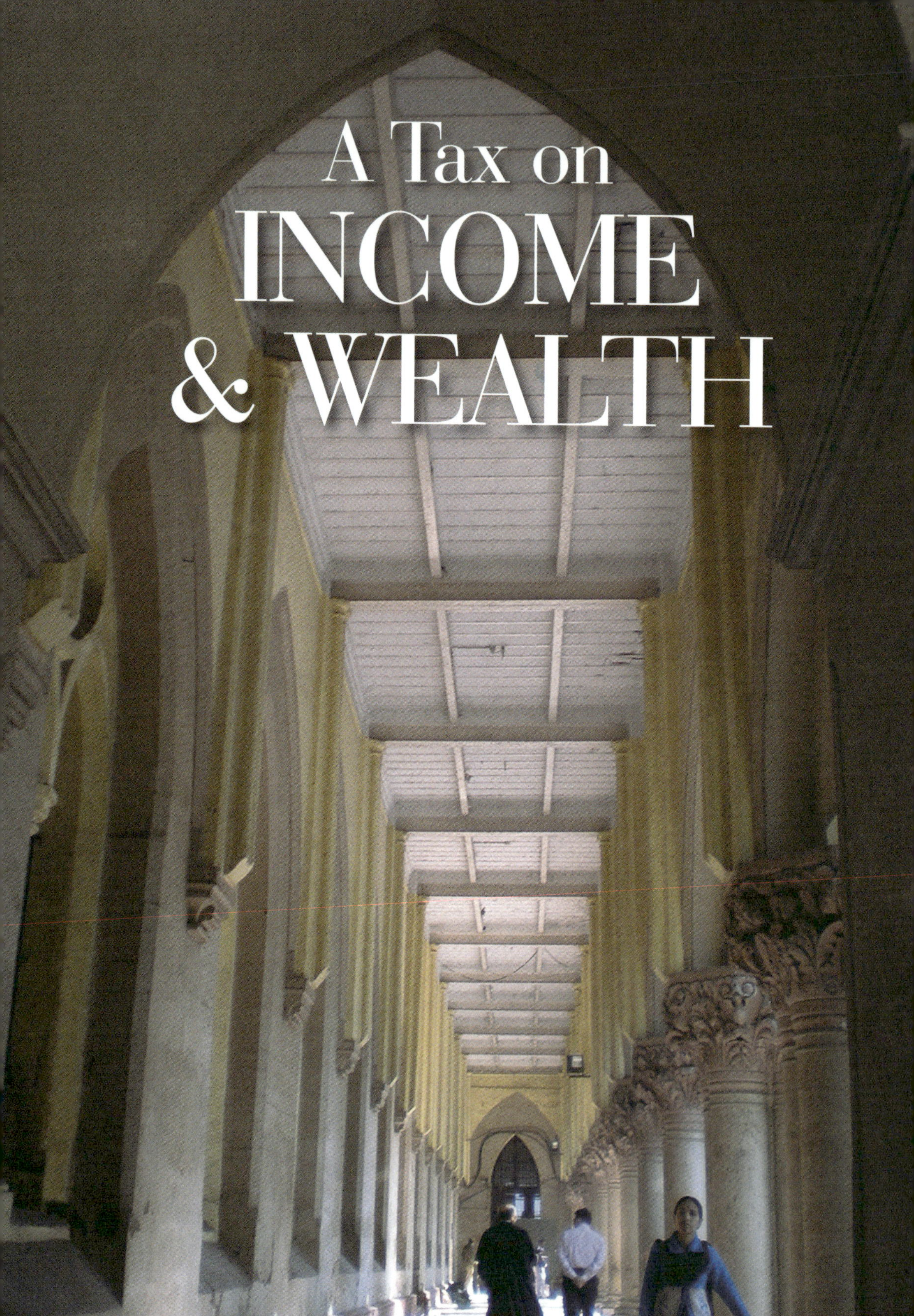
A Tax on
INCOME
& WEALTH

*'It was only for the good of his subjects that he collected taxes from them, just as the Sun draws moisture from the Earth to give it back a thousand fold'.* — **Kalidas** in *Raghuvansh* on King Dalip

It is incorrect to say that there was no concept of taxation in India prior to the advent of the Income Tax Act, 1922. Kautilya's *Arthashastra* provided an authoritative account of how public finance should be administered and what the fiscal laws of the land should be like. There were clear discussions on tax revenue, which were considered essential for the stability of a regime and critical for practising statecraft, but the Income Tax Act and its practice in India is far removed from the wisdom that Kautilya preached. Once the formal IT Act was established in India, it meant good business for legal practitioners. Truth be told, Kautilya notwithstanding, legal matters for the Marwari community, which supplied the largest number of clients for the fledgling KCo in 1911, concerned disputes amongst members of a Hindu Undivided Family; amongst partnership firms; disputes relating to acquisition of land, urban or rural; disputes relating to

## Income tax avatars

Income tax has been levied in India since 1860 and in its first avatar the Act had a reign of five years, whereafter it was replaced by Act II of 1886. It was this Act that introduced the definition of agricultural income and granted exemption to it! It was followed by the Act VII of 1918, which recast tax laws purportedly for correcting inequalities in the assessment of individual tax payers under the 1886 Act. The Act introduced the scheme of aggregating income from all sources for the purpose of determining the rate of tax.

The Indian Income Tax Act, 1922, which came into being as a result of the recommendations of the All India Income Tax Committee, is a milestone in the evolution of Direct Tax Laws in India. Its importance lies in the fact that the administration of Income Tax hitherto carried on by the Provincial Governments came to be vested in the Central Government.

testamentary dispositions; certificates of succession; disputes amongst traders for goods sold and delivered; disputed money claims amongst moneylenders and borrowers and such like. There were virtually no disputes with regard to revenue matters because there was no effective revenue law and, most certainly, the government was hardly a litigant.

Matters changed drastically after World War I, when India completely overwhelmed Britain with its dedicated support to the war effort: British and Indian soldiers (about a million of them) fought like brothers to uphold the cause of the 'Empire' but the camaraderie of the front lines disappeared into thin air once the war was over and the ruling and the ruled returned home, back to a native-sahib relationship. All but forgotten was India's contributions to the War effort, including the shipment of about £80 million worth of military equipment and almost five million tons of wheat of about £40 million worth, to Britain. They also supplied other materials such as silk, mica, tungsten.

## Taxation Enquiry Commission

The Taxation Enquiry Commission of 1953-54, headed by A.V. Vishwanath Shastri, saw the active involvement of KCo because several of its clients were referred to. They included the Birlas, Surajmull Nagarmull, Daulatram Rawatmull, Aminchand Pyarelal, Khuswant Rai and many others. KCo represented the Birlas, assisted by two very senior Birla executives, Anandi Lal Goenka and S.N. Gupta. It was also baptism by fire for young RKC, who was then acting as no more than Bhagwati Prasad Khaitan's personal assistant and, quite at sea with the complicated accounts. BP promptly sent his young assistant to Singhi & Company to learn accounts even before he learnt law. The young man learnt fast and well but that was not the secret to his popularity. 'On one occasion, A.V. Vishwanath Shastri leant on my shoulders while getting down a step and everyone thought it would be a good idea to hire me because they thought I was close to the chairman of the commission'. Whatever be the misconception, what was not in doubt was KCo's handling of the Birla case, which was quite masterful and won a lot of respect from clients old and new.

raw jute, rough-tanned hides, cotton goods, manganese, saltpetre, timber, rubber, and oils. The Government of India paid for all its troops overseas and, before the War ended, the viceroy presented an imperia tax in the form of a gift, of £100 million to the British. The political fallout was dramatic in terms of animosity between the two sides but the economic fallout of the War was something else. A virtually broke British government desperately needed to shore up its finances.

Explains Ram Kishore Choudhury, KCo's taxation expert: 'In the Indian Income Tax Amendment Act, 1916, corporate bodies were treated as separate taxable entities and the dividends paid by them to its shareholders out of the taxed profits were not taxable in the hands of the recipient shareholders. In the 1916 Act, the companies with income of Rs 1,000 or above per annum were charged at the full rate without any abatement. The Act also contemplated a system of differentiation between small and big companies, prompting some litigations relating to subdivision of companies with a view to enjoying tax benefits'. That was all it took to usher in the era of tax litigations even though they were not very worrisome at first. World War I changed all that and the government introduced the Super Tax Act, 1917. 'The Super Tax Act, 1917, was in addition to the income tax payable on the entire profit of the corporate entity. This introduction of the Super Tax Act gave rise to numerous conferences, discussions and planning for reduction of the taxable income by corporate entities', says RKC.

Indians had already started getting involved with manufacturing industries. There were entrepreneurs such as Prince Dwarakanath Tagore, who set up numerous technology companies; Prafulla Chandra Ray, chemist and entrepreneur, who set up Bengal Chemicals & Pharmaceuticals and others who were keen to buy established manufacturing units from the British. RKC says that it was 'to protect branches of foreign companies. The Excess Profits Duty Act, 1919, specifically provided that the companies paying excess profit duty in England were exempt from the levy'. By1920, the commercial community of India had had enough of the super tax and girded its loins to fight against it, successfully achieving what was a landmark in the financial history of the country. The Super Tax Act, 1917, was amended and a tax more akin to a modern 'corporation tax' was introduced.

'Over the years', says P.L. Agarwal, partner: 'KCo has been pre-eminently creative in devising various innovative options for corporate restructuring, including demerger and hiving off of undertakings either by way of family arrangements; by way of succession plans; or to avoid disputes or tax restructuring. Considering the usefulness of these innovations to the commercial world, the tax authorities eventually accepted such innovations and made some tax neutral arrangements. These are now followed by the commercial world to its advantage'.

To go back in time, the Indian Income Tax Act, 1921-22 provided that income-tax and super-tax would be charged 'in respect of all income, profits and gains of the previous year'. RKC explains: 'In computing such profits and gains, certain expenditures were allowed to be specifically deducted from gross revenue, such as rents and rates on business premises; repairs and depreciation on buildings, plant and machinery and furniture; terminal allowances on plant and machinery; insurance premia, interest on borrowed funds and any other expenditure incurred solely for the purposes of the business'.

A company for such purpose was one in which the public was substantially interested, or not less than 25 per cent of its voting power was beneficially held by the public, and its shares were the subject of dealings in any stock exchange or were freely transferable by its holders. It was further proposed that in fixing the control of the company by a

## Report of the Company Law Committee, 1952

'No law, however well-conceived or well-drafted, can be altogether fool-and-knave proof and it is impossible for any law to protect the fool from the consequences of his acts or omissions. Nevertheless, we consider that it is the function of law to prevent dishonest and unscrupulous people from creating conditions and circumstances, which will enable them to make fools of others. The powers of inspection and investigation into the affairs of a company, which the Companies Acts of most countries confer on Government or a quasi-independent authority, are intended primarily as a check on the activities of such people. We recognize that, in some cases, the use of the powers of inspection and investigation may, initially, tend to shake the credit of a company and thereby adversely affect its competitive position, although the allegations against the company may in the end be found to have been largely unfounded. It is, therefore, necessary that the investigation provisions of the Act should be so conceived as to reduce this threat to the credit of companies to a minimum. This risk should not, however, deter us from considering the desirability of conferring adequate powers on an appropriate authority to investigate the affairs of a company, where such investigation is prima facie called for. On the contrary, we consider it to be in the long-term interest of the trade and industry of this country that such powers should be vested in a competent authority and exercised energetically, albeit with due caution and fairness in all cases which require investigation'. (Page 133)

few persons, the shares held by relatives and nominees of a person would be taken as his own holdings. The additional tax liability of a member in respect to the undistributed profits of a company was proposed to be recoverable only from the company. As a measure of safeguard, the Income-tax Officer was allowed to invoke the provisions only with the permission of the Assistant Commissioner. Also, no assistant commissioner could accord approval to the proposed order without first hearing the company.

Section 23A of the Indian Income Tax Act, 1922, as introduced by the Indian Income Tax (Amendment) Act, 1930, which came into force with effect from April 1, 1930, provided that if the ITO was satisfied that the profits and gains of a company were allowed to accumulate beyond its reasonable needs, existing and contingent, having regard to the maintenance and development of its business, without being distributed to the members, to prevent the imposition of tax on any of the members in respect of their shares in such profits and gains, the ITO, with the previous approval of the Assistant Commissioner, could pass an order that the company as such should not be assessed for tax but the proportionate share of profit of each shareholder would be deemed to be distributed to the shareholders and taxed in their hands.

Agreed, the tax authorities were getting more and more difficult but they had ample reasons for doing so. The judgment of Justice J. Banerjee, in the New Central Jute Mills case (August 4, 1965), makes a telling point: 'The Indian Companies Act, 1913, which was extensively amended in 1936, and thereafter further amended from time to time, called for a drastic revision after the end of World War II...Apart from the experience gained in the actual working of the Act, which threw up many points necessitating its amendment, large changes had taken place in the organization and working of joint stock companies and, over a wide sector that was dominated by new elements in trade and industry, the character of company management had also materially altered. In many cases, conventional methods of company management were discarded in favour of less orthodox and more venturesome techniques, which the existing company law was unable to control adequately'. (Report of the Company Law Committee, 1952, Page 3). The lacuna in the Act left the way open for some businessmen to misuse and at times to pervert the provision of the

Smiling solicitor; satisfied clients: It was a difficult tax regime but the Birlas had excellent counsel.(From L-R) G.N. Khaitan, G.P. Birla, K.K. Birla, S.K. Birla, M.P. Birla, B.P. Khaitan

## Speech of C.D. Deshmukh, Finance Minister, 1955-56

The Taxation Enquiry Commission of 1953-54:

'Before I go on to deal with the detailed proposals, I should like to make a brief reference to the report of the Taxation Enquiry Commission (1953-54)… It is a massive and historic document covering the entire field of taxation – Central, State and Local – and the recommendations cover a very extensive field. The report has just been printed up and copies, together with a summary, are being made available to Hon'ble Members...

'…The present Commission's report will deeply colour and affect taxation policy for some time to come. The lines of future policy have been indicated by the Commission but the steps that we take each year or from time to time must necessarily be considered in the light of economic and budgetary considerations of the time.

'Another important change proposed is that losses of business should be allowed to be carried forward indefinitely instead of only for six years as at present. A number of other changes affecting the tax liability are being included in the amendments to the Income Tax Act embodied in the Finance Bill for the coming year in accordance with the recommendations of the Taxation Enquiry Commission... Some of these involve bringing into the net certain incomes which were not being taxed. Others give concessions recommended by the Commission. I would like to mention the more important among the former. The value of any perquisite or benefit, whether convertible into money or not received by salary earners drawing over Rs 18,000 per annum and by directors of companies, and entertainment allowances of all kinds are being made subject to tax'.

law to serve their private ends.'So long as the Second World War lasted, the pull of war economy on domestic production masked these malpractices but the end of the war exposed them to the full view of an increasingly critical public. Thus arose the demand for amendment of the Indian Companies Act…', the report said.

In October 1935, a committee was appointed to make an investigation of the Indian income tax system in all its aspects and to report upon both the incidence of the tax and the efficiency of its administration. The committee was headed by Khan Bahadur J.B. Vachha. The result of the investigation was submitted to the Government of India in a report on December 24, 1936. It pointed out that the Dividend Duties Act, 1902, of Western Australia defined a dividend in the following terms: 'a "dividend" shall include any dividend, profit, advantage or gain, intended to be paid, credited to, or distributed ...' This working was held by the Privy Council to cover an issue of bonus shares. The

## To believe or not to believe

Calcutta Discount Company had been assessed for income tax for the years 1942-43, 1943-44 and 1944-45 by three separate orders dated January 26, 1944, February 12, 1944, and February 15, 1945, under Section 23(3) of the Indian Income Tax Act on returns filed by it with statements of account. Suddenly, on March 28, 1951, three notices under Section 34 of the Act were issued, calling upon it to submit fresh returns for the said assessment years. The appellant filed the returns but applied to the High Court under Article 226 of the Constitution for writs restraining the Income-tax Officer from initiating assessment proceedings on the basis of the said notices on the ground, inter alia, that he had no jurisdiction to issue the said notices. In his report to the Commissioner of Income-tax for obtaining sanction to initiate the said proceedings the Income-tax Officer had stated: 'Profit of Rs 546,002 on sale of shares and securities escaped assessment altogether. At the time of the original assessment the then ITO merely accepted the company's version that the sale of shares were casual transactions and were in the nature of mere change of investments. Now the results of the company's trading from year to year show that the company has really been systematically carrying out a trade in the sale of investments. As such the company had failed to disclose the true intention behind the sale of the shares as such Section 34(1)(a) may be attracted'. The question for determination was whether, in the circumstances, the Income-tax Officer was right in issuing notices on the assessee under Section 34(1)(a) of the Act.

Justices S.K. Das, K.C. Das Gupta and N.R. Ayyangar held that two conditions precedent must co-exist before the Income-tax Officer could issue a notice under Section (1)(a) of the Indian Income-tax Act: He must have reason to believe (i) that income, profits or gains had been under-assessed, and (2) that such under-assessment was due to non-disclosure of material facts by the assessee. The case was a fascinating one because it led to several offshoots in several courts of the country by several corporates, who believed that the rampant reopening of cases by ITOs was more to harass than to detect any real escapement of income.

committee, therefore, recommended that a similar provision be engrafted to the Indian Income Tax Act.

The most important amendment proposed related to the taxation of closely held companies. In deference to the recommendations of the Income Tax Enquiry Committee, the bill sought to introduce a simple arithmetical criterion for the determination of the applicability of the section to the circumstances of a company in any year. The proposed formula provided that to avoid the penal provision contained in the section, at least 60 per cent of the assessable income of the company should be distributed as dividends. Where the accumulated reserves exceeded the paid-up capital, the entire profit should be distributed in dividends. Thus, the provision virtually restricted the expansion of closely held companies beyond double the size of the paid-up capital by ploughing back internal resources. The point being made is that taxes were penal and induced evasion.

The Taxation Enquiry Commission of 1953-54 advised the broadening of the excise duties base to have a stable tax and more and more commodities became excisable. By 1976, all Indian commodities, including industrial inputs and capital goods, were brought under purview of excise duties unless specifically exempted, but the structure was far from stable with often mindless changes in the tax regime. The obsession with taxation was triggered off by the government taking a close look at the excess profits that certain companies made during the War. The mindset then spilt over to the original sector and all corporates were suspect, with the ITOs eagerly reopening assessments that had long been dealt with. A chain of litigations against the department was bound to follow. Section 34 of the old IT Act that pertained to the reopening of concluded assessments (later covered by section 147 of the IT Act 1961) provided the opportunity for IT intervention.

The Act said that such assessments could be reopened if the officer had 'reason to believe' that the income of an assessee had escaped assessment. The challenges posed to the notices of the authorities and the debates over terms and phrases make for riveting legal discussion around what constituted an 'opinion' and what was adequate 'reason to believe'.

Calcutta Discount Company, a KCo client, had come to Krishna Prasad Khaitan with this problem. Kishan Babu and RKC, who was asked to deal with the matter, chose to consult Radha Binod Pal, arguably amongst the sharpest taxation minds of the time. Fortunately, the language of the Act left room for debate and the courts were made to delve into the connotations of the phrase 'reason to believe'. What made such reasons conclusive and relevant enough to conclude that there has been escapement of income was the issue that was finally decided in the Supreme Court by the most eminent bench, comprising justices K.C. Das Gupta, S.K. Das, M. Hidayatullah, J.C. Shah, and Rajagopala N. Ayyangar in the matter of Civil Appeal No. 197 of 1954; appeal from the Judgment and Order of March 25, 1953, of the Calcutta High Court in Appeal from Original Order No. 54 of 1953.

Probably the sharpest of minds for all taxation matters: a bust of Dr Radha Binod Pal in the corridors of the Calcutta High Court

In the Supreme Court the matter was argued on behalf of Calcutta Discount by Sachin Chaudhuri, Sukumar Mitter, S. N. Mukherjee and D.N. Ghosh. 'Kishan Babu had asked me to ensure that Sachin Chaudhuri was properly briefed because the matter was of critical interest to the firm, the client having lost the case in the Calcutta High Court on an appeal by the authorities against a favourable trial judge ruling', says RKC.

Justice Shah held that the expression 'reason to believe' in Section 34(1)(a) of the IT Act 1922 did not mean a purely subjective satisfaction of the ITO but predicated the existence of reasons on which such belief had to be founded.

## The anatomy of an opinion

Amongst the trickiest traps that corporate India found itself was section 237 of the Companies Act that empowered the government to order further investigations, if, upon inspection, the authorities were of the opinion that there was such need. Numerous such notices were served to companies and were challenged in High Courts and even the Supreme Court. The section affected many of KCo's clients including New Central Jute Mills, Sahu Jain Ltd, Jeeyajirao Cotton, Barium Chemicals, Ashoka Marketing and others. That the clients finally won their cases winning much accolades for KCo was not the story; it was the mind behind the victory that matters. Counsel in the matter were R.C. Deb, Subrata Roy Chowdhury and Biswaroop Gupta and it involved long sessions at No. 12 Clive Row where a Shital Prasad Jain and Ashok Jain would give the lawyers a tough time. It was R.C. Deb, of course, who said that it would be good strategy to pin the department on what constituted 'opinion' and it was this strategy that won the case in the Supreme Court. 'The drill was a tough one: first Biswaroop would prepare a draft, Subrata Roy Chowdhury would settle it and R.C. Deb would resettle it finally only to have Shital Jain tear it to bits. We called him super counsel!' R.C. Deb, of course, had the last laugh when the court decided in favour of KCo's clients and opened up even more doors for the firm.

That belief, therefore, could not be founded on mere suspicion but had to be based on evidence. Any question about the adequacy of such evidence was wholly immaterial at that stage. 'If there is disclosure of some facts but not all, a taxpayer cannot resist reassessment on the plea that such non-disclosure was due to the negligence or inadvertence on the part of the Income-tax Officer to scrutinize the materials before him…', Justice Shah said.

Khaitan's case was that the under-assessment was not on account of any non-disclosure on the client's part. The judgment said: 'As admittedly the appellant had filed its return of income under Section 22, the Income-tax Officer could have no reason to believe that under-assessment had resulted from the failure to make a return of income. The only question is whether the Income-tax Officer had reason to believe that "there had been some omission or failure to disclose fully and truly all material facts necessary for the assessment" for any of these years in consequence of which the under-assessment took place'. Sachin Chaudhuri was able to persuade the judges that, in terms of what the assessing officer was saying, the only non-disclosure was that the company had failed to disclose 'the true intention behind the sale of the shares', which, he argued, was not an omission to disclose a material fact within the meaning of Section 34. 'The question whether sales of certain shares were by way of changing the investments or by way of trading in shares had to be decided on a consideration of different circumstances, including the frequency of the sales, the nature of the shares sold, the price received as compared with the cost price and several other relevant facts'.

The judges further held that it was 'the duty of the assessee to disclose all the facts, which have a bearing on the question; but whether the assessee had the

## Indian I-T in the US?

The love-hate relationship between the Income Tax department and Ashok Jain of Sahu Jain Group of Companies has been legendary. Thus one day, in 1961, Ashok Jain, sitting in the US, found himself facing an officer deputed by the income tax authorities in India. He was being served with summons under Section 131 of the Income Tax Act, 1961. The officer had been sent all the way from India and the client had to be advised from Kolkata. Bhagwati Babu and his boys put their minds together, and did extensive research on how to resist the service of summons, before BPK prepared an opinion that the provisions of the Income Tax Act, 1961 had no extra territorial jurisdiction and as such the provisions of Section 131 of the Act could not be invoked against a person residing abroad; nor could he be summoned for deposing there. BPK's signature on the opinion was then notarially certified by L.P. Agarwala (Notary and Solicitor) and RKC was asked to travel to the US. There he apprised the Income-Tax Officer that he had no jurisdiction to examine his client. The officer had to return to India without enforcing the summons. In recent months, the opinion has been echoed by a Supreme Court judgment in a matter featuring G.V.K. Industries Ltd vs the ITO.

intention to make a business profit as distinguished from the intention to change the form of the investments is really an inference to be drawn by the assessing authority from the material facts taken in conjunction with the surrounding circumstances. The law does not require the assessee to state the conclusion that could reasonably be drawn from the primary facts. The question of the assessee's intention is an inferential fact and so the assessee's omission to state his "true intentions behind the sale of shares cannot by itself be considered to be a failure or omission to disclose any material fact" within the meaning of Section 34 of the Act of 1922'. It was, therefore, held that 'the Income-tax Officer who issued the notices had not before him any non-disclosure of a material fact and so he could have no material before him for believing that there had been any material non-disclosure by reason of which an under-assessment had taken place'.

The judges concluded by stating: 'We are, therefore, bound to hold that the conditions precedent to the exercise of jurisdiction under Section 34 of the Income Tax Act did not exist and the Income-tax Officer had, therefore, no jurisdiction to issue the impugned notices under Section 34 in respect of the years 1942-43, 1943-44 and 1944-45 after the expiry of four years as they restored the order by the trial judge, J. Bose. Justice J.C. Shah and Justice M. Hidayatullah differed with the judgment of the majority but the day had been won by KCo. Tax clients flocked to Emerald House!

The saga of reopening cases, however, continued and the offices of Daulatram Rawatmull found themselves slapped with IT notices at 5, Synagogue Street, that were literally sent on jhakas (large circular cane baskets carried by coolies on their heads). They were voluminous and obviously prepared in haste: 'there was no signature on many documents and the notices were full of errors', recalls RKC about the matter that he had been asked to handle by B.P. Khaitan. The case (Commissioner of Income Tax vs Daulatram Rawatmull) was decided in March 1964 by a Supreme Court Bench comprising J. Shah, K.S. Rao and S. Sikri. It was a rather complicated matter featuring cash deposits, intra-bank transfers and creating new credit instruments to help an associate. Justice J. Shah held that the circumstances relied upon by the IT authorities 'do raise suspicion but suspicion cannot take the place of evidence'.

Recalls Ram Kishore Choudhury: 'This was a Nopany family matter and they were important clients of KCo and there were six partners, all independently important men of business'. RKC himself was one of the arguing lawyers in this matter, along with B.P. Maheshwari, assisting S.K. Kapur, senior counsel, with his characteristic intensity. The judges held that while the tribunal had rightly pointed out that the similarity of the transactions relating to certain cash credits and the proximity of time were matters that could raise suspicions that could be strengthened, it was held that

RKC, encouraged by BPK to handle the trickiest of legal cases, travelled all over the country, learning from experience; meeting the top legal minds

Sri Hanuman Sugar Mills, the ultimate beneficiary of the amount deposited … 'was an associate but these facts did not justify an inference that the assessee had anything to do with the deposit in question out of its "secreted profits". The circumstance relied upon fail to establish the one link, which must be established by evidence that the assessee was concerned with the transaction…' .

Says RKC: 'Today, the Income Tax Act, 1961, reflects a sorry state of affairs because there is no instance in Indian jurisprudence of an act or statute mutilated by more than 3,500 amendments in barely 50 years. Simple provisions like Sections 11 to 31 (dealing with exemption of the income of charitable trusts) have suffered not less than 80 amendments'. Referring to the KCo opinion in the Ashok Jain matter under Section 131 in the US, RKC explains that in 2011, the Supreme Court of India, inter alia, held in the G.V.K. Industries vs ITO matter that the 'Parliament is constitutionally restricted from enacting legislation with respect to extra-territorial aspects or causes that do not have, nor are expected to have any, direct or indirect, tangible or intangible impact on or effect in or consequences for: (a) the territory of India, or any part of India; or (b) the interests of, welfare of, well-being of, or security of inhabitants of India and Indians'.

However, the Parliament may exercise its legislative powers with respect to extra-territorial aspects or causes – events, things, phenomena (howsoever commonplace they may be) resources, actions or transactions and the like – that occur, arise or exist or may be expected to do so, naturally or on account of some human agency, in the social, political, economic, cultural, biological, environmental or physical spheres outside the territory of India, and seek to control, modulate, mitigate or transform the effects of such extra-territorial aspects or causes, or in appropriate cases, eliminate or engender such extra-territorial aspects or causes, only when such extra-territorial aspects or causes have, or are expected to have, some impact on, or effect in, or consequences for: (a) the territory of India, or any part of India; or (b) the interests of, welfare of, well-being of, or security of inhabitants of India, and Indians'. In effect, any laws enacted by Parliament with respect to extra-territorial aspects or causes that have no impact on or nexus with India would be ultra vires Parliament and would be laws made for a foreign territory.

Tiresome though the complication of the IT Act and its numerous changes were, they made for good custom for the legal fraternity. Every time KCo got a verdict in favour of a client, it gained a dozen others. There were several important and challenging cases around wealth tax too, not the least among them being the interesting and subtle distinction between ornaments and jewellery that RKC worked on to spare hundreds of middle-class women from having their ornaments taxed under wealth tax, which was a decision of great social import.

The sharpest business minds sought BP's counsel. He never disappointed. B.P Khaitan with Radha Kishen Kanoria

Recalls RKC: 'Earlier, wealth tax assessment was guided by a provision exempting jewellery up to a certain value, meant for personal use'. The question arose during the assessment of Aditya Birla's wealth tax (then being done in Calcutta) whether ornaments included jewellery. 'I successfully argued that jewellery did not include ornaments', says RKC. The matter went to court because, in the assessment year 1970-

## Dealing with Section 52

Explains RKC: 'The ITO was permitted an "objective satisfaction" because the use of the expression "if in the opinion of" made it abundantly clear that the said sub-section (2) of Section 52 had conferred unfettered and unguided power upon the ITO, which was necessary for invocation of sub-section (2) so the disparity between the market value and the said consideration to the extent not less than 15 per cent could be taxed. Once this artificial and arithmetical disparity was subjectively satisfied, the legislature took it as a conclusive proof of understatement of consideration and empowered the ITO to proceed with the computation of capital gain on the basis of the value so determined by the officer. In a number of cases the assessing officers found that, by invoking Section 52(2) of the Act, fair market value was more than 15 per cent of the consideration declared and they taxed the difference as capital gain. The action of the assessing officers was upheld by the lower authorities'.

71, Aditya Vikram Birla, did not include jewellery intended for his personal use in his net wealth on the ground that on the relevant valuation date such jewellery (intended for personal use) was exempt, under Section 5(1)(viii) of the Wealth Tax Act, 1957, from inclusion in the assessable net wealth.

The judgment in the matter makes for interesting reading. Justice Dipak Kumar Sen observed that the question of law that has been referred to his court under Section 27(1) of the Wealth Tax Act, 1957, at the instance of the commissioner of wealth tax, West Bengal-I, Calcutta, is as follows: 'Whether, on the facts and in the circumstances of the case and on a correct interpretation of Section 5(1)(viii) of the Wealth Tax Act, 1957, as it stood before and after amendment by Finance (No. 2) Act of 1971, the tribunal was right in holding that ornaments intended for personal use not studded with precious or semi-precious stones were not liable to be included in the assessee's net wealth for the while. The Wealth Tax Officer accepted the Birla contention in exercise of his powers under Section 25(2) of the Wealth Tax Act, 1957, but the additional commissioner initiated revision proceedings in view of the amendment of Clause

(viii) of section 5(1) of the Act by the Finance (No. 2) Act of 1971'. The Act amended the clause with retrospective effect from April 1, 1963, so as to exclude jewellery from the scope of the exemption under that clause. 'By the same Act, an Explanation 1 was inserted in the clause with effect from April 1, 1972, to give an extended meaning to the word jewellery', explains Ram Kishore Choudhury.

The additional commissioner held that the assessee's ornaments of all descriptions were jewellery and liable to be included in his chargeable net wealth in the assessment year in question and directed the Wealth Tax Officer to modify the assessment accordingly. Aditya Birla preferred an appeal to the tribunal that noted the difference between 'jewellery' and 'ornaments'. It held that ornaments were included in jewellery with effect from the April 1, 1972. An explanation was added to Section 5(1)(viii) of the Act by the Finance (No. 2) Act, 1971. The tribunal followed an earlier decision of another bench in the case of Rajashree Birla vs the Wealth Tax Officer for the assessment years 1969-70 and 1970-71, where it was held that ornaments for personal use, not containing precious or semi-precious stones, should not be included in the assessment of wealth tax and set aside the order of the appellate assistant

## No room to tax

The 1981 case of K.P. Varghese vs the ITO [(1981) 4 SCC 173)], decided by the bench of P.N. Bhagwati and E.S. Venkataramaiah, had a major impact on Section 52 (2) of the Income Tax Act, 1961, which dealt with consideration for transfer in case of understatement of value. The case featured a house bought in 1958 for Rs 16,500 and sold by the buyer to his daughter-in-law and his five children in 1965. The ITO, however, held that the fair market price of the property would be Rs 65,000 and that the seller would be assessed for capital gains. The full bench of the High Court, by its majority decision, concurred with the ITO's view after the single-judge bench had allowed the assessee's contention. KCo intervened in this matter on behalf of some of its clients and Ram Kishore Choudhury was sent to the Supreme Court. (see box dealing with Section 52)

commissioner. The appeal of the assessee was allowed. There was an identical question being asked in Ahmedabad in the Arundhati Balakrishnan (a Mafatlal relative) case. Nani Palkhivala did not agree with RKC's argument that jewellery and ornaments could be treated separately. The matter went up to the Supreme Court, which ruled that jewellery did not include ornaments and the Act was subsequently amended. This was a historic victory for KCo.

There was, however, trouble galore over Section 52(2) of the Income Tax Act, introduced by the Finance Act, 1964. The idea was to rope in transactions in respect of transfer of capital asset, effected with the objective of avoidance or reduction of the liabilities of the assessee vis-à-vis capital gain tax: if the full value of the consideration for such transfer exceeds the full value by an amount of not less than 15 per cent of the value so declared. Employing the Act, the ITO realized that fair market value was more than 15 per cent of the consideration declared and taxed the difference as capital gain with such action upheld by the lower authorities.

The impact was severe on the Birlas and several assessments of the Birla group of assessees were reopened under Section 147 of the Act and revision proceedings commenced under Section 264 of the Act. RKC was asked to handle the matter and appeared before the assessing officer, inspecting assistant commissioner of IT, commissioner of IT, appellate authorities and the tribunal arguing on behalf of the Birla group of assessees contending that (a) Section 52(2) should be construed as having regard to the object and purpose for which it was enacted. It was not to be given strictly literal construction, which would lead to it being declared as ultra vires; (b) the section should be so construed as to suppress the mischief and evils sought to be remedied and not to hit bona fide transactions; and (c) to attract applicability of Section 52(2), two conditions have to be fulfilled, namely, that fair market value of the asset exceeds the declared consideration by 15 per cent or more and that the consideration has been understated by the assessee with the object of avoidance or reduction of tax. The revenue had the burden of showing that all these conditions had been fulfilled and each of these conditions had to be viewed and established independently.

Serendipitously, RKC went to Delhi, where he came across the case of K.P. Varghese vs ITO in the monthly list of the Supreme Court. He had known about the lower court judgment in the case of K.P. Varghese and set the strategy in motion: urgent calls went to Swaroop Narain Gupta, the GP/KK Birla tax executive and G.P. Birla himself instructed RKC to intervene immediately and also assist the counsel appearing on behalf of K.P. Varghese. In Delhi, RKC obtained a copy of the paper book of the case and contacted K.P. Varghese's counsel, supplementing his preparation with the assistance

## Colourable ordinance

The government of Bihar was especially harsh with its sales tax levies: it would impose sales tax in Bihar by promulgating successive Ordinances while bypassing the State Legislature. C.M. Ghorawat was asked to tackle the vexatious problem under Pinto Khaitan's guidance. Article 213 of the Constitution of India empowered a state Governor to promulgate an Ordinance at any time except when the Legislative Assembly of the State was in session but Article 213(2) provided, inter alia, for the Ordinance to be laid before the Legislative Assembly and that it would cease to operate at the expiration of six weeks from the reassembly of the legislature. The Bihar government would allow its ordinances to lapse and pass a fresh ordinance with retrospective effect from the date of expiry of the previous ordinance, covering the interregnum. This practice continued for years and had been unsuccessfully challenged in the Patna High Court. KCo reviewed the matter afresh and C.M. Ghorawat differed from the two Division Bench judgments of Patna High Court. He held that the levy of sales tax in the aforesaid manner was colourable exercise of power by the government; was ultra vires and bad in law. Subsequently, similar views were expressed by the Supreme Court with reference to an identical situation and the views expressed by KCo were supported thereby. Ultimately this practice was stopped in Bihar.

of Dr Debi Pal and also argued the matter. Justice P.N. Bhagwati, who presided over the bench, upheld the contentions, which were agitated by RKC before the lower authorities in the case of the Birla group of assessees. This success meant that numerous re-assessment proceedings, revision proceedings and appeals were dropped, and tax demands, which were raised by invoking Section 52(2), were knocked off.

Dr Debi Pal was the cat's whisker, coming up with brilliant solutions. (L-R): R.N. Jhunjhunwala, Dr Debi Pal, Justice Padma Khastgir and Justice Kania of the Supreme Court of India

Every day, there were new kinds of cases and KCo soon found itself handling the first demerger case in the country. The old Companies Act provided for amalgamations but not for demergers. That was when Balrampur Chini had to be demerged from BCCI owned by Hari Das Mundhra. Balrampur Sugar Company Limited and Tulsipur Sugar Company were acquired by Pannalal Saraogi and Matadin Khaitan respectively and had to be bifurcated into Balrampur and Tulsipur. The scheme was approved by the Calcutta High Court on July 1, 1959, under Justice P.B. Mukherjee's order. What made this achievement remarkable was that KCo had got the demerger approved even though there was no provision for it in the Companies Act. Not surprising, for arguing the matter for the firm were the stalwarts, Ranadeb Choudhury, assisted by S.C. (Koilu) Sen.

There was yet another development following the demerger, when a 10-rupee share became two 5-rupee shares of Tulsipur and Balrampur. The IT department started proceedings under the Gift Tax Act, which has since been abolished. 'KCo's opinion was that in mergers and even demergers, there is no transfer involved inter vivos (transfer or gift made during one's lifetime, as opposed to a testamentary transfer). The vesting of property by the transferrer in favour of the transferee in this case was courtesy an order of the High Court. A written submission had to be prepared quoting leading national and international judicial authorities to establish that the sanction of a scheme for merger or demerger did not amount to a 'transfer' within the meaning of the Gift Tax Act. The opinion was submitted to the chairman of the Central Board of Direct Taxes by Bhagwati Prasad Khaitan along with the client's representative, Pannalal Saraogi, who appeared before the CBDT. The gift tax proceedings were then withdrawn', says RKC, who recalls spending hours preparing the submission. Gobindlal Saraogi, brother of Pannalal Saraogi, recalls the friendship between his family and the firm for the past 63 years. It began as a business relationship and blossomed into a relationship with Ram Kumar Saraogi's daughter getting married to Bhagwati Babu's son.

Bhagwati Prasad Khaitan himself had said that post 1930, when he became an attorney, the character of the legal space started changing in India; more so after World War II. Prior to that there were few companies and some phutka-related matters; there were also breach of trust and limitation matters. Then came the war and that marked the advent of the Defence of India Act; the shortfall in essential commodities led to the Essential Commodities Act, said BP in a storytelling mode at a meeting with friends.

'By the time India was independent, the Income Tax Act had become quite evolved... There was also the excess profit tax on the one hand and, on the other, people were taking over companies and wanting to become directors. Others wanted wholesale agencies and even to establish managing agencies and only lawyers could interpret the new laws and help clients with their new aspirations.... Personally, I got busy from morning till evening and KCo's reputation spread by the day... Then came the five-year plans and as the

Always a smiling visage; never mind the work pressure: International and domestic work came by. Party for J.F. Bartos by Bata Shoes; November 17, 1961

government got active, so did the private sector. It started setting up new industries. There were foreign collaborations too and even government work came our way. Then came the labour laws and I realized that this would mean even more work for us because the maliks would want to protect their turf, and the workers, theirs. The government would, of course, want to be populist'.

Whatever may have been the nature of the law, KCo had mastered the art of protecting the client's interests. Nonagenarian Jolly Mohan Kaul, former district secretary of the Communist Party of India, who was sometimes asked to represent labour in these tribunals, would find a Khaitan on the other side. He recalls: 'There we were, all excited and angry about labour rights and ready to agitate and there would be Mr Khaitan, smiling, unexcited and patient. Even in our most excitable frame of mind, we could not but help notice that'. That smiling visage, one suspects, was that of Bhagwati Prasad Khaitan.

# HONESTY
## is the Smartest Policy

As upright as it gets: the Calcutta High Court is a beautifully crafted building

*The Hon'ble judge looked askance. There was the venerable Bhagwati Prasad Khaitan standing before him along with some distinguished looking gentlemen. 'What are you doing here, Mr Khaitan? Certainly, I had exempted you from making a personal appearance?' The court – generally associated with the baser aspects of humanity – experienced a humbling moment. 'How could I allow myself to be exempted when my brother directors have been asked to be present?', responded the redoubtable BP, then on the board of Nicco, a company with which he had been associated almost from its inception in an advisory capacity and, later, as director. The judge promptly exempted every director from any further personal appearances.*

Bhagwati Babu looked up in dismay; even horror. No he was not confronted with a difficult case of law; nor a difficult judge. He was confronted by one of his brightest protégés, Sita Ram Jhunjhunwala, a slip of a boy in his twenties, sitting before him with a dilemma quite shocking for those times. Sita Ram was being groomed by Bhagwati Prasad Khaitan to be an attorney and he had absolutely no doubt that the young man would come out with flying colours at the forthcoming examination; never mind that it would be a very tough one; conducted by the High Court of Calcutta, with the registrar himself in charge and the examination run by the gora sahibs.

BP's favourite disciple: Sitaram Jhunjhunwala, whose sons and grandson work with the firm even today

Sita Ram had come to him with a scandalous piece of paper. Bhagwati Babu looked at it and his face showed his consternation: this was the question paper of the attorneyship examination that was yet to be held. Someone, somehow, had

managed to leak it and one such paper had landed in the hands of young Sita Ram. Brought up in the now-forgotten tradition of honesty is the best policy, the young man struggled with his own conscience and, finally, went to his mentor with his predicament. The resolution was clear and instant: 'you will not sit for the examination this time'. So Sita Ram had to bide his time; sitting for the next round of the examination to get his certificate and promptly be made partner at KCo, where he turned out to be amongst the brightest stars.

Sita Ram Jhunjhunwala, whom one has met in the earlier chapter, had joined KCo as an accounts assistant. Possibly his beautiful handwriting and his grounding in commerce prompted the firm to place him under the strict cashier and paterfamilias of KCo, 'Lukkhi Babu', the burra babu of the firm. From him Sita Ram

## Sita Ram Jhunjhunwala

As Hindu Muslim riots broke out in Calcutta in 1942, SRJ, who stayed in Poddar Chhatra Niwas on Chittaranjan Avenue near Mahajati Sadan, found himself caught in the crossfire. Everyone was fleeing and SRJ managed to save himself by hiding in the rooftop water tank. Then when he found a Sikh regiment patrol going by his building and offering to escort the extremely scared hostellers to safety, SRJ and few others jumped on the military truck from the balcony of the first floor. SRJ took two dhotis, tied one around his head to save it from possible injury and the other around his waist and jumped into the truck, suffering minor cuts and bruises; and managed to reach the Howrah Station and take the earliest train to Deoghar.

He was then getting Rs 400 a month in KCo and was yet to become a partner. After three or four months things were back to normal in the city when he received a telegram from BPK to the effect: 'Sita Ram where are you? Come back immediately. Situation is normal. Sending Rs 1,600 by telegraphic money order; confirm safe receipt' and so on. This was followed by remittance of Rs 1,600 for the four months that he was away. The family was delighted and its reverence for the Khaitans increased considerably. When Sita Ram became a partner at KCo, it was a matter of historic importance to the family in Deoghar; bringing them great pride and joy that was shared by the entire community, recalls younger brother, RNJ.

learnt the basics of how firms were run. It was, however, B.P. Khaitan who realized the potential of the young man and put him through the attorneyship paces with excellent results, guiding him whenever he was in a quandary.

For Brij Mohan Khaitan, uncle BP was a mentor and guide. B.M. Khaitan seen here with M.P. Birla

BP was equally supportive of his own family, his friends and his many wards at work. The legal scene in India was becoming more and more complex and Indian firms were taking over multinational enterprises on the eve of the departure of British interests. Sitting on the top floor of his headquarters at 4, Mangoe Lane, in downtown Calcutta, Brij Mohan Khaitan, chairman of the world's largest tea plantation group, was in a reminiscent mood: 'B.P. Khaitan was not just an uncle and legal advisor; he was my mentor and guide. I lost my father in 1963 and I would turn to BP for all matters financial, legal or otherwise. He helped in reorganizing my company and in this he was ably assisted by his son Pinto, whose forte was a blend of law and economics. They made an excellent team'.

Although related to KCo by lineage, a nephew to Bhagwati Babu, his father's younger brother, BM's professional association with the company began in the early 1960s. BM was the Indian partner in Williamson Magor; the other partners were in London and they, along with Gladstone Lyal, were looking after Ellerman Lines, a major shipping firm that looked after tea exports. The custodians of the entire holdings of Williamson Magor were the senior partners of Orr Dignam and Lovelock & Lewes, Silverston and Lang. 'I was looking for a one-third shareholding in the company and that was proving a ticklish problem', BM recalls. 'There was the issue of a conflict of interest as Orr Dignam were also the solicitors of Gladstone

Lyal. It was then that I turned to my uncle, B.P. Khaitan, who had an extraordinary knack of solving problems without going to courts. Through across-the-table negotiations with Silverston of Orr Dignam, he settled the matter in my favour in a trice'. Although in the thick of the legal profession, BP was vehemently opposed to litigation. Strange as it may sound, he was always one for amicable settlements, he would never advocate long-drawn-out legal battles'.

Bhagwati Babu had a special place for Sita Ram Jhunjhunwala as did most other seniors. When Tulsi Prasad Khaitan, who had just got married and was planning to shift to Delhi, wanted Sita Ram to accompany him, Bhagwati Babu told him that he would have a much brighter future as an attorney in Calcutta than as an accountant in Delhi. So Sita Ram stayed back and fulfilled the dreams of his mentor and more. Amongst the most important lessons learnt by him, which he had passed on to his son Arvind, in due course, was that 'one fought to win cases for clients and one never judged the case. One just assessed the points of law. Judgment was for other authorities and, of course, the divine one'.

Meanwhile, the office became a training ground for any Marwari boy who wanted a career as an attorney. Two of the new recruits of the 1950s continue to be with the firm: Ram Niranjan Jhunjhunwala (Sita Ram's younger brother) and Ram Kishore Choudhury, both of whom one has

Minutes of Partners Meeting dated 28th December 1999, Page 1

**MINUTES OF MEETING OF THE PARTNERS OF KHAITAN & CO. HELD ON 28TH DECEMBER, 1999 AT 4.00 P.M. ON THE 8TH FLOOR AT 9, OLD POST OFFICE STREET, CALCUTTA 700 001.**

Present:

1. Mr Ram Kishore Choudhury
2. Mr Pradip Kumar Khaitan
3. Mr Purushottam Lal Agarwal
4. Mr Ram Niranjan Jhunjhunwala
5. Mr Nand Gopal Khaitan
6. Mr Gouri Shankar Asopa
7. Mr Padam Kumar Khaitan
8. Mr Rajiv Khaitan
9. Mr Arvind Kumar Jhunjhunwala
10. Mr Aniket Agarwal
11. Mr Haigreve Khaitan

1. Working of Calcutta, Bangalore and Delhi offices :

Mr Pradip K. Khaitan briefed the Partners that there appears to be a slow down in work in Calcutta and Delhi offices and effort was needed from all the Partners to procure new work as well as upgrade the talent amongst the existing lawyers to be able to do new types of work. Mr Pradip K. Khaitan pointed out that in many cases existing clients are not giving all their work to us. It was also pointed out that in many areas such as industrial disputes, intellectual property and computer law, the existing people in the Firm did not have adequate knowledge and expertise. Mr Pradip K. Khaitan suggested that existing persons in the Firm be identified and encouraged to specialise in such areas.

The Partners discussed the points made by Mr Pradip K. Khaitan and agreed with the same.

2. Reduction of expenses :

Mr Pradip K. Khaitan briefed the Partners that in the current year the profitability of the Firm was much lower than earlier years and there is a need to cut down costs and expenses in all areas. The Partners discussed and agreed with the same.

met earlier in these pages. RKC was placed under the tutelage of Sita Ram Jhunjhunwala. 'I joined KCo in December 1951, although I was not qualified to be admitted as an articled clerk within the meaning of the Calcutta High Court Rules (original side). In December 1955, a formal agreement of articleship was executed with Sita Ram Jhunjhunwala and filed with the Registrar, High Court (original side). The office then was in 1B, Old Post Office Street, 2nd Floor, and the four partners: B.P. Khaitan, Krishna Prasad Khaitan, Sita Ram Jhunjhunwala and Makhanlal Jhunjhunwala, whose father was Chiranjilal Jhunjhunwala from Ranigunge'.

MINUTES OF THE MEETING OF THE PARTNERS HELD ON 25TH JANUARY 2001 AT THE CONFERENCE ROOM ON 8TH FLOOR, AT NO.9, OLD POST OFFICE STREET, KOLKATA – 700 001 AT 4.30 P.M.

| | |
|---|---|
| 1. Attendance | Mr R. K. Choudhury<br>Mr Pradip Kumar Khaitan<br>Mr P.L. Agarwal<br>Mr R. N. Jhunjhunwala<br>Mr Pramod Kumar Khaitan<br>Mr Gouri Shankar Asopa<br>Mr Padam Khaitan<br>Mr O. P. Jhunjhunwala<br>Mr Rajiv Khaitan<br>Mr Arvind Jhunjhunwala<br>Mr Aniket Agarwal<br>Mr Haigreve Khaitan |
| 2. Chairman | Mr R.K. Choudhury took the Chair at the request of Mr Pradip K. Khaitan. |
| 3. Preparation of Minutes | Mr Haigreve Khaitan was requested to take down the notes of the meeting and prepare minutes of the meeting for Mr R.K. Choudhury's approval and circulation thereafter. |
| 4. Opening of a Mumbai Office | Mr Pradip K. Khaitan mentioned that the future in West Bengal appears dim and while cost curtailing is being implemented in Kolkata, it has become necessary to look at opening an office in Mumbai. He stated that opening an office in Mumbai would mean commitment in terms of manpower as well as money. It will mean that at least having one senior person in Mumbai and one person from Kolkata on a whole-time basis in addition to other persons from Kolkata devoting substantial time in Mumbai. He suggested that if an office is to be opened, it should be opened at a proper level otherwise no office should be opened at all. He mentioned that senior partners of successful law firms in Mumbai have been approached as to whether they would be willing to join the Mumbai office.<br><br>Mr R.K. Choudhury mentioned that the principle decision as to whether to open an office in Mumbai or not should be taken first. If a decision is made to have an office in Mumbai, then proper space could be located, a budget made out and people from Kolkata selected to be moved to Mumbai. Following this local people including senior |

Minutes of Partners Meeting dated 25th January 2001, Page 1

Makhanlal Jhunjhunwala, a bachelor, was as hardworking and meticulous as he was jolly, recalls RKC. Though more than law he handled the office administration and finances. His constant refrain was: 'Raising bills on time is very important; it can increase the firm's realizations many times over!' Around 1959-60, both he and SRJ were given Ambassador cars. For the youngsters, it was quite a treat watching him learn to drive with the learner's licence hanging next to the number plate. 'He was so nervous that he never did learn to drive', recalls RKC. Tragically though, he collapsed in court one day and passed away soon after. RKC also remembers a Mukherjee Babu (K.P. Mukherjee), apart from himself and Niranjan Singtia, the two assistants. 'We shared a small office space at 1B, which also housed our library and record room'.

Bhagwati Babu had an eye for the right candidate: he did not follow a recruitment policy; nor did he particularly care for brilliant academic results, even though most members of his family were academically gifted. 'I was not an exceptional student; my brother-in-law, Krishnanand Jalan, son of Ishwar Das Jalan, who was a solicitor, requested Sita Ramji to take me in. Bhagwati Babu was the sole deciding authority for all appointments. He did not follow a hire and fire policy but he would ensure that those that stayed were motivated, inspired, learnt the job well and worked hard', says RKC. Indeed, the trainees had to work hard: 'take out the bundles of cases from racks, clean them, place them on the seniors' tables. There used to be a small telephone exchange box in the hall with the telephone operator turning the handle to power it. There was no dialing in those days. The partner's assistant would have instruments without any dialling facility, the operator would answer the incoming call and connect it to the desired extension', recalls RNJ.

Minutes of Partners Meeting dated 13th April 2001, Page 1

MINUTES OF THE MEETING OF THE PARTNERS HELD ON 13TH APRIL 2001 AT THE PORTICO, TAJ BENGAL, KOLKATA AT 11.00 A.M.

| | |
|---|---|
| 1. Attendance | Mr R. K. Choudhury<br>Mr Pradip Kumar Khaitan<br>Mr P.L. Agarwal<br>Mr R. N. Jhunjhunwala<br>Mr Pramod Kumar Khaitan<br>Mr Nand Gopal Khaitan<br>Mr Gouri Shankar Asopa<br>Mr O. P. Agarwal<br>Mr Padam Khaitan<br>Mr O. P. Jhunjhunwala<br>Mr Suman J Khaitan<br>Mr Arvind Jhunjhunwala<br>Mr Sanjay Khaitan<br>Mr Aniket Agarwal<br>Mr Haigreve Khaitan |
| 2. Chairman | Mr R.K. Choudhury took the Chair at the request of Mr Pradip K. Khaitan. |
| 3. Absence | It was noted that Mr Rajiv Khaitan could not attend the meeting as he was out of India. |
| 4. Merger with AMSS | The proposal for merger with AMSS was discussed. Fourteen of the Partners present were in favour provided the terms were right.<br><br>Mr Arvind Jhunjhunwala felt that rather than merge we should first concentrate on Delhi office and later extend to Mumbai on our own.<br><br>It was decided that we would listen to the representatives of AMSS and later take a decision. |
| 5. Unification of three firms | Even though merger proposal with AMSS is under consideration the Partners present unanimously agreed to the unification of the three firms into one. |
| 6. Mumbai Office | If the merger with AMSS does not materialize then efforts would be made to establish a meaningful presence in Mumbai by collaboration with some other Mumbai firm. This could be in addition to efforts to be put in making Delhi profitable. |

RKC, his senior by nearly a decade, says: 'It was not till Pinto Khaitan took charge that modern employment practices, letters of appointment, gratuity, provident fund and all that were introduced'. The traditional old office started transforming itself into a modern solicitor's office after 1965. 'Separate chambers were built, furniture was changed, sitting arrangements, library and record-keeping were overhauled. The entire office was air-conditioned with window ACs. The wooden shelves hanging from the ceilings were removed', recalls RNJ. When RKC saw Pinto arrive, he would tease: 'toofan aa gaya (the storm has arrived)' because Pinto was transforming things. There was a complete face-

## The other Ghanshyam Das

'Starting from my days in school, Ghanshyam Das Kejriwal took great interest in me and in making me a lawyer. I accompanied him on his visits to his factory, on his business trips all over India and abroad. This is how I acquired first-hand training in all facets of business, dealing with banks, collaborators, suppliers, setting up of units, acquisitions and so on. He not only bore all the expenses but paid a fee too'.

— *Pinto Khaitan*

lift. Indeed, KCo was modernizing itself in letter and spirit to deal with the slowly changing business climate.

'The business arena then was peopled by merchants and traders and all our important clients were from this field. Most legal work was limited to drafting of deeds and documents and the practice was limited to the high court', reminisces RKC. There were some criminal cases but hardly any corporate clients for the firm. The character of work was quite different because there were hardly any taxation matters. Calcutta was, of course, the centre of action then. 'KCo was well known and respected in the merchants and trading community and our lawyers spent most of their time in the courts. This is an important difference from today: we were required to spend at least 80 per cent of our time in the courts. Today, of our 200 lawyers, 180 would be working on their desks and no more than 20 would be in courts at one time. The practice has changed with the passage of time as our clients started acquiring companies from the erstwhile British owners'.

In Sita Ram Jhunjhunwala, RKC had a hardworking mentor. He would get into the depths of the matter; try and understand the problem and look at the solution from different angles, which no one had possibly thought of in some remarkable instances of out-of-the-box thinking. More importantly, he had a vision for himself. 'When the new Companies Act came about in 1956, he mastered it and made it his area of specialization. It became his forte. Even in those days he thought of an USP for himself because he believed in providing value addition to every service', recalls son Arvind Jhunjhunwala. Every junior flourished under him: R.K. Choudhury, Pinto Khaitan and Om Khaitan, among others. He had a lot of matters and the young trainees could not but be well trained, putting in hard work of excellent quality. It was this specialization that endeared him to industrialists of the 1960s. Among others was S.K. Birla who would come to him for advice, big and small. 'For whatever little understanding I have on the subject, I have always acknowledged him as my guru', says S.K. Birla.

The Kanoria family's relationship with KCo goes back to the 1930s or maybe earlier. Recalls H.P. Kanoria (of the Srei Group): 'Even as a student in Presidency in 1959-60, I looked after my father, Kedar Nath Kanoria's business. He and I would meet Bhagwati Prasad Khaitan, our counsel and Sita Ram Jhunjhunwala. We were on "hello" terms with Kishan Khaitan. We would first visit them at Emerald House and then on the sixth floor of 9, Old Post

## Sibling-like: the Singhanias

Ever since I remember, from the early 1950s, I have been associated with KCo, which was our prime agency for handling all our legal work. There was also a family connection. My elder sister married Tej Narayan Khaitan, D.P. Khaitan's son. Then Krishna Prasad came into the picture and his son, Nand Gopal. There was Om's father, Sree Mohan Khaitan, who was not with KCo but would take me to watch football matches in Calcutta. There was also Kali Babu's son, Nilu and his son Suman Jyoti.

However close our personal relationships were, there was no compromise with professional relationships. They did their best. 'Bhagwati Babu nay dekh liya; Kishan Babu nay keh diya (Bhagwati Babu has checked it; Kishan Babu has said so)' and we were sure that the matter would be dealt with competently. We had the highest regard for them.

*— Hari Shankar Singhania*

## The 60s office

In the sixties, the main practice area was court litigation of all types. There were only two single chambers: one for Bhagwati Prasad Khaitan and the other for Krishna Prasad Khaitan. There were five or six big rooms to accommodate tables for four or more persons. SRJ shared his chamber with his solicitor assistant, R.N. Mullick and his two clerks; probably Hazra Babu and Nanku Tiwari. Behind his table was the 2nd floor balcony as we see it today. When I joined, I got the seat of his junior clerk. Makhan Lal Jhunjhunwala too had a similar chamber that he shared with his legal assistant and two others, including his court clerk. Later, one of them made room for Pinto Khaitan. The atmosphere was informal though everyone worked hard: some members of the staff, like the typist and record keeper, would work with their shirts off. The sweat soaked shirts would hang on the arm of the chairs as they worked in their vests. One of them was Sachin Babu, the managing clerk of KPK. Jatin Babu, the record keeper, was a very honest and sincere person, Tripura Babu was the head accountant while Bibhuti Babu was the head typist, recalls RKC.

Office Street. At Emerald House, BP would sit in the corner office (extreme right as one entered). Even in those days, the office looked like a modern solicitor's office. Sita Ram Jhunjhunwala sat in the chamber next to Kishan Babu's. I remember the firm assisting us over a property matter at Hastings – the khajna (tax) which had not been paid because the notice had been suppressed by another party. This was in the 1950s and KCo was engaged for the case. The matter went to the Supreme Court where we won. My office is still there: at 3, Middle Road, Hastings'.

There was much that H.P. Kanoria learnt from SRJ. 'There was a trademark case in 1960 and KCo did the entire documentation work for a major acquisition that we were doing: the Bengal Flour Mill Ltd, whose erstwhile owners were Balmer Lawrie. SRJ dealt with the case along with P. L. Agarwal. There was one clause in the agreement that I was uncomfortable with and he assured us that even if we signed it no harm would be done. His very simple reasoning was: "Suppose I give someone a statement in writing saying that 'you can shoot me' and he does so; does it absolve him of criminal offence?" The argument was a great lesson for me', says Mr Kanoria.

Not only did Sita Ram serve clients, he brought in new lawyers into the firm regularly. At the age of 88, barrister, Mr S. Tibrewala unhesitatingly says: 'I am a product of KCo and will continue to be so. Sita Ram Jhunjhunwala brought me into the profession that I would never have thought of otherwise and, over the years, I have enjoyed the total trust of the firm'. Mr Tibrewala recalls going to Delhi on a Birla matter with the celebrated Koilu Sen as his senior. 'The case had attained some notoriety with the Birlas being accused of purchasing a company on the cheap but we won the case'.

Sita Ram's younger brother, RNJ, had an interesting encounter with destiny, courtesy KCo. He wanted to be a doctor or an engineer, but circumstances and a gentleman by the name of Bhagwati Prasad Khaitan, holidaying in Ranchi for the Durga Pujas, met him and intervened. The ambitions of being a doctor were defenestrated when he fainted in a dissection room. All hopes of pursuing a career in mechanical engineering were buried when BP 'commanded' that he come to Calcutta for his graduation, followed by law and attorneyship. Older brother, Sita Ram, would support whatever his mentor said; so to St Xavier's for BCom did RNJ go with the proviso that he attend the firm between 11 a.m. and late evening, after college hours (6 a.m. - 9 a.m.). 'I would return home with my brother after attending conferences and doing whatever else was asked of me'.

The thought of becoming a lawyer did not appeal to RNJ because of his rather unpleasant experiences with lawyers in Deoghar and Ranchi and he kept working on BP till he agreed to let him study chartered accountancy instead of law. 'BP even helped me get articled with Singhi & Company,

### Men in black

'When I joined in 1960, there was no written dress code but it was understood that one needed to be in formal dress with a tie jacket and, preferably, a suit; not a combination of blazer with trouser, for every working day, including Saturdays. While going to court one had to put on a black coat, irrespective of whether one was a lawyer or law student. Court timings were 10.30 a.m. to 6 p.m, save for the duration of the China and Pakistan wars in 1965 and 1971 respectively. The risk of bombardment prompted the authorities to advance the timings. After things settled down, the final office timings were 10 a.m. to 5.30 p.m.'

— *R.N. Jhunjhunwala*

chartered accountants, on the fourth floor of 1B, Old Post Office Street. When Singhi & Company refused to give me leave for two months to prepare for my BCom finals, BP advised me to give up the job. By then I had no option but to take up law for future studies. My brother wanted me to study in Patna where the course was shorter than Calcutta's three-year course but by that time admissions to the Patna Law College were closed. So, I returned to Calcutta. I had already lost a year but was allowed a six-month reduction in the three-year LLB course'. The career thus chose itself for RNJ who enrolled as an advocate and practised independently for one year till Bhagwati Babu insisted that he join the firm at Rs 750 per month. Also, at BP's insistence – and against SRJ's objections – he was financially supported while he was articled with the firm under PK. This was contrary to the high court rules that did not permit remuneration for those articled for becoming an attorney but 'Bhagwati Babu said that he would certify that I was being paid only out-of-pocket expenses if any questions were raised'.

The faith in the young man was well placed for RNJ passed all the three exams: preliminary, intermediate and final with first class firsts and secured the highest ever marks in the history of the Calcutta High Court attorneyship exam, and won the maximum number of awards and prizes. 'BP was so delighted that he accompanied me to the prize distribution ceremony at the attorney library in the high court', where the Chief Justice Sankar Prasad Mitra, was giving away the awards.The performance of the KCo youth did not escape the attention of Sankar Prasad Mitra, who had found KCo candidates securing gold medals and the bulk of the prizes in all attorneyship examinations. Presenting the gold medals on this occasion, he turned around to BP and enquired: 'Mr Khaitan, how come all the candidates from your office take away all the gold medals and prizes?'. Pat came the response: 'That is my professional secret, which I can share with you if you are willing to be an articled clerk with us'. Everyone burst into laughter and the Chief Justice promptly garlanded BP with a gold medal and a prize in a spontaneous gesture of appreciation of his wit and contribution to the legal fraternity. The other winners were happy to await their turn to receive their medals and prizes, recalls RNJ.

Meanwhile, elder brother SRJ had attained great maturity within the profession. Mr S.K. Birla recalls the takeover of OCM in 1973 from its foreign owners when Sita Ram Jhunjhunwala's 'guidance turned out to be invaluable'. SRJ would delegate work and train his juniors well, for he

One secret BP did not share: how come all KCo candidates walked off with all the awards. From (R-L) Pinto Khaitan, P.L. Agarwal, BP (fifth from right) and Om Khaitan, next to BP. KCo boys with their awards

## Babu culture

'There were only four partners and around 10 lawyers and far more typists and peons. Each partner had a separate personal peon who would wait downstairs until the 'babu' arrived; collected his briefcase and, in the case of some partners, a large suitcase full of briefs. Sita Ram Jhunjhunwala, who handled the maximum number of litigations and had volumes of briefs to be carried home, had a leather suitcase, the maximum permissible size of the cabin baggage in aircrafts today. Not all the partners had cars in the beginning. The first car was allotted in 1959-60 to SRJ; an Ambassador (with overhead valve in the engine) that was bought for Rs 12,500'.

— *R.N. Jhunjhunwala*

handled a great deal of cases. He would work in the office and also take work home – a suitcase full of briefs. Without computers or even photocopiers in those days, everything had to be typed on manual typewriters. Recalls son Arvind: 'He would sit and correct all the drafts at home after dinner and take them back to office the next day. That was the evening routine, everyday, for two or three hours. There was no margin for mistakes for there was no question of retyping'. Understandably then, he was overworked and, therefore, stressed; often coming across at work as an unsmiling person. 'Once away from work though, he was a different person; full of jokes and always with something funny up his sleeve at all social gatherings'.

There were lessons for his children even upon retirement. Says Arvind: 'After my father had retired, he would go for evening walks and sometimes I would go along. On one such occasion, a person literally accosted him; checked if he was Sita Ram Jhunjhunwala and then accused him of ruining his life. My father dealt with him absolutely calmly. Later, I asked who the man was and my father explained that he was on the opposing side in a matter in which KCo's client won'. 'You fight to win without worrying about the consequences. As lawyers, we are not to judge', SRJ told his young son, just as he advised his clients.

As a human being too he took all his personal responsibilities seriously. Times were hard and Sita Ram had six sisters and two brothers. As the eldest and the only earning member of the family for some time he had to take care of their education and general upbringing and also ensure that the sisters got married off into good families. Even after that, the responsibilities were not over for Sita Ram. He was the paterfamilias and remained engaged with the families, playing an active role in the nurturing of his nephews and nieces and getting them married too. So Arvind had a lot of company when he was growing up. Hard work and responsibilities took their toll and Sita Ram had a nervous breakdown, retiring at the age of 54. That was when the loyalty to KCo paid off because the firm continued to pay his wife a monthly Rs 2,000 as chamber rent that saw his family through, says Arvind.

Time flies and it was almost in a flash that the firm had to get set for its golden jubilee. Recalls R.N. Bajoria: 'My first encounter with the Khaitans was in 1961, the firm's golden jubilee year. BP, the senior-most partner, was a close childhood friend of my father. Some other members of our families were also friends. We were a business family and we suffered a severe adversity on

## The Chittaranjan connection

Justice Manjula Bose recalls: 'My family has been associated with the firm for at least a hundred years. I recall Dadu (Chittaranjan Das) working with Bhagwati Babu. Even in those days, around 1911, he had a roaring practice of Rs 50,000 a month. I remember Bhagwati Babu and Sita Ram Jhunjhunwala coming to No. 2, Beltala Road. They wore sparkling white clothes and Sita Ram Jhunjhumwala wore a pink pugree. They would both have a tika on their foreheads. Three generations of our families have been associated and my brother, Siddhartha, did all the big cases of the Birlas. B.K. Birla went to college with dada (S.S. Ray) and entrusted him with all his legal work. You will find many reported judgments of the Supreme Court'.

## 'Matters sort themselves out'

Bhaskar Gupta says: 'BPK was the patriarch and we all looked up to him; he was indeed the father figure to all juniors in the profession. I first met him when I was very young and hardly received any matters. He asked me how many matters I was getting and I said that I was getting about four a month and he looked disappointed. I said that I took a week to prepare each matter and I was quite comfortable. Besides, I hated to be caught in a situation when two of my matters appeared at the same time. I would get flustered and upset. BPK gave me a piece of advice that I remember to this day: He said: "If such a thing happens, the first thing to do is to remain calm and sometimes matters sort themselves out. Cases adjust themselves". I did get a lot of briefs from the firm after that'.

account of certain disputes and litigations with our relatives, which had a disastrous effect on the business. My father was attending to these litigations and I was assisting him. My experience with the state of legal affairs left me quite disenchanted with the profession and I was keener to join the Indian Administrative Services. However, when it came to choosing a vocation for myself, I finally opted for law, in which decision I was guided, in a parental manner, by BP. He advised me to take up this profession, considering our family's position, and that advice definitely had a major influence on my final decision'.

Not only did the firm encourage youngsters, it seems to have actively encouraged independence of spirit, even when it occasionally went against established norms. In an excise matter on packing and wrapping paper and printing and writing paper in connection with the assessment of Orient Paper Mills, a G.P. Birla company, RKC was entrusted with drafting the petition to be filed in the Supreme Court. BP, the perfectly cultured person that he was, had insisted that his juniors never use harsh language, especially against the government of India and its authorities. 'I had used the word "mockery" vis-à-vis the functioning of quasi-judicial authorities', recalls RKC. BP baulked at the idea of using such a strong word and forbade his junior from using it but RKC slyly put it in anyway.

'When the Supreme Court delivered its judgment reported in AIR 1969 SC 48, I found that it had used my term, "mockery", to describe any direction from the higher authority to the adjudicating authority as making a "mockery" of the judicial process. I showed the judgment to BP'. Was he upset? 'No. He was delighted that notwithstanding his advice, I had used the harsh word, which the Supreme Court had thought fit to borrow. I had appeared in that case along with Siddhartha Shankar Ray and a very proud BP explained the entire circumstances to GP Birla in my presence'.

R.N. Bajoria has been associated with the firm from the day he joined the profession without being an employee. He was a junior to Elias Meyer, bar-at-law and senior counsel but was briefed by them in several important cases. 'I have also always received tremendous support for my chamber facilities and other assistance,

## Governor and the client

Mr Subimal Ray's fine legal mind made its mark on the advocates sitting for a conference with him, around 1967. An important KCo client, a colliery owner from Bankura, had been arrested. Those were the days of the Defence of India Rules and Article 226 of the Constitution was not available to the citizens. The order of arrest was passed in the name of the Governor of West Bengal, the venerable Padmaja Naidu, then serving her third term. Clearly there was a crease on Bhagwati Prasad Khaitan's forehead for the client was an important one. The best legal minds were consulted – E.R. Meyer, R.C. Deb, Siddhartha Shankar (Manu) Ray and, of course, Subimal Ray, the nephew of the West Bengal Chief Minister, B.C. Roy.

In the course of the conference, Subimal Ray came out with his master stroke: 'Manu', he told young Siddhartha Shankar: 'giyay dekho (go check) the terms of the Governor's appointment'. Siddhartha Shankar did so and hit pay dirt! Padmaja Naidu's appointment for the third term was not registered in the Gazette of India; there was no warrant of appointment though it was obligatory for the President of India to issue a

which enabled me to conveniently carry on the profession', he recalls. There was, of course, the guidance from 'Bhagwati Babu, Krishna Prasad Khaitan and M. L. Jhunjhunwala during the initial years' that gave him a firm foundation. 'As I worked with the firm, my understanding of legal processes increased and it was KCo that gave me an opportunity to work with such stalwarts of the times as R.C. Deb, Somnath Chatterjee and S.N. Bose. Even as a youngster, I was entrusted with leading cases of the firm; sometimes as the "junior-most" lawyer'.

Yet another young barrister who remembers getting his first major arbitration work (on a Kusum Product case) from the firm is Bhaskar Gupta. The firm also gave him the opportunity to go to the Supreme Court on work that was exciting for the young barrister. What made the work doubly interesting was that he got to work with the eminent C.K. Daftary! Not only did promising young lawyers get a chance to hone their skills under Bhagwati Babu; promising youngsters working with clients too got the best possible on-the-job training. A graduation and an LLB degree in his

fresh warrant of appointment after the expiry of each five-year term! It was, therefore, invalid; so was any order passed in her name!

Her appointment was duly registered for the first and second terms but not for the third term and Siddhartha Shankar had the material he needed to settle the matter. Under Subimal Ray's advice, it was decided to file a writ of habeas corpus and quo warranto under the Specific Relief Act, challenging the appointment of the Governor. Probably all administrative hell broke lose in the state and Niren De, the then Attorney General of the country, rushed down from New Delhi to argue the matter on behalf of the Union of India.

The hero of the hour, Subimal Ray, being the Chief Minister's nephew, of course, did not appear but there was a battery of lawyers comprising Messrs Meyers, Deb and Ray, with KCo as advocates on record. When the Governor came to know of the fiasco, she chose to resign. The client was saved and the matter was later settled amicably. 'The important point here was that even during the suspension of Article 226, a writ of habeas corpus and quo warranto could be filed', says RKC, who had been asked by Bhagwati Babu to deal with the matter.

Even during the suspension of Article 226, a writ of habeas corpus and quo warranto could be filed as agreed by the Calcutta High Court

pocket, young Pramod Chand Agarwal came to Calcutta from Allahabad, where he had done a bit of legal practice. Calcutta was then the land of golden opportunities and the company that wanted to interview the young man was Birla Bros, then operating out of 15, India Exchange Place.

The person interviewing the young man was none other than B.M. Birla. When it came to testing his legal acumen, however, BMB wanted his solicitor, Bhagwati Prasad Khaitan, to interview the young man. It was 1956 and Pramod Chand was in his twenties as he sat in a fourth-floor room at 15, India Exchange Place and found himself answering questions on filing a suit in the matter of a trust. Having cleared this viva voce, the young man had to answer a written test and he recalls questions on private companies and rights of directors. BP must have liked what the man wrote, for soon he was given the position of legal adviser and secretary to Birla Bros!

For Pramod Chand Agarwal, no break could have been better. While he was serving the Birlas, he was, for all practical purposes, an assistant to the sharpest legal mind of the times, Bhagwati Prasad. There was an enormous amount of work to be done; there were a host of important companies in the group and Birla Bros were the managing agents to them. This entailed dealing with a great deal of legal issues and extensive correspondence. Pramod Chand would examine everything, prepare drafts and then, almost on a daily basis, take the papers to 52/2, Ballygunge Circular Road in the morning, where Bhagwati Babu would give him exclusive time. 'His uptake was absolutely brilliant', says Pramod Chand Agarwal. 'He would normally make a small correction but that would make a dramatic change in the quality of the draft. This was possible because of his grasp of the law and practical approach'. The other Birla who had to sit with a Khaitan partner regularly was M.P. Birla who needed a session with Sita Ram Jhunjhunwala. From 1968 to 1971, prior to his illness, SRJ would go to Birla Building between 4 p.m. and 5 p.m. every evening and sort out all of MPB's matters.

Not only was the office modernized; so were minds. More importantly, the firm was welcoming ladies into its fold. Recalls Justice Leila Seth: 'In Calcutta, I joined the chambers of Sachin Chaudhuri at 52/5, Ballygunge Circular Road in the 1960s and I remember Pinto sending me my first brief mentioning three gold mohurs. It was from a querist and I worked very hard on preparing an opinion. I referred to every book that I needed from Mr Chaudhuri's substantial library. I sent it to Pinto but he did not get back to me; nor did any fees arrive. Three or four months later I met him at a party but did not want to raise the issue...however, Pinto himself came up to me and told me the truth: The client wanted a male opinion and not a female opinion. Pinto Khaitan explained the lawyer's credentials but that cut no ice with the client and he was forced to send it to the top-most lawyer in the company, who kept it with him for months and, after receiving several reminders and a substantial fee, wrote: 'I fully endorse the opinion of Leila Seth'.

Says Mrs Justice Seth: 'I must confess that KCo was a liberated firm and promoted women and I worked with them quite closely'. Mrs Deb Burman agrees: 'B.P. Khaitan knew my father and they were directors in various companies. I first interacted with him in Delhi, when he came for a conference with Siddhartha Ray in whose chamber I was a junior. He asked me to draft a letter, which I did, and that he greatly appreciated. He then gave me many matters'. Good work got more work and, as Mrs Deb Burman says: 'BP was essentially a very straight person. When Ramnath Goenka came to him for an appointment during the holidays, he passed on the work to Rajesh Khaitan saying that I should be briefed in the matter. Ramnath Goenka came to my house to brief me and gave dictation for eight days. Bholanath Sen was my senior and we moved the matter and got a rule and stay. Ramnathji was so pleased that he gave the firm a lot of cases', says Mrs Deb Burman.

Indeed, BP had inspired the first Marwari women to study attorneyship and one of them, Kusum Dadoo, still works with KCo. What the firm insisted on was that the articled clerks take their business seriously and do well in the examinations. No one had appreciated the class of BP's legal mind better than the Birlas and those who were personally mentored by him realized the difference it made when one was trained by the best. 'B.M. Birla had absolute and implicit trust in the advice of Bhagwati Prasad Khaitan. Other Birlas too held him in very high esteem. Personally, there could have been no better mentor for me', recalls Pramod Chand. 'After we successfully defended the forged import licence matter, he told B.M. Birla that I had worked very hard and had given valuable support for winning the case. B.M. Birla called me

Justice Leila Seth thought Khaitans were a liberated firm. Seen here, in the centre, with Umesh Khaitan to her right.

and repeated what had been reported to him. BP gave me the credit where most others would have taken the credit'.

As far as the Birla-Khaitan relations go, Pinto Khaitan sums it up: 'The association with the Birla family started from the inception. Each and every member of the family supported us to the hilt in every way. They grew at a fast pace in every direction – industry and commerce and philanthropy. We grew alongside them and they were a pillar of strength'. As far as the bonds of client-firm trust are concerned, Hari Shankar Singhania sums up the relationship that started from the 1950s: 'I still consult the family and am in touch with Pinto and Nand Gopal, who is on the board of our company. That is the extent of faith and confidence we have in them. They have the right to say what is good or bad for me and the courage to say that I am wrong. I have never questioned their service; when things appear to take unduly long, I ask them and they explain the reasons and we never question them'.

# OVER THE ROPES
## for a 50

*'The first thing is that we worked as a professional company not as a business company. If a case came to us we tried to fight the case to the best of our ability and only charged our fees. We did not try to make money in any other way through the case'* — **Bhagwati Prasad Khaitan**

The 1960s were particularly interesting times for the firm: it was set to enter its golden jubilee year in 1961; the second generation had begun to join its ranks – Bhagwati Babu's son, Pradip Kumar, came into the profession in 1961 as an articled clerk for becoming a solicitor – and there were some breathtaking cases that the firm was handling, beginning with Haridas Mundhra to Shanti Prasad Jain, which had spilled over from the end 1950s. Birla Bros were the biggest client, of course, but the firm enjoyed the confidence of such other houses as the Bangurs, Juggilal Kamalapat and the Kanorias, amongst others. In those days KCo had four partners and six associate lawyers, who had to cater not only to the needs of the clients but also work on institution building. Such institutions as the

## Still going strong

'The first case that I handled for KCo featured Ganesh Properties. Even then they were a leading firm of solicitors. Though the dual system has been abolished and many solicitor firms have been wound up, KCo has grown in stature with branches in Delhi, Mumbai and Bangalore and is amongst the biggest law firms in the country', says S.B. Mookerjee.

'Since then I have been briefed by them in several cases, amongst the interesting ones, that of Indian Express Ltd, when the original company was divided and there were proceedings under the Companies Act and suits filed in various courts. Fortunately, litigation has come to an end in this matter.

'I was also briefed in the Surajmull Nagarmull matter while I appeared against KCo clients in the Turner Morrison matter… the litigation started in the 1970s and is still going on though I am no longer associated with the matter'.

Calcutta Stock Exchange, the East India Jute and Hessian Exchange and, later, the Indian Chamber of Commerce were literally structured by the partners of KCo. These institutions, in turn, trusted the firm completely; some of them were even competing firms. KCo retained their confidence because of the Chinese walls that it had built around each matter, and clients had no hesitation in confiding in the firm.

Reminisces Pinto Khaitan on the occasion of the centenary celebrations: 'In 1961, KCo had just about 10 to 12 lawyers. People worked in a leisurely style. Letters were replied to only after clients came to see you and personally discussed matters. You came to office at a time that suited you. One lawyer never came to office before noon because he had to have a meal before coming to work and his wife could not get the meal ready before that. Raising

## Messrs Bhagwati and Kishan

Dipankar Gupta recalls: 'Clearly BPK and Kishan Babu were holding the firm together in the 1950s. Each had excellent qualities and handled a wide clutch of clients. While the firm was one, each partner handled a group of clients. Bhagwati Babu was, of course, the head and the principal architect. I recall Swami Gokulananda of the Ramakrishna Mission once publicly describing him as a flower and going on to explain why he thought so.

'I remember Sita Ram Babu and am still in close touch with his brother RNJ. There was P. L. Khaitan, who was a very pleasant man and his son Padam, who was very efficient. He instructed me in the Burn Standard vs McDermott matter in the Supreme Court that was handled by Padam and OP. There was the quiet and very efficient P. L. Agarwal and the reticent Umesh. OP was a lot more colourful and took me around Singapore when I went for a matter there. I remember going to Sentosa Island with him. Then there was Nilu, who knew his law inside out. You could depend on him to do his research and suggest arguments and his drafting was superb. Only he was not comfortable standing up and arguing before the court. All of D.P. Mandelia's work was done by Nilu Babu. His son Suman was then only a child, whom I was very fond of. Then there was Bhabraji's grandson, Asopa, Chand Mal Ghorawat and, of course, Pinto, RNJ and Nand Gopal'.

bills was not a priority either. Once in a year, during the Pujas, the clients would come and pay for services rendered during the year and that was when the firm paid its counsel. The firm grew at its own pace and yet was a leading firm in Calcutta. The other leaders included Orr Dignam, Sandersons & Morgan.... The relationship with rival firms was cordial. My father used to go for a walk in the evening along with Mr Dunderdale of Sandersons & Morgan. The firm rarely accepted a change; never accepted a change unless the client had cleared the previous solicitor's bills'. Also, it was customary for clients to become friends.

Kishan Khaitan played a leading role in holding the firm together in the fifties. Seen here with former Indian President, R. Venkataraman and son NG

The Bangurs had a very special relationship with the Khaitans that transcended the realms of law. There were units in the group that gave loans and the firm was called in not just to do the documentation work for the loans given and maintain the deposit of the title deeds but Narsingdas Bangur wanted to be personally advised on the reliability of the borrower, his assets and his capacity to repay.

There are stories galore concerning the clients. The Government of India had declared the peacock as its national bird but why would that lead to complications between client firms? Very simply, two of KCo's closest clients, Orient Paper of the B.M. Birla group and the Singhania-owned J.K. Paper, used the peacock as their logos and were ready to defend their turf. Says Ram Kishore Choudhury: 'It took all of Bhagwati Babu's wiles to bring the two parties to a consensus around making minor changes in their logos so that Orient had a dancing peacock and JK a more stylized one. Of course, the groups have since outgrown their earlier logos. There was equal heartburn over both the Bangurs and the Birlas having different group concerns named Jayshree! Yet again BP was the honest broker, bringing about an understanding between the two. It was, however, the establishment of the "Companies Act 1960 raj" that made the cash registers ring for many legal firms, thanks to the overwhelming curiosity of the government in all matters corporate. BP's only word of caution to his younger colleagues was to be restrained while billing so that the client would return'.

The Companies Act, 1960, meant more cases for the firm. S.B. Mookerjee recalls: 'If memory serves, the first case in which I was briefed by KCo pertained to proceedings under the Companies Act in 1960, featuring Ganesh Properties Private Ltd. I was the fourth junior in the matter that had several leading lawyers of the times; none of them survive. The litigation has, however, survived

## Mundhra matters

RKC recalls: 'The success of round one made Mr Mundhra a permanent client of KCo. He acquired Alcock Ashdown & Company Ltd and Lodna Colliery (then not nationalized). Once again, HDM wanted a receiver appointed for Lodna and KCo made an application. Sachin Chaudhuri had been engaged to argue the matter but soon there were differences between the barrister and the solicitor, Kishan Khaitan, and the former gave up the brief. The problem was that Justice U.C. Law refused to adjourn the matter and Kishan Khaitan requested RKC to proceed with the argument. It needed three or four days of arguments in the court of Justice Law before KCo got an order appointing a receiver. For RKC, it was a matter of great faith reposed on him by Kishan Khaitan for he was still a junior who was asked to step into the shoes of the stalwart, Sachin Chaudhuri'.

Shoe on the other foot: When business took him across the shores, Bhagwati Babu often allowed his nephews and grand nephews to show him the ropes; often 'swallowing his uncleship'

them all and is still an ongoing one'. This litigation was under sections 397 and 398 of the Companies Act, 1956, regarding control over a huge property at Tirreti Bazar, owned by the Maharaja of Burdwan that had been let out to Ganesh Properties. The litigation featured the management and affairs of Ganesh Properties, some aspects of which have been settled. The pending dispute is around the sale of the property by the Maharaja to one of the fighting shareholders. There were three of them: the Jajodias, the Sarafs and the Acharyas. 'They are still fighting against the Estate of the Maharaja of Burdwan and while I am no longer involved in the litigation, my son is involved in this', says Mr Mookerjee.

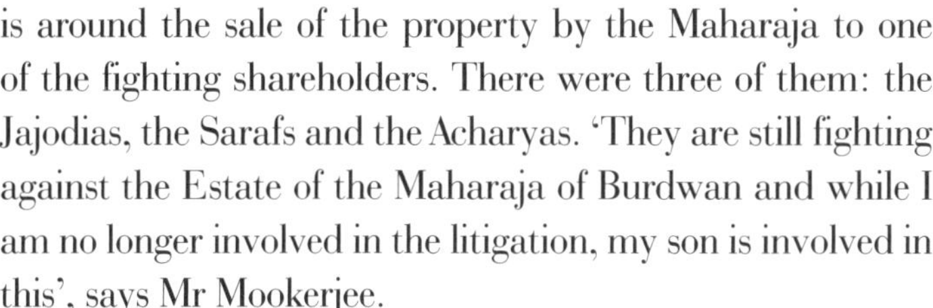

C.K. Dhanuka, barely 16 then – a college-going boy – would accompany his grandfather Ram Kishen Dhanuka and father Shankar Lal Dhanuka to work and that was when he became familiar with the firm and its ways. 'B.P. Khaitan and Kishan Khaitan used to be on the board of Jaipur Polyspin and Naga Hills Tea Company Ltd. All the legal advice that we needed since then has been received from them and they have never disappointed us. I remember going to Jaipur with B.P. Khaitan, where we would have some of our board meetings and he had a lot of stories to tell me. All of them had a moral, though his main message was around the importance of honesty and not to cause pain to anyone', recalls CK.

R.N. Bajoria talks of the early 1960s: 'The first case that I handled was of Ratnakar Shipping, relating to the levy of

## Back to the future

Jaideep Gupta recalls: 'In 1988, I was involved in the Turner Morrison case that had a history dating back to the 1960s, when the British India Corporation was going down the tubes. There was a round of dispute with the Birlas and the fight then shifted to the Hari Das-owned Hungerford Investment Trust and the Sahu Jains. There was a big round of litigation with a section of Turner Morrison shareholders acting against the management under Section 397 of the Companies Act. The HIT vs Sahu Jain matter of the 1960s went up to the Supreme Court in the 1980s. The end result was that HDM was declared bankrupt and the Sahu Jains took over Turner Morrison. At that point of time there was a Nirmaljit Singh Hoon, a British citizen, who had allied with the Sahu Jains but, in 1988, possibly propped up by HDM, filed a Section 397 against Turner Morrison. The ad interim matter was heard for eight months without affidavits by Mrs Justice Manjula Bose, who passed an order superseding the Turner Morrison board.

Justice Manjula Bose, who passed an order superseding the Turner Morrison board

'Two parties filed separate appeals. We went on appeal in the court of Justice Ajit Sengupta and the other party appealed in the court of Justice Bimal Basak and matters took a turn for the worse because Justice Basak refined his earlier judgment and superseded the board and the management was thrown out. Turner Morrison was then the prime shareholder in Shalimar Tar Products, then a thriving company that continues to do business even today. I was rushed to Delhi and worked through the night to prepare an SLP. In Delhi, the matter was mentioned by S.N. Kakkar before Chief Justice Mr R.S. Pathak. He gave an ad interim order and the matter proceeded. That was my first appearance in the Supreme Court.

'The important thing is that I learnt all my company matter in this case. We had the brilliant K.K. Chakravarty, who had renounced the world and become a sadhu, who came back to supervise the case for Turner Morrison. I did all my work under him and knew that if he did not object to what I was drafting, I would be in safe territory. He was meticulously thorough and I even learnt simple things like: "no director could be nominated by a shareholder. One could only propose names and, with necessary shareholder support, it would be accepted"'.

a stamp duty. Then there was the Shanti Prasad Jain case, a foreign exchange case that went up to the Supreme Court…' It was, however, the Hari Das Mundhra case of 1961 that held the nation enthralled, being the first major share market scam that sucked in the Indian finance minister and the Life Insurance Corporation into its vortex. R.N. Bajoria recalls the story that came to be known as the 'Mundhra share kelenkari' in the vernacular press but not before the earlier rounds went to the young and aggressive businessman.

Even today, a meeting with Hari Das Mundhra is very interesting; his eyes sparkle and his lips smile, though he does not want to go over the past. He still has theories about how to tackle black money though, and he spends an evening chatting with us at 8, Loudon Street. HDM is as unconventional as he was half a century ago, when he visited Krishna Prasad Khaitan: it was 1961 and he wanted a suit to be filed against Hungerford Investment Trust Ltd, represented by Nirmaljit Singh Hoon, for specific performance of an agreement for the purchase of Turner Morrison Company Ltd. Kishan Babu summoned Ram Kishore Choudhury, who engaged Mr Somnath Chatterjee to draft the plaint and petition. The matter was moved by R.C. Deb (suit no. 600 of 1961) and the trial was held by the then Justice A.N. Ray, later Chief Justice of India.

The matter featured hearings for more than 30 days and HDM deposed before Justice Ray. He was also cross-examined by the much acclaimed Sachin Chaudhuri, barrister, who later became the finance minister. Hoon was then questioning HDM's ability to pay, but Mr Mundhra was quite sure that he did not have physical possession of the shares. In course of deposition, HDM came up with an idea: instead of wasting the time of the court, Mr Hoon, the defendant, should produce the shares in the court and he would produce the consideration money agreed to be paid.

They would exchange the shares against money and save everyone's time. Mr Mundhra had thus established that he was 'ready and willing' to purchase. Sure enough, Mr Hoon could not produce the entirety of the Turner Morrison shares. He was 780 shares short and Turner Morrison was taken away by the receiver appointed by the Delhi High Court. Justice A.N. Ray directed that in view of failure of Mr Nirmaljit Singh Hoon to produce the agreed quantity of shares there would be an order permitting Mr Mundhra to control the affairs of Turner Morrison. Thus, Mr Mundhra continued to manage the affairs of Turner Morrison without paying for the shares.

The story took a different turn thereafter. Hari Das Mundhra had agreed to purchase the controlling interest of Turner Morrison. He had acquired 49 per cent and he was to take the remaining 51 per cent. However, before he could do so, Mundhra got embroiled in a duplicate share scandal that sucked in the Life Insurance Corporation and the then finance minister of the country,

## Jub pyar kiya tow durna kya

Bhaskar Gupta reminisces about a case that he handled for the firm in his early days: 'It was a complicated one featuring Orient Paper that had a plant in Madhya Pradesh and it involved an important constitutional matter. Lalit Poddar was the instructing assistant in that case and we all travelled to Jabalpur by train. There was A.C. Bhabra from Khaitans and the tax expert R.N. Bajoria. We had expected the matter to be over in a couple of days at the most but it went on for 10 days. The interesting thing was that there was nothing that one could do in the evenings and even after discussing the case in detail, Mr Bhabra would have early dinner and go off to bed by 7.30 and we were at a loose end. We stayed at the Jackson Hotel and there was a movie hall nearby to which we all trooped after 7.30: R.N. Bajoria, Lalit Poddar, myself and the client's representative. The movie playing there was *Mughal-e-Azam* and around the time that we went into the hall the same song would be playing: "jub pyar kya tow darna kya". This happened for seven days in a row and though I had neither interest in Hindi movies nor songs, I do know that one song. Then, when we were really falling off to sleep, we would come out of the hall and retire'.

eventually leading to his imprisonment following a high-profile trial in New Delhi. Mundhra conducted his litigation from jail to exercise his right to purchase the 51 per cent but Turner Morrison had by then started removing the blue-chip companies from the parent's fold by diluting the shareholding of its owned companies. Essentially, the managed companies were increasing the share capital because the purchase contract was with the managing company.

Thus, ultimately, even if Mundhra got the company, he would not get the blue chips. The litigation was filed for the purpose of challenging such dilution of the company managed by the Turner Morrison group and an injunction was granted by the single-judge bench and upheld by the division bench and further upheld by the Supreme Court. 'We handled every case of Haridas Mundhra till 1991-92. We left due to personal reasons', said RKC.

The point was that imprisonment could not really dampen Mr Mundhra's spirits. From the jail he called for RKC to implement the agreement for acquisition of shares of Sajjan Cotton Mills in Bombay (now Mumbai). 'The necessary deeds, powers of attorney and the consideration were signed and executed by HDM while he was in jail', says RKC. In all his matters, KCo would brief R.C. Deb assisted by Mr Somnath Chatterjee. There were several property acquisitions that the firm handled: immovable properties in Bombay at Bank Street, Narain Dhabolkar Road and such others. One of the buildings was to be acquired by the Maharashtra government to make residences for its ministers and another for some other purpose. We got both the orders for acquisition quashed', says RKC.

The relationship with HDM did not please everyone; certainly not M.P. Birla, whose Birla Jute HDM was eyeing. 'Mr Mundhra acquired substantial number of shares of Birla Jute', recalls RKC, who was asked to convey to Hari Das Mundhra that even bulk acquisition of Birla Jute shares would not help him in his mission. RKC then arranged a meeting between Hari Das Mundhra and Mr B.K. Birla and HDM agreed to offload the shares that he had acquired, but the undercurrent of animosity remained.

Interesting though these details were, here too Bhagwati Babu demonstrated his sense of fair play vis-à-vis his boys. Hari Das Mundhra had by then become Ram Kishore's principal client in both civil and criminal matters but Bhagwati Prasad had been told that the Birlas did not appreciate RKC taking up his cases in view of the conflict (or likely conflict) between the Birlas and Mundhra. The Birlas, of course, were the prime clients of KCo. RKC promised that save for a criminal matter that was going on in sessions

## Catch the Khaitans

When Bacchu Pal joined the Bar in 1967, KCo was a big name in the Calcutta High Court. 'Mr Dipankar Gupta (former Advocate General of West Bengal and Solicitor-General of India) was a promising name. I had been advised to join his chamber for devilling and I did. Mr Gupta's work was then mostly confined to the original side of the high court, which meant that a dual system was prevalent as in England. It comprised two classes of lawyers: the barristers and the solicitors. Basically, the former argued in court while the latter acted. The prevailing norms or etiquette carried from the Inns of Court, England, where the barristers had to qualify and be called. The implication of this was serious for the barristers who were new entrants in the profession and could not have a direct client; only the solicitors could. The clients instructed the solicitor who selected the barrister to plead the case in court. The fees were collected from the client by the solicitor, who would be responsible for paying the barrister. The solicitors who happened to be in court rooms watched their performance and made their own assessment of the barrister's qualities. Unlike in other professions, where clients were laymen, a barrister's clients, in essence, were experienced lawyers and the new barristers were under the solicitor's scanner. One day, almost a year after I joined, still actually briefless and taking a lift back from court, I was not surprised to hear from a collegue, a few years senior to me and reasonably well entrenched, that I should "catch" KCo, the busiest firm of solicitors in 1967, when they come to the chambers of Mr Dipankar Gupta. He was right. I had to do something.... but what and how?'

court he would not take up any HDM civil matters as, under the law and legal professional ethics, it would be unfair on his part to give up a criminal matter. 'BP knew that my work was upsetting M.P. Birla but, instead of getting annoyed with me, said that he was pleased with my stand and explained the legal ethics and principles to MPB'. That was the last that RKC heard of the matter.

Bacchu Pal (second from right) knew he had to 'catch the Khaitans' to succeed in the profession. In the photo are Subrata Roy Chowdhury (L) and Justice Kalyanmoy Ganguly

KCo would continue to be engaged in the Hari Das Mundhra matter for decades and several years later, in 1988, Siddhartha Mitra and Jaideep Gupta would deal with it again and indeed learn a great deal of law from the case and about how solicitors had to work to protect client interest. An adverse order in Calcutta saw Pramod Khaitan and P.L. Agarwal literally hijack Siddhartha and Jaideep from the corridors of the Calcutta High Court and take them to Delhi. Roopa Sheth was assisting in the matter, preparing an SLP, working through the night. Jaideep recalls: 'I learnt all my company matter in this case in which the point of law was whether, in a rights issue, a foreign shareholder could be offered shares without Fera clearance'.

There were many equally interesting even if not always headline-grabbing cases. Mr R.N. Bajoria recalls the nationalization of the Oriental Gas Company during B.C. Roy's time that was challenged in 1962 on the ground that the state had no power to nationalize the gas industry that fell within the exclusive domain of the Centre. The matter centred around the gas industry being subject to dual entries under both the Central and the state lists on jurisdiction.

## Pal makes a pal

It was Bacchu Pal's lucky evening. A KCo solicitor entered Mr Dipankar Gupta's chamber with a banking matter and he quietly watched the 'proceedings'; listening and trying to follow the discussion. 'The problem before them was, when a customer of a bank deposits money to the credit of his account from time to time and also withdraws money from the same account from time to time, does he withdraw the first credit or the last credit entered in his account?' Suddenly, a bell rang in the young man's mind: it was Clayton's case and the lecturer was none other than Mr Robert Edward Meggary, a multi-faceted man and a great scholar as well as a teacher-cum-lecturer explaining to overflowing students in the hall at the McGgghea Hall of the Council of Legal Education at the Gray's Inn, London. Quite unwittingly he volunteered: 'Clayton says what was to be done'. Mr Gupta called for the report looked at the case and, though, not much of an assistance, was generous enough to tell the solicitor that the principle laid down in Clayton required serious attention and reading as a starting point because the rule 'first in and first out' enunciated in Clayton could have relevant implications; they would follow it up'. These words were good enough to impress the solicitor; none other than RNJ. Says Mr Pal: 'I did not quite "catch" KCo but at least made acquaintance with one of them'. RNJ had better ideas: he would try out the young man, and briefed him in that very bank case and in many other cases subsequently and continued to instill confidence in the young barrister. 'This was of immense importance to me as I was a rank outsider. The association with RNJ still continues. He was a perfectionist as far as work was concerned and I took serious note of that'.

'The Parliament had by legislation taken control of certain industries of importance and had the sole power to legislate with regard to these industries. Gas was one of them and our case was that since the nationalization had been under a state government enactment, it had to be struck down', recalls Mr Bajoria. The state government's contention was that there was an entry in the state list that read Gas and Gas Works, in view of which, despite the industry being under the Central list in general terms, the state could also nationalize. This position was upheld by the Supreme Court.

Young lawyers who were briefed by the company would inevitably go places. One of them went on to be the Solicitor General of India. Dipankar Gupta recalls first meeting

Bhagwati Babu in the chamber of Siddhartha Shankar Ray, where Bhagwati Babu was a regular. The barrister had just returned from England in May 1955, enrolled at the Calcutta High Court on August 5, 1955 and joined Siddhartha Ray's chamber. 'The hours were long, from 6.30 in the evening often till 1 in the morning. Juniors were never paid a dime in those days but Siddhartha Ray was special. He would ask us to prepare drafts and opinions and then when the client was there, he would ask us to be present and, after the conference, would tell them... so-and-so has prepared this and has done an excellent job. That commendation to the client would be worth much more than any money that we could have got'.

Siddhartha Ray must have had some special words of praise for his junior for, over the years, KCo was amongst his best benefactors, giving him many opportunities that contributed tremendously to the consolidation of his career. 'Siddhartha Ray and Bhagwati Babu were personally responsible for much of this. Indeed, I have had a very long association with KCo and some of the very interesting details still come to mind. There were, of course, the cases but the experiences on the personal side are more enduring'.

If relationship-building was the key to client-solicitor business, the firm excelled at it for even as the firm was building its relationship with Mr Dipankar Gupta, it was establishing links with the next generation too. Says Jaideep Gupta: 'My association with KCo goes back to my childhood, courtesy my father (Dipankar Gupta), who would be taken for long arbitrations during court and our own holidays and very often we would accompany him. I remember spending a month in the Ashoka Hotel when I was barely 10, when I was brought to Delhi by Kishan Khaitan during the Hidayatullah arbitration matter. I spent a summer at the Oberoi Intercontinental in Delhi in 1966 on a Hindustan Motors matter as well. Siddhartha Shankar Ray and Dipankar Gupta were all there and I got to know Delhi well then. Normally, we would come with Kishan Khaitan or Pinto Khaitan; never with BP. There was a third holiday in 1970-72, when Om and Nilu Khaitan were here. Thereafter, I went off to England to study law at the Jesus College, Oxford University'. To Jaideep's joy, Mr Pinto Khaitan turned up at his college with friends and wanted to be shown around

## Introducing Rajiv

Little knowledge can sometimes be an 'undangerous' thing! It was a 16-year-old bragging to his granduncle about his ability to get things done that was to determine the career of Rajiv Khaitan. B.P. Khaitan was having problems getting the family zamindari bonds issued by the Government of India to be mutated to the names of the heirs. The Reserve Bank of India's regional office at Patna was giving him the usual run around. That was when this teenager, who seemed to know everyone in Patna – where he went to college – stepped in. His friends comprised the sons of much of the Bihar bureaucracy and he offered to sort out the matter at a chance meeting with his granduncle who was then visiting Patna. The bemused senior Khaitan asked the young man to do his best. It transpired that he did not have to look very far. Teaching him at a study circle that he had joined at that time was the secretary of the Reserve Bank's Employees' Union, who had once told him that he could get things done at Reserve Bank of India, Patna. Young Rajiv asked his teacher to live up to his words: 'Help me to sort out this for my dadaji', the young man urged.

The teacher went to the concerned department, found out where the file had got stuck and realized that the Reserve Bank of India needed an indemnity or a surety for processing the mutation and that the application was otherwise acceptable. Rajiv arranged to submit the surety and the bonds were returned after mutation in seven days! The granduncle was delighted and advised him to complete his graduation in Calcutta rather than waste his time in Patna. Young Rajiv's fate and future was sealed.

Post matriculation, Rajiv had got stuck in mid-session of college because of the Jaiprakash Narayan student's movement. Colleges had been closed for long periods. That was when BPK advised him to come to Calcutta. He could not get a transfer certificate at Patna because the Patna University was non-functional. With some help from BPK he managed to get a provisional enrolment in the Calcutta University, which would have to be regularized once the transfer certificate was procured from Patna. Rajiv then joined the second year BCom at Bhawanipore (evening college) and the Jogesh Chandra Law College thereafter, for LLB. The deal was that he would come to work with BPK every day before or after college.

the college. 'Those were still days of a personal association. The professional association started much later in 1985. KCo was the largest litigation law firm in Calcutta and, given our old association, I worked with them and with every partner'.

Pinto Khaitan: guiding professionals, parenting their children; seen here with Mr Chandra Sekhar of ICICI and Mr V.D. Jain of Birla Jute

Back to the 1960s, amongst the most interesting cases that the firm handled in those days was the lungi case, which was also amongst the first trademark cases in the country. Bhaskar Sen recalls: 'In one of the earliest trademark litigations that I was involved with in the late 1960s, when I had a standing of no more than six months, a dispute arose around whether the trademark Ganga Jamuna (the name of a lungi) was registerable. My seniors were Bholanath Sen and Ajay Mitra. The other side had Gouri Nath Mitter, A.C. Bhabra and Dipankar Ghosh. It was a matter featuring two lungi makers: one named Ganga Jamuna (makers: M. Misbauddin and Co.) and the other Ganga Jamini (makers: Md Amin and Co.). The matter came up in court no. 12, before Justice Sabyasachi Mukherjee. My senior not being there, Gouri Mitter argued at length that, by using the name, Ganga Jamini, his clients had not infringed the trademark of our client.

When Gouri Mitter completed his arguments and I realized that none of my seniors were present at court and that I would have to speak. With a faltering voice and trembling legs, I opened my mouth, looking at the clock to strike the hour for lunch. I was familiar with the matter but was afraid to speak. Next to me sat R.N. Jhunjhunwala, the instructing

## Beating bank nationalization: round 1

It was a Saturday, July 19, 1969; fairly late in the afternoon. The business community was struck with a bombshell. The then Vice-President of Imdia, acting as the President, promulgated an Ordinance in exercise of powers conferred under Article 123 of the Constitution, transfering and vesting the undertakings of 14 commercial banks. These included the Birla family-controlled United Bank of India and the Sahu Jain family-controlled Punjab National Bank Limited, both KCo clients.

In Mumbai, there was the Central Bank controlled by the Tatas and a certain R.C. Cooper, who held shares in Central Bank of India, challenged the Nationalization Act in the Supreme Court of India. The bankers pooled their resources and agreed to have Nani Palkhivala argue the matter, supported by a battalion of lawyers. KCo was instructed to watch and assist Mr Palkhivala and deputed R.K. Choudhury to do so. Eventually, the Ordinance and the Act based in pursuance thereof were declared ultra vires and the government was forced to amend the Constitution.

advocate from KCo, providing me with the courage to go on. Post-lunch, Bholanath Sen arrived but the judge wanted me to continue. I thought that I had said whatever I needed to in half an hour but had to continue till the end of the day's hearing, certain that I had ruined the case. Thankfully, Mr Bholanath Sen took the matter over the next day. However, my friendship with Mr RNJ had got cemented for life with that experience around 1969-70'.

The judge upheld KCo's contention that by reason of long usage of the trade name 'Ganga Jamuna' and use being prior in point of time, the mark had become distinctive and its maker (KCo's client) had acquired better right over the opposing party that was ordered to stop using the 'Ganga Jamini' trademark.

KCo had by then become a 'brand' with immense goodwill. Till 1969, the goodwill of the firm belonged to Bhagwati Prasad Khaitan but he chose to pass it on to the firm without consideration that it holds to date. As the firm prospered; so did some of its solicitors. Around 1975, Mr

Bholanath Sen, senior barrister, became the PWD Minister, West Bengal, and the chairman of the newly-formed Second Hooghly River Bridge Commissioners (under a special act for construction of the second Hooghly Bridge). He requested BP to undertake the work of advising HRBC regarding construction contracts to be entered into with various parties. This would involve preparation and approving of documents, contracts and such others in connection with the proposed project. The work was assigned by BP to RNJ under his and Pinto Khaitan's supervision and the firm acted as HRBC's principal and sole solicitors from its inception. Importantly, the firm rendered honorary services. 'After the bridge was constructed and inaugurated, the HRBC authorities felt hesitant to come to us for our services unless we charged our fees. After that we agreed to charge a token fee of Rs 100 or Rs 200', says RNJ.

Trouble broke out when a dispute arose with the Bhagirathi Bridge Construction Company, Gammon India, Gannon Dunkerley and a joint venture of all these companies, BBCC Ltd. HRBC was faced with claims running into several hundred lakhs of rupees from BBCC and its sub-contractors. The matter was referred to arbitration and HRBC got it conducted through their in-house dealing officials/engineers and some retired engineers, who were familiar with arbitration procedures. One day, their vice-president and two directors came rushing to RNJ with a plea to save the company because an award of several hundred lakhs of rupees has been passed against HRBC.

RNJ considered the papers and advised them that normally such an award would be final and binding with no appeals lying against it. A very strong, prima facie case had to be made out to have it set aside and there were limited grounds for doing so. 'For challenging the award one would have to establish that (1) the award is perverse in law or on facts on the face of it; or (2) the arbitrator is guilty of misconduct; or (3) the arbitrator has misconducted the proceedings. It would be a herculean task as the papers involved were huge and voluminous and the matter was highly technical. It was also a difficult task to accept responsibility for, particularly when a government agency is the client, because the involvement, commitment and the need to give time beyond the call of duty is very demanding'.

KCo accepted the work, subject to the commitment of the HRBC vice-chairman and the three directors that they would make themselves and the dealing officials available on Sundays, holidays and beyond office hours on working days, apart from the regular working hours and, that they would extend their fullest cooperation and provide all necessary papers expeditiously and not in the way government companies function. The matter was taken up and the proceedings for challenging and setting aside the award were begun in the Calcutta High Court. After strenuous efforts the firm succeeded in getting the award set aside on the ground that there were flaws on the technical aspect of the matter.

The other side went to the Supreme Court on the ground that the appeal did not lie in the high court where the case was

## Banning sub-conferences

There were times when KCo conferences represented astounding agglomeration of IQ. Sparks would fly and wit would permeate the environment. RNJ recalls one in which he was no more than a fly on the wall in the 1960s. It was a case featuring Ramnath Goenka over a Rs 25,000 hundi for which he was in a conference with Subimal Roy. Along with him were S. Tibrewala, Sisir Mookerjee, Salil Roy Chowdhury and Sita Ram Jhunjhunwala and there were arguments flying across the room... sometimes in hushed undertones. The counsel and client had quite forgotten the great presence that they were sitting under: Subimal Ray who reprimanded them: 'No sub-conference in my conference' and even the mighty Ramnath Goenka squirmed.

heard for several days. 'Fortunately, the judges were inclined to accept our contention that the award under challenge had to be set aside as the reasoning given in some of the places appeared to be faulty vis-à-vis the technically authoritative propositions. However, in view of the huge claim and on grounds of public policy, the court decided to appoint a new sole arbitrator, acceptable to both sides, preferably a retired Supreme Court judge. The judges wanted senior lawyers from both sides to suggest names, which was very tricky but the name had to be suggested on the spot. HRBC and their officials not being used to litigation or familiar with lawyers and judges to the extent that the other party (contractors and sub-contractors) were wondering how to get a person of impeccable background. RNJ then came up with the name of Justice A.N. Sen, retired judge of the Supreme Court and former Chief Justice, Calcutta High Court. This name appealed to the judges but they asked for Justice Sen's consent; also on the spot.

'I persuaded the judges, through senior counsel, to give us time till 2 p.m. The judges declined. It was 11.30 and we succeeded in persuading the judges to defer the matter till the rising of the court for lunch recess at 1 p.m. I rushed to the Supreme Court Bar Association and made an STD or lightning call to Justice Sen's residence, I remembered the telephone number. Mrs Sen told me that Justice Sen was in the Taj Bengal holding an arbitration meeting and was scheduled to have lunch there'.

RNJ then got the Taj phone number and called them only to be told that no phone calls were allowed. 'I said that I was talking from the Supreme Court and that the line had to be given to Justice Sen. They asked who would talk to him and I identified myself, saying that Justice Sen was required for some Supreme Court purposes. Justice Sen was given the phone, recognized my voice and asked 'tumi okhanay ki korcho (what are you doing there?)'. I explained the urgency and, finally, managed to extract his consent that I conveyed to our senior counsel, G.L. Sanghi. The judges asked twice whether Justice Sen had given his consent, asked for my statement to be recorded and then passed an order confirming his appointment. More than 100 sittings were held by him, the papers pertaining to the earlier arbitration were permitted to be brought in and we succeeded ... The entire award was set aside'.

It was the Birla business that kept Bhagwati Babu personally busy. The 1960s were particularly troublesome times for Indian industry. One of the most important cases of the time was a 1966 charge against Hindustan Motors of importing some material/car components under a forged import licence. Not only was the charge serious; top managers of the company were being implicated, including vice-president, finance, and vice-president, manufacturing, D.C. Lahoti and N.K. Birla, amongst others. Thanks to Bhagwati Babu's handling of the case – that lasted for quite a long time – it was dismissed', recalls Pramod Chand Agarwal.

Dipankar Gupta, second from the left, was a KCo favourite; seen here with Justice M.H. Kania and R.N. Jhunjhunwala, second and first from the right

In 1967, there was yet another important case around Hindustan Motors' booking of forward exchange, following the devaluation of the rupee. The charge was that HM had manipulated the booking without a proper contract being in hand after getting prior information that devaluation was going

## Legal Aid

Says Justice P.N. Bhagwati: 'KCo subscribed to the concept of legal aid schemes fathered by me and one of its partners was instrumental in organizing Lok Adalats in West Bengal. Bhagwati Prasad Khaitan was also one of the pioneers in lending support to the National Law School of India University, Bangalore, to promote legal literacy and create legal awareness. He also conceived the idea of establishing a charitable trust known as the "Law Research Institute" for the purpose of promotion of jurisprudence and helping upcoming lawyers in different ways'.

to take place. 'I remember Dipankar Gupta being the senior counsel in this case and R.N. Bajoria assisting him. After complete investigation it was held that the allegations were not true', recalls RKC.

The 1960s continued to be notorious for the 'raid raj'. In 1969, there was a massive search of the offices of the Birlas in which truckloads of paper were taken away by the enforcement branch. This was a charge under the Foreign Exchange Act. The search and seizure were challenged. R.N. Bajoria was one of the counsels and Subrata Roy Chowdhury was the senior counsel. The company failed in the first court but succeeded in the appeal court of Justice Sabyasachi Mukherjee who ordered the return of the files. The Enforcement Directorate went to the Supreme Court that almost upheld the division bench's order but said that if there were some papers that the directorate required, it could keep them. Recalls RKC: 'Of the 5,000 files seized they returned 30 or 40. The scrutiny of the files led to at least a dozen cases but, under BP's guidance, we succeeded in all the cases. In not a single case was there conviction or fine'.

Mrs Hansa Deb Burman recalls working on this case 'almost round the clock'. Her seniors were Anil C. Mitra and, later, Gouri Mitter, then Advocate General in 1970. 'We lost the first round in Calcutta, won on appeal and the

Directorate of Foreign Enforcement went to the Supreme Court. Mr Setalvad was appearing against us. Since I was in the case from the inception and had read every paper from the trial court, I realized that, apart from the legal aspect, even the factual matters stated by the opposition were contrary to what they had said in the high court and on affidavit. I pointed these out to Gouri Mitter who pointed out the contradictions to the court. The other side withdrew'.

Pramod Chand says that the point is that 'B.M. Birla had absolute and implicit trust in the advice of BP. Other Birlas too held him in very high esteem' and Pramod Chand was a regular at 52/2, Ballygunge Circular Road. There he would see a young man, the son of Bhagwati Babu, sometimes coming into the room; quiet and well-behaved. This young man must have been soaking up everything legal that went on around him for he seemed to have picked up all his father's traits and learnt to marry them with the circumstances of his times. After his father withdrew from active practice, Pramod Chand would have occasion to deal with the son.

'After BP, I mostly interacted with Pinto, P. L. Agarwal. By then the Birla group had been divided and I was a part of the GP and BM Birla group. I would go to Pinto Khaitan's office. He has the same quality of being knowledgeable and practical, with a very sound commercial sense. He knows the art of overcoming problems without transgressing the law'. He was also young, adaptable but very, very, hardworking as would be many other Khaitans to follow', says Pramod Chand.

With Mr Pinto Khaitan, my relationship has been much more than a lawyer-client one, says Sanjeev Goenka: 'He has been my mentor and guided and literally tutored me through all processes of negotiations. He would coach me on what to say and what not to say; he would caution me against losing my cool and I particularly recall one negotiation in London, when one member from the other

## The principle of hard work

Samaraditya (Bacchu) Pal 'came to know Bhagwati Babu (as he was lovingly and respectfully called) closely in 1973, on the heels of Indira Gandhi's nationalization of the non-coking coal mines'. BPK asked RNJ to brief him to draw petitions under Article 226 of the Constitution – literally overnight – and move the High Court at 10.30 a.m. It was done. 'This is hard work, keep at it', he was told.The point that Mr Pal makes is that 'Bhagwati Babu laid down the principle of "hard work" as the criteria for briefing a junior and not the mere desire of a particular senior or any outsider for that matter. He was balance personified and enviably pragmatic'.

side lost his temper, got rather abusive and one could hear his voice from two floors above. I was not going to take it but Mr Khaitan placed his hand on my thigh; it had all the authority and affection to rein me in. It was the touch that could only come from an affectionate elder in the family that communicated to me what I had earlier been taught: in a negotiation, it is not important to score little points; it is not about personal egos; it is important to conclude the transaction; it is important to keep the big picture in mind and not to get waylaid by little distractions'.

There are stories galore about BP's son. Dipankar Gupta recalls being brought to Delhi by Pinto Khaitan on a case and they were supposed to be staying at the newly opened Oberoi. At the reception they were told that there was no reservation. 'That is when I saw how resourceful Pinto was: he took one of the cabana rooms (rooms around the swimming pool) and we made do'. The important thing here is that both the firm and its counsel were so adaptable. The work was important; a convenient location was important; not the room description.

Adaptability was again on display when Dipankar Gupta was required to go to Patna, along with Siddhartha Ray, on a Pratappur Sugar case. 'We had to go by train. Siddhartha

## Client first

So strong was the clients' faith in the firm that some even entrusted it with cases against parties with which the firm was closely associated. In 1968, Bank of India approached B.P. Khaitan to file a suit against the National Iron & Steel Company Ltd and its director guarantors, G.D. Agarwala and others, knowing full well that they were close relatives of Nil Ratan Khaitan(son of Kali Prasad Khaitan). The Bank of India chairman, regional manager and general manager requested BPK to accept the case on their behalf. 'BPK accepted their brief, a receiver was appointed, the suit heard, the decreed matter went up to the Supreme Court and the bank's claims were satisfied', says RNJ, who handled the case.

Ray was in the thick of politics in those days and asked us to leave for the station saying that he would follow. He could not make it and then there were instructions given to me on the phone that I hope I carried out. The matter went right up to the Supreme Court, where Ashok Sen appeared for the client. The case was possibly about allotment of sugarcane for sugar mills in Bihar', recalls Mr Gupta.

The renowned homeopath, Dr Bholanath Chakrabarty experienced another instance of the famed KCo adaptability. It was around 1976-77, at about 7.30 one evening, there was an SOS from Tapas Banerjee, barrister, which took RNJ rushing to his chamber, where he found Dr Chakrabarty in a tizzy. The state government had suddenly said that it would take away the land allotted to the good doctor for a Homeopathy Hospital & Research Centre, with 50 free beds. Worse, the land acquisition collector would take back possession by 11 a.m. the next day. It was one thing preparing the writ application overnight but it had to be moved before the appropriate bench of Justice R.N. Pyne at the first sitting of the court at 10.30 a.m. The difficulty was that Justice Pyne's bench never sat before 11 a.m. By the time the petition could be moved, a stay obtained and the order taken to the site, the collectorate officials would have taken possession. Extraordinary circumstances demand extraordinary service and RNJ, in consultation with Tapas Banerjee, took the original petition to the residence of Justice Pyne at St George's Gate at 8.15 a.m. and explained the circumstances to him. He appealed to him to sit at 10.30. Justice Pyne agreed and the petition was moved; the stay granted and, liberty was given to RNJ, as the attorney, to communicate the order by letter with direction on all parties to act on the basis of such communication.

'I rushed with my handwritten letter to the site with Dr Bhola Chakrabarty and others; handed over the letter to collectorate officials at the site and the crisis was averted'. After several months, Dr Chakrabarty landed up at the KCo office along with Mrs Lina Chakraborty, the then health secretary, and requested him to withdraw the writ application. 'I was taken aback'. An embarrassed Dr Chakrabarty said that the PWD Minister had got the government to offer a Rs 2-crore grant to his hospital trust to purchase land at Barasat. 'The case was withdrawn; the Rs 2-crore grant received and the hospital and research centre was completed'.

Pinto Khaitan too was in the thick of things. 'I am not a litigations person but during the initial years I handled various litigation cases, tax cases, industrial disputes, arbitration between the Government of India and Sahu Jain, when shares of Jessop & Company were purchased by the government from Sahu Jains and the valuation of the shares determined through arbitration, a murder trial and other criminal cases. Then there were various litigations in courts and Tribunals', he says about himself. However, for many clients it was the personal Pinto touch that was more enduring. Yadu Hari Dalmia says: 'There was the famous Dalmia-Jain case in which PK was involved. In the early days we had many complex matters involving our businesses in Pakistan and over repatriation of funds. There were matters that went up to the House of Lords and, finally, when we did get the order, the rupee was devalued'.

There were some unique matters of law in the resolution of which only KCo participated – those around Railway Rates Tribunal, for instance. 'To the best of my knowledge and information no law firm having practice in Calcutta dealt with the Railway Rates Tribunal situated in Madras', says RKC. The Railway Rates Tribunal hears matters relating to fixation of rates and any other charges mentioned in the Railways Act, 1890. There was a dispute concerning the Dhanuka-owned Belsund Sugar Company with regard to fixation of rates under the Railways Act, which was referred to the Railway Rates Tribunal. Bhagwati Babu asked Ram Kishore Choudhury to handle the matter with Mr R. Subramaniam assisting him in Madras. The arguments were long and detailed and the points raised by Belsund Sugar were upheld and certain rates re-fixed by the tribunal. The Union of India, however, preferred an appeal before the Supreme Court and Bhagwati Babu wanted the matter to be settled once and for all. He advised RKC to brief Ashok Sen on behalf of the Dhanukas. Mr B.P. Maheshwari was the advocate-on-record and Ashok Sen was the senior counsel. There were hectic parleys between RKC and Ashok Sen, including a telephone discussion during the lunch break on the day the celebrated barrister was to address the court. The matter was called before Justice K.N. Wanchoo and Justice V. Bhargava at the fag end of the court hour... but where was Ashok Sen?

BP taught his son not to be litigious but when he had to fight he would goad his boys to give it their best shot. The photo shows BP giving his son Pinto a warm send off on his first business trip abroad

## The art of being precise

Yadu Hari Dalmia says: 'Professionally, I came in touch with the firm when I was doing commerce at St Xavier's. I became close to Pinto Khaitan and also developed an interest in law, especially taxation law. I worked on two very interesting cases with KCo. In one we realized that we had to meet Mr Nani Palkhivala. It was a very complex case and it was quite impossible to get an appointment with him. We were at the Oberoi, Delhi when we got a 15-minute slot with him and I was worried that we would not be able to convey our case and get his opinion in that short time. Pinto Bhaiya advised me to come along and to make the most of the time. Sure enough, in that short time, he could not only communicate the matter to Nani Palkhivala but also get a clear opinion on the matter with an advice for us to fight the matter right up to the Supreme Court even though he would not be able to represent us for want of time'.

RKC broke out in a cold sweat and kept turning his head towards the door of the courtroom but there was no sign of his senior counsel. Justice Bhargava, who was far more experienced than the young advocate, knew exactly what was going on and made a telling remark: 'Mr Choudhury, if you are looking for Mr Sen, I think he has gone out of Delhi'. A perplexed RKC rebutted: 'No, Your Lordship, I spoke to him at the lunch break and he said that he would be here'. The judge knew better and advised the young man that his senior was out of the city and that he would not permit an adjournment on that ground. RKC would have to proceed with the matter. Next to RKC sat his mentor, Bhagwati Prasad, who said in a sharp undertone: 'Ram Kishore, proceed'. The still nonplussed lawyer said: 'The clients will be very upset, if I do'. There was a sterner command that even the judge heard: 'I said, proceed'. The judge advised him: 'I suggest you listen to Mr Khaitan'.

Willy-nilly, RKC put on his bravest face and proceeded with the submissions. The following day too Ashok Sen was engaged in another matter and again Justice Bhargava insisted on RKC continuing and concluding arguments on behalf of Indian Sugar Mills Association. Senior ISMA executives had all but given up hope and were in jitters, even though they were gradually warming up to the arguments of the young substitute. Finally, Ashok Sen came to make the final arguments and then it was the client's turn to be overwhelmed when the judgment was in their favour. 'After the successful handling and appearances before the Supreme Court in relation to the Railway Rates Tribunal all matters relating to fixation of tariff by the Railways were entrusted to us and BP gave me several other matters relating to Central excise and sales tax'. Of course, he found great pleasure in talking about the prowess of his young team at KCo to the growing world of clients.

BP was uniquely qualified to run a legal firm and train his young wards; talking about his young team to the growing world of his clients

If Bhagwati Babu was uniquely trained by circumstances and upbringing to run the legal firm and mentor the young, his son too had a very special training that transcended the basic legal education and the modern, 20th-century schooling, complimented by a global exposure. This began with the very process of socialization involving charity and charitable organizations that were an important part of the firm's legal services too. Many of its clients took their charities very seriously. 'I remember, Narsingdas Bangur and my father walking barefoot in a procession, carrying the holy books on their head to the Vaikunthnath Temple', says Pinto Khaitan. This was only one aspect of the learning that, while appearing irrelevant to a legal career, was critical for the psyche of the lawyer who would be dealing with family firms of a particular bent of mind.

Says Dinesh Himatsingka, 'My personal relations with the firm go back to Pinto Babu, who is uniquely placed to assist and advise us. That he knows the law is a given; he also knows the psyche of a Marwari family, which is critical for advising a family-run enterprise such as ours and the one receiving it. He is the best advisor one can find and I have consulted him and have been guided by him on so many issues from the time I started the business'.

BP was equally a man of religion. Narsingdas Bangur and he would walk barefoot in a procession, carrying holy books on their head to the Vaikunthnath Temple, recalls Pinto Khaitan

There is equal praise for the firm and its other members from Mr B.K. Birla: 'The Khaitans are a well established family in Calcutta and we have a close relationship with several members of this family... Of them, Pramod and Nand Gopal Khaitan are amongst the top lawyers of Calcutta. One can close one's eyes and accept their advice and opinion. The legal relationship apart, our families are very close and the senior member of the family, Bhagwati Prasadji, had been associated with the Birla family for nearly 60 years. We received the greatest legal assistance from him, the likes of which we have received from no one. His son Pradip Kumar Khaitan is today a very experienced lawyer...', Mr Birla wrote in his autobiography. In a world of trust deficit, to be able to accept any advice with 'one's eyes closed' is bliss.

# BENGAL
## and the art of
# 'GHERAO'

KCo's silent corridors, on Emerald House's first floor, are lined by rooms where minds work overtime

*America had sent a man to the moon and the world was rejoicing but why would a legal firm in distant Calcutta want a day off to celebrate? Pinto Khaitan thought the idea was ridiculous and made no bones about expressing his mind to the KCo union that had demanded 'chhutti'. Armstrong's day quickly became a day for strong-arm tactics and the union resorted to a pen-down strike. While Bhagwati Babu managed this crisis, the message had gone out: Emerald House would not be the one big happy family for some time to come.*

Bengal was in a state of ferment with labour-management disputes taking on violent proportions and the Labour Minister, Subodh Banerjee, of the United Front government reportedly saying that he would not 'allow the use of the police' in case of labour agitations. 'I have allowed a duel between the employees and the employers in West Bengal and the police has been taken out of the picture so that the strength of each other may be known'. Industrial action in the state was taking on menacing proportions with managers being forcibly confined for hours and even days on end.

For any storyteller to be objective about a phenomenon that was at once inevitable and disastrous, it would seem safe to describe the tale as told in the courts and by the

### A strike that Roopa recalls

A rookie in the early eighties, Roopa Sheth was confronted with what to her seemed to be a scandalous poster on the walls of the office, running down her bosses, whom she looked up to in those days. A union problem at KCo was not something that she could accept. Yet there are amusing memories: 'I remember pulling down the posters at the entrance; something that I would not repeat ever. I was new and naïve then. I also remember some of my seniors being gheraoed and confined to their rooms. I even had to smuggle in Paan Bahar for one of them'.

judges. In fact, when all of Bengal was in a tizzy over the gherao phenomenon, KCo decided to advise its clients, Jay Engineering, whose managers had been at the receiving end of gheraos time and again, to go to court and have the legality of the labour action and police inaction settled once and for all. Jay Engineering was not the only victim of worker recalcitrance; all of Bengal was strewn with such examples, made worse by police inaction.

If the whole of Bengal was in a tizzy, could the honourable justices have been immune from it? It was only after considerable debate in the courts that the judges came to an understanding of the term 'gherao' but the final judgment itself was a commentary on the evolution of industrial legislation in India and the ways of both management and labour. These applications under Article 226 of the Constitution were first moved before Justice B.C. Mitra but, given the sensitivity of the matter in Bengal and the enormous public interest, a larger Bench was constituted to hear the matter.

The petitioner no. 1 in this matter was Jay Engineering Works (a limited company) that made sewing machines and fans in Calcutta. It had a sales office known as the 'Eastern India Usha Corporation' at no. 26, R.N. Mukherjee Road in Calcutta where around 365 workmen and other management staff were employed. The petitioners were Ram Nath Gupta, the manager of the office; Anand Prakash Goel, superintendent; Srikesh Lahiri and Sudhir Kumar Mukherjee, area supervisors; and Baijnath Kapur and Babulal Toshi, supervisors. The respondent (no. 8) was the Jay Engineering Workers Union, registered under the Trade Unions Act, 1926, of which Raghunath Kushari was the executive member.

Matters came to a flashpoint at Jay Engineering when on or about January 17, 1967, 18 employees of the sales office, including some union members were retrenched. The judges were not concerned with the legality of the retrenchment

## Courting strikes

The Calcutta High Court too has had its own share of strikes: once in 1998, when the High Court Employees' Welfare Association struck work and resorted to agitation, shouting slogans against the High Court Administrative Body, when Justice Samir Mukherjee was the Acting Chief Justice. The employees, demanding implementation of the Pay Commission recommendations, apprehended that that the high court would not send a favourable report to the Government of West Bengal. 'As far as I can recall, there was no judicial work for a day and the pen-down strike continued for three days', says RNJ. There was a more recent incident before the Puja vacations in September 2010, also over the Pay Commission's recommendations, when there was total disruption and no judicial and administrative work could be done. All the gates of the high court were locked, including the court rooms and no one was able to enter the court premises. The situation continued for a week or so.

but the legality of the confinement and the police inaction. On January 27, 1967, at about 1 p.m., the retrenched employees, along with 70 others, blockaded the sales office premises, completely obstructing the passage of personnel and goods, including food for the barricaded persons, who were wrongfully confined therein. The blockade was lifted at 3 a.m. on January 28, 1967, after police intervention.

The judgment went into the political background of the matter; to March 1, 1967. The United Front government had just come into office. On March 2, 1967, the retrenched workers, together with around 200 other employees, 'gheraoed' Ram Nath Gupta and other officers at the office from 1 p.m. The 'gherao' continued for 33 hours and was lifted at 10 p.m. on March 3. All the while the beseigers tampered with the company's property, defaced the walls and continuously shouted insulting and humiliating slogans against the confined. A minimal quantity of food was provided to the managers and the police at the Hare Street police station, informed about the siege, stayed inactive.

On April 17, at 11 a.m., the retrenched workers along with some 100 or 150 others once again gheraoed the manager and other officials and repeated their acts of trespassing, damaging office property and abusing the officers. Once again, the besiegers allowed little food to be brought in and the police remained inactive.

Finally, an application was made before the chief presidency magistrate, Calcutta, under Section 100 of the Criminal Procedure Code. The magistrate ordered the officer-in-charge, Hare Street police station, to search and rescue the confined persons and produce them before him. The confined persons were rescued at about 10 p.m on April 18. After 10 days, the gherao was repeated on May 29 and the manager and other officers were confined to the office for more than five hours, from 10.30 a.m. to 3.30 p.m. with the police once again choosing not to act.

Such police inaction was probably being perpetuated by some extraordinary communications from the government, including one signed by the Chief Minister, Ajay Kumar Mukherjee dated June 9, 1967: '...government would like

Three generations of Kanorias have been well-served by the firm. H.P. Kanoria (behind President Kalam) recalls KCo helping him act against seven employees at a time when even acting against one was considered risky

## Growth amidst gherao

Mr H.P. Kanoria recalls: 'KCo were particularly helpful when we had our labour problem in the mid-1970s. It was the gherao era but we purchased the biggest flour-processing mill in the country, the Bengal Flour Mill, at that time. People warned us against buying because a lot of people were migrating to Rajasthan and elsewhere but my father showed great guts and ventured to acquire the firm. Immediately after the takeover we had a labour problem and under the advice of KCo, we dealt with the problem legally without having much loss of production. We summarily dismissed seven members of the watch and ward staff. Taking action against one workman was considered a great catastrophe but we did it against seven of them and the firm helped us to solve the problem legally'.

to impress upon all officers specially those connected with maintenance of law and order, that the police must not intervene in legitimate labour movements and that in case of any complaint regarding unlawful activities in connection with such movements, the police must first investigate carefully whether their complaint has any basis in fact before proceeding to take any action provided under the law'. Even earlier, there was a Cabinet decision on March 14, 1967: 'Cabinet considered the situation created by the "gherao" of industrial establishments by their workers resulting in the confinement of the managerial and other staff and directed that in such cases the matter should be immediately referred to labour minister and his directions obtained before deciding upon police intervention for the rescue of the confined personnel'.

It was quite clear that the latter communication virtually interdicted the police from taking action in case of 'gherao' without permission of the labour minister who, in turn, held that 'gheraos' were included within the expression 'legitimate labour movements'. The judges went into the connotations of a strike, which is lawful and is a recognized instrument in the hands of labour, which aids them in any concerted movement to improve their position vis-à-vis the management. While a gherao may or may not amount to a strike, accompanied by violence or the commission of any offence, it could 'never be lawful'.

'It has by now become notorious that gheraos … have been happening widely in West Bengal and also of the part that is being played therein by the trade unions. We cannot shut our eyes to what is by now general information that as a result of indiscriminate gheraos attended with violence, industry, trade and commerce in West Bengal are coming to a standstill. Expansion of industrial undertakings have been stopped; industrial undertakings are closing one by one and we have the dismal picture of thousands of workers being thrown out of work just when the food situation had become perilous and prices have soared beyond the means of the common man. Instead of labour profiting by such movement, thousands of them are today on the verge of starvation. It is the lesson of history that whenever trade unionism has exceeded bounds and become militant, for example the strikes in England in 1926 and the civil disobedience movement in 1932, when trade unions tried to take advantage of the same, there has been a retrogression in the forward march of trade unionism'.

The court found history repeating itself. 'So far as the ministers are concerned, we are prepared to concede that mala fides on their part has not been established. So far as the Chief Minister is concerned, although he seems to have used the word "gherao" somewhat indiscriminately, even the press reports show that he has referred to peaceful gherao where all the workers were pursuing their legitimate trade union rights within the bounds of the law', the judges said.

It was eventually held that the Council of Ministers of the state of West Bengal, in issuing the directives in the impugned circulars, had clearly violated Article 256 of the Constitution. It was held that they had no jurisdiction or authority to issue the two impugned circulars, which must therefore be struck down. It was also held that while no fundamental right of petitioner no. 1, Jay Engineering Works, had been violated, those of its managers and officers had and they would have been entitled to relief on the ground that their fundamental rights to move freely (guaranteed by clause (d) of Article 19(1)) and to carry on occupation, trade or business, guaranteed by clause (g) of Article 19(1), had been violated; 'but for the fact that by reason of the proclamation of Emergency the fundamental rights guaranteed by this Article cannot be enforced'.

The three judges were in agreement on all scores and

The era of strikes took its toll of KCo's Calcutta office as well and it took a while for the spirit of bonhomie to return. KCo Calcutta staff in the library

giving his opinion Justice B.C. Mitra said that 'gherao', as practised in this case, must be held to be unlawful. The question of whether the respondent workmen were guilty of the charges and deserved punishment must be determined in other proceedings and in other fora. He also held that the government's circulars on the role that the police could play were unlawful and that if the commissioner of police and the officer-in-charge, Hare Street police station, failed to perform their duties in obedience to the two circulars, they had 'failed to discharge the duties imposed upon them by law' induced by the questionable directions and instructions.

It would be worthwhile to revisit Lord Denning in the case of R. vs Metropolitan Police Commissioner (1968; 2 Q.B. 118): 'I have no hesitation, however, in holding that, like every constable in the land, he should be and is, independent of the executive. He is not subject to the orders of the Secretary of State... I hold it to be the duty of the Commissioner of Police, as it is of every chief constable, to enforce the law of the land. He must take steps so to post his men that crimes may be detected; and that honest citizens may go about their affairs in peace. He must decide whether or not suspected persons are to be prosecuted; and, if need be, bring the prosecution

Pinto Khaitan with V.D. Jain and executives of Birla Jute in Satna

or see that it is brought; but in all these things, he is not the servant of anyone, save of the law itself. No Minister of the Crown can tell him that he must, or must not, keep observation on this place or that; or that he must, or must not, prosecute this man or that one. Nor can any police authority tell him so. The responsibility for law enforcement lies on him. He is answerable to the law and to the law alone'. This, if nothing else, was upheld by the Jay Engineering case.

Industrial strike affected so many of KCo's clients. Recalls Keshav Mathur of Ratnakar Shipping: 'I am reminded of the years when my company had to resort to a lockout (1969-1971) along with the entire Birla group of which my company, Ratnakar Shipping, was a member. Certain actions on the part of the staff were most regrettable and I met two stalwarts of Khaitan, P.L. Agarwal and N.C. Shah, on how to address the problem. They were both experts in their field and helped me deal with a situation that I was poorly experienced to handle. With their help, we managed to keep the company running as was necessary for a company with ships sailing the high seas and attended to their logistics and supplies, on a daily basis.

'Mr Ram Kishore Choudhury's help was invaluable on many matters of tax and in certain matters concerning lease. His quick grasp always resulted in the least amount of time spent on explaining the problem and he always went into great detail before making suggestions. There was also RNJ, who bailed me out of a tricky situation with regard to yet another barge repair, this time in the Haldia docks. RNJ took the matter up with the party in Dubai who had rejected the barge as being not seaworthy and sorted out the problem. Albeit, the barge was not fully ready but we went unscathed'.

In hindsight, possibly the most amusing story of KCo's involvement with striking workers was RNJ's act of rescuing the receiver. This time RNJ was in the police van! No, he was not arrested but the KCo partner was helping the police rescue a court-appointed receiver from the hands of an angry mob in the 1970s. The right to strike hit industry in many ways, even when a company's own employees had no problems. Thus, on the eve of Holi, when sales would be particularly sizzling, a Bata India consignment to Mokameh was held up by the workers of the transporting company. On Bata India's suit, Justice S.C. Ghosh of the Calcutta High Court appointed barrister, N.N. Debnath, to take possession of the consignment, lying at the transporter's godown at Burra Bazar near Mahatma Gandhi Road and have it despatched through some other transporter. Easier ordered than executed.

When RNJ and N.N. Debnath went to the godown to execute the order they were trapped by a hostile mob threatening them with dire consequences. 'The situation became both volatile and aggressive, when I managed to convince them to let me out of the premises to respond to nature's call; proceeded straight to the nearest Jorabagan thana and sought help from the officer-in-charge. The OC regretted his inability to help without a court order so I had to plead with him to call the registrar, original side, Calcutta High Court, because the life of the receiver was in danger'. Once the registrar was contacted, RNJ impressed upon him the need to convey to the judge an oral prayer for police help, which Justice S.C. Ghosh allowed. He also instructed the registrar to ask the OC to render sufficient police help. RNJ, the OC and the police then travelled in the thana van to rescue the barrister. Alongside, the goods were lifted by another transporter in an operation that continued beyond midnight.

# A CAPITAL MOVE

*K.K. Birla was setting up the Zuari Agro fertilizer plant in Goa and needed to source technology globally. He also needed a legal mind that would understand the nature of the deals and contracts. That was when he thought of Bhagwati Babu's son. So he sent off Pinto Khaitan to the US to interact with lawyers there representing the technology suppliers and to familiarize the young man with the prevalent practices of international law. For the second-generation Khaitan it was an eye-opener of a different sort. 'There I not only met lawyers and saw law firms but met American businessmen, the US State Department that was running the USAID programme and the World Bank. I saw how cutting-edge law firms ran their businesses; most importantly, I realized that they were present in the capital of the country and in important commercial centres. New York and Washington were essential locations for US law firms and I started dreaming of our office in New Delhi'.*

As Chris Smart, an Englishman, sat sipping coffee at a corner shop in London, he was teaching his Indian friend an important lesson in life. Never be late for a meeting. It was the early 1970s and Pinto Khaitan was in the UK to handle a shipping litigation for K.K. Birla. 'This trip exposed me to English lawyers and their professionalism. Mr Chris Smart who accompanied me would ensure that he was early for his meetings, choosing to spend time over a cup of coffee at a corner shop if he was too early, rather than being late for meetings'. The idea was never to make another person wait for you.

The ways of global business and international law were just opening up for Pinto Khaitan, who was sent to Spain to resolve a matter involving a bill for repair of the client's ship by a Spanish shipyard, recalls the client, Keshav Mathur, former chief executive, Ratnakar Shipping. Indeed, shipping was a fascinating business but, as Mr Mathur realized to his great consternation, one in which one had to deal with different nationalities and not all their practices were straight. A Ratnakar ship (a tanker) was undergoing repair in Cadiz, Spain, in a famous shipyard known in history where the Spanish Armada was based. There was a dispute over the cost of repair and the tanker was seized by the shipyard.

'I failed to make any headway, when Pinto Babu was requested to help. He accompanied me to Spain, where we appointed a local firm of solicitors to handle our case. We were together for over three weeks and, were it not for him and his interaction with the local solicitor, I would have stood no chance. His advice and methods were even appreciated by the Spanish solicitor, Senor Pando. Eventually, we got what we wanted and I thanked Pinto Babu heartily because a loss here may have cost me my job. Pinto Babu not only salvaged the matter but even put in a good word for me to my chairman. I thus retained my job!' For Pinto Khaitan, it was another day at office and an 'exposure to how the Europeans ran their legal practice and their negotiating skills that are needed in any business', as he put it.

Contrast it to how the firm was conducting its business in the Calcutta of those days: There would be B.P. Khaitan sitting at a long table with all his clients seated in front of him. The person whose case he would be discussing would come to the seat in front and discuss his concerns within

## Principled growth

That the firm would grow was a given but there would be some cardinal principles to be adhered to when the firm went in for the expansion. Says Pinto Khaitan: 'That the firm's interest would be the motivating factor, not an individual partner's. Even when it led to some conflict of interest and some partners chose to go their own way, we chose to stick to this policy because we believed that, in the long run, the interests of the firm were more important'. However, the firm's infrastructure would be available to every lawyer so that he or she could achieve his potential to the full extent and develop his career.

## Training Om

On his third day at work, Bhagwati Prasad Khaitan asked his grandnephew, Om, to fetch the AIR of a certain year. 'I had no clue what that meant save that AIR meant All India Radio, which I knew was not too far from the office. So I went off to All India Radio Station with that chit of paper saying on which he had written AIR and the year. People saw it and looked at it strangely…till some man familiar with the law said that I would find it at a lawyer's office. I argued that I had come from a lawyer's office, whereupon he suggested that I go to my library and look for the book. I went back, got the book out and went to him'. Bhagwati Babu, who was wondering where the young man had disappeared for an hour, asked him where he was. 'I told him the truth and he had a big laugh but then prepared a schedule for me to work in each department, including the despatch department, to see and understand how a law firm operates. In the despatch department I saw the Despatch Register that had the record of everything that was going out of office. He advised me not to be shy about asking questions but to take the opportunity and learn what I could. To my mind that was the best part of my training'.

*— Om Khaitan*

everyone's earshot. Interestingly, everyone chipped in with suggestions and it was like a community resolving a problem together. This was a far cry from the conference rooms in which client-lawyer meetings would take place at an international level; where confidentiality was maintained strictly and there was no question of any breach. Pinto Khaitan realized that if he were to take the firm places, he would have to change the way it conducted its affairs.

Bhagwati Babu's famous long table is a story that many like to talk about, especially the youngsters that he initiated into the business, including members of his extended family. Recalls Om Khaitan, grandson of Lakshmi Narayan, who started coming to office even before joining law college. He was only a final-year student of commerce at St Xavier's when Bhagwati Babu met him and said that if the young man wanted to become a lawyer, he should report for work after morning college. 'He took me on as an articled clerk. I sat in his chamber and had a ringside view to some of the most interesting legal discussions of those days in the

1B, Old Post Office Street office. There was a world of VIPs visiting him in his simple room where he sat on his swivel chair and at his long table that had four or five chairs in front, where his clients sat. There was a small chair on the side, in which he asked me to sit. Some of the clients came personally; others sent their law officers. The top clients he would visit himself but I do remember some very important people coming to the office: Manturam Rampuria, B.P. Bajoria, the senior Mr Bharatiya, Mr M.L. Mittal…'

Life was not easy for the youngsters at KCo: Om got no stipend till he had served for five years. Bel Chamber's Rule 88 provided that an articled clerk was required to serve a full period of five years before admission as an attorney, a provision later amended with the court being empowered, under special circumstances, to allow a shorter period of articled clerkship. From 1967, the full court reduced this period to three-and-a-half years. So Om Khaitan had to bide his time and, when the time came, he got Rs 50 and his wife got another Rs 50. 'While we had to pay no rent nor pay for our food, clothes and entertainment were on us and I did have some high-society friends to keep up with. I, however,

## The legal one-stop shop

C.K. Dhanuka talks of Mr Pinto Khaitan taking over the company and becoming equally active in the affairs of Dhunseri. 'He joined the board of Dhunseri Petrochem and Tea Ltd. His many virtues include his quiet charm; his complete frankness; his commercial sense that impacts on every solution. He is a veritable one-stop-shop for all legal matters. In fact, everyone with KCo is quite vibrant and totally concerned about the client's welfare. Mr P. L. Agarwal too was most helpful and serves on the board of Dhunseri Investments and continues to be one of the finest minds in Company Law. Thus, though we are not much of a litigating company, we have benefitted a great deal from their corporate advice across a spectrum of matters. I do not recall a single instance of having suffered a loss on account of advice received from them; we have actually gained a great deal from our association in every manner. As far as client satisfaction is concerned, I give them cent per cent'.

## BPK's edicts

'I remembered BPK's advice: (a) Master all your facts and the law becomes easy to apply; (b) Never be afraid of a personality appearing against you; (c) Never be afraid to tell the truth; (d) Be patient, let the other side finish before you proceed to rebut. You will find the other side contradicting itself; (e) Never overstate your case; do not go to a height from which you cannot backtrack; give yourself room to fall; (f) Counsel who shout in court are not necessarily the best counsel; (g) The person who talks too much is usually a shallow person; (h) The biggest strength is your strategy in litigation or in negotiating a contract'.

— *Om Khaitan*

rode a scooter and my wife and I even managed to see a movie once in a while. It did not matter then and as BP told me: "In the eyes of your wife, you will always be a fool". He truly was an unforgettable influence in my life. Even when I branched off on my own, I drew from the lessons that I had learnt from him. Branching off on my own gave me more energy'.

Not just BP, every senior helped and it was Sita Ram Jhunjhunwala who made Om go through the paces. 'I worked very closely with Sita Ram Jhunjhunwala who was an extremely hardworking man. When he sat at a table there was no joking or chatting; it was work, work and work and he kept on passing files to me; four, five...one after another. He was extremely intense and said that handling a client depended on how well one knew the case. That meant reading, reading and more reading. Even when I went to him with some work that he had asked me to do, I would find that he knew all about the matter. He also had complete mastery over the art of drafting'.

Justice Ruma Pal, who had met Sita Ram Jhunjhunwala in her early years as a junior in Siddhartha Ray's chamber, recalls being told by SRJ that if he received some papers from a client, he could not sleep till he had examined them; never mind how late it was. 'Such devotion to duty was most remarkable about him'.

In the office, the youngsters that Sita Ram Jhunjhunwala had trained were flowering: amongst others Ram Kishore Choudhury, who had for quite some time caught BP's attention. SRJ had loads of work and Ram Kishore had to attend court every day, honing his skills. BP saw the potential and sent him to work with the eminent Radha Binode Pal, who later on became a judge of the International Court of Justice, the Hague. 'I started attending the chamber of Radha Binode Pal and in course of such attendance I became acquainted with Debi Prasad Pal and Balai Lal Pal'. Between handling these cases, RKC became a master and BP would then entrust him with the trickiest of matters.

Recalls RKC: 'In 1972, Mr B.K. Jhawar came to consult BP in connection with a litigation to be launched in Houston, US. BP advised me to proceed to Houston along with the client's representative. At Houston, I realized that the lawyers there would take inordinately long to prepare an exhaustive plaint. In my view, the plaint could be on the ground of dishonour of Bill of Exchange and I shared my opinion with BP, who agreed. The suit was filed and I had to visit Houston three or four times and, when the suit was heard and the decree passed in favour of our clients, BP promptly talked about it to his other clients; to the Birlas, in particular K.K. Birla and G.P. Birla. There was pride in his firm and his boys, and he never lost an opportunity to show them off'.

Modernism was in the air; technology was in the offing; BP's son was going overseas and the entire Calcutta office wished him bon voyage

The boys, in turn, delivered almost without fail. Recalls Mr H.P. Kanoria: 'The firm showed great foresight when we were acquiring the property in New Alipore for our residence in 1974-75. A land ceiling Act was in the offing but KCo envisioned the possible enactment

## Dhotijora; single tax

Around 1972-73, there was the famous Dhotijora case, involving levy of excise for which KCo briefed Hiralal Sibal (father of the Union Education Minister, Mr Kapil Sibal) from Chandigarh. Excise was levied on dhotis that always came in pairs and were treated as a single unit. The government wanted to levy excise on each dhoti and 'we argued that the name of the product was dhotijora. Hiralal Sibal was a very dynamic lawyer and argued the matter for two or two-and-a-half months, finally winning the case for us. The department did not appeal', recalls Om Khaitan.

and took necessary precaution so that no land ceiling would affect us. Apart from legal acumen, the firm has great vision as well. In that matter too we were assisted by Sita Ram Jhunjhunwala, P. L. Agarwal and N.C. Shah'.

For a company that was winning cases internationally, surely an office in the national capital was a must. As moves for starting the Delhi office were debated seriously, there was yet another important realization: that KCo could not remain a family-run business; that it could not conduct discussions with clients in public places; that it would have to have offices in the capital of the country and other centres. Recalls Pinto Khaitan: 'My father did not dampen my enthusiasm. Over time, he saw the benefits that were being brought to the firm with the changes that I had initiated and, over time, everyone started to support what I was doing'. The only criterion was that the growth should be principled and those who were not happy with these principles were welcome to function independently. Many others shared these sentiments.

Says S.K. Kapur: 'The younger generation has grown up entirely before me. My good fortune has been that all Khaitan associates have been extremely fond of me as I am of them. Indeed, I regard Khaitan like my private property and it offends me if I see anything that borders on impropriety in any shape or form on the part of any of its associates. That offends me personally. I do not expect that they would at all be irregular in any way'. Those that were prepared to abide by the principles were encouraged in every possible way and given every facility to flower.

Principles were accompanied by technology and it was the induction of modernism that gave the firm an edge when the rest of Calcutta was desperate to shun technology. Technology was the killer of jobs but Pinto Khaitan points out: 'We were quick to pick up technology even in the early years. We had the teleprinter, the EPABX and the electronic typewriter and then computers, as soon as they came into the country. We were the first to have computerized accounting… of course, a lot more can be done even today. We always laid great emphasis on a good library'. Roopa recalls the arrival of a state-of-the-art photocopier; an imported machine that occupied a large room. 'It had 20 stacks and magically arranged 20 sets of photocopied documents. It was almost an object of wonder for us'.

## A house for GD

In 1975-76, KCo handled the purchase of the Amrita Sher Gill Marg property for G.D. Birla. His daughter-in-law, Sarala Devi, was very keen on the property that was close to the Lodhi Gardens and she wanted it for GD, so that he could go there for his walks. The seller was P.C. Sawhney, who was parting with two acres of his four-acre plot. Her enthusiasm was so apparent that the sellers managed to negotiate for a rather good price of Rs 13 lakhs. Mrs Birla would, however, continuously phone Mr Sawhney to ensure that the deal was sealed. Recalls Om Khaitan: 'I finally had to tell GD that if she continued to intervene, I would not be able to conclude the deal and he promised me that she would not speak to Mr Sawhney again; but she did'. By then the Sawhneys had realized that they could hold out for more even though I argued that it was unfair to negotiate after the price had been settled. He asked why the solicitor was coming in the way of his getting a better price. I said that I had to protect my client's interest. Then I suggested that he should sign on the dotted line of the contract but I would leave the amount blank and that he would have to have faith in me that I would eventually put in a sum higher than Rs 13 lakhs'. Sawhney agreed and signed on the documents and Om put in the sum of Rs 13,50,000. The deal was sealed for that amount. The property is worth Rs 800 crores now!

Meanwhile, his international exposure had informed Pinto Khaitan that a professionally managed firm would need more than lawyers. 'While lawyers could handle the legal aspects of the business, the firm would have to be run by professional chartered accountants, human resource people or MBAs who would have to handle recruitments, training, accounting as in any other standard global firm'. That was the beginning of a formally adopted learning process for all KCo lawyers – a function that is overseen by one of the members of the executive committee.

Pinto Khaitan, a trusted advisor to the Birlas. Seen here with Mr B.K. Birla and Mrs Sarala Birla

Significantly, while there was no formal human resource training programme in the days of Bhagwati Babu, the training that the youngsters received under him was comprehensive; the motivation first-class. Admits Pinto Khaitan: 'Today, we train freshers professionally; something that my father had taught us. He had no time for those with a clerical mentality and would push people to accomplish things on their own. He inspired dynamism and supported it. KCo believes that the young lawyers should all be achievers and be supported by the firm as they do so. Indeed, this made my father an object of admiration for all those that he had nurtured… such people came back on his birthdays and reminisced over old times'.

Most importantly, the firm had an excellent system of documentation that Harish Salve recalls to this day. Mr Salve is another jurist that KCo has been briefing since his 'days as a youngster at Soli Sorabjee's chamber, when the practice of briefing counsel prevailed. It was very important to know the original side practice in the chartered high courts and to appreciate how meticulous KCo was, he says: 'the manner in which everything was noted; every letter carefully written, every pleading carefully studied. There was the stamp of commercial law and not just writ court law. There were carefully documented and evidenced paper trails and at a time when there were no computers'.

Senior advocate Arun Jaitley links up the Khaitans of the yesteryears and the firm as it obtains today: 'When Calcutta was unquestionably the hub of Indian industry during British India, KCo was the firm of choice for industrial houses. Later, Calcutta stopped growing as a business centre; old firms went into insolvency; there was commercial and company law litigation and Khaitans became a pioneering law firm in that environment. However, even when Calcutta ceased to expand, KCo continued to grow nationally, while retaining its premier status as a solicitor firm in Calcutta. There is hardly a Calcutta judge who has not been briefed by KCo and only a few in Delhi, who have not grown out of KCo. There is hardly a counsel, who has not been extensively briefed by KCo. The old Indian industry, including some old Marwari firms, swore by the firm. A lot of them still do'.

As the company chose to start a Delhi office, it was doing

## Buying Rallis

When Mr S.K. Birla wanted to buy Rallis India, a foreign company, he found a condition that prevented any Birla or its associate from buying the company. SKB was very keen on the acquistion so Om examined the papers and advised him to go ahead and buy, saying that one would deal with the consequences. To Om Khaitan's mind the condition was illegal because while, under Fera the court could put general conditions around Indians not being allowed to buy something, it could not discriminate under the Act, disallowing only one company. Nevertheless, when G.D. Birla heard about the advice he informed BPK about Om's advice to SKB, despite such an order. 'It did not matter to GD that we had taken Ashok Sen's opinion and he told Om in BPK's presence that he was doing something illegal'. 'I countered: if he said I was doing something illegal, he was wrong. If he thought I was doing something not totally moral, he was probably right. However, if he wanted me to stop doing something not totally moral he should ensure that no company did anything that was wrong because I believed that the order was wrong and could be challenged', says Om. The matter was settled in S.K. Birla's favour in the Supreme Court.

so under some well-established business principles. The shift was, of course, hastened by the flight of capital from Calcutta with the communists taking over and, in the first flush of success, resorting to a gherao raj that saw industrialists quit the city in hordes. Going to Delhi was no great shakes for the firm: several cases had taken many of its lawyers to the Indian capital numerous times. Ram Kishore Choudhury, amongst the more frequent travellers, was asked to take charge of 'Project Delhi'. He was, in any event, there for long stays and, at that particular point of time, was working on a case for B.M. Birla's firm, Blackwood Hodge.

When RKC told B.M. Birla that he had been asked to urgently locate space for a Delhi office for the firm, the bait that BM held out was: 'You win this case for me and I give you space'. He did not wait for victory though. He handed over the space in his office at 12, Hailey Road. All RKC had to do was buy some furniture and the office of KCo was up and running. Bhagwati Babu thought that P.L. Agarwal, one of his brightest sparks, should take charge of the Delhi office and all was set for PLA to move but that was when Om Khaitan, who had just lost his father and saw no reasons to stick around in Calcutta, threw the hat in the ring. Bhagwati Babu decided to give the young man a break. Nil Ratan Khaitan was requested to move to Delhi too and he was happy to move with his clerk. 'We worked in the two rooms and I stayed at a guest house belonging to Mr B.M. Birla, at 208, Jor Bagh and later moved to rented (at Rs 900 a month) apartments in Chirag Delhi', recalls Om.

The strategy in Delhi, where the firm was new, was to get known in the business circles using the chamber of commerce network but it was a family connection that helped matters the most. Om Khaitan recalls: 'The Calcutta office had given me a princely sum of Rs 20,000 to manage all our expenses for the entire year. Of course, we had a rent-free place and had no electricity bills to pay. That year (1970), the accounts of the firm were all hand-written by me'. As luck would have it, Ashok Birla wanted to purchase what was then Burma Shell House on Kasturba Gandhi Marg (now ECE House) and wanted the firm to handle the entire transaction, the due diligence, the documentation and the conveyance – everything. Om quoted a fee of one per cent of the costs and Ashok Birla readily agreed. The deal was for Rs 80 lakhs and the firm got a fee of Rs 80,000. It never had to ask Calcutta office for funds since then. BP was quite shocked to hear the huge fee quoted but was told that since the client was happy to pay, he should have no problem.

Watching the firm as a client in those days was Sharad Vaid, currently partner. He was a chartered accountant and company secretary working with Dalmia Cement (Bharat) Limited and taking law classes in the evening, when his association with the firm began in Delhi, in 1972. Heading it then was Om Khaitan, by then well known in Delhi's business and legal community, while Umesh Khaitan was a fresher. The person who really mattered though was Om Khaitan's stenographer, Uma Kant Gupta. Recalls Sharad: 'A stocky person, carelessly dressed with dishevelled hair, he had a great deal of authority in the office. Beneath the disorganized exterior, however, was a highly sincere and orderly person, who could find any piece of paper from the mess on his table. The only problem was that in his absence no one else could locate any paper; he was totally protective about them. He handled administration and gave appointments and all advocates would be submissive to him since, on office matters, Om Khaitan relied on him completely'.

In KCo, industrialist Charat Ram found a salve for all his wounds. Seen here with Om Khaitan

Another source of influence was M.L. Khaitan, chairman of Bata India, who was close

## Courtcraft pays

If there was one quality that KCo had instilled in its lawyers it was the ability to think on their feet. In the early eighties, the K.K. Birla-controlled Upper Ganges Sugar Mills, which also made Morton toffees, found itself facing prosecution, when the Inspector of Food Industries in Uttar Pradesh alleged non-conformity with the prescribed manufacturing norms at the Morton plant. The inspectorate started prosecution not just of the manager, (Ram Krishan Rohatgi) but also the directors that included K.K. Birla and R.K. Choudhury. The company challenged the prosecution by way of revision under Section 482 of the Code of Criminal Procedure Code and succeeded at the high court. However, the Municipal Corporation of Delhi went to the Supreme Court [Corporation of Delhi vs Ram Krishan Rohtagi (Upper Ganges Sugar Mills)], challenging the order.

Upper Ganges Sugar Company engaged a battery of lawyers: Fali Nariman, Kapil Sibal and M.C. Bhandari to defend its case. There were heated arguments in the court of justices S. Murtaza Fazal Ali and E.S. Venkataramiah and matters were clearly not going well for the defendants with the judges openly making statements from the bench to the effect that 'how can everyone go scot free?' That was when smart thinking did the job: RKC suggested that not everyone needed to go scot free; the inspectorate could continue to prosecute the factory manager but spare the directors, who had little to do with the day-to-day affairs at the factory. Given the near deadlock in the arguments, Justice Fazal Ali agreed. Having been spared, K.K. Birla then called RKC and said that no effort should be spared to get Rastogi (the manager) off. Needless to add, the matter went back to the magistrate for trial and was dismissed as the inspectors could not establish their case.

The moral of the story lies elsewhere though. On the day that the directors of Upper Ganges were released, in an identical matter, featuring DCM, before the same bench, Purshottam Lal Jhunjhunwala and other directors were facing prosecution but the outcome was different. Their counsel, U.S. Desai, refused to budge from the position that everyone prosecuted against should be spared and the judges refused to give DCM a favourable order. It only needed a little mental agility for KCo to win the case while an exactly similar case went against DCM.

to several businessmen and who chipped in with vital help. In Delhi, he stayed at the Oberoi Maidens and, when he had little to do, he would spend time at the KCo office, asking the lawyers 'not to mind him'. One day, Om got a call from the Oberoi saying that MLK would like to come down to see him with Charat Ram. 'I suggested that I would go up to his office but I learnt later that Dr Charat Ram's credo was never to call the lawyer to his own house but to go to his'.

Charat Ram came straight to the point. Those were the days of the Steel Control Order under which firms were allowed to import steel for their own consumption but never to sell. Somehow, one of his Hyderabad factories had sold imported steel. Explained MLK: 'Dr Charat Ram had rebuked his son and staff in the severest manner and, save for making them bleed, had punished them in every way. The question was how we could save them from being sent to jail. He was happy to pay the penalty but shuddered at the thought of jail'. Om asked for two days to think over the matter while he read up every book on the case. 'I found to my delight that in one book the words "may not" sell appeared as "may". It was obviously a misprint but I took the book to Ashok Sen and pointed out the matter. As he was wont, he pulled out his own book and said: "No it says 'may not' here. Konta thik? (Which is correct?)". I admitted that his book was correct but insisted that our client's mistake was bona fide'. On the basis of that misprint KCo developed the argument that the client could be penalized but not prosecuted because its action was based on an error in printing. 'Charat Ram became our client

## Talent is for keeps

'I joined the firm in 1995 and soon learnt that partnership and co-operation was not a choice but the only way here. I have voiced my opinion, right or wrong, in these many years freely and fairly even when I was an associate, before I became a partner in 2004 and can vouch for the fact that my words never went unheard', says Gauri Rasgotra. 'What touched me most was that when I had to leave in 2006, to accompany my husband to the US for a three-year assignment, the firm never said "bye" to me. At a grand send-off dinner for my husband and I, Pradip Khaitan simply said that you will remain a part of us and will come back to us. He kept his word, as he always does, and I returned in 2009 to become, once again, a part of his exciting vision to forge a growing, more professional presence in the legal landscape. I found a place here to use the experience gained at the India Centre of the George Washington University Law School'.

for ever. Till his last days, he would climb up the stairs of my office – much after I had branched out on my own – and never did he call me to his office'.

As the firm secured important clients, it made friends with the large community of budding lawyers. Says Arun Jaitley: 'In my younger days, I would visit Himalaya House. The firm was already connected with my father, who used to appear in the trial court in Delhi. He was known as Panditji. I too have been briefed by the firm extensively, especially after I became a senior, by its Calcutta, Delhi and Mumbai offices. I have seen it as a lawyer from some 34 years ago. My friend Rajiv Nayyar used to be a junior with KCo and I would visit him and go for lunch at Connaught Place'. Some of the KCo traits stand out in his mind. 'In Delhi, the firm had a trade dressing; a blue binding on the files, which would distinguish the Khaitan brief amongst a pile of files', Mr Jaitley recalls.

Amongst the most important clients was D.P. Mandelia, who handled all G.D. Birla matters, who wanted advice on a Renukoot case, where Hindalco had its plant. Aluminium needs continuous power and the plant was being starved of power though there was a guaranteed contract for power. There was no captive power in those days. The Birlas wanted a stay on the disconnection as soon as possible and GD wanted C.K. Daftary as counsel. 'I felt that was a bad idea because the counsel would have to read volumes of material and Mr Daftary was too old to be asked to do that. GD did not like being contradicted and reprimanded me: "Young man, are you telling me whom to brief? Go to Daftary and give him the papers".

So off went Om first having sent the papers to C.K. Daftary's office and followed it up with the visit along with Mr Mandelia. There was the senior counsel smoking his pipe, who was introduced to Mr Mandelia. He heard his visitors and asked: 'Do you think I can do this?' Om said he did not think so but G.D. Birla believed so. The senior counsel advised: 'No, gentlemen, take the papers back and give it to someone who will do justice to them'. Om countered: 'Sir, but Mr Birla has faith only in you', at which point the senior counsel turned round and said: 'Mr Birla can pay me money but not my life' and that was that.

When D.P. Mandelia reported the discussion to GDB in Om's presence, the senior Birla said that Om must have asked him not to take the case. 'I was a hot-headed man and walked out of the meeting. GD then called up BP and asked: "What kind of a person have you got in Delhi". BP heard me out and said: "Never confront a Birla. They do not like to take no for an answer. You should have handled him tactfully". Shortly after that Om got another call from Mr Mandelia asking him to come over. Om promptly informed him that Bhagwati Babu was in Delhi and could come along but D.P. Mandelia insisted that he came alone. So Om went and was asked who the best person to handle this matter would be. He answered: 'A.C. Bhabra from the Calcutta office'.

A.C. Bhabhra (R) and Om Khaitan in Delhi

'Mr Bhabra came from Calcutta and everyone worked round the clock without sleep, at the office, including Dipankar Gupta and Nil Ratan Khaitan. The papers were prepared, everything was cyclostyled in the office and the party went off to Allahabad. They came back with a stay and order for immediate power connection'. Om returned home and went off to sleep, asking his wife not to wake him up. While Om was asleep there arrived a distinguished-looking gentleman with flowers and a message asking to meet him and hand over the flowers and letter in person. Since the spouse would not wake up the tired husband, he waited patiently. He was under instructions not to give it to anyone. 'When I woke up, I found G.D. Birla's secretary waiting for me. He handed over the flowers and the envelope to me. I opened the envelope and there was a handwritten note from

## Delhi dosti

In the Delhi office there was great bonhomie between the seniors and juniors. They would meet over lunch and tea in the library – KCo had an excellent library – and, invariably, there would be discussions around different points of law and different cases. 'It was a great learning experience for the youngsters. Everybody was encouraged to participate fully with their knowledge of case laws and it was a very enriching experience'. *— Parag Tripathi.*

GD: "Om, you were right; I was wrong"'.

The Birla connection continues. Says Arun Jaitley: 'In more recent times, I have been briefed by NG whom I find work-oriented, focused and professionally very competent. So do I find many others in the firm. Most importantly, its client confidence is excellent; its clients have stood by the firm. NG has briefed me on the Birla-Lodha matter and I have handled dozens of cases briefed by Krishna Kumar, Malini, Kumkum and also by OP and Suman. I have worked with Pinto Khaitan and his son, Haigreve', says Mr Jaitley.

Not just the clients, the youngsters in Delhi loved working there. Kumkum Sen, currently heading Bharucha & Partners in Delhi, joined KCo, New Delhi, on July 5, 1983, 'less than two months after getting married and moving to a new city (from Calcutta)', thanks to the good offices of her Calcutta seniors and Justice Leila Seth, as she admits. She had, of course, known of the firm because even as a junior in the chamber of a renowned barrister in Calcutta, a junior brief from Khaitans was regarded as a very important step forward.

'I still remember the elevators of Himalaya House not working and walking up the entire flight of stairs to the seventh floor on a hot and humid morning. I also remember Bhagwati Babu making his rounds of the office on his Delhi visits, a serene smile on his face and, on one occasion, accompanied by a school-going Haigreve. There was great work from Indian business houses, such as Birla, Modi, Dalmia, Shriram and Thapar groups. The work ranged from textile, cement, heavy engineering, power, media and took us to the Supreme Court, Delhi High Court and other high courts, in Lucknow, Chandigarh, Allahabad and Jaipur. Largely, the work was high-quality litigation'.

It would have had to be interesting, for keeping her company were some sparkling colleagues. There was young Rajiv Endlaw (brought in by Ishwar Sahay) who was thorough with his work and became an independent arguing counsel in two to three years. There was Manmohan (son of the former Union minister Jagmohan) and the sparkling Sanjay Kaul, who trained with the company for seven years. These gentlemen are honourable justices now and must have enjoyed fascinating times. There was also Parag Tripathi, currently India's additional solicitor general and between them they dealt with some very exciting cases. Recalls Kumkum Sen: 'In those days of a closed economy, very few lawyers had the opportunity to do international arbitrations and corporate advisory work but both these skill sets were picked up by me in KCo'.

The serene smile the juniors saw on Bhagwati Babu's face must have hidden many a care and worry. Even when there was no litigation to fight, GD would manage to generate work. One day he called BP and said: 'Madho (M.P. Birla) ko woh ghar de dow (referring to a substantial Delhi property)'.

## Infallible Fali

There were some hilarious times as well, especially with Fali Nariman whose language could be unparliamentary at times. Everyone took him in their stride but not D.P. In a Hindalco matter, D.P. Mandelia had gone over for discussions with Fali Nariman who told DPM that he was talking 'through his hat'. The Birla boss, used to reverence, was shocked and was ready to leave and Om Khaitan had to save the situation because he knew that Mr Nariman had not meant anything personal. He charged back: 'You are talking through your hat and what Mr Mandelia is saying is correct' and the discussions continued. Once the dust had settled the solicitor told Fali Nariman that DPM was not used to such language; the contrite Fali apologized and all was forgotten.

The complexities around transfer of property in India were just as frustrating as some complicated legal battles. 'It took all of BP's grey hair and my not-so-grey hair at that time to structure a deal transferring the property to one of M.P. Birla's investment companies while also ensuring that he retained his personal stake in the property'.

These assignments, which KCo had been receiving from its early days, however, gave the firm perfect knowledge of realty laws of the land and how they had to be used to benefit the client. A former legal officer of Carritt Moran, Mr S. Guha Roy, recalls how the firm helped the tea-broking company to acquire its building from the Old Mission Church at 5, R.N. Mookerjee Road 'We wanted to buy and the church was happy to sell and my uncle, Subrata Roy Chowdhury, asked me to meet Mr RNJ at KCo to handle the matter. Sure enough, he found that the church had no clear right to the property; it had just been occupying it for some 400 years. Then came an elaborate process of establishing the church's property rights through creation of documents from whatever records existed, securing legal clearance for the sale of property. Only then did Carritt Moran get its own home at a prime location in the city'.

Home-building seemed to be a part of Khaitan's daily routine in more senses than one and in quite unexpected ways. Bhaskar Gupta asked his young assistant to wait in front of court no. 13 to pick up a brief from a Khaitan attorney. 'You will recognize her... she is tiny'. Was the barrister setting up his young junior for a date? He was, but he did not know it then; nor was that his intention. All he wanted was his junior to talk to the lady, fix up the conference, collect his formal brief and the case for opinion, whereafter the barrister would guide his junior on how to take the matter forward. Siddhartha Mitra had just joined the profession in 1983 and was a junior in the chambers of Bhaskar Gupta, who 'would be briefed by KCo, especially in constitutional law, indirect taxation and arbitration matters. He and his elder brother, Dipankar Gupta, also did a lot of opinion and advisory work for KCo and my first brief in the profession was from the firm', recalls Siddhartha.

'An opinion was to be given by Mr Bhaskar Gupta and me on a matter relating to penal proceedings initiated by the West Bengal Fire Services Act against Philips Carbon Black Limited. The question was whether certain licences were required to be obtained by the company for its carbon black factory in Durgapur. Our opinion was that the penalty provisions were not applicable and, eventually, the proceedings contemplated by the authorities were withdrawn'. What continued though were proceedings outside the purview of the matter. The lady who briefed Siddhartha was Roopa Mitra, a young attorney, encouraged to join the profession by Bhagwati Prasad Khaitan. The two chose to take the brief beyond what the seniors had advocated and press suit for a lifelong engagement. As Mr Pinto Khaitan was to state later: 'He (Siddhartha) is our jamai babu' and continued to treat the young barrister, who had married his colleague, with 'the greatest of affection', as Siddhartha recalls. Siddhartha has remained a counsel for the firm ever since.

Meanwhile, the group was expanding with the Birlas forever bringing in fresh matters as they went into joint ventures and collaborations. Many of these matters would also be handled by RKC under Bhagwati Babu's guidance; the latter, of course, treating him as a member of the Khaitan family. Over all these cases, the firm was building up a reputation for itself and as in the days of yore, bright youngsters were making their way to the firm for training. 'It was clear that the company was an excellent nursery for young lawyers. It had several distinctive and endearing traits: it gave young lawyers the courage to think independently; it filled their working lives with a sense of camaraderie – there was neither pettiness nor unhealthy competition; credit was

## Cess excess

Yadu Hari Dalmia remembers the Indian Cements case with a seven-judge bench in Tamil Nadu on a cess matter. 'This was around 1988-89 and we were facing a liability of some Rs 40 crore to Rs 50 crore and had lost the matter in the Madras High Court. This was a very complicated matter and Nilu Khaitan was asked to assist us. We did all our research and prepared a very good case, developed several arguments and at the end knew that we had a 50:50 chance. Mr Pinto Khaitan kept our spirits up saying that sometimes one's luck played a very important role in decisions. Generally, in tax matters courts do not like to strike down levies. This was a very complex matter and involved constitutional issues and centre/state powers. The matter first came up before a two-man bench featuring one judge who had ruled against the state government. The matter then came before a seven-judge bench. The question was whether tax on land would be levied with reference to royalty on minerals or the minerals themselves. The attorney general personally argued in this matter but, finally, we won the case'.

freely given and shared; information and knowledge were readily exchanged amongst peers and between the seniors and the juniors over lunch and tea; it taught the young lawyers how to handle clients; how to impress them. It also allowed young lawyers to choose the senior counsel to be briefed and, having allowed them to do so, the seniors would back them up. They would be protective of the youngsters as well and not really allow senior counsel to rough them up. It engendered a sense of belonging. Had there been no parting of ways with some senior partners, this would be a fantastic company because the people who were there then have all risen to positions of great eminence – some as senior counsel and others as judges', says Parag Tripathi.

There was a manner of dealing with clients, especially the finicky ones. Recalls Parag Tripagthi, 'I remember having just returned from Harvard with an LLM and joining the firm: I was called into O.P. Khaitan's chamber, where there was a foreign client sitting. He called me in and asked: "Have you not just returned from Harvard" and even before I said a bewildered "yes", he turned to them and said:

"These are the kind of boys who work with us all the time". As far as training was concerned, essentially, the idea was to throw the young lawyers at the deep end and get them to swim ashore. Recalls Parag Tripathi: 'One day Om Khaitan handed over some documents to me and made a firm statement: "Fera may yay nahi ho sakta hai (this cannot happen under Fera)". Then he added: "Tow kaisay ho sakta hai?(so how can it happen?)" and then advised me to get to work. Totally foxed but not wanting to look like a fool, I quietly went to his secretary, Uma Kant Gupta. I confessed that I had no idea about what exactly I had been told or what I was supposed to do. He said: "All I can say is that he means that mens rea is not always relevant if you are acting with bonafide intent. You may be in the clear". I wondered how that logic worked but was shooed off with a: "that is what I make of it…now you decide what you want to do".

'I worked on those lines and found the relevant judgment, prepared some opinion and then went up to Mr Khaitan meekly saying that I had done the job…He asked: "Ram Singh wala judgment liya na… buss jao". O.P. Khaitan recalls: 'My objective was never to allow the youngsters to get fixed ideas. Encourage them to do research, point out the feasibility of the exact opposite of what they were thinking to ensure that

The Delhi partners with Mr Pinto Khaitan. Standing (L-R): Bharat Anand, Sanjeev K. Kapoor, Ajay Bhargava, Manish Mishra, Asim Abbas, Rajat Mukherjee, Atul Shanker Mathur Sitting (L-R): Dr P.K. Agrawal, Vanita Bhargava, Pradip Kumar Khaitan, Gauri Rasgotra, Sharad Vaid, Manas Kumar Chaudhuri

they looked at the issue from all perspectives'. The world of law was complicated and twisted and such exercises allowed one to develop the ability to look at any question holistically.

There was the equally brilliant Ashutosh Patra. Parag Tripathi recounts Rajiv Endlaw's equally interesting experiences with him. 'Mr Patra called him in one day and asked him to do some research on a matter. He always gave us full freedom to make up our minds and Endlaw came up with an opinion where he held that though the Supreme Court had decided on the issue, in his (Endlaw's) view it was erroneous. Mr Patra heard him out and asked: "How long have you been in the profession?" The answer came "Two years". He nodded his head and then said: "Excellent, in two years you have overruled the Supreme Court". He then emphasized: "What the Supreme Court has held is the law!" Endlaw came out, having learnt a lesson... or had he?'

Mr Patra asked him to prepare an opinion on another matter... and Endlaw did his research and prepared an opinion and justified it by saying that the Supreme Court had held so in a similar matter. Mr Patra looked at him and asked: 'And what makes you feel that the Supreme Court ruling cannot be overruled?' The point again was to make the junior question an issue or a ruling from every angle. The idea was to provoke them, explains Mr Patra.

'It was an interesting matter where there was a provision in Companies Act that prevented the company from making certain investments without government permission. We told the client to go ahead and make the investment because under that section the word "prior" was not affixed to the approval. Mr Ashok Sen agreed with us and he argued the case in the court of Justice A.N. Sen of the Calcutta High Court, saying that the company would seek approval of the government but after the investment was made. The important thing, however, is that all arguments must be

The entrance to the plush KCo office on Barakhamba Road today

logical because if they are not, they would be overturned'.

Mr Patra was equally protective about his juniors. Once Parag Tripathi was asked to prepare a petition under Article 32, that would have to be moved urgently, and show it to a very senior counsel by 5 p.m. The counsel asked him to accompany him to Madras (where he had to attend to a very important Jayalalitha matter) and promised to finalize it in the aircraft. He slept in the aircraft, did not find time to see the junior in Madras and took a different return flight. Says Parag:'We met at the Delhi airport and I told him that we would have to file it the next day and there was no time for him to settle it. He said: "Shove it in". So the matter was filed. He was free the next afternoon around 12 or 12.30 and called us to settle the matter. I said we had filed the petition as he had asked us to. Then he started reading the petition and found fault with every line: "What is this?" he asked: "Idli? Dosa? When are you coming to the point?" He went on in this vein and, finally, dismissed it saying that there was nothing in the petition'.

Ashutosh Patra, who was quiet throughout, pointed out that there was the Naresh Shridhar Mirajkar judgment, AIR, 1967, page 1; by a nine-judge bench and the surprised senior counsel conceded: 'Ayee Ayee Yow; you know your law'. He then asked when the matter was coming up for hearing? On being told it was on the 21st, he jumped again: 'What? 21st? I am not there...' Mr Patra had had enough and said in his own mild manner: 'Sir, the other day I was with Fali and he said that he would not be able to come for a matter but that I could take some other donkey along'. One could hear a pin drop but then the senior counsel laughed aloud... 'Fali said that, did he? Smart fellow!' Then Mr Patra continued in his unabrasive manner: 'I agree that the draft could have been better but your junior drafted it and you have a cheque from KCo'. The point that Parag Tripathi was making was that KCo would not allow its juniors to be pushed around.

Leila Seth, still not a judge, had meanwhile moved to Delhi and continued her association with the firm. 'When I came to Delhi, once again I received much of my work from KCo and was, in fact, sitting in their office in Himalaya House, for which I paid no rent. While Umesh and Om were there, it was Pinto who had asked them to brief me. I worked closely with the lawyers there: A.K. Sen's daughter was there, T.M. Sen was there, Nilima Thakur joined too, P.V. Kapur was there and Nilu Babu, a very competent lawyer. It was a nice working environment. I had excellent relations with Nilu, he was very particular and very good and it was very helpful discussing cases with him. He was very good with his drafting too though he was never an arguing counsel. Pinto himself was very well respected though I did not have much dealing with him. They had very good counsel; for the bigger cases, of course, they had Manuda (S.S. Ray) with whom the firm had a long-standing relationship. Amongst the important cases that I remember was the Bennett Coleman case on the supply of newsprint'.

There was excitement galore for those in the Delhi office; sometimes with the complexities of the case and sometimes with the fun and games played by counsel. Ashutosh Patra was at the receiving end of Ashok Sen's antics. Ashok Sen was as brilliant as he was unpredictable. 'One would never know if he would appear in your matter or allow himself to be hijacked by another client. I took him to the Patna High Court on a matter but there was the rather sensational case of the Ananda Murti, Prabhat Ranjan Sarkar, who was not being granted bail. His people got hold of Ashok Sen and hijacked him to appear on the bail matter leaving us without a counsel. Our sales tax matter, in which we were seeking an exemption, got adjourned but Ashok Sen got bail for the Ananda Murti. When I told him that our matter had got adjourned to the next day he said that he could not stay back and went back to the judges seeking to be heard. The Patna High Court being strict on these matters said that it could not make an exception for Ashok Sen, who was an outsider, when it made no such allowances for the local lawyers. Making an exception for him would annoy the others. Mr Sen then argued: "Who is the outsider? I am from Bihar", he asserted and convinced everyone present that he was a local man. Then, turning to the rest of the lawyers in court he asked: "Do you consider me to be an outsider? Will you get offended if they take up my matter?" Of course, no one said anything and then he turned to the judges who, in deference to his tremendous stature, allowed him to argue the matter', recalls Mr Patra. Ashok Sen got KCo the exemption!

While the world of professional practices in manufacturing, governance and even law was making a mark in India, there still remained the business of the old-fashioned trust, especially when it came to family settlements and lawyers. Also, many professional relationships between the firm and clients have lasted over three generations as has that between KCo and the Dalmias. 'My personal relationship with them transcends the business relations that our companies have. I think BP and my father were classmates at Chidwa and he often came and stayed with us. All of us would regard him as a family elder and touch his feet when he came. My sister who got married into a Calcutta family considered Pinto Bhaiya as her own brother', says Yadu Hari Dalmia.

Not by law alone: The Khaitans took part in other joys of life. Rama Prasad Goenka seen here with NG at a Bengal Rowing Club function.

There are several leading entrepreneurs today, who trace their relationship with the Khaitans for several generations. Amongst them is Harsh Goenka, the elder son of R.P. Goenka: 'As a family, we have been close to the Khaitans for over four generations; my great grandfather, Sir Badridas Goenka, had known Bhagwati Khaitan. From him to my son, Anant, who is 29 and actively deals with KCo, it has been a relationship of more than four generations. Earlier, it was a matter of trust and confidence, which are a given today. Now, it is about how much knowledge one brings to the table and how good one is'. Harsh says that there are people from his office at KCo and people from the firm at his office 'all the time', though not necessarily for litigations. These interactions cover a range of issues of a personal or corporate nature.

The 'personal' level of interaction is in continuation with the times of Bhagwati Babu. Like his father, Pradip Kumar Khaitan's forte has also been around resolving family disputes because he enjoyed the confidence of various family members. 'In this space, I have assisted with succession planning of a number of families. This expertise in succession planning was acquired when I assisted in community services, working with people like Radha Krishan Kanoria or Kishorilal Dhandhania, who would do community service in sorting our family disputes. People need a lot of counselling when planning their succession; they need to provide for their children, for their charities, do some tax planning and the entire matter has to be handled with delicacy and tact', says Pinto Khaitan.

'Mr Pinto Khaitan has been a particularly close friend of my father who regards him very highly. To me, he is a revered uncle and whatever he says is almost like the law', says Harsh Goenka. 'What helps in our dealings is that the firm knows the history of each company in the group and while briefing it, we do not have to start from scratch; we can come straight to the point. The firm actually knows most of the nooks and corners of our office. Indeed, when we need to examine our own history and the people concerned have left, we ask KCo and they provide the necessary records because as lawyers, their documentation has been better'.

The bottom line is trust. Says the redoubtable Mr R.P. Goenka: 'I find them sincere and earnest. Today, if I do not consult Pinto Babu, I feel legal advice is not complete. Any knotty or complex problem, I seek his advice. You cannot get a more loyal client and I am proud of that'.

# FREEDOM FROM FERA

*There were some very distinguishing qualities about Bhagwati Prasad Khaitan. He was a lawyer who hated litigation and would always advise me to minimize litigation and ask us to resolve all issues between parties through dialogue and compromise. Not that he was shy of fighting deserving cases; but he would rather give dialogue a chance. At other times, he would argue, persuade and use every legitimate instrument to get the other side to come round.* — **Rajive Kaul**

The 1970s were ushering in an era of excitement. The state of Emergency was yet to come but Indian business was going places and Indian governance was being questioned. Socialist India was forcing Fera companies to dilute and that meant considerably enhanced scope for legal work. Pinto Khaitan recalls: 'Since Fera came into being and was being implemented, many sterling companies were being converted to rupee companies. Some sterling companies also chose to quit the country rather than dilute. I handled many such cases. Now the transactions have taken a full circle. Earlier foreigners divested; now they are coming back and investing in India'. Curiously, some companies that were multinationals then – and are under the public sector now – are being served by KCo. Indo-Burma Petro-

Facing page: The easing of the Fera restrictions meant a spirit of freedom; a spirit that KCo had engendered in its ranks; gruelling work is balanced by laughter and light-hearted fun: the Delhi KCo boys show how

## Kudos for clients

If B.M. Khaitan has kind words to say about his uncle and cousin, the sentiments are entirely reciprocated. Says Pinto Khaitan: 'BM's reliability, honesty and fair dealings won him the trust of his international partners. Indeed, the foreigners invited him to become partners or buy their business. They lowered their expected price and gave convenient terms so that he could accept because they believed that he was the right man to look after their interests and business. I had the honour of working for him and I learnt a lot from him. BMK knew how to encourage his people to give their best without flogging them. At times, in his kindness, he backed the wrong horse'.

leum (incorporated in 1908 and predating KCo) for instance that later became IBP and is currently merged with the Indian Oil Corporation. Says K.K. Banerjee, general manager: 'We have been working with KCo for a long time and they helped us immensely during our Indianization process and subsequent merger with IOL. Once Mr R.N. Jhunjhunwala got involved with us, he took charge. There were so many legacy issues, so many statutory compliances required, so many employee issues. Everything had to be done in a time-bound manner. The point is, the firm understood our concerns and timelines. Today, I work with them from Mumbai and have no problems on any score'.

PK's cousin, B.M. Khaitan, talks of two significant business acquisitions, which shaped the destiny of his group – experiences that were greatly satisfying. 'Macneill & Barry was to be merged with Williamson Magor & Company sometime in 1974. The Tatas owned 20 per cent, the other major shareholder was the Inchcape group. I was keen on buying the Tata holding, which would put me at par with Inchcape in the merged company but there were too many obstacles. We were endlessly discussing and arguing to no avail. Finally, I requested B.P. Khaitan to take charge. He went to Mumbai and met JRD, who put him on to Satarawala and Palkhivala. BP battled it out with the two Mumbai House stalwarts and, to everyone's surprise, in the end, took out a cheque book from his coat pocket and wrote out a cheque. He had left the Tatas with no option; they could not question the authenticity of a cheque from a leading law firm. Thereafter, I bought the Nizam's holding and became the major shareholder'.

From then on, 'it was Pinto who was advising me on all matters, particularly in the takeover of India Foils, and Metal Box. He showed his true colours in the Mcleod Russell takeover. The way Pinto structured the deal was simply brilliant. That deal is the cause of much of our success today'.

Even so, being in business in the 1970s and 1980s was very difficult: 'There were so many restrictions – MRTP, Fera – and it was Pinto who kept my radar on course through the turbulent years, always by my side, guiding, advising'. The firm has never quit his side since the mid-1950s. 'From the smallest to the most complicated, everything goes to KCo. Now Padam looks after our entire group. My sons are very comfortable with him, there is great rapport between them and we are very happy with the relationship'.

Yet another young man in business coming in close touch with BP around the early 1970s was Rajive Kaul. The executive chairman, Nicco Corporation, remembers a 'gentle, humble and distinguished personality' to whom he was introduced, when he came to wed his bride in 1971. Over the years the association became stronger because BP was a mongst the most revered members of the Nicco board that he joined in September 1949, the year Rajive was born. 'He must have been our advisor from the time the company was first conceived of as the National Insulated Cable Company of India Ltd'.

Friendship between the young director and the senior benefactor blossomed. 'I naturally got to know him much better as he was our senior-most director on whom all of us relied. He was a man of few words but when he spoke all

## Brother director

Rajive Kaul, who met the towering legal personality, BPK, at his wedding was to be beholden to him for more reasons than one. Five years after the initial introduction, the two were slated to serve on the board of the same company. Those were the days when all board appointments had to be cleared by the Company Law Board and somehow the name of Rajive Kaul was not getting cleared. It was B.P. Khaitan who used the good offices of KCo to get to the bottom of the mystery. Not only did he identify who was unhappy over the naming of the 27-year-old to the board but overcame all opposition from some senior members of the company to his becoming a director of the company.

## Raising Haigreve

'My grandfather has been a great influence on my life', declares Haigreve Khaitan. 'His strongest quality was that he was always calm and collected and I never saw him lose his temper. Even, when he was in great pain towards the end of his life; he never was upset. I was the favourite grandchild and since our birthdays were around the same time; his birthday on July 9 and mine July 13, the birthdays would get celebrated together. BP said: never run after money; do not work for money… and I never saw him work for money. Since, our father had little time to spare, grandfather gave me a lot of his time'.

Haigreve came closer to his father when they started working together. As children, he and his siblings would help PK with his work at home…making photocopies, running errands and 'come to office on Sundays because he would be working over weekends too. We would be given Thums up, muri (puffed rice) and sandesh (a Bengal sweet). That was how he bribed us', recalls Haigreve.

Between BP and PK, a first-class job was accomplished in terms of raising the third-generation Khaitan

of us listened. His advice and wise counsel was invariably the last word on the subject', says Rajive Kaul. There must have been an especially soft corner for Rajive in his heart for Nicco was the last company whose directorship he gave up. 'He would tell me that he wanted to leave and had already left other boards and I would go to his house to persuade him to continue. He would argue that he was getting old and that we did not really need him and I would tell him how useful his advice always was and he stayed on till August 8, 1990!' says Rajive. 'Throughout, he served with exceptional sagacity. I remember a rather interesting import case, when Nicco imported lead from Russia and was asked to pay an unreasonable duty. BP took the matter up with the government and got the unjust demand revoked. For me, he will always be a friend, philosopher and guide but the personal trait that made him stand out was his humility'.

Justice Ruma Pal too recalls the supreme grace with which Bhagwati Babu would conduct himself: 'I recall a tall person with a shock of white hair. He spoke so softly and yet commanded such respect. Every action, even pulling a chair, was gracious. I also remember the excellent meals that we had with him; once at the Bengal Rowing Club when we had an excellent sit-down meal with a full silver service. It was probably his birthday'.

BP's diverse interests brought him in touch with a host of interesting people. Retired Justice D.R. Dhanuka recalls interacting with him closely when there was a move in Mumbai to do away with the dual system that involved the client paying three sets of fees: the lawyer's fees for the senior and junior counsel and the solicitor's fee. The government wanted a committee to examine how the system was working in Calcutta and Justice Dhanuka travelled to Calcutta with the committee, interacting with the likes of Bhagwati Babu and P. D. Himatsingka. 'Siddhartha Ray was the Chief Minister of West Bengal then and we met him and were very warmly taken care of by BP and Sita Ram Jhunjhunwala. Later, I met him again at Madhusudan More's daughter's wedding. Post-retirement I have done some arbitration work with KCo, Mumbai'. This is the office headed by BP's grandson, who believes that his grandfather was amongst the greatest influences on his life.

Managing legal cases, growing complex by the day, might have been meant for men of sterner stuff but women were making a mark as lawyers and judges. Also, cases had multi-state implications that meant escorting barristers to courts across the land. Om Khaitan recalls a very important matter around determination of the sugar cane area allotted to a sugar mill for Pratappur Sugar of Kanoria Chemicals. The area was partly given to the Thapars. Mr Shyam Sundar Kanoria had come to BP for filing a writ petition, who handed the matter over to Om. Siddhartha Shankar Ray and Dipankar Gupta were briefed and the matter was to be filed in Patna. 'In those days the Patna High Court was very strict about granting stays in such matters while the Allahabad High Court was more amenable', says Om. 'The dilemma was that while the land allotted to our clients was in Bihar, the plant itself was in Uttar Pradesh. I suggested to S.S. Ray that we file in Allahabad, to which he pointed out that Allahabad would not have jurisdiction. Yet we decided to take a chance and prepared two identical petitions. The three of us then went to Allahabad by train. I remember playing bridge to while away our time, creating a dummy for the fourth player… While playing, S.S. Ray asked what was up my sleeve? Why were we moving Allahabad first? That was when I told him that we might be able to get a stay on merits in Allahabad and it would be an ex-parte decision because the opposing side would not expect us to file there. If we did not get it on the jurisdiction issue, we would withdraw and go to the Patna High Court with the Allahabad High Court order on the stay on merits'.

## Encounter with English law

There were cases big and small: Indian Fibres Ltd was an interesting litigation that C.M. Ghorawat handled on behalf of the RPG Group. In June 1984, the company exported guargum (used to make ice cream) to an English company. The consignments of guargum were allegedly contaminated with pesticides and rejected by the ice cream manufacturers, Lyons Maid. A claim for damages ensued. KCo succeeded before the Calcutta High Court in getting the claim of the English company struck down but the English court (Chancery Division) declined to follow the Calcutta High Court judgment and allowed the petition of the English company to extend time to commence arbitration proceedings. The letter written by KCo defending its clients Indian Fibres was, however, cited before the Chancery Division and was quoted extensively in the judgment delivered by it on November 22, 1985 (reported in LexisNexis under the cause title: Arthur Branwell & Company Ltd vs Indian Fibres Ltd).

The legal team was taking a chance but a winning one it proved to be. The other side moved on the jurisdiction issue and 'we promptly withdrew and told the judge that we were happy to withdraw. That was a Friday and the judge said that he would release it on Monday. We had tickets to Patna and, when we moved the high court there, the court said that it needed confirmation that the matter had indeed been withdrawn in Allahabad. Telephone lines being what they were in those days, it was almost impossible to get the lawyer who was in court in Allahabad handling the withdrawal. After great difficulty I got him over a very poor connection and got, what I thought was, a confirmation that the case had been withdrawn. I told Manuda that I had confirmation. He went to court and argued the matter and we got a stay. He went home to rest and well after that I got a call from the lawyer from a clear line and he said that what he was trying to say was that the judge did not sit that day and the case would be withdrawn the next day.

'I did not know what to do. I tried to get in touch with S.S. Ray but Triloki, his assistant, had instructions not to disturb him. So I called up Mrs Ray, who was with him and told her that Manuda would have to be woken up in a matter of great urgency. She did so and when he heard what had happened S.S. Ray was furious. However, we decided to go to the judge's house and explained what had happened. The judge respected S.S. Ray's position and agreed to let the stay continue'.

The 1970s also marked the beginning of the firm's relationship with the Goenkas and Mr R.P. Goenka. 'He was a leader in industry and his association brought the firm to a new plane. With the growth of industry and commerce, many new business houses emerged and the firm was fortunate to continue to enjoy their confidence and support. Their support led to Haigreve attaining maturity in the profession and success', says Pinto Khaitan. Mr R.P. Goenka himself

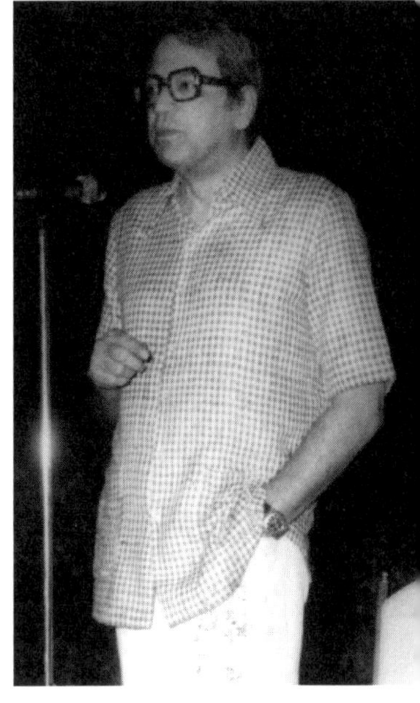

Manuda to the Khaitans, S.S. Ray would even allow himself to be disturbed at odd hours if there was urgent work. Seen here speaking at a KCo Delhi party

recalls: 'B.M. Birla asked me to meet B.P. Khaitan, when I was one of the two arbitrators for Surajmull Nagarmull and B.M. Birla was the umpire. I took B.P. Khaitan's guidance to resolve the matter'. As far as the next generation is concerned, it was not till the 1970s that RPG came in touch with Bhagwati Prasad's son and soon transferred all his business to KCo. No better testimonial is required.

However, if BP's son was firmly taking charge, it was not so much due to the pedigree but because of competence. Recalls C.K. Dhanuka: 'Pinto Babu had helped with the negotiations for the sale of Jaipur Polyspin to L.N. Jhunjhunwala. He wrapped up the deal for me and we managed to sell at the right time and the right price. Had we not done so at that time, we would have lost heavily. Pinto Babu not only concluded the deal for us but he did so at a time when I thought that we had lost the deal. He restored the matter through some very smart negotiations and moves and, finally, salvaged it'.

In the early 1970s, Pinto Khaitan was to recruit a very interesting young man, who had just obtained his Master of Laws (LLM) from the Delhi University. His scholarship was obvious from the curriculum vitae presented. Pinto Khaitan's style was, of course, a bit different from that of his father's but BP was dealing with uncut diamonds; his son was dealing with processed carbon. The discussion was unambiguous: 'You either know the law or you do not. If you do, go ahead and do what you have to do; if you do not, learn what the law is and do what you have to do. There is no other option'. There was a lesson no. 2. 'If you do not understand something, ask as many times as you need to. Once you have understood the matter, there is no room to repeat the question'. The new recruit had a third instruction; 'KCo has a good library in Calcutta; look after it and the legal research'.

## Protecting the boss

BPK's habit of sticking his neck out for his friends had rubbed off on his son too and Pinto Khaitan found himself at the receiving end of a rather unpleasant litigation featuring a Ramananda Agarwal over Richardson Hooghly Holdings Ltd, an English company whose shares, in the Indian company, he and the Poddars, were keen to acquire. Permission to acquire shares in an English company meant clearances from both the Reserve Bank of India and the Bank of England. Both had given their permission but the terms were at variance and the deal did not fructify. Meanwhile, the Poddars gained possession of the company, much to the angst of Ramananda Agarwal. There were unhappy allegations and KCo agreed to represent the foreign company in the numerous litigations and proceedings, ranging from those at the Alipore Munsiff Court to the Calcutta High Court and the Supreme Court. Worse, everything seemed to be going against the client. At that point Mr Pinto Khaitan requested C.M. Ghorawat to handle the matter.

C. M. Ghorawat: handling matters for the boss

Having read up on the innumerable cases going on, the principal question that pointed itself out to CMG was whether the RBI permission that Agarwal had originally obtained to buy the shares, was still good because Ramananda Agarwal had since passed away and his heirs were conducting the litigation. That meant another round of reading but the persistent lawyers found his answer in an unreported Supreme Court judgment, which laid down the proposition that a statutory permission is personal to the person to whom it is granted; it does notsurvive the death of the person; it dies with the death of the person. 'The point taken was that the RBI permission to purchase shares was granted to Ramananda Agarwal. Upon his death, the said permission also lapsed and did not survive and his heirs were not entitled to the benefit of the said permission for purchase of shares in Richardson Hooghly Holdings Ltd'. Matters started turning around miraculously since then; only it was not magic: it was the knowledge of legal precedence that held sway. 'Our contentions also found support in a subsequent Supreme Court judgment in the case of Needle Industries (India) Ltd vs Needle Industries Newey (India) Holding Ltd reported in AIR 1981 SC 1298'. As CMG went about winning every case thereafter, the heirs of Ramananda Agarwal ultimately proposed to settle the matter out of court and, accordingly, the matter was set at rest. The terms of settlement were filed in the Supreme Court, the Calcutta High Court and various other courts, which resulted in closure of all the proceedings.

Indeed, he was placed in the library itself. Today, questions, some outlandish in nature, around a piece of legislation or a judgment or notification or legal proposition, from any office of KCo can be referred to this not-so-young-any-more man and the oracle does not disappoint. C.M. Ghorawat (CMG) joined KCo in November 15, 1972, and believes that the past 39 years have been 'a pleasant, gratifying and an enriching experience'. His legal mind has been allowed to travel over the entire canvas of law as it has evolved and experienced some rather dramatic moments in courts featuring the country's top jurists, made possible by sheer reading of legal developments.

It was around October 1977. It was at about 4 in the afternoon and leading counsel, Siddhartha Shankar Ray's furrowed brows suddenly smoothened out; his eyes glistened with the sense of excitement and, despite being present before a division bench of the Patna High Court comprising Chief Justice K.B.N. Sinha and Justice B.S. Singh, there was this involuntary exclamation that attracted the attention of the judges. Sitting behind him were his barrister-at-law spouse, Maya Ray, M.J.Z. Mowla, then Bata's senior law officer and a young colleague from

## Manager as occupier

This was one provision of the Factories Act that had considerable inconvenience value: the 'occupier' of a factory, for purposes of compliance with the provisions of the Act, had to be a director, which was quite a problem for directors, who did not usually stay at the factory. The Inspector of Factories insistence in the matter led to numerous cases in the country and it was KCo's engagement with the issue in the late 1970s over a Orient Paper Mill matter that brought matters to a head because the Chief Inspector of Factories refused to renew the Orient Paper licence for its Orissa plants unless the renewal was sought in the name of the directors as opposed to the factory manager. Finally, Justices R.N. Misra and B.K. Ray of the Orissa High Court held that a person who is not a director can be nominated occupier. Hundreds of firms and their directors breathed a sigh of relief!

The Kolkata senior management team
Sitting (L-R): O.P. Jhunjhunwala, N.G .Khaitan,P.L. Agarwal, R.N. Jhunjhunwala, Padam Khaitan, C.M. Ghorawat

Standing (L-R): Roopa Sheth Mitra, Arvind Jhunjhunwala, Aniket Agarwal, Ajay Gupta, G.S. Asopa, Kusum Dadoo, Arvind Baheti

KCo, who had just passed on a judgment for him to peruse.

This was a Bata India excise matter, challenging an explanation appended to an exemption notification. The opposing counsel, a senior Central government advocate of 30 years' standing was quoting a Gujarat High Court judgment (Jamnadas vs C.L. Nangia, reported in AIR 1963 Guj. 215) that was making mincemeat of S.S. Ray's submissions. The team of S.S. Ray, Dipankar Ghosh and S.K. Kapur, had done their homework but the Gujarat judgment had not occurred to them. Would Manuda lose this one? It certainly seemed so till a magical document was thrust into his hands. Years of legal research and library work had paid off for C.M. Ghorawat, whose mind raced to the Supreme Court judgment that had clearly overruled the Gujarat one. Would the young man dare to presume that his illustrious seniors were not aware of the latest judgment? Hesitatingly, he located the judgment and passed on the law report to Mrs Ray who considered it, flashed her most happy smile; and nodded her head, encouraging the young man to pass it on to her husband. Siddhartha Ray could not suppress his glee.

'What seems to be the matter, Mr Ray?' the Chief Justice asked. An apologetic S.S. Ray said: 'My Lord, I do not normally interrupt the opposing counsel but he is perhaps unaware that the judgment that he is so assiduously quoting as a clincher has been overruled'. Saying so, he handed over the law report AIR 1970 S.C. 755 (Hansraj vs H.H. Dave) containing Supreme Court judgment in the matter. The judges considered it and 'within five minutes the matter was over and decided in favour of Bata India Ltd', recalls C.M. Ghorawat. It was not an easy matter to connect the two judgments for the names of the parties involved had changed and the latest judgment was couched in difficult legalese but not enough to escape the attention of a studious examiner of the law. Bata, already a client, was to be a client many times over for KCo.

Even as CMG was being eased into high-profile cases, so were other young barristers such as Sudipto Sarkar. Amongst the earliest ones that they both handled, as CMG assisted Pinto Khaitan, were 13 arbitration matters featuring Port Shipping Company Ltd, a goods transporting company, against Hindustan Steel (now Sail). Mrs Hansa Kumari Deb Burman was the senior counsel, assisted by a very young Sudipto Sarkar, who had just started his practice as chamber junior of Mrs Deb Burman. The matter related to HSL's claims for shortage of iron ore and steel material loaded in Port Shipping barges and the claims from Port Shipping for hire charges for the barges. Not only did KCo win every matter but CMG had begun to sink his teeth into practical law.

At about the same time, Pinto Khaitan asked him to help him with various matters of India Steamship Company pertaining to its litigations with Stelp & Leighton litigated in London and the subsequent Foreign Exchange Regulation

## When directors are liable

Bhaskar Sen recalls a 1973 case for which he was briefed by Pinto Khaitan to appear on behalf of Vishnu Hari Dalmia: 'I had to shift to Delhi for the case that was tried in the special court there. Kundan Lal Arora, senior advocate, was my leader and the matter continued for several months. For me, it meant moving to Delhi with my wife and son in 1973. Relations with the solicitors were almost filial but my son missed my mother. So Pinto brought him to Calcutta to meet his grandmother and brought him back'.

The case was around vicarious liability of directors of a company in respect of offences committed. Today there are many judgments on the directors' liabilities and responsibilities but in those days there were virtually none. Dipankar Ghosh's arguments were based on a judgment in the 1925 matter of City Equitable Fire Insurance Company Ltd (Chancery Division 407), which followed a 1901 judgment of Dovey versus Cory (appeal case 477). The hearings were held at the Tees Hazari Court.

The court, however, held that the directors would be responsible only if they played a role and would be vicariously liable only in respect of specific statutory offences of the company and Vishnu Hari Dalmia was acquitted.

Act proceedings arising therefrom. Stelp & Leighton were freight-forwarding agents of India Steamship, who would collect freight and were required to submit accounts, which they failed to do. Instead, they alleged fraud against India Shipping to evade Indian taxes. KCo briefed Fali S. Nariman, Dipankar Gupta (still not a senior) and S.K. Kapur (yet to secure his senior gown) at different stages of the proceedings. Stelp & Leighton's position was not accepted by the English high court and the company eventually went into liquidation. The Fera proceedings, an offshoot of the London proceedings, before the Fera board, exonerated the client. 'We won in all the matters', says CMG.

Meanwhile, P. L. Agarwal was coming into his own and S.K. Kapur has the most amusing stories to tell about him. 'PL must, of course, be specially mentioned if only because we shared so many whiskies together and neither of us is either ashamed or embarrassed to admit it. He is a gem of a lawyer and a friend. I recall his taking me to Madhya

Pradesh to do a case. We flew to Delhi at midnight and he put Biswarup Gupta and myself into a non-air-conditioned third-class compartment, and took us sitting throughout the night to some unmentionable place for a hearing on an arbitration proceeding the following day. The clients wanted a stay that we successfully obtained. I have grave reservations if the fees for that were ever paid'.

S.K. Kapur has another interesting story, as much a commentary on the times as on the firm: 'I recall PL and I, with the whole team from Hindustan Motors, headed by the late Dipankar Ghosh, landing at the Mumbai airport at

## P stands for Perry

It was P.L. Agarwal at his Perry Mason best. Law breakers were getting smarter over the years; so was crime detection. In the 1970s KCo found itself immersed in a murder mystery. The Jaipuria family of Calcutta sought its counsel to defend its son-in-law against a charge of killing his elder brother and two others. The deaths occurred in Assam, where the two siblings were embroiled in a dispute over the encroachment by the older brother on the younger one's tea estate in Nowgang. This was headlined as the Sutodiya Barapani Triple Murder Case and P.L. Agarwal, quite a rookie then was called upon to handle the matter.

The story as pieced together by the police was simple: the accused allegedly waylaid the car in which his elder brother was travelling with his friends; shot all the occupants dead with his pistol; drove the car into the Barapani Lake near Shillong; dumping the vehicle and its dead occupants in the lake. It so transpired that the car did not quite drown completely and one of the occupants was not quite dead. The survivor managed to come out and testified!

It was now time for KCo, led by P.L. Agarwal to bring to bear the latest technology on the investigation and establish through fingerprinting, forensic and ballistics reports that the police conclusions were too simplistic and, therefore, incorrect. It took great expertise to establish the over-zealousness of the police; the tampering with a lot of evidence and misreading the ballistics reports vis-à-vis the distance and direction of fire. The lower courts, not entirely savvy with the latest in technology, convicted the accused but the High Court reversed the finding, giving the accused the benefit of doubt, which was later upheld by the Supreme Court. Young PL's performance is something that his seniors talk about even today.

3.30 a.m. Our flight was 14 hours late. The arbitration for which we had gone was to take place the following morning. We went into what is now the Trident and were told that there was a 45-minute waiting line even in the coffee shop. The next afternoon, after the first session of arbitration, the whole team trooped into the French restaurant to which PL insisted on taking us but Dipankar Ghosh took one look at the menu, saw nothing on it cost less than Rs 150 and said: "At these prices, I cannot digest anything at all and I am going to the coffee shop". The whole team had to follow'.

Mintu Sen recalls working with P.L. Agarwal on several matters, including 'a very important one featuring the JK Corp Ltd in the Orissa High Court. The year was 2001; we had to go to Orissa regularly and PL along with Roopa Mitra from KCo would accompany us. My junior in the case was Siddhartha Mitra. Essentially, we were praying for sanction of the high court for a scheme of compromise/arrangement between J.K. Corp and its lenders, bankers and shareholders and the Central Paper Mills Limited and its shareholders. The objective was to restructure J.K. Corp through a restructuring of its debts, including transfer of its paper division to the Central Paper Mills. What seemed to be an easy case turned out to be a long-drawn one with the foreign bankers to JK objecting. The scheme was finally sanctioned after a two-year battle by both the Orissa and the Gujarat High Courts'.

O.P. Jhunjhunwala, son of the ailing Sita Ram Jhunjhunwala – who fell seriously ill at the peak of his career – recalls the days of the Naxalite movement with delays in the Calcutta University examinations and more delays in publishing the results. The young man was desperate to get the article for attorneyship because of his father's illness. 'With no other option, I made an application to the Calcutta High Court, stating the cause of delay, to allow me to become articled for attorneyship prior to the publication of the university results'. The application was considered by the full court meeting of the high court judges. All, save one, permitted him to get articled before graduation. 'It was a historical resolution by the Calcutta High Court, which helped me save a precious year'.

There was more drama in the offing. While he was doing his articleship, the Advocate's Act was suddenly amended and the practice of attorneyship was abolished from December 31, 1976. That was another shock but the Chief Justice of the Calcutta High Court, Sankar Prasad Mitra, rectified the situation by permitting the article clerks at that time to take the final examination before the amendment came into force on January 1, 1977. 'It was a blessing in disguise and I worked very hard and qualified as an attorney-at-law in December 1976. Ours was the last batch of qualified attorneys. The attorneyship examination has since been abolished by the Calcutta High Court, original side'.

As far as the practitioners of the law were concerned, many of the present-day leaders of the bar were getting into the profession by the 1970s and KCo, as leading solicitors, were picking up the sharpest. Recalls Sudipto Sarkar: 'I was enrolled in 1970, started serious practice in 1973 and got my first brief from the Khaitans soon after they saw me in action in a case when I was appearing against them. My cross-examination of their witness must have impressed them for, thereafter, they started sending me briefs. I started working with KCo when my fees were no more than Rs 34 and the firm was very active in Calcutta. Over the years, I have been very close to the company and its senior partners and, even today, if there is a personal matter, KCo are my solicitors. I continue to enjoy a warm relationship with the seniors', says Sudipto Sarkar.

'I also appeared in the Hooghly Ink matter; a company in which Mr Pinto Khaitan was a director. It was a company matter in which R.C. Nag and S.P. Sen were my seniors.

KCo chose the sharpest from the emerging ranks of young lawyers and barristers. Sudipto Sarkar (C) with Subrata Roy Chowdhury (R). Justice Kania and Vishwanath Vajpayee former Chairman, Bar Council of India at a KCo event

Hooghly Ink was a foreign company that, post Fera, had to offload its shares. We were representing the foreign company. The Agarwala group (Arun Agarwala of Christian Mica, a company that has since gone into liquidation) had entered into an agreement to buy those shares but the foreigners did not want to sell to them. They had asked Pinto Khaitan to be on the board and the Agarwalas had brought about several allegations against the company and against Pinto Khaitan personally'. It was a matter before Justice Salil K. Roy Chowdhury, featuring allegations of oppression of the majority by the minority along with mismanagement and misappropriation of funds and other issues. 'I had to defend Pinto Khaitan and ultimately our clients got control of the company. Interestingly, the court also decided that in a corporate mismanagement action the court could give relief to the respondent, which it did in this case'.

Not only were clients and lawyers warming up to BP's son; so were his partners. Recalls Padam: 'I qualified in

1976. Pinto Khaitan was then the managing partner. Since I only handled litigation earlier, it meant going for conferences to senior counsel's chambers every evening. My father sometimes gave me a lift in his self-driven car but that was not quite convenient. I asked Pinto Khaitan if the office could allot me a car because it was difficult to manage with my father's car and then I forgot about it. Getting a car could be quite a chore in those days; Ambassadors were not so difficult to get but a Fiat meant a substantial wait. I was pleasantly surprised one morning to be woken up by our help who said that the driver from no. 52 (where Pinto Khaitan stayed) was at our house. I asked him what the matter was and he said that Pinto Babu had sent the key. "To what?", I asked. "To the new Fiat", he said. Lo and behold there was a brand new Fiat for me. I quickly got into a shirt, first went to the temple and then called Pinto Khaitan. He had booked the car for himself but was happy to give it to me!'

Recipient of his cousin's affection: Padam Khaitan (in the cockpit here) got his first Fiat from PK

Senior counsel talk of PK with affection: 'I remember working with Pinto both for and against him. In the Jalan family dispute it was a matter of both money and ego and finally it was the second generation that settled the matter. The method and manner of the settlement was the subject of many conferences with Pinto at S.B. Mookherjee's house', says Mintu Sen. A lot of other people too were appreciative of Pinto Khaitan and his team: Mr P.T.J. Knaapen, chairman of Bata India, amongst others. The regimes of V.P. Singh as Finance Minister and, subsequently, the Prime Minister of India, were not kind to Bata India that found various proceedings initiated against it. Some six separate show-cause notices for alleged Fera violations were issued to Bata and its chairman, managing director, other directors and officers. Mr Pinto Khaitan was guiding the matters, some of which were won before the Fera board and some came to less fortunate conclusions.

CMG, who was handling the matters, recalls: 'During

Senior lawyers and associates, KCo, Kolkata office. The library holds the key to many a KCo success

a conference with Mr R.N. Bajoria and Mr S.K. Bagaria in New Delhi, I came upon a Mumbai High Court judgment in the case of Shree Kanti Oil Mill, reported in Mumbai Court Reporter, a copy of which we needed. The matter was of such great import that the company flew down Mr D.N. Banerjee, senior law officer, to Mumbai to get a copy, which was just as well because it helped in getting one matter decided in favour of Bata, first before the Fera board and thereafter before the Calcutta High Court'. All the proceedings were taken to the Calcutta High Court in second appeals (judgments are reported in AIR, Company Cases, Company Law Journal).

A division bench presided over by Justice Ruma Pal said: 'The important point considered and decided was that even when penalty gets mandatorily attracted the moment there is violation of the provisions of Fera, the adjudicating authority still has and ought to exercise its discretion and consider the conduct of the party while deciding the quantum of the penalty. If the violation was unintentional and there was no mens rea involved, no penalty should be imposed'. Says CMG: 'KCo won in all the matters and Bata India was exonerated of the charges and allegations'. An appreciative Mr Knaapen complimented Mr Pinto Khaitan on the firm's defence of Bata.

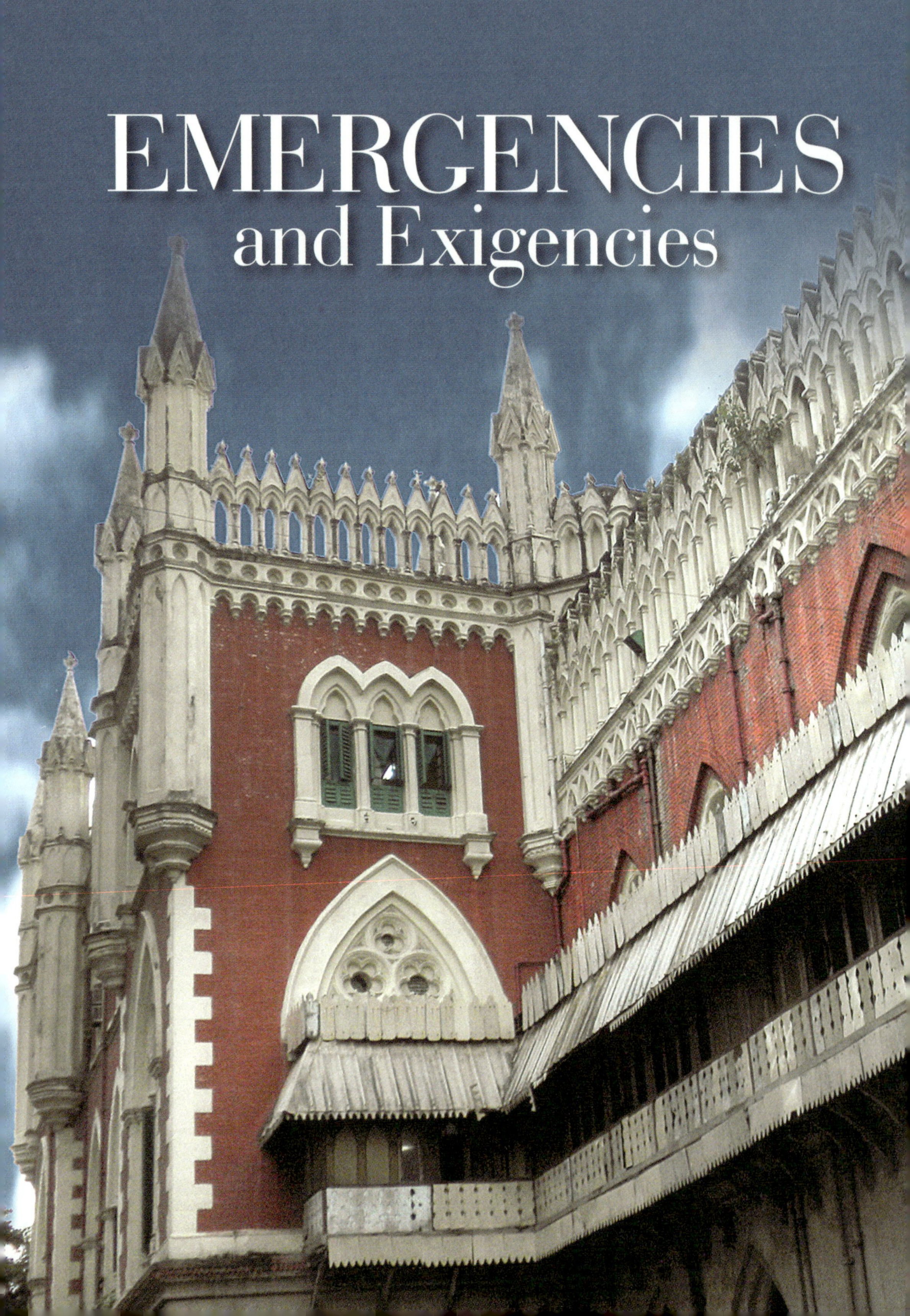
EMERGENCIES
and Exigencies

*It was Thursday, July 5, 1979. There was an inconspicuous group making an appearance in the court of Hon'ble Mr Justice T.K. Basu; traditionally being (the interlocutory court) no. 12, on the first floor of the Calcutta High Court. Hon'ble Justice Basu, who suffered from vertigo, could not sit on the dais. Instead, he had the lower bench, along with his officers. Mr Ram Niranjan Jhunjhunwala, appearing in his capacity of an advocate, made an oral application seeking permission to move an urgent court application before the lunch recess. Justice Basu asked what the urgency was about and RNJ said that he wished to move an application on behalf of his client, former Prime Minister Indira Gandhi, to which the judge reacted with a rather sharp tone: 'The name of your client does not impress this court. That is no ground for urgency'.*

A chastened RNJ submitted that the urgency was occasioned by a radiogram message that his client had been served with by the special court of Justice M.L. Jain, Delhi High Court, communicated to Indira Gandhi in Darjeeling through the superintendent of police. The former Prime Minister, holidaying there with her family, had been asked to appear before the Special Court at Patiala House, on Monday, July 9, 1979, to be tried for offences on account of 'Emergency excesses' under the Special Courts Act, 1979.

RNJ told the judge that he and his client had worked through the previous night, preparing a writ petition under Article 226 of the Constitution of India that was still to be finalized and there would be no time left if he was unable to move the application on that day. Justice Basu nodded his head, acceding to the prayer. 'Come before one o'clock', said the judge. It was 1 p.m. and the papers were still not ready. The formalities of taking the oath commissioner from the high court to the Park Hotel, where Mrs Gandhi was staying with Maneka Gandhi, Sanjay and little Varun had to be completed. RNJ had taken the oath commissioner, Jeeban Babu and his office clerk, Sital Ganguly, to the meeting where waiting for them were a lawyer, Madan Bhatia and Kamal Nath. Indira Gandhi was going through the petition that she had been asked to sign in various places. 'Sub theek hai tow (everything all right)?' she checked with RNJ, who assured her: 'Ji (yes)'. For once the lady signed without demur: 'Indira Nehru Gandhi'. Jeevan Babu promptly pointed out that her name in the petition was Indira Gandhi and that she should sign accordingly. Once again she obliged.

The team wrapped up the work and could report to the high court only post-lunch. Sailen Dutta, RNJ's junior, had got the court's permission for a post-lunch submission. The court may have been indulgent but other problems remained. Who would represent the former Prime Minister given that the charges of Emergency excesses of 1975 were still fresh in public memory? Which counsel would take the case up? Most senior counsel had declined the brief for no one wanted to get dragged into any political controversy for a case that they suspected would not fetch a reasonable remuneration. With counsel refusing what they thought was a thankless job, RNJ was in a fix

The Radiogram Message No.1148/3/1/78-SIU (SIB-1) dated 2.7.79 from S.P, SIB -1, SIU, CBI, 5, New Delhi, addressed to Superintendent of Police Darjeeling. A copy, forwarded to Indira Gandhi read: SPL Court No.2 has issued a notice under chapter XXXVI of Code of Criminal Procedure requiring the presence of Smt. Indira Gandhi, formerly Prime Minister of India in person or by pleader in his Court on 9.7.79 at 10 a.m. at Patiala House, New Delhi in Case No.1 of 1979 State vs. Smt Indira Gandhi and others. Smt. Indira Gandhi has been away from Delhi. According to her personal staff she is presently staying at Darjeeling. Request intimate Smt Gandhi about the issue of notice by the Spl. Court and signal action taken immediately.
Dated - Darjeeling the 3rd July, '79.
IMMEDIATE
GOVERNMENT OF WEST BENGAL
Office of Superintendent of Police
Darjeeling.
Memo No.8043/7-79. Dated, Darjeeling the 3rd July 1979
Copy forwarded to:-
Shrimati Indira Gandhi
Former Prime Minister of India,
Richmond Hill, Darjeeling
For Information
Sd /-R.C.Sharma
Superintendent of Police, Darjeeling

and running from pillar to post. He finally persuaded Subrata Roy Chowdhury to appear but not without trepidation that the normally reliable counsel may not turn up. The sentiments against the case were very real. Not surprisingly, Subrata Roy Chowdhury, waiting in the corridor outside the courtroom no.12 to ascertain the mood of the judge, pushed RNJ to go inside: 'Tumi Maa Durga Durga bole aage jao. Petition present koro, judger mood dekho. Ami courter baire aachi, cholo na dekhi. (You go in, taking Ma Durga's name, present the petition and check out the judge's mood. I am waiting outside. Let us see what happens)'. So RNJ found himself alone placing the application and facts before the judge. 'It was an extremely tense situation for me as I moved the application and placed the facts and legal proposition that the infirmity of the order lay in clubbing together Emergency and non-Emergency offences and offenders, which amounted to treating unequals as equals and did not have a nexus with the object of the Special Courts Act'.

THE HINDUSTAN TIMES

Laldenga held in Capital; Mizo Front is banned

Zero hour on night of July 11

He was for 'non-Mizos' expulsion

Skylab death risk minimal

Youth speeds up wedding, woman deserts husband

Police stir to dominate session

Socialist consensus to remain in Janata

Facilities, perks raised for BSF

Congress-I civil stir from Oct. 2

All Cong-I MPs want Sanjay in party

Mrs Gandhi alleges statute violation



*Hindustan Times* bottomspread on the Indira Gandhi case

The argument was that it was contrary to the opinion of the Supreme Court of India expressed in the presidential reference made to it under Article 143 (1) of the Constitution of India on the validity of the provisions of the Special Courts Bill. 'The point appealed to the judge who thought that the petitioner had a good prima facie case for an interim order for staying the notice and the proceedings proposed to be initiated thereunder'. While all this was going on, Subrata Roy Chowdhury quietly entered the courtroom and, prompted by the judge, joined in making submissions. Finally, Justice Basu asked the court officer – the assistant registrar – to take down: 'Rule nisi as prayed for issued, interim order of stay as prayed for granted for a week only. Returnable next Thursday (July 12). Petitioner's advocate to serve copy of the application and the order forthwith on the respondents and the Central government's solicitors'.

Recalls RNJ: 'As soon as we came out of the courtroom Subrata Roy Chowdhury created a high voltage atmosphere with the press reporters'. They surrounded the two counsel, as SRC briefed the press with his typical flourish. The legal reporter of the *Statesman* wrote on July 6: 'Special Courts to show cause: On an application moved by Mr Subrata Roy Choudhury, on behalf of Mrs Indira Gandhi, Justice T.K. Basu of Calcutta High Court on Thursday directed the Union of India and Special Courts (Nos. 1 and 2) to show cause why the Special Courts Act, 1979 should not be declared ultra vires the Constitution and the Union of India should not be restrained from issuing any declaration under the impugned Act and the Special Courts should not be prohibited from acting under the impugned Act or any declaration issued or that might be issued under the impugned Act by the Union of India'. The court also issued an order of injunction 'restraining the respondents from acting under the impugned Act or any declaration made under the Act or giving effect to the summons dated July 2, 1979'. The injunction was for a week with liberty to the respondents to ask for variation

Getting the former Prime Minister back to her seat. KCo chose to help Indira Gandhi when many others were afraid to

## RNJ Recalls

The Union of India raised serious objection to Indira Gandhi's invoking the jurisdiction and powers of the Calcutta High Court after successfully avoiding service of the notice at New Delhi in Union of India vs. Indira' s application. In fact, the Deputy Secretary in the Ministry of Home Affairs in New Delhi sought to have the injunction/stay vacated and the Writ Application dismissed by telling the court the facts inter alia as: On June 27, 1979, Special Court No 2 (case No.1/79) issued a notice with a letter dated June 28, 1979 'for appearance by person or through pleader on 9th July 1979 to hear parties on the question of limitation'. On June 29 1979, notices were served on two of the accused R.K. Dhawan and D. Sen. Indira Gandhi could not be served the petition as she was reportedly in Darjeeling. After waiting for a couple of days, an inspector visited her residence again but learnt that she was still in Darjeeling and may not return for a few more days. Thereupon a wireless message was sent to Darjeeling to inform her about the date fixed for her appearance either in person or through the pleader on 9.7.1979. On July 4, a CBI inspector left for Darjeeling by air for service of the notice but found that Indira Gandhi had left Darjeeling by the time the inspector reached Darjeeling. 'In view of her departure from Darjeeling to Calcutta on 4th July, 1979 it was not possible to serve notice upon Smt. Indira Gandhi in Darjeeling and the same was returned unserved by the Chief Judicial Magistrate, Darjeeling'.

### Statute ignored: Ex-PM

Continued from page 1 col 4

..der around 4.15 p.m. from former West Bengal Chief Minister S. S. Ray, on coming out of the Calcutta High Court building after finishing his arguments in the two cases Hoping that one of the standing counsels would like to contact him regarding the Maruti case, Mr Kacker did not leave his hotel room till late that evening. But no one turned up. Even after his return to New Delhi, no Government agency appears to have approached the Solicitor-General for advice.

Mr R. N. Jhunjhunwala, who has filed the writ petition in the Calcutta High Court on behalf of Mrs Gandhi, has basically attacked Sec. 5 of the Special Courts Act. This section permits the Union Government to declare that a case will be tried by the Special Courts.

He argues that in conferring this power Parliament has gone beyond its legislative competence and has bestowed a judicial power on the executive. This destroys the basic feature of the separation of powers among the executive, the legislature and the judiciary laid down by the Constitution.

...gating and prosecuting offences committed by people in high public or political offices even though under the Constitution the police and the courts are State subjects. The vagueness of the term "high public or political office" has also been attacked.

Further, as no opportunity to be heard is given by the Union Government before making a declaration under Sec. 5, principles of natural justice are violated. Mr Jhunjhunwala concludes that as Sec. 5 is the core section, its unconstitutionality renders the whole of the Special Courts Act illegal.

The Calcutta High Court's jurisdiction to entertain Mrs Gandhi's writ petition and grant her a stay was based on the fact that the notice for appearance in Delhi in the Maruti case was served on her in Darjeeling in West Bengal. It seems that the notice was served on Mrs Gandhi orally over the telephone.

According to the CBI, as Mrs Gandhi was in Darjeeling, a radiogram was sent from Delhi to the Superintendent of Police, Darjeeling, for service of the notice of Special Court No. 2 asking Mrs

On July 6, on learning that Indira Gandhi had returned to Delhi, another inspector went to serve the notice on her but it could not be served as the injunction order of the Calcutta High Court was shown to him prohibiting any action. The next day, the unserved notice and the report of the police officers were submitted to Special Court No 2. In the circumstances the statement that the Petitioner was personally served a notice in Darjeeling was untrue and Calcutta High Court's jurisdiction had been wrongly invoked.

## Emergency experience

'My association with the Khaitans goes back to 1967', says S.K. Kapur. 'During the first decade, I must have done many small litigations, which were then the in thing. Then came a very important case, during the Emergency. It featured proceedings before the CBI director against a prominent business house. The case was inspired by an attempt to control the editorial policy and news reported by the *Hindustan Times*. The powers that be wanted to start a completely frivolous and unwarranted litigation with an underlying threat of criminal prosecution at that point of time. Pinto and I were involved in that case and he made me work very hard for my living. There were some 17 separate files; bulky and all important. I had to first make an index of the files in order of importance. Pinto was a hard task master and had the advantage of handling that litigation for at least three years before I came in. It meant that he got all the foreign jaunts and the paper work was parked on my table and became my baby.

'My leader was Fali Nariman, who was a handful himself, making all sorts of demands in the conferences. He made the mistake at the very first conference of being uncharitable about KCo and Pinto sulked throughout. It was left to me to handle Fali. There are many small incidents in that case that are worthy of independent reporting but I recall that when we were going up the lift to the director's office, I directed Fali's attention to a board on the wall that read: 8, Tolstoy Marg. Fali's response was: '"that is what you have been spinning for the last three days?". The point was that we won. In fairness to Pinto, there is a footnote to the story. I had worked my fingers to the bone and on the flight back for the last time, Pinto asked me what my fees would be and I told him what my current fees were. To that he said: "You cannot charge me that". Then after a pause, he said: "You charge me six times the amount". That was a practice that he has not maintained and an action that he has not duplicated ever again. The matter came up in appeal and the Memorandum of Appeal was drafted by me. I remember the first conference with Mr Dipankar Gupta, who had just come into the case. When we walked into his chambers, Pinto told him: "You do not need to read anything if you read Mr Kapur's memorandum".

'That was followed by a token of appreciation from Bhagwati Babu himself. He came back from a visit to London and brought me a YSL tie, which was a very big thing in those days. I do not know of very many people who could have got it for me'.

Subrata Roy Chowdhury (C) and R.N. Jhunjhunwala (L) teamed up to defend Indira Gandhi

or vacation of the order on notice to the petitioner. 'The petitioner challenged the impugned Act on the grounds that it violated Article 14 of the Constitution. The summons were served on the petitioner on July 3, in Darjeeling, within the jurisdiction of Calcutta High Court', the *Statesman* said.

Thus began Indira Gandhi's fightback to power and public life. For RNJ, it was amongst the most sensitive cases ever. Special arrangements were made to fly down the superintendent of the concerned department of the high court, Amar Babu, to the capital for serving the copy of the application and the notice on the Union of India and other respondents. By 5 p.m. the news spread and public interest in the matter was aroused though Indira Gandhi had still not lived down the unpopularity of her Emergency raj. Reporters were milling around in the court and RNJ was surrounded for his sound bytes.

The matter had come to KCo courtesy Kamal Nath on whose board (EMC Steelal) P. L. Agarwal served. Kamal Nath, an Indira loyalist, had sought PL's help

The Supreme Court did not stay proceedings in the writ petition pending in the Calcutta High Court

and PL requested RNJ to handle the matter. 'I went to BP because the matter was sensitive and no one was keen to take up the case. BP believed that no one should be denied legal service, it was decided that I would do the case in the appellate side where the firm could not act as the advocate but an individual could', says RNJ. The Congress party paid two account payee cheques in the name of RNJ, which were signed by Pranab Mukherjee and Buta Singh on behalf of AICC as secretary and treasurer.

The *Statesman* again reported on July 18 under the heading: Special Courts Act Challenged: 'Mr Subrata Roy Chowdhury resumed his arguments on Tuesday…he said that the Supreme Court did not have any occasion to consider the final enactment (the Act) after the amendment introduced by the Rajya Sabha'. Had the Supreme Court any occasion to examine the Act, it would have struck it down for 'over-inclusiveness' and impermissible classification under Article 14 of the Constitution of India, said Subrata Roy Chowdhury. While the additional solicitor general did obtain an ex-parte order from the Supreme Court staying the Calcutta High Court order on July 20, the apex court gave the government special leave to appeal against the Calcutta High Court order.

On August 13, however, the Supreme Court heard the matter again for clarification of the earlier order and said that while granting the ex-parte stay of the high court's order, the Supreme Court did not intend that further proceedings in the writ petition pending in the Calcutta High Court should be stayed. It would, therefore, be open for the High Court to proceed with the hearing of the writ petition filed by Mrs Gandhi and parties would be at liberty to move the high court for early hearing. The apex court hoped that the high court would take up the writ petition for hearing as early as possible and dispose the matter off expeditiously, adding that it would be open to either party to apply to the high court for referring the writ petition to a division bench of two judges.

As luck would have it, Indira Gandhi got the added advantage of the confusion prevailing in New Delhi in the Union Ministries of Law and Home. 'The Union Ministries of Law and Home – the two Ministries directly concerned with the stay order of July 5 given by Mr Justice T.K. Basu of the Calcutta High Court on the Maruti case – have yet to decide as to the legal steps they should take in connection with the case', wrote the *Hindustan Times*, New Delhi, on July 9, 1979. The rest is history as the party in power failed to stay on and fresh elections were ordered and Indira Gandhi returned to power.

KCo has somehow worked well with the Gandhis; Indira Gandhi and then her daughter-in-law, Sonia. The photo shows BPK with the former Prime Minister

The Emergency provided KCo an opportunity to show its ingenuity in many ways. Om Khaitan recalls a very interesting case when the Haryana Chief Minister, Bansilal, wanted a trust, being managed by Murli Dhar Dalmia, to do something that it was not possible for him to do. Bansilal was very angry and with both Cofeposa and Misa prevailing, had an arrest warrant issued against him under Misa. Murli Dhar Dalmia also happened

Calcutta High Court, where the Indira Gandhi hearings took place

to be a relative of Mr Mandelia and was in charge of one of the Birla companies. 'Mr Mandelia took a personal interest in the matter and came to our office. We decided to take the matter to the Delhi High Court and took the matter to Mr Soli Sorabjee, who quickly saw the merits of the case and was furious', says Om.

The problem was that the police were getting ready to nab Murli Dhar Dalmia and 'we had to smuggle him out of Haryana, take him to Soli Sorabjee's house and then take him to the court in Mr Sorabjee's car', Om recalls. The police were waiting at the entrance of the court and Mr Sorabjee told the senior officer that even if they touched him, he would move against the entire police force. Then he went into the court and told the judge that he would argue the matter but that the hon'ble court would need to instruct the police outside not to touch his client. The judge summoned the chief of police and told him to clear the high court premises of police. 'The matter was argued and we got a stay', Om says. Hearings continued for two or three years; Bansilal tried his best; so did we. In those days, Mr Mandelia would come to our office and have lunch with us. He said: 'You are earning so much out of us that you should be serving us meals on silver thalis'. I retorted that we need one more client like Murli Dhar Dalmia and we would indeed be able to afford silverware for our clients'.

There was yet another person, R.K. Dhawan, whose wish was command during the Emergency. Corporates were told that he was under instructions from the Prime Minister to ask them for advertisements in a souvenir, for Rs 5 lakhs a page. He also wanted jeeps to be supplied to the Congress party. When the Congress lost and Charan Singh became home minister, he asked the corporates to come clean. Many did but those that did not were in trouble. K.K. Birla, R.P. Goenka, P.C. Sethi and R.K. Dhawan were all asked to come and depose. 'KKB came and gave his statement, RPG was in Nainital and we advised him to take a stay against arrest on the plea that he would cooperate with the investigators', says Om. 'I remember P. C. Sethi coming to our office and sitting outside my room when I came out and found a former minister sitting there. I asked him how we could help him and he said that he wanted us to handle his case as we were handling the cases of Mr Birla and Mr Goenka. When the Congress party came to power, he threw a party that Mrs Gandhi attended. I was invited too and when Mr Sethi introduced me to her saying that we had represented him, she remined him that we had been her lawyers too'.

The Emergency, however, meant enormous hardships for Calcutta's merchant community as elsewhere, and the company constantly found itself defending clients who were feeling threatened with so many warrants of arrest being issued. There were, of course, liberal judges who would be considerate. Says R.K. Choudhury: 'I recall moving an oral writ application before Justice Durga Das Basu for issue of writ of mandamus restraining the Government of West Bengal and the police authorities from issuing warrants of arrest and the police from executing them. Justice Basu did not accede to the counsel's submission at first but Mr Meyer's arguments finally won the day for the client and mandamus was granted'.

The state of Emergency, like a bad dream, too came to an end. It was for KCo to participate in the act of getting its chief protagonist – dethroned temporarily – back in the seat of power. Several years later the firm would help Indira Gandhi's daughter-in-law too.

# ENTER THE EIGHTIES

Looking for the law: the library inside the Calcutta High Court; much-used books stacked up every day

*The structure of a law firm in India is like a pyramid. There is a huge base of litigation, criminal or environmental law, and then there are the huge corporate law firms that supposedly give you a bevy of services; they treat the client like a business and do not go beyond the churning out of a legal document. KCo will look at family law, family values, family intent and then paint a landscape of the future with all the possibilities and options and help you take a better decision and execute it. It arrives at specific understandings of firms by asking you what you want and why; what would you want at the end of the day and help the client and themselves come to a fairer understanding of what the eventual objective is. This the firm does successfully by competently straddling both areas of law and family business.* —

**H.B. Jairaj**

O.P. Agarwal was a teenager, planning to study medicine in Calcutta, where his elder brother was a surgeon, when he realized that he could not stand the sight of blood. 'Medicine would not be for me even though I had got admission into a medical college. Fortuitously, Mr P.L. Agarwal suggested that I get articled with KCo and prepare for my attorneyship examination. I was studying at St Xavier's having earlier gone to school in Kishengunj, Bihar'. A Bel Chamber's Gold and top marks in all the three attorneyship examinations set the young man up for a career in law.

'Mr Pinto Khaitan first placed me under Mr S.K. Lath, who handled all property transactions and conveyancing. I was quite in awe of the office and yet had all the rebellious immaturity of a youngster. One day I chose to argue with Mr Khaitan himself, insisting that I was right and that it did not matter that he did not agree with me', recalls an embarrassed OP today. In hindsight, he says that the incident provided an insight into the psyche of the organization and the people who ran it: 'Mr Khaitan, whom the entire office was in awe of, did not say a word, allowing me to understand the import of what I had just done and learn my own lessons. Not for a day did he hold that initial rebellion against me. Instead, he gave me responsibility and the full freedom to do what it takes to handle important cases'. At some point the young man realized that he had erred; and even if he had not, he should not have said what he did. 'Today, I appreciate that, even on the merits, I may not have been correct!' Yet this was the young man who was allowed to handle the high-voltage Texmaco matter.

The Texmaco matter (around 1980) was about invocation of a commercial performance guarantee under section 124 of the Contract Act, 1872. This was an application in Suit No. 562 of 1972 whereby the petitioner, the Birla-owned Texmaco, asked for an injunction against the State Bank of India (SBI), State Trading Corporation of India (STC) and the Projects and Equipment Corporation of India (PEC), restraining the SBI from releasing or making any payments to the STC and the PEC under – or in respect of – the performance guarantee issued by the SBI. 'Pinto Babu showed great confidence in giving me the matter. Even today, I cannot delegate such matters to juniors. The legal point was whether a bank guarantee could be invoked irrespective of an underlying dispute. Eventually, the Supreme Court in its landmark judgment ruled that if the bank had given a guarantee on someone's behalf, it had to

## Music copyright

Gopal Mookherjee recalls: 'I had been briefed on a copyright matter by Arvind Jhunjhunwala and Ajay Choudhry, featuring Sa Re Ga Ma. The legal questions were:

Was it only the right to make the record assigned to the company (Sa Re Ga Ma) by the producer of the film or whether the copyright was also assigned with regard to the literary, artistic and musical work?

Whether the assignment permitted Sa Re Ga Ma to only manufacture and sell records or other contrivances (digital) as well.

honour it, according to its terms'.

Justice Sabyasachi Mukherjee seen with Justice Kania, Roopa Mitra and Pinto Khaitan at a KCo organized law lecture

The court held that though the guarantee was given for the performance by Texmaco of their contractual obligation in an orderly manner, the obligation was taken by the bank to repay the amount on 'first demand'; 'without contestation, demur or protest; without reference to Texmaco; and without questioning the legal relationship subsisting between STC and Texmaco. The decision of STC about the liability of the bank under the guarantee and the amounts payable thereunder shall be final and binding on the bank'. There was a further stipulation that the bank should forthwith pay the amount due 'notwithstanding any dispute between STC and Texmaco'. In that context, Justice Sabyasachi Mukherjee said, 'The moment a demand is made without protest and contestation, the bank has obliged itself to pay irrespective of any dispute as to whether there has been performance in an orderly manner of the contractual obligation by the party'. The firm 'lost the case but the Supreme Court had set a trend on all bank guarantee matters', says OP.

There was continued excitement over several Birla matters. KCo had been acting as advocates and solicitors for Hindustan Aluminium Corporation (now Hindalco, a Kumar Mangalam Birla company) and handled all its litigations in Calcutta, Allahabad, Mumbai and the Supreme Court around taxation and Central Excise and other matters from any other business controlled by D.P. Mandelia. Sometimes, Mr Askaran Agarwal, general manager, would come to KCo and, even on matters handled by a senior partner, BP was kept posted because he would be briefing GD. For taxation matters, he would generally rely on a team of R.K. Choudhury, Debi Pal and R.N. Bajoria, in the high courts of Calcutta or Allahabad. There was a major matter vis-à-vis aluminium price fixation and a writ petition was filed in the Calcutta High Court. R.C. Deb, Siddhartha Shankar Ray and Dipankar Gupta were all briefed. Dipankar Gupta recalls the matter going up to the division bench of the Calcutta High Court where the judgment went against the company and Askaran Agarwal collapsed in the courtroom.

O.P. Agarwal recalls many small and interesting cases: one in which the firm went to the extent of attaching the UBI Dalhousie Square Branch and, yet another, around 1980, when it took on a very resourceful fellow law firm, Dube & Company, which had taken a bank loan and then used every trick in the book to delay repayment and adjudication of the matter. 'We retaliated by creating an equal number of difficulties in his way and forced him to settle the matter. Mr Dube has since become a friend and acknowledges that we

## Regal legal

Between 1989 and 1991 KCo advised the Secretary of the Trustees of Nizam of Hyderabad on the valuation of the fabulous jewels of the Nizam for Wealth Tax purposes. RKC recalls making several representations for and on behalf of the Nizams before H. M. Patel, the then Finance Minister. The Government of India brought global experts for such valuation when the Nizam refused to pay the entire amount of Wealth Tax demanded by the government. The jewels were finally acquired by the government in 1995 for Rs 206 crores after a prolonged legal battle that went up to the Supreme Court. The sale proceeds were apportioned amongst the beneficiaries of (16 sons and 18 daughters of the Nizam) according to their specified shares. There are now two sons and three daughters besides 104 grand children. 'KCo withdrew when the disputes amongst the siblings became too difficult to handle', says RKC. The firm was also consulted by the Maharaja of Tripura in connection with his property on Ballygunge Circular Road and was advised that Tripura House be retained as residential house. 'Besides, KCo rendered legal services through N.A. Palkhiwala to the Concord of Maharajas in connection with abolition of Privy Purses. I held several conferences with Maharaja of Jaipur, Bhawani Singh, the one and only Maharani Gayatri Devi, Maharaja of Coochbehar, Maharaja of Bikaner and other contenders for Privy Purses. Some of the meetings were help amidst spectacular grandeur', reminisces RKC.

had done something that no one else had done against him'. There was also a major matter of recovering a Grindlays Bank loan from Hindustan Pilkington. 'The company had big lawyers appearing for it and essentially we persisted and finally affected recovery. Mr Ashok Sood was so happy with us that he threw a party at the bank. Sudipto Sarkar represented us and Pratap Chatterjee was on the other side'.

Not every case may have been exciting but many were concerned with the everyday life of the not-so-important businessman. Mr G.S. Asopa recalls a 1980s case, featuring a one-time champion boxer, Nathmull Agarwal, who had a big retail textile shop near the Sealdah station. He suffered a paralytic attack that incapacitated him for a while and permanently damaged an arm and a leg. Nathmull had a partner, a certain Saraf, who was supposed to look after the business when Nathmull became sick but actually took it over, depriving the ailing Nathmall of even his salary and share as a partner. He also fudged the accounts and skimmed off the profits, which is when the ailing boxer came to KCo.

The matter was handled by Mr Asopa, who advised the client to file a suit for dissolution of the partnership for appointment of a receiver and for accounts. 'The proceedings went on for some time and though some negotiations took place, greed got the better of the other partner, who would not consider any fair scheme for settlement. Thereafter, the matter was referred to arbitration at our suggestion'. Justice A.N. Sen (retired) was appointed sole arbitrator and after a prolonged hearing, an award was made in Nathmull's favour, entitling him to repossess his shop as even the premises were originally under his tenancy. 'Fortunately for the boxer, he had not thrown the shop into the partnership firm', says Mr Asopa.

There were other matters big and small. Recalls Mr

Kanoria: 'In the 1980s, KCo advised us when we were acquiring a property in Jaipur but, more importantly, they were the legal advisors for the launch of Srei International. Mr P.L. Agarwal has been helping us from 1980. My son, Hemant, started visiting them as a BCom student along with me and has more or less taken over the management of the business. I have interacted with all the senior partners like Ram Kishore Chowdhury, RNJ, P.L. Agarwal, Pinto Khaitan and N.C. Shah but our main dealing in recent years has been with Mr N.G. Khaitan, PL, RNJ and, at times, with Mr Pinto Khaitan. I still visit the firm and have discussions with NG and PL on various matters'.

BPK would go by pedigree; welcome children of friends to join the profession. RNJ was amongst the earliest; Roopa Sheth followed two decades later. The photo shows BPK (R) with RNJ and colleagues

The 1980s were when KCo started donning truly globalized colours with even entry-level recruits screened for academic excellence. Elsewhere, old family connections were put to good use in getting the right people for the firm. There was yet another Zakaria Street connection that existed between the firm and one of its advocates: Stock broker Bhupatrai Maganlal Sheth lived on Zakaria Street and would occasionally take an evening walk at the Victoria Memorial with Bhagwati Prasad Khaitan. One day, their sons met. Pradip Kumar Khaitan met MRB Sheth over an insurance deal; the latter handled all Bangur insurance claims. It was 1980 and MRB's daughter was planning to study law and he said so to the senior Khaitan. Thus was sealed the career of Roopa Sheth, quite unknown to her. BP wanted the young lady working at his office the following Monday. 'My father took me along to meet Bhagwati Babu on the

## Lifting the corporate veil

O.P. Jhunjhunwala recalls a Grindlays case, featuring a bank executive, Ipsita Singh, who had colluded with certain parties and given vehicle loans in the range of Rs 70 lakhs or Rs 80 lakhs: very large amounts in those days. She was a very well-connected lady who then quit the bank and went off to Singapore. 'We had to file cases against her and had to lift the corporate veil to establish that she was the kingpin in the fraud and finally got her to settle'.

seventh floor of 9, Old Post Office Street on a Saturday and I found a warm and welcoming man. S. K. Lath, the KCo property expert, was sitting with him then and was asked to be my mentor from the following Monday, when I was asked to join as a trainee. There was no letter of appointment; till date there is none, even after 30 years but when associations run deep, a formal piece of paper is of little value'.

The young lady was put through the paces first learning the art of training under S.K. Lath at 1B and then to train under N.C. Shah, the labour and criminal expert. Thereafter, she was under BP and PK's wing and asked to sit in the library at 9, Old Post Office Street, where Mr Ghorawat started giving her work. CMG mainly handled BP's and PK's work in those days and for the young recruit it meant learning indirect taxation, foreign exchange and MRTP matters. 'He was a hard taskmaster but I am grateful for the many ways in which he trained me. I was encouraged to write opinions, do research work and attend court regularly. BP would say that a good lawyer need not remember every bit of enactment but should know where to find it when it is required: he must know his library well'. KCo thus had a first-class library that its advocates were encouraged to build up. 'PK was particularly encouraging'. The training was hands-on and intense and in about three years Roopa was independently handling cases.

Carrying on the family legacy: Haigreve Khaitan, son of Pinto Khaitan, Rabindra Jhunjhunwala, son of R.N. Jhunjhunwala and Aniket Agarwal, son of P.L. Agarwal. All partners at KCo now

Yet other family connections came in handy. Sita Ram Jhunjhunwala's younger son joined the firm as well: 'I had two stints with KCo, first as a CA in 1981, when Mr Pinto Khaitan asked me to join the Delhi office after I qualified as a CA in 1981. I stayed with the company till 1984 and though it was a comparatively privileged position, with a company flat and car, I did not enjoy the stint. I returned to Calcutta, studied law and then chose to rejoin the company at a rather low salary, choosing to sacrifice some much better-paid offers because by then I was a CA, a CS and a lawyer. Bakelite Hylam offered me the position of a company secretary at Hyderabad at a salary of Rs 10,000 plus a car and a flat. Yet, I opted for KCo for a salary of Rs 3,500 that even I felt was very meagre'. At times blood is thicker than water and the work was exciting because Pinto Khaitan threw the young man into the vortex of an exciting Bangur family settlement. 'I worked on it and showed it to him. He looked at my work and said that he had made an error. Henceforth, I would be paid not Rs 3,500 but Rs 5,500. Thus began my stint as a corporate lawyer. At that point of time, I had no intention of being in litigation'. Fate and the company had other things in store for him.

'I did three or four agreements of joint ventures or takeovers of companies with Pinto Babu and then I got sucked into litigations when one such agreement went into litigation. It was for control of Mollins of India Ltd (cigarette machine makers with a factory at Mohali, Chandigarh). I had done the agreement for the transfer of shares from ITC (that held 60 per cent in the company) to the Rasoi group. When the matter went into litigation, I was the natural choice, first as a briefing lawyer for the litigation and then got drawn into the litigation itself'.

The first case that Roopa Sheth handled independently was a Duncan's tea cess matter in 1982, even before she had qualified as a lawyer (in 1983) but the case took her to Delhi in the company of Mr S.K. Bagaria, junior counsel from Calcutta, to challenge the constitutional validity of the levy. 'I recall briefing Siddhartha Shankar Ray. SSR gave us time at 11 p.m. He took one look at me – I was puny then – and suggested that I spend the time with Maya Ray, while he took care of my clients. Of course, I did not leave; we had the conference and the SLP was admitted in the Supreme Court the next day with an order passed in favour of the clients. I recall Mr Krishna Kumar of our Delhi office who handled the bulk of the firm's Supreme Court litigation, taking wonderful care of me in Delhi, giving me a tour of the various courts in Delhi, guiding me, taking me out for meals and really making me feel at home'.

The 1980s was also the decade of Rajendra Sethia as far as corporate news was concerned; one that made it to the headlines was his acquisition and subsequent loss of control over the blue-chip Jokai, an Indian tea major. While Sethia had acquired controlling interests in Jokai, Rajiv Lochan Kanoria too had substantial holding in the company through Parasmani Investments. Once Sethia's Esal Commodities, ran into serious trouble internationally, Parasmani needed to secure its investments in the Indian firm Jokai. Recalls Siddhartha Mitra, who was briefed in this matter by KCo: 'The Kanorias filed an application under sections 397, 398 and 408 of the Companies Act, alleging mismanagement of the affairs of Jokai through its holding company, Esal that had gone into liquidation and was under receivership. The court took cognizance of our complaint of oppression and appointed a nominee of Parasmani Investments, the petitioner, as a director on the board of Jokai!'

Roopa's greater learning experience came when Mr Ghorawat was on his annual leave for a month during the puja vacations and Roopa had to deal with the many petitions that had to be moved during the vacation – right from advising clients, briefing counsel, finalizing petitions, filing and finally getting favourable orders for clients. 'This then became the routine for the next five years, when I handled such clients as Worthington Pump India, Kesoram Industries, Bata India, Andaman Timber, McNeill & Magor, Ratnakar Shipping, India Steamship, Wimco Limited and many others. 'I remember signing the vakalatnamas for the Bata India Limited Fera violation case… although CMG was my senior in these matters as by that time I was enrolled as an advocate. The only people around my age group then were Rajiv and Suman Khaitan and there were three senior ladies: Kusum Dadoo, Shrutkirti Purohit and Sudha Agarwal'.

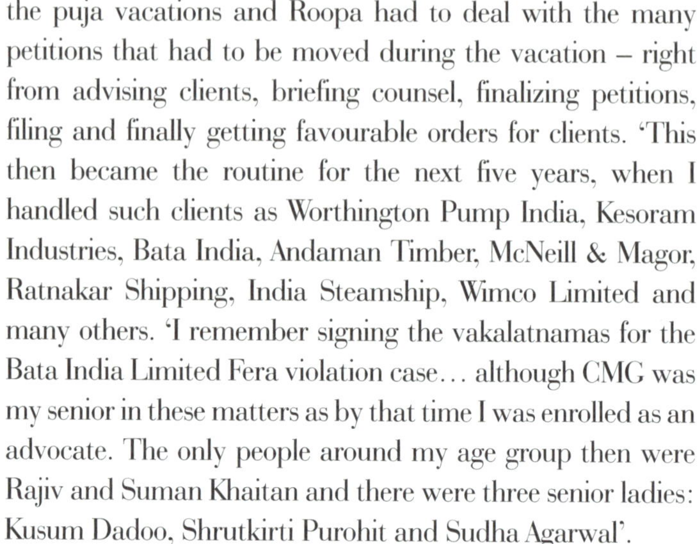

Hemant Kanoria

In 1987, Roopa was given a car by the office that she would drive herself. 'PK also gave me a lot of work to handle independently. These were important arbitrations

## Third generation client: Hemant Kanoria

'I have personally been dealing with KCo since 1980-81, when I was no more than 17 or 18. I would accompany my father and, in those days, would interact with Mr P.L. Agarwal, Mr N.G.Khaitan and Mr R.N. Jhunjhunwala'. The discussions would be around litigations, contracts, legal advice and the teenager would lap up what the various partners were discussing. 'It was an excellent experience for a youngster like me. I was exposed to a group of very intelligent people, who had the ability to think laterally and come up with solutions. That is why a client goes to a lawyer; when he has a problem that has to be solved. So first, the association with KCo has been a very good learning experience. Then came the listing of Srei on London Stock Exchange in 2005. This was done entirely with Mr P.L. Agarwal's help. We became the first Indian non-banking finance company to get the listing and Mr Agarwal did the entire documentation, working day and night to ensure that everything was ready on time. Eventually, it was a very successful listing and there were zero legal issues. Indeed, Mr Agarwal went out of his way to assist us; not in a lawyer-client manner but as a partner, ensuring that we succeeded. That, in fact, has always been our experience with the firm. It is not that we have been successful in all matters but we have seen them putting in their best efforts'.

such as Macnally Bharat and a Central Excise refund for Andaman Timber. This was a major victory that led to a timely refund of Rs 25 lakhs, considered a very big sum in those days. Had the refund not come when it did it would have made things impossible for the client because the law was scheduled to change. My standing counsel for almost all matters was Sudipto Sarkar. One day in 1988, I was waiting in his chamber for a matter, when I got a call from Mr P.L. Agarwal asking me to wait there because he was sending another client to Sudipto's chamber. The client turned out to be Turner Morrison, representing whom was a K.K. Chakravarty', says Roopa.

The job at hand was to have the interim order passed ex-parte on an application made by Hungerford Investment Trust of Nirmaljit Singh Hoon, varied. The matter came up before Justice Prabir Majumdar and KCo successfully got the order varied. This was in 1988 and the Turner Morrison case has been concluded only recently. 'Thereafter I started assisting Mr P.L. Agarwal on all litigation matters. That was another excellent learning experience: PL was a very good teacher, a thorough person and a perfect gentleman. Just sitting in his chamber and watching him deal with clients, one could pick up a great deal about the nuances of law', Roopa says.

There was also an interesting case of Anglo India Jute Mills, in which a winding up petition was filed against the company in respect of a money decree passed against it by a foreign court. That matter was being handled by Mr Ghorawat, who briefed Siddhartha Mitra. 'The question was whether the jurisdiction of the company court could be exercised to wind up a company on the basis of a decree passed by a foreign court on a debt payable by the company', recalls Siddhartha. 'We had no answer on the merits of the decree but our contention was that since it was an ex-parte decree passed by a foreign court in our absence, such a decree could not be considered to be a debt for which winding-

GD's grandson, Aditya continued to repose faith in BPK (L). Seen here at an Hindalco AGM

up proceedings could be initiated. The court accepted this contention especially because the defence of the company had not been tested by the court passing the decree'.

There was never a minute's respite from newer challenges; if the client was not in trouble, the partner was. In 1989, Mr Pinto Khaitan found himself in a legal tangle for an offence that he did not think he had committed. He had resigned as director of Katihar Jute Mills quite a while ago and, after his resignation, the company had defaulted on some promised payments to its workmen. To the dismay of the firm there was a non-bailable arrest warrant against Pradip Kumar Khaitan, in the matter: Case No. 399/77, in the court of the chief judicial magistrate, Katihar. He had also been declared an absconder. The matter was finally resolved with a court order from Justice Manjula Bose, who said, 'It appears that indisputably the petitioner was not a director of the company, viz., Katihar Jute Mills Ltd (in Liquidation) at the time when the offence ... is alleged to have been committed... inasmuch as he had resigned long prior to the said date'. The Calcutta High Court revoked the order of the Katihar court and ordered that the other processes be recalled as far as Pinto Khaitan was concerned.

Mr Pinto Khaitan himself, of course, continued to provide a sense of security to his clients in Calcutta or out of the country. Recalls N.R. Kulkarni of his days as C.K. Birla group finance head: 'At Birlas, we depended on the Khaitans as friend, philosopher and guide. Quite often, we had to deal with international parties when the firm's help was valuable. I remember one instance when we were dealing with an MNC in Singapore and had to take a final decision on valuation of a business. After a lot of discussion in our team, we ultimately telephoned Pinto in Calcutta and derived great comfort from the fact that he concurred with our opinion and told us that we were on the right track'.

Dinesh Himatsingka, grandson of P.D. Himatsingka, who had started his own solicitor's firm around the same time that the Khaitans did, is today a KCo client. 'The important thing is that I have never fought any litigation; I have taken KCo's advice on various issues that are required by law. Lawyers today help companies complete legal formalities; not necessarily fight legal battles. My understanding of a legal firm is quite precise. Three of India's Chief Justices worked with our firm... I have watched the legal process very closely. My father had told me: "Do things so that you do not have a legal case in your hands". It is like the good family doctor who ensures that everyone in the family stays healthy; where no one has fallen sick rather than one who has cured a sick person – important though that is. As far as the legal advice is concerned, you trust that the advice that your lawyer has given will be good for you; that he has navigated the legal path professionally and with your best interests at heart', says Mr Himatsingka.

# THE LAW
# AND LIBERALIZED INDIA

Liberalization meant more laws for more freedom, even as many statutes were dropped. Things looked good for KCo that took the opportunity to expand. Even laid back Calcutta saw growth

*KCo has worked with a great sense of tradition, as did Mulla and Mulla in Mumbai, for instance; or Gagrat & Company and Kanga & Company. A lot of such tradition is being lost but we benefited from working with very senior counsel and their taking an interest in the juniors' work. A special quality about the firm was the kind of commitment that each case got. I worked on small cases to very large cases but the degree of commitment was the same. It was as if the firm was on trial; the firm's reputation was on test; so you put out your best effort.* — **Harish Salve**

It was the 1990s and the time to liberate India under Dr Manmohan Singh as Finance Minister but where would India be without its royal heritage? So royalty continued to occupy mind-space and drive courtroom drama. Mrs Hansa Deb Burman mentions the Cooch Behar Case, which P.L. Agarwal was handling for KCo around 1992. The dispute was over the successor to the maharaja: his widow or the son of his only brother, Virajendra Narayan. Mrs Deb Burman, then a young lawyer, recalls: 'His widow was a lady of foreign origin, Gina Narayan. Virajendra Narayan, whom I was representing, wrote to the government that he was the successor and that he should be thus anointed. Gina Narayan too wanted to be named successor. The government refused her because she had not even been recognized as the maharani. However, while the privy purse for the late maharaja was Rs 10 lakhs, for Virajendra Narayan (VN) the government reduced it to Rs 4 lakhs. Gina Narayan produced a will that said that she had been left everything and had applied for probate in the Calcutta High Court'.

In all probate cases, there are two witnesses to the will and any one of the witnesses has to come to the witness box to prove the will. Says Mrs Deb Burman: 'None of the witnesses came but one Jane Narayan did. I had briefed

PL: from corporates to maharajas... handling all cases with panache

Somnath Chatterjee on this matter but when it came up, he was in another court. So I had to cross-examine Jane. I asked if she had seen the maharaja sign the will and she said that while she was familiar with the signature she had not been witness to the signing. This did not work in the court and, finally, the wife and the nephew had to settle the matter mutually'.

In the course of the hearings, one morning, Mrs Deb Burman was in the corridor of the court when she saw PL rushing towards her, saying that the other side was moving a petition in court no. 8. 'I found Rathin Deb, Gouri Mitter and some others, representing Gina Narayan, moving a petition in the court of Justice R.N. Dutt. Fortunately, I had a postcard in my hand from the IT department saying that Gina was selling off the property in Alipore. Essentially, the other side wanted a stay against VN from interfering but when I produced the notice from the IT department establishing that she was disposing off the property, the court gave me a stay against them. Everyone in the court congratulated me. The important point is that one must know all the facts of the matter; the law would follow. One must master the facts', says Mrs Deb Burman.

Equally, one needed to master the law; not only Indian but international law as well. Thus, after the passions of nationalism and the exclusive focus on Indian enterprises had died down, it was necessary to get international investors and their technology into a liberalized India. It was also time for KCo to change tack and work actively to help global enterprises play their role in providing the country with state- of-the-art technology. Thus, when in 1990s Kerr-McGEE Corporation of Oklahoma City engaged the firm to assist it in playing a role in India's underdeveloped oil and gas space, KCo guided it through the process of establishing units in strategic locations in India. This was on behalf of Reading & Bates, a large Texas

## Exide excitement

In the early 1990s, Sudarshan (S.K.) Birla, had, through various Malaysian companies, bought over the controlling interests in Exide in a much-reported case. The financing was done jointly with the Rahejas, who had involved a Swiss company in the matter. The Malaysian shareholders went into liquidation, thanks to a palm oil industry crisis in which they were caught up. 'In view of this critical situation, the Rahejas wanted their nominees to come into the Exide management to pre-empt the Malaysian liquidators from taking control of the Exide shares', says Siddhartha Mitra. Birla Eastern, represented by KCo, filed a litigation in Calcutta to prevent the Rahejas from holding a requisition meeting in which they intended to pass certain resolutions for removal of the Birla nominated directors on the Exide board. 'We won the first round of litigation in the Calcutta High Court. The matter went to the Supreme Court but before the suit was finally decided, the parties settled and the Rahejas, through some of their companies, bought over the interests of the S.K. Birla group in Exide', says Siddhartha Mitra.

oil firm headquartered in Houston, US, and involved not only knowledge of Indian laws but also a comprehensive knowledge of Delaware (US) Company Law. It meant having to steer the company through a veritable legal labyrinth as it implemented its project in India in harmony with this country's stringent Foreign Exchange Regulation Act, 1973. Says RKC: 'Once this was accomplished, the firm got other international assignments'.

Cases came in various shapes and sizes; forever fascinating. There was the headline-grabbing Renusagar case that had been going on from the 1960s – when the first generation of the Gupta (Dipankar Gupta) barristers was involved – and ending with the second generation in 1995, when Dipankar Gupta's son, Jaideep, was engaged by the firm. Jaideep Gupta recalls the most interesting Hindalco vs General Electric matter in what was a 20-year dispute. Mr Venugopal appeared for Hindalco and Jaideep was a junior. The case was about General Electric setting up the Renusagar power plant in the 1960s for which there was a payment dispute that needed arbitration under the ICA in Paris. Renusagar did not pay; nor did it participate in the arbitration process. The award went against it and was challenged in India. Says Jaideep: 'In the first round in the Mumbai High Court L.M. Singhvi appeared for us; the matter was finally decided by the Supreme Court in December 1995; and the award was upheld. A large amount was payable to General Electric. Matters were made worse by the exchange rate going against our clients. I believe that that case changed the Birla policy against litigations. They started opting for settlements'.

The Hindalco matters saw more than one father-son duo being engaged over time. Mr Abhishek Manu Singhvi's first intense interaction with the firm happened over the celebrated Renusagar case: 'It was one of the biggest of its times: international commercial arbitration was nascent, stakes were high, egos of two dominant multinationals even higher; and I was merely a junior counsel, watching and trying to absorb from the "greats" of the profession: Nani Palkhivala, my father and, later, Shanti Bhushan, Venugopal and others'. From the firm there was Nilratan Khaitan, always the 'best prepared amongst the junior counsel; very intense, ready with copious notes in impeccable and organized calligraphy', says Mr Singhvi. Many others share the opinion of this meticulous person who 'represented an unusual tribe: virtually in-house to KCo, though he was not yet a solicitor and did only counsel's work', recalls AMS. The trouble was that the case was 'rather weak on our side but we valiantly fought Renusagar II and III through six rounds of the high court and apex court litigation'.

For AMS, the case was memorable for more reasons than one. It was bang in the middle of the final round of Renusagar III being argued by special consent of both sides in the May-June 1993 vacation, before a special bench

## Ashok Sen and the disappearing page

During the hearing Ashok Sen, appearing for the temple authorities and the trustees cited various books and authoritative texts showing that historically, the practice of Sati did not involve burning of the bride on the death of her husband and that the act of Sati was a divinal one. Horror of horrors, one of the books handed over to the court, brought by the Trustees from Rajasthan, which was being cited before the court on how Shree Rani Satiji became Sati, had a full page photograph of a newly-wed bride sitting on her husband's pyre, being lit by some body standing close by: exactly what Ashok Sen was trying to refute. Thinking on his feet Ashok Sen tore the page out in a flash and tucked it into his trousers. The Additional Advocate General saw what happened and brought it to the court's attention and wanted the book to be handed over to the judges but no one could find the offensive photograph and no one dared to do a body search of the redoubtable barrister!

presided over by Justice Venkatachaliah, that his father became the Indian High Commissioner to the UK and he was designated India's youngest senior advocate at age 34. 'I received my designation over a telephone call when I was actually sitting next to our senior counsel in the Supreme Court that summer and arguments were on in full force!'

Probably the most socially-disturbing case of the late 1980s pertained to the burning of Roop Kunwar of Deorala, newly-wed and widowed, forced to sit on the funeral pyre of her deceased husband and burnt alive by her in-laws. The village looked on in the belief that she would become Sati, an incarnation of Goddess Durga. A country-wide protest followed this revolting incident and the Parliament passed a law prohibiting commission and glorification of Sati. The government also decided to enforce the Act by applying it to the various Sati temples throughout Rajasthan in particular and other states in general. Shree Rani Satiji Mandir, one of the biggest Sati temples in Rajasthan, was a prime target. The Rajasthan government served notices to all temple authorities, including Shree

Rani Satiji Mandir, which had its registered office at 12, Government Place (East), Calcutta, where the notice was received, directing it to close down the temple. Its trustees were amongst some of KCo's biggest clients.

The order stated that government officials with police force would be there to monitor compliance of the order. No one could enter the temple and offer seva puja or hold any other form of prayer or celebration. These notices were served a few days before the temple's annual function, when several lakh devotees were expected to gather for the annual celebrations. The trustees, office bearers of the Temple Society and the Trust, rushed to KCo with the notice, urging it to take immediate steps before the Calcutta High Court to have the order stayed. The task was to argue before the court that Sati had very wide socio-religious connotations and should not be equated with the horrendous widow-burning phenomenon.

The state of Rajasthan appealed to the Supreme Court, which had the matter transferred to the apex court in view of the public importance of the issues involved. There it was heard by a two-judge bench of Justice Ranganath Mishra and Justice M.N. Venkantachaliah. On behalf of the temple, it was argued that the festival was to commemorate the patriotism of the Rajput women, who 'specifically' upon the heroic Rajput rulers of the times, 'meeting death at war, would commit "Johar" to pre-empt the enemy from enslaving them. This could not be an offence or objectionable in any way'. It was argued that reducing the meaning of 'Sati' to 'widow burning' would be a great injustice. The word 'Sati' had different connotations, according to the context it was used in and had been recognized as 'Satya' (chastity), connoting a woman of virtuous character. It acquired special importance when the wife of Maryada Purushottam Shri Ram was named Mahasati, a name connoting great honour.

As such, the ordinary meaning of 'Sati' is not only widow-

## Sati and the law

R.N. Jhunjhunwala, who handled the case, says: 'A writ application was prepared and moved before Justice Pratibha Banerjee. Mr M.I. Khan, Additional Advocate General, appeared on behalf of the Rajasthan State Government and opposed the application. At the telephonic request by the Rajasthan Chief Minister to the then Chief Minister of West Bengal, Jyoti Basu, Mr Nara Narayan Gooptu, Advocate General of West Bengal, was also briefed by the government to oppose the application. Justice Banerjee refused to grant any stay'. In anticipation, appeal papers had been kept ready, the memorandum of appeal and stay application were hurriedly completed and moved before the Appeal Bench of Justice Ajit Sengupta and Justice K.M. Yusuf. The eminent barrister Ashok Sen, fortunately available in Calcutta then, agreed to appear before the Appeal Court and notices were served on the government, including the advocates on record for the states of West Bengal, Rajasthan and the Union of India. RNJ says: 'The matter was moved at 2 pm in view of urgency, the Appeal Bench allowed Ranisatiji Mandir Authorities to issue notices stating that mela or the annual general meeting would be held subject to further orders that the Appeal Court would pass the next day. The State of Rajasthan prayed that the hearing be postponed to enable its Additional Advocate General Mr M.I. Khan to be present but the judges refused any adjournment, heard the case following day, August 18, 1988 and passed a further order that the annual religious mela of Shree Rani Satiji Mandir at Jhunjhunu may be held if the court sanctioned it and, in the mean time, the usual daily worship, puja inside the temple could continue. The government could not interrupt the daily puja or harass devotees, the court said, while directing the temple authorities not to hold the annual

burning; it related to virtues of a lady or her character and if taken to be an offence or an attitude of offence, it would amount to mental bankruptcy. The court should take judicial notice of the public conviction and that Mother Sati was worshipped in every house and not confine the meaning of the word to being offensive and pertaining to widow-burning only. As such, simply being a Sati temple or worshipping Sati could not be an offence in the Act nor it shall be an offence at any time.

The judges passed an order to the effect that 'one fact, which is not in dispute is that the temple has been in existence for centuries …we find that regular puja is performed five times a day in this temple. Apart from what is disputed to be an image of Sati there are images of Lord Shiva, Hanumanji and other deities within the temple whom Hindu tradition accepts to be Gods. It is not for us at this stage to take a final view one way or the other. Yet, there is a prima facie case for examination and it cannot be said that the petitioners' claim is such that it can be rejected at the threshold. It would be difficult to rule out the contention of the temple authorities petitioners until the matter is adjudicated and a final decision is reached. Petitioners have alleged interference with their pujas. That criminal prosecution may be launched against them. We direct that for the puja offered within the temple no prosecution be started against those who offered puja until the matter is finally disposed of and the correctness or otherwise of the plea taken by the petitioner is finally examined in the writ petition', the judges said.

## Roop Kanwar and women

Says Kumkum Sen: 'Looking back, I wish I had kept a detailed record of my work experience, products and creations, whether petitions, appeals, advices on evidence, contracts, the first FIPB application or whatever I had accomplished during my years in KCo. One important case stands out in my memory: an offshoot of the Roop Kanwar Sati case of a young widow, who was burnt alive on the funeral pyre of her husband in September, 1987. This case, described as a voluntary decision on the part of the widow who was hailed as a Sati, was challenged only at the insistance of women's organizations. The acquittal of the accused coincided with a petition made for holding of a puja allegedly commemorating the 400th Anniversary of Shri Sati Devi organized by the Rani Sati Mandir Trust, Jhunjhunu. This was assailed by the women's groups in the Supreme Court Appeal and KCo, accepted the brief for the Mandir and the Trust, as most of its clients were its promoters. I, as senior associate, was asked to handle this case. Going through the records on the file however, I felt a sense of discomfort as I was attempting something contrary to my personal beliefs. In 2011, I would have no hesitation to accept a similar brief but, in 1996, I was younger and possibly more sensitive. The important thing was that and at no point did the partners try to pressurize me'.

On the Bhadra Amawasya, which would fall on the 10th of September that year, there would be an annual mela near the temple. The judges held that 'Offering of puja inside the temple and holding up a mela outside are certainly two different aspects and the mela may give rise to problems of law and order… we direct that no mela shall be held either on the 10th of September or at any time until further orders. … since there is apprehension of disturbance of law and order, the state authorities are free to regulate the gathering of people around the temple even for offering of puja'. The judges also held that those who intended 'to offer puja within the temple may not be physically obstructed and no impediments other than for regulating may be placed … in the matter of offering puja within the temple'.

There were equally sensational cases of different kinds. The Ring Tong Tea Estate matter, which taught young Arvind Jhunjhunwala the lesson that BP had been dinning into the hearts and minds of his team, is worthy of mention. Arvind recalls: 'The Ring Tong Tea Estate in Darjeeling, which was one of the finest learning experiences that I have had, featured a family dispute featuring a father, two sons and a grandson. The father, one son and grandson (Desraj, son Sushil and grandson Sanjay Choudhury) were on one side and Vinod Agarwal (as he chose to call himself), the other son, was my client. Ring Tong was an excellent tea estate owned by the Choudhurys. This was a Section 397 matter and came to us because of our experience with Company Law', says Arvind.

The fight was over control of the tea estate. Prior to the dispute, everyone was managing the garden. However, the grandson and Arvind's client, Vinod, did not see eye to eye. 'At the behest of the grandson, the family increased the share capital and made Vinod a minority', says Arvind to whom it seemed like an open-and-shut case because he could easily prove to the court that the share capital increase was malafide and motivated to reduce an equal partner to a minority. He thought that this would be an easy one.

'On day one, I went to the CLB with Sudipto Sarkar and Gopal Mookherjee on my side. On the other side were R.C. Nag and Mintu Sen. On the first day there was a pre-lunch session and the matter was to continue post-lunch at CLB, Delhi. It so happened that during lunch break I found a big green file on the table that I opened. Lo and behold, there was a bunch of case law papers supporting the other side. At that point of time I had not realized that it was Mr R.C. Nag's file. I realized that later when he came looking for the file. It was an unintended bonus for me and I thought I would prepare my arguments against all the case laws that the other side would cite. Indeed, the matter was bitterly fought over six months but it was, finally, P.C. (Mintu) Sen's persuasive arguments that won the case for the other side'.

The point of law was that while the Company Law Board accepted that there was oppression, it followed the principle of the Sindri Iron Foundry case that the oppressor being in the majority should buy out the oppressed. 'Our point was that the courts could not give their blessings to an act of admitted illegality' but, with Mr Mintu Sen at his best that day, the judge was swayed by his persuasive power'. As far as Arvind himself was concerned, he learnt that little or large bonuses, obtained accidentally or illegally, did not matter; only the power of argument did. Any adverse order puts one back by two years. What provided a soothing balm for the young man, who was possibly licking his wounds, was a chance meeting with the grandson on the return flight. They were taking the same flight home and Sanjay Choudhury came up to Arvind and said: 'Arvindji, in the next matter you will be my solicitor'. Even in loss, there was a touch of glory.

## Enter telecom controversies

If there were some cases of a traditional nature, there was some absolutely new ground that KCo was treading. Tata Cellular vs. Union of India is a landmark judgment in more ways than one, marking the entry of cell phone technology, which has transformed India. Kumkum Sen recalls working on a matter that was totally new in those days: 'I have to confess to my naiveté; when the clients came with the proposal of challenging the decision of the Selection Committee in respect of the bids in the financial tenders invited by the Department of Telecommunications for circle operators for grant of licence for cellular phone services, I had a very faint concept of a cellular phone and its functions. The entire litigation involved two years of continuous work, first before the Delhi High Court and then the Supreme Court. The judgment, which runs into 155 paragraphs, at para 80 expounds on the Wednesbury principle – now common knowledge, in 1994 a revelation – encapsulating "that a decision of a public authority can be judicially intervened with only if the court concludes that no authority properly directing itself on the relevant law and acting reasonably could have reached it". Of course, the client, India Telecomp, lost the case but it was a great learning curve', says Kumkum Sen.

Gopal Mookherjee and Arvind made a good team. The barrister recalls an interesting Company Law matter featuring the dispute between the sons of Harbanslal Malhotra, a matter in which he was briefed by P.L. Agarwal and Arvind Jhunjhunwala. The matter was finally resolved and Gillette offered to buy the company. This was a family concern, making the Topaz blade, in which there were three sons. The younger son had moved out of the family business and started his own company, Vidyut Metalics Ltd, which made the Supermax brand of blade. He had also asked for a third of the family business for which he wanted the business to be split into three, something that his brothers resisted. The whole case was around the younger brother wanting a third of the company with the intention of splitting the family business to benefit his own company. This was opposed by the other brothers, who were happy to pay him for his shares but refused to hurt the established brand. KCo represented the two older brothers. The legal point involved was whether a limited company could be partitioned for a family dispute to the detriment of the company and its shareholders. The matter was eventually settled privately. The younger brother got a factory in Thane while the older brothers retained the Topaz brand name.

Arvind recalls an interesting aside in the case relating to one Mr P.S. Bawa, who was on the boards of both the companies. Thus when the matter went to court, there was P.S. Bawa, director in both the petitioner and the respondent companies. The client had opted for Iqbal Chagla in Mumbai whose junior used to be Zia Mody, then an independent counsel. 'I went to brief Iqbal along with our barrister, Gopal Mookherjee, and Mr Bawa. At the beginning of the conference Zia started by telling Iqbal that the real villain here appears to be a Mr Bawa, who is playing on both sides, without realizing that Mr Bawa was sitting right there. The

## From banking to engineering

Jaideep Gupta acknowledges that he picked up banking work from RNJ: 'My first matter was with Bacchu Pal and RNJ and it was a Grindlays Bank matter, when I learnt to prepare bank suits. RNJ had another client, Swapan Paul, for whom we did several matters and I visited his Camac Street office then. In P.L. Agarwal, I found the most knowledgeable company specialist that the Khaitans had. He was quiet, unobtrusive, very thorough and totally clear in his mind. I also worked with O.P. Jhunjhunwala on small labour matters and with C.M. Ghorawat and RKC, who was a trustee in many institutions and took my opinion in trust matters. Besides, there was Ramesh Chowdhry. With Mr Padam Khaitan I did small interlocutory matters, commercial disputes and winding up petitions, small arbitrations and chamber matters and I did some 391 schemes with Suman Jyoti. When I came to Delhi in 1992, at least 50 per cent of my work was with KCo. There were SLPs to be filed in the Supreme Court. There was a Kesoram Industries cess matter featuring a rural development cess on coal that was sent from Calcutta. There was also a Sirpur Paper excise matter that was a dispute around fixed or movable assets – depending on whether they were grouted to the ground or not!'

embarrassment and the laughter that ensued was something to remember and the misunderstanding was cleared'.

'There were changes in the legal regime and Groz Beckert Saboo, an Indo-German partnership firm, manufacturing specialized hosiery needles, became the first case to be tried by the principal bench of the Company Law Board, New Delhi, after the jurisdiction of the high court was transferred to the CLB under the 1992 amendment', says Siddhartha Mitra. The complaint by the Indian party, Saboo, was that the foreign shareholder, Groz Beckert, was running the Indian business to promote its worldwide group interests at the cost of the local operations. Recalls Siddhartha: 'Material was being supplied by the overseas company to the Indian operations at much higher than the international market prices and profits were being squeezed in India. Since the chairman, who had to be a German, had the casting vote under the articles of association of the Indian company, all protests made by the Indian shareholder were being turned down by use of this casting vote, as "an instrument of oppression".

The CLB passed an order that since the German partner was in the majority and providing the technology essential for the future of the company, it could be given the option to purchase the shares of the Indians by a method of valuation agreed by both parties'. This was done and the Germans ended up buying out the Indians at a rate 'much higher than what they had originally offered when they wanted Saboo to sell its stake before the litigation', recalls Siddhartha. Of greater interest was the fact that the matter came to the Khaitans because of the competence with which the firm had handled the Jokai matter for Rajiv Lochan Kanoria, who referred the firm to Saboo. The firm did not disappoint, though arrayed against them were such stalwarts as I.M. Chagla assisted by Darius Khambata. 'Our team comprised S.B. Mookherjee, Sudipto Sarkar and myself, along with P.L. Agarwal and Roopa from Khaitans', says Siddhartha.

Gopal Mookherjee recalls another international arbitration featuring Stone India for which he was briefed by Arvind Jhunjhunwala. 'It was a tribunal of three judges presided over by a Hong Kong judge though the arbitration took place in Calcutta. The matter was around an intellectual property dispute and featured an infringement of a licence agreement that restricted Stone India from modifying or improving a licensed product. It got resolved through arbitration'. The facts of the case are interesting and complicated: Stone India was faced with a claim by Faiveley Transport (erstwhile GEC Alsthom) who were the successors in interest to a licensing agreement between Stone India and one Sab Wabco (erstwhile Westinghouse American Brake Company).

In 1972, Stone had entered into a technical knowhow arrangement with Wabco that makes railway braking systems; a knowhow that Stone acquired. Globally, there are two braking systems: the American design and the UIC (European design). The Indian Railways follow the UIC and Stone had an agreement for the UIC design owned by Wabco Stone in 1972, based on which it made these railway braking system. In the late 1970s, the European operations of Wabco were taken over by a European company called Sab Wabco.

In 1981, Indian Railways introduced a variation in the braking system with the introduction of a special feature: a pressure-limiting device. Stone India designed the device and incorporated it in the brake valves and secured Railways approval in 1991. The brake system was cased in aluminium (every carriage has one and when the engine driver applies the brake it applies uniformly on every carriage). Since the aluminium casings were being stolen from the goods trains, the Railways wanted to convert them into cast-iron casing for goods trains. Stone, which was till then supplying the aluminium-cased brakes, developed the technology for the cast-iron casings. This happened in 1991 and the Railways said that the supplier would need an agreement with either

## Mody vs Tata

Delhi continued to be a hot bed of activity as India liberalized. Jaideep Gupta reminisces: 'In my first few years in Delhi, I got a huge amount of work from KCo. The office at Himalaya House had a transit office for Pinto Khaitan and I often worked there. I remember, Kaushik, son of Sudhir Chandra, who owned the premises at Himalaya House, working there too. I handled a big arbitration for R.N. Mody of Hindustan Development Corporation, who had a dispute with Ratan Tata, then in charge of Nelco, which had supplied components of automation for its wire mill at Malanpur (Gwalior). The acrimony went on for 10 years after which the matter fizzled out because by then the machinery had become junk and R.N. Mody sold out. There was also the ANZ-National Housing matter, which at that time featured the highest claim of between Rs 50 crore and Rs 60 crore. Besides, I handled some stock exchange cases'.

Sab Wabco or Knorr-Bremzie, the authorized suppliers.

Stone already had a knowhow agreement with Wabco since 1972; the technology had been fully absorbed; the agreement had expired; and it had to go in for a fresh agreement to conform to the 1991 requirement. It approached Sab Wabco and settled the deal for a sum of $30,000 to be paid in three instalments for which it would have licensed use of the updated technical knowhow. However, Sab did not have the technology for cast-iron but for aluminium casing only though the agreement said that it was for updated aluminium/cast-iron distributor walls. All that Sab Wabco did was to resend the original 1972 designs, incorporating all the modifications that had been made by Stone, with new drawing numbers and their stamp. Since these were old designs, they did not feature the pressure- limiting devices that Stone had developed on its own. However, since the Railways insisted that suppliers have agreements with their two approved designers, Sab Wabco or Knorr-Bremzie, the agreement was entered into and two instalments had been paid although no new technology had been received. Even Sab Wabco did not insist on the third instalment.

In 1993, the Railways came out with fresh specifications for the brake systems and this time there were four approved designers with whom the suppliers had to have technical collaboration. Thus another licensing agreement was needed. In 1993, Sab Wabco did not have a presence in India but by 1997 it had been taken over by Faveley Transport, which also acquired controlling interests in an Indian company that was a competitor of Stone, Railway Products India Ltd, a Saroj Poddar company. Once the two became competitors for Railway orders it was not in the interest of Faveley to allow Stone to continue with the supplies, Arvind recalls.

The old agreement had a clause saying that Stone could not modify any product without Sab's approval. In 2001, Railways wanted another modification: to integrate the two valves (the brake and the relay valve) into one. 'We approached Faveley Transport for technology to integrate the two and they refused saying that this was a new product and had to be covered by a new technical agreement. Stone developed the product on its own and got it approved. Ever since, Faveley has been asking the railways not to approve the Stone's product, because the modifications had violated the agreement'.

Since the product had been approved by the Railways, Faveley initiated an ICCR arbitration. 'Our point was that we

## The rival's respect

Impressing the opposition was the name of the game. Mr Vinod Krishna of Metal Box got to know and respect the firm that had been on its opposing side more than a decade and a half ago. 'It was in 1995, on a transaction where the opposite party was represented by KCo, Calcutta, where Mr P.L. Agarwal played a vital role in understanding our complexities and, in turn, addressed our concerns'. The association has been fortified by the professional services provided by the firm in Mumbai for the past decade. 'KCo Mumbai represented us in a transaction, which was then extremely vital for us. Since then, our relationship with the firm has steadily grown from strength to strength', says Mr Krishna.

had an agreement for the aluminium distribution valves since 1972 from Wabco and did not need the 1993 agreement for the new railway requirement. In any event, no technical knowhow was received and the 1972 drawings were stamped by Sab Wabco and it was not the updated valve because it did not have the pressure limiting device… which meant there was no updation as was clear from the drawings'. The arbitration hearing was held over three days: on May 22, 23 and 24, 2010. The arbitrator came on February 23, 2011, and held against Stone on most points. 'When the hearing took place, for seven days we would sit with Gopal from nine in the evening till four in the morning… and we got ready to challenge the award with an application for setting aside the order'.

The Mody family was another steadfast client. Raghu Mody (L) seen here with Pinto Khaitan

'We produced a witness during the arbitration who was asked: "If no technology was received by Stone from Sab Wabco, why did Stone enter into an agreement?" He answered in Bengali: "eshob shob dhappabaji (all this is an eyewash)" and this had to be explained to Mr Anthony Houghton, the umpire. The cost of the arbitration was huge but all standard agreements have the ICCR arbitration clause. The cost of the technology was $30,000 but the initial provisional cost of the arbitration was $112,000!'

There was also the Mollins experience that Arvind recounts. 'Our client, Rasoi Ltd (a Raghu Mody company) had acquired controlling stake in Mollins and had to vote at the AGM to remove the existing board that did not take kindly to the sale. I went to Mohali with the officers of Rasoi and the proxies to cast the vote. We had anticipated trouble and I took along Preetam Singh Saini (a local lawyer) and a photographer to document developments'.

The AGM was to be held at Mohali at a time that Punjab

was disturbed around 1990-91. At the main entrance to the company there was a crowd of workers who refused to allow anyone in. At the gate, there was a union leader holding a meeting against the Calcutta businessman who wanted to take the company over. 'Preetam Singh Saini saw the crowd and said: "Arvindji bhaag chalo…yeh tow marengay (Arvind, let us run. These people will beat us up)". I said that I had not come from Calcutta just to run away. Instead, I went to the person who was addressing the crowd and asked him what the problem was and if they had any objection to my going inside to attend the AGM. The man was so shocked at the direct approach that he made way for us to go in. Inside, however, there was the local police station officer, who had instructions not to let us in. He pointed to his gun-bearing men and said: "This is Punjab and there could be an encounter any time". The message was clear and we had to leave. This was all photographed though'.

The group came out, went to the police station where they refused to lodge the complaint. 'When I showed them my ID card as a lawyer, the person in charge took down my GDR and gave me the number. Only after I received my GDR and was coming out did I see the officer, who had refused me entry to the AGM, returning. I got away quickly because my job had been done'. Based on the diary and the photographs and documentation, Arvind got an order of injunction against the meeting. 'It was the ability to think on the spur of the moment that had seen me through!' The legal issue here was around the transfer of the purchased shares – the law for which has since been amended to allow free transferability of shares in a listed company. The board had at that time refused to transfer the shares on some flimsy ground, though ITC had sold 60 per cent of its shares to Raghu Modi's Rasoi.

If Sita Ram Jhunjhunwala's sons were giving an excellent account of themselves, so were others, quietly learning the ropes and awaiting their turn. More importantly, they were

## Best yet to come

'KCo has grown and grown: first within Calcutta, then within the eastern region, then in Delhi and the north and finally in other parts of India, including Mumbai and the South. They have retained their USP, an indelible link with some of corporate India's oldest and most respected families, a bond of trust and confidentiality, an old world charm style of lawyering and an ability to hold relationships. I have no doubt that the best is yet to come'

— *Abhishek Manu Singhvi*

all enjoying the work. Says S.K. Kapur: 'There have been large and small pieces of work and all of them were fulfilling. It meant hard work and it was good, clean fun. All law is not musty or old or stale; it can be happy too and the joie de vivre with which my juniors in Khaitan have worked will always remain with me. If I may name those who have given great pleasure by permitting me to associate with them, they are RNJ, NG, Padam, Ghorawat and Roopa. I must not forget another KCo doyen, who is currently a consultant, Ram Kishoreji. I also remember Haigreve and Sudip Mullik, who came all the way from Mumbai to brief me for an arbitration matter in Ahmedabad. I went at least 30 times on a pollution control matter that we finally lost'.

Indeed, sometimes justice demanded thinking on one's feet, especially when Bhagwati Prasad Khaitan's personal interests were hurt, as it was sometime in 1988. On a complaint from some non-teaching staff and teachers of the Shri Shikshayatan School, the government issued notice on a Friday, appointing an administrator to take control of the management of the school and possession of its campus (that housed the Shri Shikshayatan College as well) by 10.30 a.m. the following Monday. Bhagwati Babu, then president of the school, asked his troubleshooter, RNJ, to take charge. The matter was clearly tricky and the school administration was in a state of panic.

The school had no time to move high court during the weekend. So special permission was obtained from the judge presiding over the bench concerned and there was a flurry of overnight activity preparing a writ application under Article 226 between Friday and Saturday. On Saturday, the papers were ready and a special permission was obtained, courtesy an application seeking appointment with Justice Padma Khastagir at her residence at Bishop Lefroy Road. A court sitting, held at her residence, heard the application and granted a stay that also resulted in Shri Shikshayatan School getting the status of a 'linguistic minority educational institution enjoying protection under Article 30 of the Constitution of India and functional autonomy', says RNJ. This, he adds, is a rare privilege enjoyed by a school in West Bengal.

Not just was Calcutta doing interesting cases, so was Delhi that was taking on new people too. Right after joining in 1996, Sharad Vaid was asked to handle a very interesting case involving a complaint required to be filed on behalf of the Sheet Glass Manufacturers Association against Gujarat Guardian Limited, a joint venture between

## Cool Calcutta

Calcutta too had it share of excitement for the young and aspiring. Hindustan Motors sold its earthmoving equipment business to Caterpillar around the year 2000. Recalls Rabindra Jhunjhunwala, 'we concluded the deal and, when the time came to raise a bill, my seniors, PK and PL, asked me to raise the bill, sign and send it under my name'. Wrote Rabindra to his client on January 10, 2001, over email: 'With reference to your telephone conversation with Mr Pradip Khaitan, please note that we are proposing to charge an in pocket fee of Rs 25 lakhs only. We, however, leave the final amount to you. The out of pocket would, however, be charged as actuals'. This was a typical KCo practice and there were pleasant occasions when the client said that the fee was too low!

'It was my first bill and for Rs 25 lakhs, a huge amount at that time. It was quite magnanimous for my seniors to give me the opportunity. That gave me a great boost and, indeed, I have retained both the bill and a coopy of the cheque that the client sent'.

Guardian Industries Ltd of US and the V.K. Modi group, before the MRTP Commission, against the restrictive trade practices and predatory pricing adopted by the latter. Guardian Industries had deep pockets and financial muscle and was undercutting the other sheet glass manufacturers and trying to throttle them in what was amongst the first of the cases of predatory pricing in the country. 'RNJ guided me and taught me the legal intricacies and procedures to be followed in this matter. The services of Mr R.S. Suri were availed for preparing the case and drafting the application and Siddhartha Shankar Ray was engaged for arguing the case before the MRTP Commission.

'We would go to S.S. Ray's house in the evening and work there till late hours, finalizing the application and, later, preparing for the case hearings. Ultimately, the matter was mutually settled and our client was saved from virtual ruin. Not just RNJ, even S.S. Ray took great personal interest in guiding me and training me but it was Mr Pinto Khaitan who kept on thrusting work on me, compelling me to learn on the job'.

The grandsons of DP and BP work in close harmony. Dhruv Khaitan, Haigreve Khaitan, Ravi Kulkarni and Pinto Khaitan (L-R)

There was also a lot of interesting international work being sent by Dhruv Khaitan that provided the firm with terrific learning. Sharad Vaid recalls: 'Dhruv Khaitan was a man of great details and a hard taskmaster and between 1996 and 1999 was involved in putting together a hi-tech venture in the field of information technology. While he was being guided by Mr Pinto Khaitan, I was required to do all the planning, documentation and execution part of the work along with Rajiv Khaitan from the Bangalore office.

I was entrusted with the full responsibility and given complete freedom of working on this complicated and multi-faceted transaction. It involved formalizing a financial and technical knowhow and joint-venture agreement with the US's Equifax Inc. for a credit card processing venture in India. I did the drafting and vetting and went into the negotiations and finalization of the agreements for joint venture, technical knowhow and software licence agreement and all other related documentation, legal and regulatory approvals and compliances. I also helped the companies in legal due diligence exercise conducted by the counsels of Equifax and in getting FIPB and RBI approvals'.

Equifax Venture Infotech Limited was subsequently funded by VISA International, IBM Global, Walden International Investment group, Worldwide Smartnet Ventures and from Warburg Pincus – amongst the biggest PE investment during that time. Subsequently, the entire Equifax Inc. interest in Equifax Venture Infotek was bought out by the Dhruv Khaitan group. 'All this involved very complicated structuring issues, extensive documentation, a number of statutory and regulatory approvals and various cross-country incorporations and compliance issues. On successful execution and completion of the entire assignment, Dhruv Khaitan had complimented Mr Pinto Khaitan and the firm extensively'. KCo had taken a confident step into 21st century deal making.

Bhagwati Babu himself had by then chosen to watch the proceedings from the sidelines because the third generation was getting interested in the legal profession and, indeed, the firm was growing at a steady pace with some heady successes in between. It was in the mid-1990s that BP's grandson started getting noticed. 'I met Haigreve for the first time when he was working with P.L. Agarwal on a transaction, which I was handling as

## The young, old firm

'In the latter part of the 1990s, the firm was still in Himalaya House on Kasturba Gandhi Marg in Delhi. The office covered some 3,000 square feet and another 1,200 square feet on the same floor. Mr Nil Ratan Khaitan sat in a separate room on the same floor and had a formidable reputation as counsel. He handled many of the important cases and, of course, a number of Birla group matters, including the Hindalco matters. Om and Umesh Khaitan had both left; the Delhi office was headed by Mr Suman Khaitan and many young lawyers – Sanjay Khaitan, Ajay Bhargava and Gauri Rasgotra – were inducted. The entire set up was virtually new with a lot of interesting work for the young advocates to learn. Foreign direct investment related work had started flowing in and I got involved in securing approvals while also working on mergers, demergers, restructuring and other corporate legal work. Much of it was guided by Mr Pinto Khaitan who gave me full freedom to learn and grow', says Sharad Vaid.

KCo's client. I was quite impressed by this young lawyer and was surprised when someone told me that he had not yet become one: he was still studying in a law college. It was amazing to see his knowledge of law, application of mind and communication skill at such a young age', says N.R. Kulkarni, who was then the C.K. Birla group financial head. The young man was soaking up not just the nearly hundred year ethos of the firm but learning how to explore the frontiers of the evolving legal practice of the 21st century.

It was an ordinary day for the greenhorn grandson of Bhagwati Prasad, sitting quietly in his grandfather's office, doing what he was asked to do, when the phone rang. It was 1994; two years after the Manmohan Singh liberalization had kicked in. It was Mr Sanjeev Goenka calling, asking for Pinto Khaitan, who was out of office. 'Those were not the days of the mobile phone and I could not get hold of him. So he asked for Mr P.L. Agarwal, who was not there too', recalls Haigreve. The next sentence was a destiny shaper. The CESC managing director told the young man: 'In that case, you come along…I need you to draw up the hard underwriting agreement for a GDR that we want to sign tomorrow'. Haigreve did not even know what a hard underwriting agreement was and had little save his genes to back him up. 'I looked around the office for a draft underwriting agreement, had it typed out and went to Mr Ghorawat for assurance but he said that it was not his forte'. So off went the young man to Duncan House with whatever he had put together. 'There I saw the stalwarts: Sanjeev Goenka, Sumantra Banerjee and Robert Mullis of BNP Paribas, who gave me the terms of the $100 million issue and asked me to draw up the agreement'.

Fortunately, back in office, he found P.L. Agarwal on his seat and secured his help to draw up the agreement for the first GDR issue for CESC. 'The agreement got signed the next day and I started work under PL's guidance. Which other third-year student would have got such an opportunity?' asks Haigreve. The point is that even the

## Impressing Hutch

Haigreve married the daughter of C.K. Dhanuka in 1996 and went off for his honeymoon. Immediately upon his return, his father informed him that Mr Prashant Jhawar wanted to see him about the Usha Martin Telekom restructuring that he wanted the junior Khaitan to handle. 'I had never worked with him before and it was a restructuring that would involve several foreign investors. I was greatly helped by Sita Khosla who had some experience in this work and had handled JVs with foreign investment. Prashant did not involve any of our seniors for this project which led to a great deal of other work and was a great learning experience for me. I recall having to deal with a senior international lawyer from Simpson Thacker Bartlet, one of the world's leading law firms, representing the Asian Infrastructure Fund, who was dissatisfied with the quality of our drafting and told us what she expected. So we worked through the night to deliver to her expected standards. I still work with her today (Anu Shastri) and she refers a lot of work to us...

'We also did the second phase of the deal that saw the company being sold to Hutchison. In fact, Hutchison was so pleased with our work that they wanted us to move to Mumbai, where they would then give us all their work. Indeed, when we did move to Mumbai in 2001, we met them and they gave us all their work and we also handled the sale of Hutchison to Vodafone'.

greenhorn must have impressed the CESC bosses because, ever since, Sanjeev Goenka has engaged him in all his deals.

Then came the World Bank financing work for the CESC's Balagarh project and Haigreve was summoned once again by Sanjeev Goenka. 'This time I confessed that I was not qualified but he asked me not to worry. We needed to go to Washington for the negotiations and I landed up there with him. He cleared immigration in a few minutes but I got trapped. The officers were a little hesitant to accept my honest answer that I was advising my client on a financial issue especially when they quizzed me about my qualifications and I told them that I was not yet qualified. Eventually, they must have realized that I could be cleared as I was let out after an at least 20-minute grill. Sanjeev Goenka patiently waited for me wondering what was keeping me and I told him what had happened. That was a group that has been a big support to me: Mr R.P. Goenka himself took me along with him to Japan, Europe, UK.... everywhere and that was a tremendous exposure for a youngster'.

There has been a lot of financing work for Balagarh since then and Haigreve credits the success to the support from the firm: 'There is no doubt that I could not have delivered had they not been generous with their support. Also, no one gave me the feeling that they resented my getting to do the work. From 1995 till today, this support continues and the kind of work that we are doing cannot be done single-handedly. The team plays such an important role: my seniors, peers and juniors, the entire team works to achieve success'.

Says C.K. Dhanuka: 'The third-generation team led by Haigreve Khaitan has been equally effective and I have no hesitation in saying that when it came to floating our biggest venture, South Asian Petrochemicals Ltd in Haldia, his assistance with every aspect of the project was invaluable. In fact, the association was instrumental in making the project a success. At a personal level too, I have the highest regard for them and have never heard anything uncharitable being told about him. In fact, we were a Rs 55-crore company when I planned this Rs 470-crore investment and I got Haigreve's support every step of the way: from finances, to planning, to commercial aspects, to EPC contracts. Had he not been there to advise us, I wonder if I could have successfully completed my project'. Haigreve has a different take on this: 'With my father-in-law to be I did a lot of demergers and mergers for he was a person doing different things… buying and selling companies, properties. He really was interested in a lot of things and he would make money with whatever he did. I would often go to his place with my father but more because the food there was excellent'.

What is Sanjeev Goenka's take on Haigreve Khaitan? 'Haigreve, I have seen him grow and it has been an amazing experience to see him achieve the stature of a top lawyer in the country. He is systematic, mature, capable and very strong on domains. My relationship with him is best described by my wife who says that Haigreve is an "emotion" for me. It is a relationship that is between a son and a brother with my having complete faith in his legal acumen'. It is a faith that Haigreve has earned and Sanjeev Goenka recalls a particular deal in the retail space where the junior Khaitan was spot on with his assessment over a joint venture that he was very excited about signing.

Haigreve had been asked to sew up the legal aspects of the agreements but he came up with a bad feeling about the prospective partners and warned Sanjeev about going ahead, only to be overruled. 'He called me up and said that he did not think that we should go ahead with the transaction. "You are not culturally matched". I thought that he was a kid who was being overcautious and advised him to go ahead with it anyway. Within a year of the JV, I was tearing my hair out because the guy was impossible to handle. That

## Trusting blindfolded

There have been other very touching events around our lives, says Sanjeev Goenka. 'When his father-in-law to be asked me if it was a good idea to consider Haigreve as a suitable groom for his daughter, I told him that if it were my daughter, I would go ahead with my eyes closed. Today, if I had to place the future of my wife and child in anybody's custody, it would be Haigreve's. Indeed, it was he who suggested my son-in-law's name when we were looking for a groom for my daughter. So we have been relying on KCo for all kinds of things. Not the least was my father requesting Pinto Khaitan to handle our own family business restructuring. He would trust no one else. This is not a relationship that is based on client-solicitor billings; it is one based on affection, respect, trust and reliability. As far as bills are concerned: we chase KCo to raise bills!'

is when I realized that Haigreve had matured far beyond his years and had sensed that the partnership would not survive while I had got carried away in my excitement of pulling it off', recalls Sanjeev Goenka. 'He understands things in a pat and I do not have to waste time explaining things and I assure you that he gets repeated briefs because he adds value; not because he is a Khaitan'.

There was yet another KCo progeny, the son of Ram Niranjan Jhunjhunwala, who started soaking it all up a few years after Haigreve had got into his groove. Upon graduation Rabindra consulted Pinto Babu about doing an LLM and was advised that hands-on learning at the firm would serve him far better than an additional degree. Rabindra has never regretted taking the advice for he had had a stint at Slaughter & May, London, where he had interned for a while and at another small English law firm. 'I had met barristers; seen how they worked, their systems and functioning styles and wanted to emulate them'. Rabindra had done law at the National Law School in Bangalore – choosing to quit Calcutta for the Bangalore school itself was a major decision for those times – and had joined the firm but realized that he did not want to be under his father's shadow. That is when the Mumbai minute arrived.

Meanwhile, the Delhi office was being modernized with youngsters joining the firm. By the mid- 1990s, KCo had become known even in Delhi student circles. Vanita Bhargava, a second-year student of Law School, Campus Law Centre, New Delhi, had heard of it when she was looking for a place to intern at. Some of her friends had interned with the firm and had good things to say about it. She had not known about her family connection with the firm then. Her father had worked in Calcutta for 16 years with Rolls Print, headed by Moti Lal Bhargava, whose son studied with Pinto Khaitan. The firm also was the solicitor to Rolls Print. Indeed, there was no avoiding KCo connection for Vanita because, when she graduated and joined the office of Bina Gupta, she learnt that her boss was a Khaitan alumnus too. There was more to come.

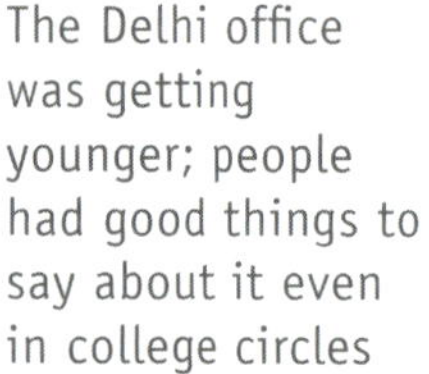
The Delhi office was getting younger; people had good things to say about it even in college circles

'I had done well in my advocate-on-record exam of the Supreme Court in 2004, securing the second position in all of India. I was to be given an award by the then Chief Justice of India at a ceremony in the Supreme Court. Ajay,

my husband, who was working in the firm since 1996, had mentioned that to Mr Pinto Khaitan. We were deeply touched when he came to the ceremony and congratulated us. I was at the crossroads of my career since I was expecting my first baby and, as with most women lawyers, was on the verge of quitting practice, since not many firms or individual lawyers would be supportive of a women lawyer, who would need to balance work and family in that crucial period. In the true Khaitan spirit, Mr Pinto Khaitan offered me not just a job but a partnership in the firm!'

In an era of job-hopping, Khaitans have minimal turnover. This is courtesy the working environment that the firm has. The hierarchy in the firm is seamless and there are no leaders with titles. Even a junior who shows initiative is given independence to service a client, which is the biggest motivating factor, even better than monetary compensation. The firm's hiring policy shows vision because it takes people in whom it can see a long-term perspective because it wants to mould its recruits into partners. It is this vision that brought the firm to its current standards of efficiency and commitment. 'Our competition is with the standards that we have set for ourselves', says Vanita.

Her husband, Ajay Bhargava, partner, had joined the Khaitans in Delhi as an intern in 1996 because the Bar Council required a one-year internship, prior to enrolment with a lawyer of 15 years standing. Khaitans was the best option. Greater openings came up after Umesh Khaitan quit the firm in 1997 and the youngsters got more opportunities to prove themselves. The office was then in Himalaya House where the five interns were permitted to sit in the chamber of none other than Mr Pinto Khaitan, when he was not around. None of them had met Pinto Khaitan, of course. Recalls Ajay: 'One day while we were in the room, some one screamed "Pinto Babu aa rahe hain (Pinto Babu is coming)". That was the first encounter with the person who would take us to our present heights'. Even serious work was fun with the seniors ordering paranthas from the Bhogal restaurant and the interns and young lawyers playing dumb charades on Saturdays.

Calcutta had its share of fun at work too. For the 25-year-old graduate, Nilanjan Ghosh, looking for employment in Calcutta in the mid-1990s, a job with KCo was almost a case of touch and go. His neighbour, Mr S.N. Kundu, was Mr Pinto Khaitan's assistant and was looking for someone to work at the office: to do some administrative work and sit at the reception. He first thought of Nilanjan, who was unfortunately not in the city then. So he picked Utpal Chakraborty, another young man, while Nilanjan had to content himself with listening to office stories from Utpal. Very soon, however, Haigreve was looking for someone similar, to assist him with his everyday work and help with administrative functions as well and this time, Nilanjan was right there. 'I met HK and PK and was asked to join the next day; on February 26, 1996'.

For a young man with zero experience, KCo was an exciting place to be in; there was a spirit of camaraderie at work and there was Samir Dasgupta, who placed the young recruit on a learning curve from day one. The young man was soon motivated to pursue legal studies, attending morning college to do his LLB under the Calcutta University. The work was demanding but the firm encouraged its people to socialize. There were social events and picnics and very soon Nilanjan was in the organizing committee and in the group that enacted plays. 'It was real fun to rehearse at the end of the day. There were a few lady colleagues and we used to get a couple of professional actresses to do the female roles that made the rehearsal sessions very interesting and, occasionally, hilarious'. The need to educate oneself was dinned into the firm by Bhagwati Prasad. There was training not just in law but basic management too as the firm progressed and managing a law firm demanded a different art form: it meant nurturing talent through personal care and formal training.

'In the 1990s I was working closely with both PK and HK. Everyone was in awe of PK but I realized very early how he took care of people. I was accompanying him to some client's office and he was making general enquiries about where I lived and how I commuted while we were in the lift. The next day he called me and asked me to buy a motorbike. It would be a gift from him! For more that 11 years, I rode that bike. I brought it with me to Mumbai when I shifted in 2001', says Nilanjan. Essentially, Pinto Khaitan would notice little signals around the workplace and see how they could be developed when he found things right and how they should be corrected when there was a jarring note.

'Around March 2003, Mr Pinto Khaitan took over the leadership at Delhi and called for a joint meeting of all the advocates with the Delhi office. His first advice was that the receptionist answering office telephone should answer promptly because the instrument was putting people on hold as he had personally experienced. "If this could happen to Pinto Khaitan what would be the plight of the clients?" he wondered. There was complete silence in the room. I ventured to suggest that the receptionist must have dropped the receiver on hearing the caller's name and taken some time to retrieve it. There was a pregnant pause and then Mr Khaitan smiled. The fear factor was finally broken'. However, client servicing 24x7 became the norm for the firm. Everyone was given laptops with internet connections to be available to clients round the clock. The entire outlook of the office changed and the increase in productivity was palpable...just as the concerns around Calcutta mounted.

On April 29, 2000, the newspapers carried a report that shook even the normally complacent Calcuttan. British Airways announced the discontinuation of its flights to Calcutta from that winter and Pinto Babu, who had been considering a Mumbai office since 1972 (ever since Aditya Birla moved base), egged on by the forever ebullient Ram Kishore Choudhury, sent off an email to all at KCo that it was a clear indication of the stagnation in eastern India. Not that people did not know it; it took the global airliner to rub in the message. Pinto Khaitan asked everyone 'to seriously look at opportunities in Bangalore, Delhi and Mumbai and invited everyone's views', says Rabindra Jhunjhunwala.

Nothing could have pleased RKC better who gave his thumbs up to the project and urged that a committee be formed to get it off the ground; the sooner, the better. KCo considered aligning with some Mumbai law firms for starters but none of the discussions amounted to much. A partner's meeting in early January next held in the conference room on the eighth floor, at no. 9, Old Post Office Street, opposite Emerald House, considered the kind of office space that would be required and it was decided to get around 3,000 square feet at a prime commercial area, preferably in central Mumbai. Rabindra was in the game though he knew that moving out to Mumbai would mean losing his father's contacts. He would not be able to capitalize on his Calcutta goodwill. 'Today, I have made my circle and did not inherit his but at that time it was a big decision', he says.

Looking for opportunities all over the country. Grabbing them and excelling: The KCo motto. KCo lawyers in the Delhi office library

'To continue to be in Calcutta with its old-fashioned ways of working did not appeal to me – a 28-year-old then – so when the opportunity to move to and start an office in Mumbai came, I grabbed it. It was also an opportunity to adopt the best practices that we had learnt and to implement them. On our part, we continue to adopt the best practices and adapt ourselves to them even today. Mumbai also came with a partnership offer that made the transfer all the more attractive'.

The Mumbai Office of KCO is a class apart

Haigreve, Prabhay Khaitan (Ashok Khaitan's son) and Rabindra moved to Mumbai in 2001. 'I had been in the profession for only two years then but Haigreve and Prabhay were well-established. The three of us were teamed off because there was a certain comfort level between us and there was the support of all the seniors in the firm. In fact, Haigreve and I had thought of moving to Delhi and had started spending time in the Delhi office. Today when I look back, I am so glad we settled for Mumbai'. Matters developed over a 2001 transaction around restructuring RPG's cellular businesses in which IFC and IL & FS were both invested. 'Haigreve and I were advising RPG and the deal was signed in Mumbai on July 3, 2001. I decided to stay back and look at office space and that effectively became the time I moved to Mumbai'. The office was opened later that year, on November 11, 2001, the 90th anniversary of the firm. 'We started in Ballard Estate in a building called Meher Chamber, which Ram Kishoreji found for us. We purchased it from his client Chase Bright, owned by Alok Jajodia. We took two floors and under four months to get it ready. We did all the work from choosing the tile to the carpet and, of course, the people. At weekends, we would go to Calcutta'.

Yet it was the Bangalore office that took off first. KCo's Silicon Valley, India, experience began in 1993.

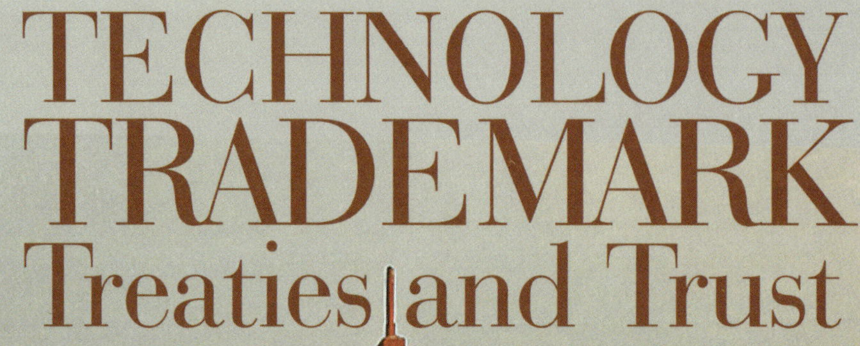

# TECHNOLOGY TRADEMARK Treaties and Trust

Bangalore, the land of even climate and brilliant minds with a scientific temper. Which other city could the enterprising firm have chosen to start its next office?

*It was a dramatic presentation. P. Chidambaram whipped out a Mont Blanc pen from his pocket and displayed it to the court: its elegance; the design; the sophisticated look and feel; and went on to explain how these elements in the pen were matters of protection under the Design Act and how the drawings made to produce the pen were protected under the Copyright Act. He explained how one filled it with ink and how the nib enabled the smooth flow of ink while writing were elements protectable under the patent law. No, the Union Minister-to-be was not dealing with any litigation involving a pen; he was dealing with an important intellectual property rights case in the country, relating to protection integrated circuits used in electricity meters. The Mont Blanc pen was only a tool to explain to the court how the same article could be protected under different forms of intellectual property laws in the country: trademark, copyrights, design, 'mask-works' and patent laws; how even an apparently simple instrument like a pen needed a unique, precise and detailed drawing that could be protected under copyright laws; how dies and tools made from those drawings and used for manufacturing the various parts of the pen could be protected under the copyright laws; even the manner in which the unique product, thus created, was sold under the name, Mont Blanc, was protected under trademark law. Finally, he went on to explain and how someone else selling a similar product could be guilty of 'passing off'. Using the Mont Blanc example, he proceeded to convince the court how counterfeited Chinese IT chips were hurting businesses that had invested billions in technology in India. P. Chidambaram was appearing in court on a brief from KCo, featuring Analog Devices Inc.*

Liberalization in the early 1990s meant a brave new world for India and for international companies seeking to do business in and with this country. The Indian diaspora had already captured hearts and minds at Silicon Valley and now Silicon Valley was planning to transplant itself in this country, at least partially. Which city could it have chosen save Bangalore, the land of even climate and brilliant minds with a scientific temper? Which other city could the enterprising firm have chosen to start its next

## Littlewoods; big experience

Says Kaiser Ahmad: 'In the early 1990s, I was spearheading varied corporate and business development assignments for Littlewoods, the UK Retail and Mail Order Chain, as part of the Eastbourne International Consulting Group. One assignment was to assist Littlewoods in its SE Asian corporate expansion, including setting up a buying office structure headquartered in Singapore, encompassing its sourcing activities in Hong Kong, Indonesia, Malaysia, India and other countries in the region. While the primary focus was on sourcing, our mandate included exploring business opportunities for Littlewoods to sell into the region, either through a joint venture, distributorship or other arrangements.

'While offices were easily set up in Singapore and Hong Kong in Littlewoods own name, India was considered a difficult country for foreign entry. So Littlewoods India sourcing activities were initially conducted through third-party agents. However, we began to explore how to take advantage of the gradual liberalization, which was taking place in India in the post-Rajiv Gandhi era to achieve approval for foreign investment, not just in a sourcing company but also in the sensitive area of retail.

'We were assisted in the business planning part by Coopers & Lybrand and were looking for legal advisers to assist us through the maze of Indian regulatory issues. A barrister friend – Mr Sudipto Sarkar – recommended KCo and introduced me to Pinto and Padam Khaitan. Thus began a professional and personal association that continues to this day.

'With the help of this impressive team of professional advisers, we achieved something quite remarkable in 1993 – obtaining approval from the Foreign Investments Promotion Board to set up a 100 per cent foreign-owned entity with two business objectives: To conduct merchandize development and sourcing activities for export; operate retail operations within India. Approval was granted for a 100-per cent owned corporation'.

office? Not only was the city becoming popular with a whole breed of information technology companies from across the world; some of India's most famous IT companies were setting shop there. There were new business, commercial and, of course, legal issues that would come up and KCo wanted to be where the action was.

Also, there was some talk of a Supreme Court of India bench coming up in the south. Common sense and commercial intelligence dictated that the firm have a base where the apex court of the land would have a bench. The apex court did not go to Bangalore but Khaitans did and with excellent results. There were few law firms there and no one had partner-level representation as KCo had, right from inception. Recalls Rajiv Khaitan: 'It all began in early 1993 when KCo considered further expansion and I was one of those doing a little of everything: litigation, corporate advice, transactions and real estate work, apart from assisting Pinto Chachaji in the administration of the firm in Calcutta. This experience made me a suitable candidate to take the responsibility of setting up our new office at Bangalore and I was asked to prepare a plan on what we needed to do'.

Competition was not tough at that time though Amarchand Mangaldas had opened an office. There was the venerable King and Partridge, which still exists; the Madras-based Rangarajan and Prabhakaran; some local firms and a host of good individual lawyers with several juniors in their chambers. KCo developed strong relations with some excellent counsel there: amongst others were M. Jayaram, R.N. Narasimhamurthy, Udaya Holla and K.G. Raghavan, who continue to be amongst the most respected counsel in Bangalore even today. Enterprising Rajiv selected himself; so did O.P. Agarwal, who had developed in to a solid, serious and hardworking lawyer. He and his wife, also a lawyer, were looking for a change of scene when Pinto Khaitan offered them the opportunity the couple accepted with alacrity. 'So it was decided that O. P. Agarwal and I would move to Bangalore and set up the office there. I made several trips to Bangalore then. We had to identify space and recruit people. We sought the assistance of Mr Pinto Khaitan's daughter and son-in-law and first booked space in an office at Embassy Square on Infantry Road. Since that building was not ready, we bought some 6,000 square feet of ready space at Sunrise Chambers on Ulsoor Road; had it fitted out and started the office in November 1993', says Rajiv.

Fortune favours the brave. Almost by magic, as soon as the firm decided to set up the Bangalore office, it had an assignment from Littlewoods, an international retail brand, 100 per cent foreign-owned, falling into its lap. It was a very new area of work for KCo and indeed for the country because organized retailing was in its nascent stages in India. Some 20 years later, when the country is grappling with the issue of global retail in India and the percentage of permissible equity, it is not a little amusing to learn that KCo had ushered in a retail chain with 100 per cent non-resident holdings into the country, through all the legal processes. Indeed, large-format retailing was thus ushered into India by KCo.

'The Littlewoods experience was an enriching one for us for we advised them on all aspects of the large-format retailing business as they went about acquiring their retailing space in several cities, setting up the supply chain logistics, finalizing the product packaging, labelling, recruiting and training the employees, getting all the legal sanctions and ensuring all regulatory compliance' says Rajiv. The Littlewoods retailing format had many features that were new for the country. Rajiv explains: 'At a time when all the stores in Commercial Street were closed on Sundays and for lunch between 1 and

## Bangalore for Littlewoods…

'One of the factors influencing the decision to locate in Bangalore was that Khaitans had started operations there and we were assured of the appropriate level of continuing legal support. It did the legal work to establish Littlewoods India Limited as a corporate entity in 1994 and Littlewoods merchandizing and retail business personnel began to arrive from England. It was the firm that helped us obtain the necessary approvals for us to hire these foreign nationals. Office premises were located and acquired; Indian managerial and support staff was recruited; and the training commenced. Site selection activity commenced for the launch of retail operations in Bangalore – premises were located and signed up, after protracted lease negotiations in which Rajiv Khaitan played a crucial role. In due course, these premises were made ready for business and the Littlewoods Bangalore store was launched in 1996.

'The sourcing operations that had also commenced, provided a rich flow of merchandize, giving the local consumer access to products developed in conformity with the highest international standards. Simultaneous search for other sites were undertaken in the major metros. By 1997, suitable locations had been identified and signed up in Chennai and Hyderabad, with KCo being actively engaged with us in all negotiations with property owners, preparation of appropriate documents and so on.

'In 1998, my five-year assignment with Littlewoods had ended. With staff and facilities, both Indian and foreign, fully in place, my role with Littlewoods had been fulfilled. I was preparing to return to New York when the close association with the partners of KCo paid unexpected dividends. Mr Pinto Khaitan, then actively looking after the overseas interests of various clients, suggested that I base myself in London to assist Khaitan clients in many areas of non-legal business services'.

3 p.m. on all days, Littlewoods wanted to remain open for 365 days without the lunch-time closure. It also had a coffee shop on the top floor, which meant getting several additional municipal licenses and complying with several additional regulatory aspects'.

Littlewoods wanted to install a water-softening plant, a central air-conditioning plant, an escalator within the departmental store, which was still a novel idea for Bangalore. The expatriates also provided world-class training to its recruits for six to eight months. Indeed, that training provided by Littlewoods laid the foundations of professional retailing and shop-floor managment in India

## The little big experience

Kaiser Ahmad says: 'A new chapter began in 1998, with me heading an organization in London – Guggenbuhl Khaitan Consultants Limited – a collaboration between the firm and a Swiss organization. For the next five years I was based in London, undertaking assignments internationally for Khaitan clients, in such varied areas as tea, engineering, manufacturing, transportation and project logistics. These assignments included serving on the boards of some of the clients' associate companies, overseas as well as in India, and required me to travel around Europe, back and forth to India and as far afield as Kazakhstan and Azerbaijan.

'In 2004, I decided to retire from full-time activity and returned to New York. However, the close professional association formed with the firm continues in occasional consulting assignments and an even richer personal bond has been forged with Pinto, Padam, Rajiv, Haigreve and others. Their help and kindness continues to this day'.

with some of the Littlewoods trainees of the early 1990s now heading the leading retail chains in the country. The experience was an international one in more ways than one and KCo learnt from it every inch of the way from setting up the country's first large format store, fully-funded and pursuing excellence. What more could a firm, seeking to hold its own in the emerging world of globalization, want? 'We spent a lot more time with Littlewoods because we did not have any other pressing engagements', says Rajiv.

Meanwhile, the other partner, O.P. Agarwal and his wife too took up the new assignment with great gusto. 'Both Rajiv and I shifted and started enjoying our work… setting up the office with Rajiv from scratch; even though I also had a lot of Calcutta matters and had to balance both places for a while. In Calcutta, we had an established organization; here the challenge was to do things from the beginning'. OP's first client was Krishna Fabrications Ltd that made automobile seats and was run by Mr Surinder Choudhri. 'We got him through a Calcutta connection. Mr Choudhri was a leading Bangalore entrepreneur who hired us to provide general legal advice on a corporate legal retainership basis.

Today his business has expanded and we handle the legal needs'. More interesting business came by way of TaeguTec, a Korean company. This was the kind of company that was going to be important for India; technology-focused and futuristic. Alok Bhartia was a shareholder in this company that was in serious trouble over its trademark around 1997-98. A certain Mr Jain of Calcutta, who made vests under the TT brand name got an order of injunction against TaeguTec from using the TT trademark in the Delhi High Court. TaeguTec's entire business came to a standstill and its lawyers, stalwarts in trademark matters, Remfry & Sagar, held that the company would have to wait for the law to take its course in terms of getting the injunction vacated.

'When they suffered the injunction, Mr Bhartia who had faith in us wanted the matter to be transferred to KCo because he thought we would be able to have the injunction vacated. This we were able to achieve within a very short time. KCo went the extra ground to provide succour. Mr Manmohan Singh appeared for us and, when we got the injunction vacated, even the Korean principals were delighted with us', recalls O.P. Agarwal. Since then the firm has been their general corporate advisors. It handles everything from property acquisition to matrimonial matters.

IT companies, global and Indian, realized that KCo would be a good firm to have as friend, philosopher and guide to establish themselves in the country. Amongst the most important companies to come to the firm was Tally, owned by Bharat Goenka, for which we handle all trademark matters. The company is constantly coming with new products and there are many tag line and brand names

The Bangalore Partners
Sitting (L): Rajiv Khaitan (R): O.P. Agarwal
Standing (L): Anindita Phukan (R): Abhilekh Varma

issues that have to be handled from time to time.

Getting the Bangalore office on a firm footing meant doing certain things differently because the firm had the luxury of starting afresh in Bangalore. 'For starters, we branded our services and worked with an advertising professional to design a logo for us. This was yet another learning experience because the advertising consultant made us think in terms of what we thought of ourselves and what we were envisaging for ourselves as a firm: he made us understand our identity even as he designed our logo and the first brochure that would set us apart from other firms. Essentially, the agency put us through a one-hour grilling session in our office and forced us to think; to clarify our purpose in our own minds', recalls Rajiv. Though the office was formally opened from April 1, 1994, the Littlewoods work had started in end-1993.

The new KCo Bangalore office. Business is good and growing

The strategy was to take advantage of the firm's heritage relationship with the country's leading audit firms. S.R. Batliboi (now E&Y) and KCo had a historic association since 1915, almost from the beginning of the firm. SRB later became auditors for the firm. This relationship was put to effective use. 'SRB had started its office in Emerald House within our office before moving out into its own office in the same building. Mr Kashinath Memani, senior SRB partner, was very supportive and introduced us to SRB's Bangalore partners, Mr Pankaj Dhandharia and Sunil Bhumralkar (check spelling) asking them to help us. Some of our early clients came through references from them. One of them was Analog Devices, an IC silicon chip manufacturer in a niche area that had just come into India.

The Analog story, one that legends are made of, saw the firm take on the first counterfeiting attack by the Chinese on an American company on Indian soil. On a more permanent basis, Analog opened KCo to technology and the firm started

## Replacement value

Alok Bhartia has known KCo and O.P. Agarwal for more than 20 years. 'We have had various official associations through many of my group companies. One of the joint ventures, where I am the Chairman of the board is TaeguTec India Ltd. We had a complex situation arising out of trademark litigation that was a snag threatening to hamper our operations at a time when the company was getting established in the country.

'We were dealing through attorneys engaged by our multinational partner. We were not getting a sense of comfort and were feeling uncertain about the entire issue. Based on my past experience, we decided to change the attorneys and engaged KCo. Ever since, we are quite happy with the way the firm has dealt with the case and kept us updated on various developments at appropriate times, enabling us to take necessary corrective actions'.

getting involved with details of licensing technology. This counterfeit story deserves detailed telling for working with Analog exposed KCo to this exciting space: high technology licensing and protection of intellectual property rights.

Analog had sponsored the development of wireless in local loop phone technology called the CorDECT system by the IIT Madras in the 1990s and KCo had to assist in licensing of the technology to four vendors in India. Thereafter, Analog developed a low-cost energy metering chip that a Chinese firm, Shanghai Belling, started counterfeiting, prompting the American firm to go after the counterfeiters in Indian courts and succeed in restraining the sale of counterfeits in India. Such chips had started entering India in 2002.

First, one had to collect comprehensive information and data about the counterfeit, some of it through investigators appointed in China and, of course, in India. One needed the complete picture and the modus operandi: who its agents were, who were its distributors in India and who were its customers. Armed with the information collected, KCo tried to have the customs department disallow import of counterfeit goods. For every step taken by Analog to protect its turf, the Chinese counterfeiters had a ploy to continue exporting fakes to India. Finally, Analog got its investigators to actually purchase the fake chip and determine its circuitry. This was then compared with Analog's own circuitry to prepare a watertight case for the Indian courts. 'In the first week of January 2004, we filed a suit against Shanghai Belling and four of its distributors at New Delhi in India. P. Chidambaram, Rajeev Nayyar and Manmohan Singh (now a judge of the Delhi High Court) were engaged for the case. It was at the first hearing that Mr Chidambaram made a very dramatic presentation to explain the complexities of intellectual property laws, the likes of which Indian courts have rarely come across', recalls Rajiv.

P. Chidambaram went on to become a Union minister and KCo engaged Arun Jaitley in his place for subsequent proceedings. We secured an injunction on January 14, 2004, and filed copies of the order with all customs offices in Delhi, where most of the counterfeit chips were being imported. Every customer of the meters with fake chips was served with copies of the injunction. While preparing the plaint and the affidavits, it was very important for us to clearly make out a prima facie case of infringement before the

## Alok Bhartia on KCo

'I know KCo and Mr O.P. Agarwal for more than 20 years. We have had various official associations through many of my group companies. One of the joint venture companies, where I am the Chairman of the Board is Taegutec India Ltd. We had a complex situation arising out of trademark litigation. This was a threatening snag to be able to hamper our operations at a time when the company was getting established in the country.

'We were dealing through attorneys engaged by our multi-national partner. We were not getting sense of comfort and were facing uncertainty over the entire issue. Based on my past experience, we decided to change the attorneys and engaged KCo. Ever since we took this decision, we are quite happy and are pleased with the way the firm has dealt with the case and kept us updated on various developments at appropriate the time enabling us to take necessary corrective actions'.

court to get an ex-parte injunction in the matter. This was achieved by making a very detailed affidavit from the person who had helped develop Analog's original chip – and in whose name the patent was obtained in the US (a Chinese gentleman named William Koon) – explaining the process of development and comparing the feature of the original chip and the counterfeit. 'The "mask work" of the original chip was analytically compared with the impression of the counterfeit chip to prove beyond any doubt that the Chinese chip was a copy and the entire process was documented for the benefit of the Indian court. During the detailed research and analysis we realized that the Chinese manufacturer had copied even a mistake (an unconnected resistor) in the original chip design', Rajiv says. This had to be proved in court for KCo to get the injunction for there was the proverbial rub.

Technology-driven office for a tech city. View of KCo Bangalore

After preparing a strong prima facie case to get an injunction, KCo was faced with a legal dilemma. There were two intellectual property laws under which infringement could have been restrained: the patent law and the mask work law. However, the application for the relevant patent was still pending before the Indian authorities and hence could not be protected in India. The 'mask work' law too had not been operationalized in this country and, accordingly, no application for registering the maskwork had been filed in India. Thus the 'mask work' could not be protected in this country. After much brainstorming with counsel, KCo decided to proceed under the common law rights of 'passing off' for the injunction. On the first day, when P. Chidambaram argued the matter, he had to convince the judge about the counterfeiting and that Analog had a prima facie case for grant of injunction.

'Not only was an injunction granted but a receiver was also appointed to seize the counterfeit goods at the distributor's premises', recalls Rajiv. This was the first case of its kind to be filed in India claiming action against passing off of an IC chip. 'The entire team had worked very hard to get the injunction. The international press covered the case widely and praised the Indian legal system'. It may have taken a year to build the case but the order created enough pressure on the Chinese firm to approach Analog for settlement. Of course, Analog had its US and Chinese lawyers helping KCo to prepare a watertight case because it was very important for Analog to stop the Chinese in their tracks. One client had been won for life and, as Rajiv says: 'From 1994, till today, we have worked with Analog Devices and done everything that they have wanted us to do amidst excellent client-solicitor relationship with them'. The personal touch came when Analog gave Rajiv an Award of Excellence in 2006.

More interesting work on global acquisitions came as well. Himatsingka Siede asked KCo to handle three global acquisitions, one in Italy and two in the US, apart from doing corporate advisory work for them. Mr Dinesh Himatsingka of Himatsingka Siede recalls: 'I had moved to Bangalore some 25 years ago and did need legal services from time to time. When KCo opened office in Bangalore, my father introduced me to Rajiv. Since then, whenever we needed legal assistance, we have not even considered any other option but KCo. It had nothing to do with the size of the firm or the qualification of the lawyers: one either worked with P.D. Himatsingka (the family firm) or Khaitans'.

KCo Bangalore: a hard-working team

## Kudos India

On May 1, 2004, Bill Roberts, the Business Trends (Litigation; Page 19), correspondent, wrote an article on the Analog victory: 'Protecting IP is among electronics companies' greatest concerns about doing business in India and China, potentially the two biggest markets in the world. Analog Devices' experience suggests that India's commitment to protecting IP rights and its judicial processes for doing so are as robust as any in the West. As for China, its commitment remains to be seen'. Referring to Analog's legal counsel in America, William Wise, he wrote: 'Once Wise's team asked the Indian courts for a hearing, the court issued the temporary order within a week. Either Analog Devices got lucky or its case signals a sea change in India. Wise told the correspondent: 'We hired competent counsel in India and got some great advice. By the time we asked for the hearing, we were pretty confident that a fair judge would give us the temporary injunction. Our evidence was compelling'.

Indian law also has an interesting twist not found in the US that will help Analog Devices in the future. Once a court issues a temporary injunction, it designates a commissioner to raid the premises of the offending party, seize all the products in question and gather any related information. In the Analog Devices case, the raid took place within a week, Roberts wrote.

The young partners must have satisfied the clients because they were being considered as more than legal consultants: Dinesh Himatsingka wanted Rajiv to join his board: 'When I wanted to take Rajiv on board, I consulted Pinto Babu and sought his approval. The idea was to select people carefully, people that you have worked with and wish to continue working with, people who would consider your interests as if they were their own. While an understanding of the legal issues would be important, the understanding of the philosophy of a business family was equally so. It is the combination of an understanding of all aspects that makes a legal firm important to a client'.

Meanwhile, the Littlewoods retail experience was proving to be more than fortuitous. Several years after Littlewoods, Mahindra Retail would come to KCo. Amar Korde of Mahindra Retail says: 'There are very few family firms that operate in an intellectual capital space; KCo is one amongst them. It is at once a family firm and also professionalized. This makes it unique: there is no other such law firm in India. For a client like myself, the family factor provides an assurance of continuity. In other law firms, there is greater likelihood of the person servicing you leaving. Then one has to start from scratch'.

What Korde finds exceptional is the firm's linear approach: it takes up issues sequentially to get a complete understanding and then gets back to the client with options. Not only does he have no reasons to complain about the KCo service, he finds the firm's knowledge resources around standards of weights and measures and packaging laws to deal with the legalities under the Metrology Act quite stupendous. 'We have been working with the firm even before our headquarters moved in to Bangalore in 2008. Earlier, we worked with Ravi Kulkarni in Mumbai. When we moved to Bangalore, we needed a local firm that would be able to service us quickly and were very happy to learn that KCo had an office here. We divided our work in three. All routine consultation, litigation and compliance work was given to Khaitan. We picked a niche consulting law firm for real estate, Anup Shah. For specialized matters relating to international bilateral agreements, FDI, we decided to take two opinions: from Amarchand and Khaitans. Thus

## Dovetailing commerce and law

Dinesh Himatsingka of Himatsingka Siede says: 'To my mind the biggest strength of KCo is the quality of professional advice that it gives, taking into account not just the legal aspects but the commercial aspects of the issues involved. Every business house needs such guidance that would dovetail the commercial interests with the legal position and provide advice that is comprehensive in nature; it needs a legal firm to go into issues that have not yet come into play and think about the consequences. KCo would go into these details; examine the options and provide us with a complete perspective that would be necessary for us to take a view'.

we really have only two firms on our radar'. Admittedly, administering the packaging law has been very difficult. It is a Central law but implemented by the states that add their own requirements and have it administered through the state police. The act has often been considered to be an income stream, which is not uncommon in the country, where packaging standards are far from uniform or compliant with the metrology requirements.

Clearly, the Littlewoods experience that had familiarized the firm with metrology laws, proved to be most helpful in the case of Mahindra Retail. In 2008, the law got teeth and was revamped in line with good practices; the department started doing larger raids with strict penalties. The first-time offender was penalized Rs 5,000 and second-time offender got three years in jail. Overall, the industry's approach was to 'manage' rather than comply. KCo advised compliance and urged the company to refuse to stock goods that were not 100 per cent compliant in a world where people chose the easy way out instead of ensuring that the packaging details conformed to the requirements. It took the Mahindras eight months to achieve full compliance and KCo helped with exercising continuous vigilance because the retail business was getting at least one new product a month.

There have also been a few trademark litigation in Mumbai around Mahindra Retails, 'Mom & Me' brand against two other older companies: Me and Mom and Mom N Me. Says Korde: 'In an ongoing case, in which no stay was enforced against us, contrary to most legal advice, KCo advised us to settle and is facilitating the settlement process'. Yet again, the firm handled 'with excellent professionalism the Club Mahindra IPO', he adds. Amar Korde finds Ravi Kulkarni's genteel manners and open-minded erudition most satisfying in a counsel. 'Yet there have been cases when the thoroughness of the legal documentation prepared by KCo has made the other party nervous about working with us. In one matter, when it came to the need for insulating the client from direct ownership of a business to be acquired, the volumes of paperwork made the other party – that had expected the business deal to be done over a handshake – quite uncomfortable. While the deal was salvaged through the personal intervention of the senior management, the takeout was that while the documentation must be thorough, it must be enforceable; if the heavy documentation leads to the breakdown of a deal… one would have to look for other options', says Korde.

What makes KCo special is that it cautions clients about the pitfalls and offers the workarounds. 'The firm tries to look at the issue from the client's perspective and provides a legally workable solution. Understandably, KCo has certain non-tradeable buckets but client's comfort with the position comes first. The firm listens, researches, asks for your position, gives you options, and advises not to litigate but settle in appropriate cases. It looks for long-term effects, it offers continuity. It may not offer too much of the English erudition; it is much too rooted to the ground. Its erudition comes out of researching; it does not jump into haan or naa (yes or no) positions', says Korde.

KCo has been a solicitor of choice for firms old and new. For a fledging technology company, Mistral, KCo, has been a friend, philosopher and guide, holding its hands from its inception till date. The relationship began after the two had met in a business deal in which KCo was helping an American company on the other side. Since then the firm has helped Mistral with its venture capital funding, 'We were greenhorns then and knew nothing about due diligence; KCo's advice helped us in understanding of the issues involved and in making our agreements. Most importantly, Rajiv was approachable and came to us more like a friend than a lawyer. The comfort factor with him was excellent and he protected our interests at all times; we

## Swamped by SWAMP rules

'Over these years, we have had no reasons to complain', says Korde. 'Indeed, when it came to the Standards of Weights and Measures Act and Packaging laws and to deal with the legalities under the metrology laws, Rajiv is extremely erudite and it was he who helped us change not only the way we did things but also the way some large FMCGs handled their packaging declaration and compliance of the Swamp law. Our company has to handle as many as two lakh SKUs (for its stores) and it was Rajiv who helped us achieve 100 per cent compliance. We were serious about our zero tolerance for non-compliance of packaging laws. This meant not only providing all the legally required declarations but putting them in the technically correct format. We had to take on major manufacturers, including leading multinational vendors, who found it difficult to fall in line but Rajiv gave us the strength to hold out. Even our sales managers opposed our zero tolerance policy and would refer to the falling sales on account of it. Finally, we prevailed and got all our suppliers to fall in line and become 100 per cent compliant. The inspector who came to check gave us the 100 per cent compliant report; something that was unbelievable. Rajiv was made a speaker of honour in the Mahindra spectrum, where we invite the experts to speak'.

valued his feedback because it was honest and the response has always been quick', says S.M. Anees Ahmed.

So excited was the Mistral team about its first venture capital funding that it was jubilant after signing the shareholder agreements; it would have been ready to sign anything in the excitement because it desperately needed star-up funds. KCo examined the various clauses, explained their significance and ensured that detailed legal due diligences was done. It taught them where to hold back; explained to the client the need to see worst case scenarios and protect Mistral against possible future issues; worry about what if something went wrong; to commercially negotiate a good contract and save itself from the bad times. Since then 'most of our documents are drafted by KCo – our vendor contracts, customer contracts, employee agreements. As we have grown, I have watched the firm grow and yet remain approachable. Rajiv does not let layers come in between him and us. For me, he is the front man but I know that there is an engine behind him'.

As technology gets complex, the law around it gets even more so. Mistral makes extremely high-end technology products that are used in critical operations from mobile command and control rooms to laser-guided missiles, aircraft systems, early warning systems and border surveillance. It developed wearable surveillance solutions that can record everything and bring down legal costs that result out of inadequate documentation. The mobile command and control rooms are used in cricket matches for instance; for VIP security. What helps KCo in dealing with this client is their understanding of technology issues. Says Anees: 'They see the legal aspects arising out of technology that we do not see because they can quickly grasp technology aspects. Then they bring out IP issues and methods to secure them as patents or copyrights and deal with contracts for royalties, indemnity aspects of the agreements that we make with our customers'. Mistral has been recently contemplating an arrangement with a Spanish company to sell the latter's homeland security products in India in return for Mistral developing designs for the Spanish: 'We get India access to their products. This involves a complex structuring of a deal. There will be tax issues, IP issues and KCo will negotiate for us and not let us get bullied into doing things that are not in our interest. They are building in protection mechanisms in the documentation', says Anees.

The firm seems to be at its impressive best when

## Mom's lounge

'There is also a case around our Mom's Lounge…a facility that we offer for expecting mothers; exerting an upwards influence with mothers, where legal issues may arise because there may be a grey area under the law, which even the authorities are not clear about. It was Rajiv who explained to us the legal positions: those in which there can be no 'unnis bees' (zero tolerance) and those where there is some scope for tolerance. KCo has the corporate and commercial understanding of the issues to tell us where we stand vis-à-vis the law that few others have', says Korde.

The Bangalore High Court: the majesty of the law

advising family businesses; where it has a clear advantage over most competitors. H.B. Jairaj of Bangalore's HRB Group admits: 'Having dealt with a lot of law firms all over the country, I found that KCo has a very unique spot: the only law firm in the country capable of advising family businesses that are corporatizing or negotiating with multinationals. In this space, it is the master. Other people are not able to muster this knowledge. The firm also has a strong understanding of how businesses function and this is not something that all legal firms have. It can look at things not only from the legal perspective but at the overall picture as well. It appreciates the commercial intent of the client and then advises on the appropriate legal structuring that should evolve out of it; what the framework should be; and also what should not be done'.

KCo's advice was with Bacardi most crucial when Jairaj was exiting an agreement to produce liquor in his premises with Bacardi. Jairaj explains: 'In joint ventures between an MNC and a family-owned company, one is looking at the union of not only two businesses but two very, very different mindsets: one is a very highly paid and smart employee on the MNC side – but still an employee – and the other is the owner. The owner remains constant but the employee on the other side changes from time to time and this makes it very difficult for the owner to establish the relationship that he had with the original employee with the replacement. The new employee does not have the same personal understanding between the partners and looks at only the documentation for future decisions relating to the joint venture. It is this cultural difference and the issues that arise from it that the legal firm must help bridge through sound understanding of mindsets on both sides'.

KCo had long realized the need for detailed and correct documentation imperative. Jairaj explains 'Since the new MNC employee does not have the same understanding as the predecessor who brought the business together, he must depend on the documentation to continue the relationship. JVs fail because of a lack of understanding of the culture and inadequate paperwork. To the MNC manager, the numbers matter more than anything else. When the MD changes the owner on the other side is talking to someone else, who thinks totally differently. Rajiv anticipated these problems. Sometimes the MNCs run out of capital or change their plans whimsically and one needs

The conference room at the new KCO Bangalore office

### The right thing to do

'We all do things that are good for us but not always do the right things. It is Rajiv's conviction that if things are morally right, legally they will fall in place. In following his advice, I have been able to give myself the ability to sleep in peace', says Jairaj. The point he makes is that KCo's relations with its clients do not depend only on billable hours; it does not want to make money only on making deals go through but by uncovering the underlying truth of what these families want and how best they can be legally assisted to achieve it. 'People like ourselves find it extremely difficult to work with firms that want our business at any cost. There are firms with lawyers who do everything except what they are supposed to do. KCo is able to focus on providing legal and strategic advice'.

to safeguard the owner's interests. He painted a landscape of an unravelling environment; he was able to see the scenario and keep the safeguards for me and, therefore, I got my due share when we parted with Bacardi. Bacardi was interpreting the agreement differently and KCo helped me negotiate from a position of legal strength. It has done that for several other companies too'.

As Rajiv Khaitan says: 'Often, while doing big deals, people lose sight of the real issues; the major things. We ensure that the critical issues are negotiated in our client's favour and, if at all, we go easy on the smaller issues' These are little nuggets of advice that clients respect. The important thing is that clients do not ever question the firm's advice.

Dinesh Himatsingka, having sought and accepted the advice, followed it. As he says, 'because we did things together. We discussed issues, when it came to taking over companies overseas we had deliberations and decisions were made over these discussions. I cannot assess the long term consequences of these decisions right now... only time will tell'. Nothing like trust to cement relationships; nothing like trust never betrayed to make relationships last forever.

# THE 21ST CENTURY

*It must have been a curious sight: three Indians – father, daughter and nephew-sitting at the Dorchester's business centre in London, dictating, typing, correcting and concentrating on what was clearly a legal document. They looked like unlikely typists; indeed they may never have done any serious typing in their lives for they were the scions of one of Calcutta's most successful business families and they were trying to swing one of the most interesting global deals of India of the 21st century. It would make the buyers the largest tea-plantation company in the world.*

The senior person in the group was a partner at one of Calcutta's top legal firms, the other his daughter and the third was from yet another branch of the family that was into big-time industry. Padam Khaitan, the grandson of Naurangrai's eldest son, and his daughter Nandini were in the company of Anshu, the great-great-grandson of Naurangrai, the great-grandson of his fifth son Gauri Prasad, the grandson of B.M. Khaitan and the son of Deepak Khaitan. For them it was to be a holiday in London but for a businessman on the move, the scent of a deal is a scent of a deal. Deepak Khaitan had heard that 17 gardens of George Williamson, Assam, were on sale and there was no way that the son of B.M. Khaitan would let this opportunity slip by.

Fortunately for him, his ever-reliable cousin, Padam Khaitan, was around and it was a simple enough matter to ask Padam to take charge while he went about his own business. Padam, a Bel Chamber's Gold medallist, was known to be a pucca professional but he had never handled a big-ticket takeover of the kind that he was being asked to. Having been thrown into the deep end, this young partner of KCo had to find his way out without himself or his client getting scalded. Deepak Khaitan had made it clear that it was the solicitor's responsibility to swing the deal.

Facing page: Work hard; play harder for that is the spirit of the 21st century at KCo

Then began a series of tiresome meetings with Magor's solicitors, Penningtons, who first asked for a formal letter of offer. That is when Padam Khaitan went into the tizzy of typing at the Dorchester, helped by his young daughter who had just passed her law and Anshu, BM's grandson. The price to be quoted for the buy would have to come from the redoubtable B.M. Khaitan himself and the letter of offer would have to await the quote from 4, Mangoe Lane. Once the offer price was available, the three were ready with the document that they promptly mailed. Then came a period of seemingly incessant wait: seven days before there was a call from Penningtons. They wanted clarifications, which was a veiled way of asking: 'Do you have the money?'

Fortunately, the then head of ICICI Bank's corporate section, a Mr Balasubramaniam, was golfing in Scotland. His services were quickly procured by the prospective buyers and when the discussions turned difficult, the banker pulled out his cheque book with a flourish: 'How much money do you want?' The banker's presence seemed to settle matters on the finance score and the parties were ready to sign the term sheet. Before the signing, Deepak and Padam went off to Harrods to buy a pen with which Magor would be asked to sign the term sheet and which would then be gifted to him. The signing went off smoothly and Philip Magor seemed happy enough with his rather expensive pen.

The solicitors, John Riddick and Leon Arnold, continued to be crotchety though, and drafts went back and forth till Philip Magor probably got worried about the bill that his lawyers who, it would be fair to assume, would want to be paid by the hour, would present. Since much of the correspondence was around the guarantees that the buyer would have to provide, he decided that he did not want any guarantee but wanted the terms of the sale to be quickly settled. Even after the term sheet was signed, there were

The fountainhead of justice: outside the Calcutta High Court

## Client Dhruv

'It was around the year 2000, during the dotcom boom, we were bringing private equity into our firm and KCo sent its people from every office to work on the deal. It was a complex deal: we were buying out our joint-venture partner, bringing in private equity and restructuring our businesses and this involved lots of people, different parties, conflicting interests, detailed due diligence and clearly we were not geared up to handle such things. The firm rolled out its resources, helping us to achieve our ends. The point is that the lawyer has to be both an insider and outsider; see things from our perspective and from the other side's point of view too. In this deal, we had international lawyers representing the other side, from US, Europe, Asia and KCo put it all together for us'. — *Dhruv Khaitan.*

other matters to be settled – warranties that the seller would have to provide in terms of tax and other liabilities – and Padam and his young team had to go to Newbury where the solicitors had their office.

It was an adventurous mission by all accounts. Padam Khaitan, busy pouring over his notes, missed the Newbury station and when the three got off at the next station they saw neither a soul nor any transport there. On closer inspection, they found a little cabin where there was a solitary guard who offered to call the Newbury station and ask for a cab to be sent from there. Thus did the party manage to reach the Penningtons.

Matters were far from cordial, with the English solicitors behaving as if they were doing the Indians a favour with their reluctant 'OK, I will give you this' and it took the normally unflappable Padam to ask them if they thought they were doing charity. Indeed, they would receive a tidy sum for the deal. Matters settled, the tired party returned to London. 'I had a tuna sandwich for the first time in my life; I was hungry but Nandini and Anshu ate nothing. They were strict vegetarians', recalls Padam.

The fatigue factor was not helped by the ways of the solicitors; not the least was the language that they used, managing to rile Deepak so much that he walked off in a huff, withdrawing from the deal, only to return to the negotiations after Magor had personally apologized. Matters then having been settled to everyone's satisfaction, the penthouse at the Dorchester was booked for the grand signing event. If Padam Khaitan had expected a gift in reciprocity for the handsome present that the Khaitans had given Philip Magor, he was disappointed. What must have compensated for this disappointment was the gala 'thank you' party that B.M. Khaitan threw for them at Queen's Park once they were back in Calcutta. Many other acquisitions followed, from Uganda to Vietnam...

There were other opposing solicitors too who made professional rivalry somewhat unpleasant. Padam Khaitan recalls the feisty Mr Heine, who represented his German clients CMT, who were selling their global businesses to B.M. Khaitan-owned McNally Bharat. Heine loved to push one-

## Litigation without end

Gopal Mookherjee says: 'From 1989, I was engaged by KCo for a spate of litigations – some 30 of them – featuring the Surajmull Nagarmull disputes over control of companies between B.P. Jalan and M.P. Jalan. Eventually, all of them, save one, got settled in the Supreme Court and every senior Khaitan was involved in the cases. Padam Khaitan took the lead in this matter'. The litigations were around Company Law matters and the main legal issues that arose were:

- Whether the affairs of a company would include the affairs of its holding companies and subsidiary companies for applications under sections 397-98 of the Companies Act.
- Is there such a concept as a Family Company?
- What makes it just and equitable for a company to be wound up?
- When are partnership principles made applicable to a company?
- Is it inevitable under sections 397-398 of the Companies Act that the minority shareholders would have to sell out or can the wrongdoer, who has oppressed the minority, be directed to sell?

'Fortunately, for me, there was a strike in the Calcutta High Court over the stamp duty issue and I could stay in Delhi for a prolonged period to handle things in the Supreme Court, where the first phase stretched for several months'.

sided agreements while the polite Padam would argue that what was sauce for the goose was also sauce for the gander. Heine held that life was not necessarily logical. Hard bargaining and negotiations were understandable, for the Khaitans were buying a cluster of companies and the CMT owner, who was in Hong Kong, wanted the buyers to meet him there. Not so the solicitor's behaviour. Heine, who was by now being referred to as 'hyena' – the sobriquet owing itself to a typing error by the Calcutta office – rudely asked: 'What if you go bankrupt in the two months after which you say you will pay?' Deepak Khaitan countered: 'What if your client goes bankrupt?'

Padam Khaitan with the local advocates at Kampala with clients representatives (extreme Left)Rajiv Takru and (extreme Right) Dilsher Sen, having successfully closed a deal for Mcleod Russel.

There were other entirely forgettable meetings in Cologne as well – long discussions and bad food for lunch were an unhappy combination. Making matters worse was the absence of eateries in the vicinity of the solicitor's office; so the choice was between eating hard bread and cheese day in and day out or fruit that one could carry in one's bag. Padam had to settle for the latter. There was a lesson to be learnt in all these verbal duels and unpleasant behaviour, apart from the finer points of law that one picked up. 'For me, I grew in confidence and felt a tremendous sense of job satisfaction after the Williamson deal', says Padam Khaitan.

'There was an equally strong lesson to be learnt during the Jalan family settlement between BP, who was my client, and M.P. Jalan. First, because of the sheer number of litigations that I had to handle and then from the manner in which Justice S.N. Variava forced the litigants to come to a settlement. The only allowance he made was that if there were one or two aspects that they could not resolve amongst themselves, they could come to his court and he would decide matters for them'. Padam Khaitan was involved with the case (that had started in 1989) in 1991. That was after cousin Suman, who was handling the matter, shifted to Delhi. 'The discussions were detailed and long sometimes in the chamber of Mr Dipankar Gupta who represented one party and Amal Ganguly who represented the other. The interesting strategy in the settlement was that under court orders, every company in the group was auctioned in an "either you buy me out or I buy you out" routine that was decided by the court. Parties had to make these offers alternatively; the court even decided the sequencing of the various auctions', explains Padam Khaitan.

Other partners too had interesting experiences. There was the famous Texmaco case following the ruling of the Supreme Court that all factories should be moved out to the National Capital Region when Justice Kuldip Singh had ruled that workers who were not able to move would have to be paid salary for six years and that 60 per cent of the factory land would have to be surrendered. Everyone was complying with this order but K.K. Birla was most upset about the ruling. Om Khaitan found it to be unfair and contrary to the provisions of the Companies Act too. When the two had a chat on the matter over tea one day, Om said that not even the Supreme Court could go beyond the law. 'Justice Singh had since retired and I discussed the matter with Mr Patra in our office and we decided to go to Mr Venugopal and ask him to file a writ petition against the Supreme Court order'. Mr Venugopal almost jumped out of his chair. No one had heard of such a preposterous thing and he shooed the solicitors away saying that they were out of their minds. However, the facts of the matter had been placed

The reception at Emerald House is placid, soothing... never mind the legal hullabaloo inside

## Tech-edge

Recalls Sanjeev Kapoor: 'Even when I joined the firm in 2004, I found that it was technologically savvy and using technology to its advantage. Every associate was given a laptop and datacard on the day of joining; something that very few firms did then because use of technology was emphasized in every respect. We have kept pace with technological advances and had tailor-made software developed for our needs in a bid to harness technology to assist us to perform better. It consciously uses technology to give itself a competitive edge by ensuring that every resource is technologically assisted to perform better. Finally, every process and resource of the firm is so structured so that every advocate can excel and be optimally utilized; they are centred on ensuring that our advocates are enabled to achieve their best and provide best services to the client'.

before him. 'That night I received a call from Venugopal. He said that he had been thinking of what I had said and was agreeable to filing the case. He was going to Madras that evening and wanted Patra to accompany him and he would settle the petition on his way up and down', says Om.

The matter came up before Justice Sujata Manohar, who apparently threw the papers back saying that the matter was dismissed; no one had heard of such a thing. Mr Venugopal argued that his initial reaction was just that but he changed his mind after examining the merits of the case. Finally, Justice Manohar agreed to refer it back to the Chief Justice and ask him to reassign the case to another bench. The Chief Justice sent it back to her and then Mr Venugopal persuaded her to send it to the same bench that had originally heard the matter and promised to convince it that there was good reason to review their judgment. This was around 2002-03.

The matter was then referred to the original bench and by then every affected party had entered the fray and there were a battery of lawyers from every one. 'We had Harish Salve appearing for us and the matter was heard for over a month and we managed to convince the court that if an illegal order had been passed by the court there should be recourse to a curative petition that could never be frivolous but would have to be filed with caution, certified by a senior lawyer with a provision for very heavy penalty if wrongly filed. This was the first time in Supreme Court history that such a thing was allowed. K.K. Birla was, of course, delighted with me and invited the entire team and K.K. Venugopal for tea. Venugopal turned around and said that it would be his honour to host K.K. Birla to tea and what we had was a sumptuous tea at KKV's house. He then admitted that it was a very hard case and told K.K. Birla that had it not been for his solicitors, this would not have happened', says Om.

It was a small well-bonded family that Sanjeev K. Kapoor became a part of in 2004. Today, there are three striking things about KCo, he says. It is a big family but the bonding is just as strong; it is an ethical company; it pursues excellence and takes pride in the quality of its work. The other distinctive feature is the immense variety of work that the firm does. The firm deals in cases across a broad

## CESC survives

Mr Shanti Bhushan remembers arguing a case for CESC in the Supreme Court in 2002 before a three-judge bench including Santosh Hegde on which the future of CESC hung on balance. 'We even had Chidambaram assisting in that matter. When the case started, the bench was hostile and if we had not been able to turn the attitude of the bench with our arguments, CESC would have gone down. Eventually, we got an excellent judgement from the Supreme Court because of which CESC survived and became a very strong player in the electricity space. It has brought down its T&D losses from 23 per cent to 13 per cent and has streamlined administration in Calcutta to deal with problems of power theft. In Noida, it has brought down T&D losses from 30 per cent to eight per cent and today CESC wins all its cases not only at electricity tribunals but also at the High Court and the Supreme Court.

'I also remember being assisted by Gauri Rasgotra in the CESC case in the Supreme Court and found her to be a dedicated officer of the firm. She knew the entire brief and could put her finger on the relevant page on every aspect of the matter. It is such thorough knowledge that helps counsel argue cases'.

spectrum of law, including constitutional law; general trade and commercial laws; laws relating to energy, infrastructure, right to information, intellectual property, environment, mining; and arbitration laws to name a few. It assists clients before the Supreme Court of India, before various state high courts, Appellate Tribunal for Electricity, (erstwhile Monopolies and Restrictive Trade Practices Commission), Competition Commission, Competition Appellate tribunal, TDSAT, mining tribunals, financial reconstruction tribunals, Foreign Exchange Appellate Board and the like. Of course, it assists clients in domestic and international arbitrations including those before such institutional arbitral tribunals as the ICC, LCIA, LMAA, JAMS, amongst others.

The labyrinth of the law: a corridor at the Calcutta High Court

'Indeed the capacity, bandwidth and reach in terms of the firm's capability are remarkable and quite unmatched. We are in a position to advise a client in any matter in any part of the country or the world. We have good working relationships with international firms and have aided clients in their disputes outside India also whether it is Europe, America or Africa apart from advising almost all leading groups in the country. The firm has expertise in handling complex and difficult cases. Amongst others, it successfully challenged the constitutional validity of Section 3(1-a) of the Chattisgarh Upkar (Sansodhan) Adhiniyam, 2004 (Chattisgarh Energy Development Cess) before the Chattisgarh High Court at Bilaspur. The state has filed appeals against the order and the matter is pending before the Supreme Court of India. These appeals are also being handled by us', says Sanjeev.

KCo Delhi handled one of the most sensitive electricity restructuring issues featuring Calcutta's CESC. Says Gauri: 'We represented CESC before the Supreme Court in tariff matters, which involved complex issues like cross-subsidy, accounting of transmission and distribution losses and such others. This was a matter where we had many eminent counsel appearing in view of the high stakes, including Shanti Bhushan (whose efforts were exemplary), P. Chidambaram, K.K. Venugopal, Dipankar Gupta and Abhishek Singhvi. The matter ran into many volumes of printed material and was a matter of survival for the company. After a lengthy and continuous litigation, our combined efforts ultimately resulted in a good order for the company. I must mention that our burden was ably shared by two very hardworking and sincere client representatives, Utpal Bhattacharya and Gargi Chatterjee, both of whom are assets to CESC'.

If these were the people front-ending the CESC case, Sanjeev Goenka talks of what was happening in the back rooms. About Hagrieve, he says: 'We have travelled extensively together and I recall creating opportunities for him to visit his fiancée who was studying in London, but for most of the time it has been very hard work. He spent endless hours in Delhi when the CESC case was in the Supreme Court, discussing the matter with counsel Harish Salve and Mukul Rohatgi and being a source of strength to me at a period of extreme tension for me because the company's future depended on the outcome of the case. Haigreve was Mr Cool and kept my spirits up when things looked bad; he kept me going. Eventually, we won the case, which paved the way for electricity reforms in India. I recall a long two-hour discussion with Haigreve before we went to court. My father wondered if it made sense to take on the government but Haigreve assured me that, on merits, we had a fantastic case and, in any event, we had no option.

KCO, Calcutta: where work never stops

## Citizen Sonia

Gaurav Banerjee recalls the Sonia Gandhi citizenship matter: 'The question was whether one could be a citizen by domicile and marriage. The matter then came to the Supreme Court as an SLP, where Justice Lahoti asked us very difficult questions but then gave a very good judgment. In the course of the matter, Mrs Sonia Gandhi's marriage records had to be produced and some other documents and I believe that the judge went into the matter at such great length because he wanted to settle the matter once and for all and ruled that the "Lady is a citizen of India".

That steeled my resolve to go ahead with the case'.

There was yet another headline-grabbing matter of the times. Indeed, KCo seems to have an affinity for the Gandhi family in a court of law. This time the citizenship of Mrs Sonia Gandhi was challenged. The Lucknow Bench of the Allahabad High Court held that three election petitions filed in the Allahabad High Court, by two losing candidates in the 1999 elections from Amethi (Hari Shankar Jain and Hari Krishna Lal) and an Amethi voter (Prem Lal Patel), challenging her election on the grounds that she, being Italian-born, did not satisfy the prerequisites for registration as a citizen of India were not maintainable. Thereafter, Jain had challenged the legality of section 5(1)(c) of the Citizenship Act, 1955, under which Sonia Gandhi acquired her Indian citizenship through registration.

Under this provision, persons who are, or have been married to, citizens of India, are ordinarily resident in India and have been so resident for a period of 12 months immediately before making an application for registration, would be eligible to apply for Indian citizenship by means of registration. (This provision was amended in 1986 whereby the requirement regarding the length of residence was made five years.) Based on her application under this section, she was issued a certificate of citizenship by the government of India on April 30, 1983, and the court held that the citizenship certificate granted to Sonia Gandhi was final and binding and, unless it was cancelled by the Central government the issue could not be questioned as part of an election petition.

Jain and Lal appealed against the high court verdict in the Supreme Court. The Supreme Court bench comprising Chief Justice A.S. Anand, Justices R.C. Lahoti and Doraiswamy Raju, in its order of September 12, rejected the high court judgment that an election petition could not challenge a citizenship certificate or the constitutionality of the Citizenship Act, but dismissed the appeals because the petitions made only bald and vague averments about Sonia Gandhi's eligibility for Indian citizenship and therefore, did not satisfy the requirements of pleading material facts under Section 83(1)(a) of RPA, 1951.

This case involved a high-profile dispute on the validity of a certificate of citizenship issued to Sonia Gandhi under the Citizenship Act before the Supreme Court, recalls Gauri. 'Milon Banerjee was the counsel briefed in the matter. I worked with him and his son Gaurav Banerjee closely to make sure that this litigation saw a positive order from the highest court. The court held that the election petitions filed against Sonia Gandhi could not be directed to be heard and tried on merits as the bald and vague averments made in the election petitions did not satisfy the requirement of pleading material facts within the meaning of Section 82(1)(a) of the Representation of People Act, 1951, read with the requirements of Order VII,

## Right to educate

KCo is representing a client who has filed a writ petition before the Supreme Court contesting the Constitutional validity of Right to Education Act (The Right of Children to Free and Compulsory Education Act, 2009) on the ground that certain provisions of the Act are not in line with the Act's larger objective. Says Sanjeev Kapoor: 'In fact, the Act is framed in a manner that it is detrimental to the working of private schools and organizations, which are doing a good work in terms of supplementing the government's efforts in the educational sector and actually sharing the state's burden. The judgment in the case is reserved after a detailed hearing'.

Rule 11, of the Code of Civil Procedure. I worked with Suman Khaitan (former partner) on this matter.'

The country had been liberalized but not everyone in the bureaucracy, certainly not some revenue officers, as W.H. Targett & Company were to realize. In a long-drawn-out matter, handled by Mr Asopa, which got resolved only in 2007, W.H. Targett & Company, which had changed its name, found the revenue officer in Delhi, where it owned a property, insisting that it was a new company and the change of name represented the transfer of a property from one company to another, whereupon he made a huge demand for a transfer fee. If a case concerns an immovable property outside Bengal, the proceedings should be filed in the state in which the property is situated. Unmindful of the fact that it was only a matter of change of name of an existing company, the officer treated the company as two different companies. The imposition of the transfer fee was challenged by a writ petition in the Calcutta High Court.

Explains Mr Asopa: 'Under the Companies Act, a company may change its name and such change of name does not affect its rights and obligations. One of the demand notices from the revenue officer, New Delhi, was received by the client in its Calcutta office. On that basis, we advised the client to file a writ petition in the Calcutta High Court, which was also what the client wanted. The high court granted interim stay and, finally, the petition and directed the officer to mutate the property in the new name of the company and quash the demand'. The officer, however, preferred an appeal, which he lost. Still not satisfied with the legal position as confirmed by the orders of the Calcutta High Court, he preferred a revision application. The revision application was dismissed. Against that too the revenue officer was advised by the legal department of the ministry concerned to prefer an appeal before the Supreme Court. Finally, the SLP was dismissed and only then was the client able to get rid of the demand of the revenue officer, having spent a lot of money and 15 years in litigation.

In 2006, Mr P.L. Agarwal asked Roopa to handle a Mr C.K. Dhanuka matter featuring a hospital owned by a family trust. The hospital, a women's hospital and the only such facility for women in the region, in Sikar, Rajasthan, was being virtually taken over by the secretary of the trust following the demise of Shankar Lal Dhanuka. The usurper wanted to change the constitution of the trust, effecting the trustees' rights, for which he had called a meeting without the knowledge of the trustees. 'This had to be stopped and we chose to file a suit in the Calcutta High Court along with an interim application and secured a temporary stay of the meeting while also filing a suit at the Sikar District Court. The judge there refused to pass any order in the interim stage, forcing us to go to the high court that directed the district judge to dispose of our application expeditiously. Regretably, the matter was disposed of against us. We went up in appeal to the high court, praying for a chairman to be appointed for a meeting to be convened by the court for passing of various resolutions with regard to the working of the trust because the secretary had, by then, taken control of the hospital, placing his cronies in key positions. That apart, there were allegations of defalcation', recalls Roopa.

The court ordered the secretary to prepare an agenda – as directed by the trustees – and appointed a senior advocate of the Rajasthan High Court Bar to chair the meeting. Accordingly, Mr C.K. Dhanuka, chairman, sent an agenda – that included the removal of the secretary – that was marked to all the trustees and the secretary, asking for the meeting to be held at ITC, Jaipur. The secretary chose to ignore it and prepared his own agenda and planned a meeting at the Rawat Hotel, while the trustees travelled to

## Have the cake and eat it too

Says Mustafa Wajid of the Meher Group: 'Having sold our biggest unit that was manufacturing power factor correction capacitors to Schneider, we are now using the proceeds to drive our future business: Meher 2 that will have an intensified activity in the technology-driven space around energy efficiency and storage. We have created an asset management company to make use of the unlocked value and efficiently manage our resources. We also developed a charity division: the Meher Care Foundation, with defined plans in each of these areas. In all this, KCo has been an integral part of our team. Rajiv personally spent hours with us, especially while negotiating with Schneider, incorporating provisions that would be beneficial to us in the sale agreements. This included outmaneuvering Schneider in allowing us to retain the right to use of the Meher brand name even after selling the main business, which used the Meher mark for sale of its products. We were ultimately able to realize the full value of the business, including the value of our brand, Meher, while managing to keep it for our other businesses. In a manner of speaking, we could have the cake and eat it too'.

How was this achieved? By Rajiv showing them the path of partial assignment of trademark that they did not take on board at first and getting the Schneider lawyers to agree that it was legally possible to achieve this. 'By holding our ground on several other issues important to us, while giving away on some minor ones and by building in features in the proposed non-compete clauses, we actually deepened our relationship with Schneider', says Mustafa.

Jaipur to attend the official meeting. 'Apprehending trouble, we had sought police protection for all the trustees because we understood that the secretary had arranged for armed troublemakers to disrupt the meeting. The meeting at ITC was held in the morning under police protection but was not attended by the secretary. The resolutions were passed and taken on record by the court-appointed chairman'.

The next part of the drama got a little more exciting: 'Since we had heard about the Rawat Hotel plans with a different agenda, I went early to the hotel with police escort; paid for a larger venue, which we had decided to attend as well along with the court-appointed chairman. This took the opposition by surprise because the altered arrangements ensured that the secretary's armed men could not access the venue that was adequately guarded by the police. So the men with lathis – who were staying in the hotel, were prevented from entering the meeting and the secretary, now isolated attended the meeting alone. Once again, the original agenda was put to vote, this time with the secretary present. One of the agenda items was the removal of the secretary, which was passed unanimously. The chairman filed the reports of both meetings with the high court and orders were passed accordingly. The trust regained control of the hospital and continues to do good work to this day. The secretary filed a suit subsequently that was dismissed.

## Teaching St Xavier's

Some clients listen to advice; others do not. RNJ recalls an interesting case featuring Calcutta's St Xavier's Collegiate School in the early 1990s. The authorities suspected that question papers for the terminal examinations had gone missing and sought the lawyer's counsel. Was a public inquiry in order? RNJ advised them not to divulge their suspicion nor call an inquiry. Instead, he wanted them to gather evidence and then proceed to take action. 'I advised them to sprinkle talcum powder around the table where the question papers were kept, duly counted, matching the number of students sitting for the exam next day, keep them stacked the previous night and, if possible, for someone to hide in the room with the lights off'. The headmaster and prefect heeded the advice and hid under the table, torches in hand and lay in wait. After midnight there was the sound of the key turning; someone entered the room and tried to switch on the lights. Out sprang the headmaster and the prefect and found that it was their departmental clerk. Caught in the act, the man pleaded guilty and prayed for pardon. The extremely agitated administrators wanted to dismiss him at once. Again RNJ counselled them to hold an inquiry, give him a proper hearing before taking any steps. 'I further advised them to pay the man a lumpsum by way of adhoc ex-gratia-cum-gratuity settlement. He also said, in writing, that he should not have been entitled to them view of his gross misconduct. This having been done, he resigned taking an ex-gratia settlement of Rs 50,000'. The clerk, however, was neither contrite nor gone: having encashed the cheque, he challenged his resignation as invalid, alleging that he had done so under threat and coercion and filed several cases, in the city civil court, with the Labour Commissioner, the labour court and the high court and dragged the school through litigation for six years. He lost everywhere but only because the school had listened to wise counsel and followed the correct procedure. The authorities still wonder what the consequences of a rash dismissal would have been.

The point was that KCo not only helped clients with legal support but provided moral and administrative support to ensure that the relevant order could be implemented in the client's favour', says Roopa.

Another important case was the Saktigarh Textiles case handled by PL and Roopa for the Hadas (reported in 1994 (1) CHN, P. 219). It had been instituted by one Sunil Jhunjhunwala against the Hadas, both being shareholders and directors of the company. 'What was challenging was that, before instituting the case, the plaintiff had retained the entire bar including all the stalwarts in company law and, when it came to defending the case, there was no one to appear for our clients', says Roopa who then went doing her rounds of the Bar Library hunting for a suitable lawyer. She badly wanted Mr Dipankar Ghosh, senior advocate, who had not been briefed by the opposite party because he was very busy with the ITC 800-crore-rupee excise matter in Delhi and spent very little time in Calcutta.

It took a great deal of convincing but Mr Ghosh accepted the brief with the promise that he would not be called upon to argue, knowing full well that there was little chance of his appearing for clients in the matter due to his busy schedule. 'We ultimately briefed Mr Subrata Roy Chowdhury and his junior Mr Tapas Banerjee but the matter was fraught with trouble right from the word go. Mr Roy Chowdhury suffered a heart ailment and had to be hospitalized, leaving only Mr Banerjee and two juniors briefed in the matter: Mr Siddhartha Mitra and Mr Sanjib Banerjee (now a judge in the Calcutta High Court)'.

The matter began before Justice A.N. Ray with the entire bar on one side and virtually three juniors for the Hadas. 'I was sleepless but PL was very encouraging and confident as we battled our way; the plaintiff's counsel was arguing strongly, I felt that the case was slipping from us and that the clients would lose control of their own company. Then fortune smiled. I met Mr Ghosh on a flight back from Delhi and enquired about his schedule. He was reluctant to do any matters in Calcutta but lady luck was in the client's favour and he agreed to give time for a conference to understand the matter without making any promise to do the matter right away, given his tight schedule. Mr Ghosh's intervention made all the difference. The judge was accommodating and fixed the matter on the days Mr Ghosh was in Calcutta. It was heard at great length and we won, bringing the plaintiff to the negotiating table. He resigned from the company as director, sold his shares to our client at a price stipulated and the company remains in the Hada fold today. They did contemplate appeal but thought otherwise. This was a greatly fulfilling learning experience and taught how strategy played an important part in litigation'.

There have been equally interesting cases around India's heritage knowledge that is becoming a big-ticket commercial proposition. O.P. Jhunjhunwala talks of an Emami case featuring their ayurvedic product, Sona Chandi Chyawanprash, under the Drugs & Cosmetics Act. The department of Ayush banned the use of prefix and suffix with Ayurveda, Siddha and Unani drugs because it believed that consumers were being misled by the use of such names and directed the drug controller to cancel the drug licence of any one violating the ban. Subsequently, the banning order was modified and Ayurveda, Siddha and Unani companies were permitted to a prefix or suffix with the name of the company only with the classical name of Ayurveda, Siddha and Unani medicines but not with any other name.

Emami challenged the banning order before the Shimla High Court as it was using the prefix 'Sona Chandi' to the classical name 'Chyawanprash' for Himani Sona Chandi Chyawanprash being manufactured at its Himachal

## Saving Savitri

O.P. Jhunjhunwala talks of the case around Sri Aurobindo's 'Savitri', a magnum opus that became a matter of controversy with Sudipto Roy, an advocate of the Calcutta High Court, 'a disciple of Sri Aurobindo' filing a writ petition in the Calcutta High Court alleging that the original text of Savitri, written by Sri Aurobindo, had been changed considerably by the Sri Aurobindo Ashram and the editors had substituted their own words, as a result of which general public were deprived of the original text. It was alleged that the writings of Sri Aurobindo were a part of Indian spiritual and religious heritage and preserving the original writing of Sri Aurobindo was a fundamental duty of every citizen. 'It was a very important case as the reputation, honesty and integrity of the trustees of Sri Aurobindo Ashram were involved and the allegations were strongly refuted on behalf of the Sri Aurobindo Ashram, Pondicherry', says OPJ.

OP, son of Sita Ram Jhunjhunwala, carrying on where his father left off

The division bench of the Calcutta High Court heard the matter and dismissed the writ petition holding that the reason given in the editorial note was convincing. The reason for the revised text was given by the editors in their words: 'Until the mid-1940s, Sri Aurobindo continued to write version after version of Savitri in his own hand, tirelessly expanding and perfecting it. However, when he began to prepare the poem for publication, he could no longer do all the work unaided and was assisted by two disciples. One of them, Nirodbaran, made the final handwritten copies. The other, Nolini Kanta Gupta, the typescripts. The deterioration of Sri Aurobindo's eyesight in these last years had two consequences affecting the text of Savitri. First, his later handwriting became increasingly difficult to read. This resulted in almost inevitable mistakes by the scribe who was asked to copy the hundreds of pages of manuscript. Second, towards the end, Sri Aurobindo came to rely entirely on dictation (to the same disciple) for the composition and revision of the poem. This opened the door to occasional inaccuracies of another kind'.

The Calcutta High Court held that a supplement to the revised edition of Savitri gave a table of amendments to show the present and the previous readings and a table of alternative readings. Any researcher or a serious student of Sri Aurobindo could very well locate the original text as well as the amended one. Surprisingly, thereafter a group of persons claiming to be scholars filed a criminal proceeding in Alipore against the trustees of Sri Aurobindo Ashram on the same subject matter. The matter went before the Supreme Court that ultimately dismissed their special leave petition.

Pradesh factory since September 2005, as a proprietary medicine using gold and silver foil in its Chyawanprash formulation. Under Section 3(h), the manufacturer of Ayurvedic proprietary medicine is entitled to manufacture a drug using the ingredients mentioned in the ancient text, even if the licensee did not follow the formulae given in the said text. The main issue was with regard to the scope and ambit of the power of the Central government (Ayush) under Section 33P of the said Drugs & Medicines Act to direct the state government to cancel the drug licence or to follow any advice contrary to the statute.

Section 33P of the Act states that the Central government could give directions to any state under the provisions of the Act and all the rules under it. The Shimla High Court held that the central direction had to be in consonance with the provisions of the Act and its rules and there could be no specific directions to the state to reject or allow any particular licence. It said the allegation that the gold and silver did not form the part of the classical formulae was not tenable and held that once the gold and silver were actually added to the Chyawanprash, Emami could not be accused of misleading the customer by using the words 'Sona Chandi' in the trade name. This did not amount to misbranding.

If this was a hard-won case, there were some amazingly serendipitous experiences too. Amongst the best thing to happen to the firm was to get the parties on the opposing/other side of a case or a deal to fall for brand KCo and its

## Default setting

'Today, we at Meher cannot think of doing anything major in our activities without taking Rajiv into confidence. He is the default setting in our business and has injected an element of alertness in our people because they know questions will be asked. We have discussions, heated debates and high-pitch arguments because we have strong personalities on both sides but there are no personal interests involved'.

— *Mustafa Wajid, Meher Group*

professionalism. Many such firms loved Khaitan and came back to give them all their business. Says N.R. Kulkarni, from the C.K. Birla group, about a deal being struck by between a Birla company and a multinational in 2000. 'I recall a discussion with an MNC at the Maurya, in Delhi, when we agreed on the draft of the term sheet. This had to be supplemented by detailed documentation. It was decided that we would first prepare our draft and ask the other party to amend it where necessary. The chairman of the company called Haigreve to know how long it would take for KCo to prepare the first draft. When he said that he would have the draft ready in four days, I was very worried as I thought that it was a very aggressive promise. Haigreve surprised everyone and the complicated document was in our computer in four days. Even the counterparty was impressed. In fact, so happy it was with our lawyers that, in a subsequent deal, it appointed KCo to represent it. This was not a unique case. It has happened quite often with the firm impressing the counterparties by its speed, quality of discussion, pragmatism and communication skills'.

H.B. Jairaj of Bangalore's HRB group acknowledges that KCo today is a full-service law firm that provides comfort at various levels: to its own people, to new clients, to first-time entrepreneurs, to family businesses on a corporatizing path and it does so with care and panache. 'For any new entrepreneur, this would be a law firm of choice. It is a law firm with a soul. This is especially important in a country where the judicial system itself is on a rocky terrain', says Jairaj. It has been felt that the judiciary-executive relationship is not entirely happy and, increasingly, companies are seeking to settle disputes amongst themselves through the mediation of law firms in what may well evolve as a parallel system of adjudication.

'Law firms are being called upon to settle disputes by

negotiation without the companies going into litigation. There are patent and trademark disputes, for instance, where law firms are helping in finding solutions by negotiating with the affected parties', says Jairaj. What he was referring to was a web of trust that had to be created and which had been accomplished by KCo. 'One needs people and firms of integrity. It becomes important for people to choose the right firms to be working with'; those that have the best interests of the client at heart.

'I was considering a strategic interest in a financial services company and was wanting a seat on its board. It was Rajiv who advised me not to seek a board position for myself but to ask for the right to appoint my nominee as a director at my discretion, while having a right to have an observer at all the board meetings so that I would be free from the exposure to the vicarious liabilities of the director and yet be informed about what is happening at the board level and to protect my interest when required. That was the correct advice that I could hardly have expected from any other source'.

Other clients share such assessments. When Mustafa Wajid of the Meher group started working with KCo (Bangalore) around 2005-06 on some routine legal matters, he realized that this was not just a conventional legal resource but a firm that saw legal work in a holistic context. 'Our interactions started stretching beyond just legal to commercial advice, which was very different from other firms that found themselves boxed within the legal context only; KCo was far more strategic in is approach', says Wajid.

He continues, 'The intensity of the association went up exponentially between 2008 late 2009 when we wanted to divest our power factor correction business (capacitors that led to efficient use of energy). We considered selling this business because we saw the trends in the industry and realized that we would be visited by a unique set of circumstances,

## Supporting one's own

Parag Tripathi recalls: 'Even when I left the firm, it allowed me to continue with the matters that I was dealing with and gave me briefs. Thus it was that, even as a 25 or 26-year-old, I was independently working on the very important Kanoria Chemicals arbitration and writ proceedings, with Ashok Desai and Mr Vahanvati. The company always encouraged its former employees and briefed them on a regular basis. This is not the practice with some other leading firms that I know of. In fact, they avoided them thinking that they would run away with their clients. They never briefed lawyers, who had left them, till they had reached a certain stature in the profession. KCo was different; in fact, lawyers who have left Khaitan are all successful and well-known names in the legal world today and the credit largely goes to the firm whose unstinted support they have had'.

whereby our business would eventually become a subset of the larger energy management space. We wondered whether we would be able to take on the big players and concluded that we could not and eventually our company would get commoditized had we remained where we were', says Wajid.

It was an interesting journey that the client and firm undertook together where the company fetched an excellent price and also got the buyer to make a commitment to convert the business acquired from within its business as a global hub. 'Over the years, the buyers kept their promise and enhanced the rolls from 250 to 800 people in the unit acquired from us; transferred the production facility from China to Bangalore and are now working on transferring their French facilities to Bangalore as well. They have further invested over Rs 70 crore in strengthening the operations and have respected our keenness to ensure and enhance local value addition. Today, the exports from the unit acquired from us have gone up too.'

What has also gone up is the element of trust between client and solicitor. Says Wajid: 'As far as KCo is concerned, we have continued our association with it even for Meher II and have involved the firm in a lot of specific and general issues. Most of our essential plans for developing the new business areas are debated at the Khaitan office. We are on the verge of signing a new joint venture and it is helping us in this as well. There are times when subjective and strategic issues crop up and the firm offers us more than one views and interpretation'. What Wajid emphasizes is that the relationship is not just about a set of legal documents. It extends into all activities. It would extend to a purchase of any property, for instance. In one remarkable deal, KCo was advisor for both Meher and the seller: 'The Calcutta office protected the seller's interests and Bangalore ours and both sides were sure that justice would be done; so high is the confidence level in the firm. It takes a lot of character for a firm to be able to do that and KCo here, at times, made life difficult for its counterparts at Calcutta; sometime Calcutta took rigid stands but, in the end, the firm

## Mentally engaged with clients

Explains Dhruv Khaitan: 'Our relationship works because I can call Pinto Khaitan or any other person in KCo any time of the day or night and can expect an instant response; not a solution but a response that will assure me that he is on the job. I know that he is mentally engaged. I have the feeling of security around accessibility; it is like having an anchor while at sea. The firm also explores alternative legal strategies and advises on what would be the best option; sometimes advising us to go for a detailed and more complex route to ensure that our objectives are met. Sometimes the advice is not to get into the litigation mode because that would be strategically inadvisable. It examines the real need and does not produce copy-pasted documents but solutions that work. Sometimes it has advised us to go for a one-page agreement instead of a 25-page one for purposes of simplicity. Yet again it has taught us how to effectively negotiate by giving in on several peripheral points while sticking to the critical ones, giving the other side the feeling that they have won on several issues so it is OK to concede a few. Providing such advice would require a perfect understanding of the client's needs and the ability to identify what matters the most. Also, KCo often comes back to us for responses and chases us rather than the other way round. Furthermore, there is never the temptation to over-involve for revenue generation. The only complaint that I may have against the firm is that while there is a sense of fun in whatever it does, the lawyers work too hard. This is one aspect of their lifestyle that I wish would change'.

ensured that the deal was concluded fairly, efficiently and quickly', says Wajid.

There were other matters where the firm represented rival clients in the same case from two different offices with great fairness. Says Mr Vinod Krishna of Metal Box: 'When we commenced dealing with KCo Mumbai, we were worried about the possibility of a conflict of interest taking place. This was an overhang of the associations of the previous Indian minority shareholders, who had been using KCo Calcutta in an advisory capacity but the firm in Mumbai acted with the highest standards of ethics and were even able to resolve a long-pending imbroglio between the previous Indian shareholders and us, with KCo, Calcutta, representing their interest and KCo, Mumbai, our interest as the current shareholders. On this issue, which had remained unresolved for several years, they played the crucial role, addressing the concerns of both sides, sorting them out and amicably having the matter concluded'.

Kushagra Bajaj too underscores this point: 'There have been some rather unique examples of our getting involved in a property acquisition in which KCo represented both sellers and buyers; it did the due diligence for both parties and was also the escrow agent for both parties. That is the level of confidence that people have in Haigreve. Personally, he has been a good friend, who is always available, though I got associated with him only after KCo came to Mumbai'.

Harsh Goenka has an interesting story about the crucial role played by the firm in the acquisition of the Ceat brand name from Pirelli. 'The negotiations started from 2009, when the first round of discussions was held in Italy and lasted till 2011. We were all pleased with the discussions and had agreed on the price and formula during our discussion. However, when we sent them the details of the agreement from India, they refused to accept their commitment and left us in a tricky situation. That was when Haigreve worked with them not only to make them return to the negotiation table but revived the discussion so that it became a win-win situation for both. KCo brought to bear its commercial knowledge and advised us to allow Pirelli to use the brand name for another year and a half, while our Baroda plant was being made ready to roll out a marketable surplus. Pirelli could use the additional time to work off the extra amount that it wanted, while it would not hurt us to wait for that period because our product would not be ready for the market. This was not an easy deal to salvage because we were quite shocked when Pirelli went back on the agreement that we had arrived at in Italy'.

There were cases when the client has been rescued from an unimaginable mess. Mr Asopa talks of Budge Budge Company Ltd belonging to the Poddar group suffering serious losses; more than 50 per cent of its capital getting eroded; and the company becoming a BIFR case. The client wanted to bring the company out of the BIFR's clutches. 'We noticed that the group had another profitable company and we advised that this company be merged with Budge Budge Company to give it an excess of assets over liabilities and the loss would be wiped off. A scheme was framed under sections 391 and 394 of the Companies Act and after following the formalities, it was heard and allowed. With the sanctioning of the scheme, the company turned to a positive net worth and came out of BIFR'. No rocket science but clever thinking.

From matters of ethics to understanding the acceptable boundaries of any action, KCo has served as the legal adviser and often as a conscience keeper of many a client. 'It has told us that we are not in the business of taking advantage of others; we are in the business to establish and follow good practices at work. Do not exploit a situation: fair play and good practices should do the work for you', says Jairaj.

## Assisting counsel

Shanti Bhushan says: 'I have always received admirable assistance from its lawyers that is hardly equalled by the assistance that I get from most other firms. This proves that KCo has been following the practice of attracting excellent lawyers and that is why it can go from strength to strength. A law firm is an extremely important entity and is a must for competently handling litigation that requires sound understanding of the law and good knowledge of different legal subjects. I find that the lawyers of KCo, who brief me, are always up to date in the knowledge of their current statutes and complete case laws on the subject involved. This gives me great pleasure to work with them and argue cases in the Supreme Court or the high courts and tribunals because I feel confident that no provisions, rule or notification or any other relevant decision have been missed while briefing me'.

The important thing, say many KCo clients, is that the firm tries to understand the client's business and mindset first. This is what distinguishes it from many firms of the MNC pedigree. Many of these firms come with the answers and try to fit them to the issue. At Khaitans they first understand the issues and then try to fit in the pieces of solutions.

There was a deep crisis at the Bagla-owned Ormech Engineering, where business was irregular and which had defaulted in filing annual returns, accounts and even holding AGM. The company was, in fact, a defaulter for 10 years, which was ground enough, prima facie, for the registrar of companies to strike its name off as a defunct company, irrespective of whether or not it had valuable assets, which could be used to revive it. When Mr Bagla found out that the company had been declared defunct, he came to KCo. Mr Asopa who dealt with the matter says: 'We advised him to do some groundwork to show that, at the time its name was struck off, the company was carrying on some business and had some properties, which could be utilized for reorganizing its business and turning it into a viable company. For this, certain advice was given and documents prepared including a viability report'.

The Sick Industrial Companies Act protects the sick company from recovery proceedings by creditors but restricts the freedom of the company and its management from carrying on its affairs. 'We made an application before the court pointing out the relevant facts justifying that the company should be revived as it had valuable property and the order of striking off as a defunct company should be set aside. The ROC appeared to oppose and also filed an opposition but the registrar could not prove that the formalities, which were preconditions for striking off the name, were fulfilled. As a result, the application was allowed and the order striking off the name was set aside and the name of the company was restored in the register', says Mr Asopa.

The lawyer's responsibility is always onerous: 'A client may come with a request but it is for the solicitors to tell him what help he needs', says Arvind Jhunjhunwala, who recalls a Balarampur Chini case of the mid-2000s. A co-professional, Mr D.P. Desai, in the indirect taxation practice, once called him regarding a matter of a client seeking anticipatory bail over a peculiar problem. The client was Balrampur Chini Mills and found itself faced with a fraud charge, the alleged fraud having been committed in relation to getting exemption in excise and customs duty. A notification from the Central Board of Excise and Customs granted excise and customs exemption for certain green projects financed by the World Bank around 2005-06. The

## A matter of results

As far as getting results is concerned, Dhruv Khaitan gives the firm full marks: 'I remember learning about an injunction application against us in a foreign country some years ago. Within minutes of hearing this, the firm had its people on the move, they took the first flight out of India on the same evening (with hardly any personal luggage) and got the order vacated in a court in a foreign country. That is what result-orientation is to me'.

condition was that the eligibility for getting the exemption would be certified by the banking institution funding this project, which would in turn be funded by the World Bank. That certificate would also have to be countersigned by the concerned line ministry.

Balarampur Chini had obtained various excise and customs benefits in relation to setting up the project that was eligible for the exemption by virtue of using its sugar cane bagasse for electricity generation, which was an ICICI project. The company was not aware of the notification till ICICI brought it to their notice and asked them to avail of the exemption. They also arranged for countersignature through a consultant who was paid his fees by cheque. Based on that Balarampur Chini availed of the exemption for two or three years. It was subsequently found that the countersignature was forged and there was a CBI notice. The CBI unearthed the scam for 20 companies; Balarampur Chini was one of them. Based on the forgery, the department started a case against them for recovery of the exemptions availed of with interest and penalty. There were 67 such cases all over India. The CBI notice prompted Balarampur Chini to visit the solicitor to arrange for anticipatory bail.

Recalls Arvind: 'When I heard this I advised them against anticipatory bail because no court would grant it and once it was refused, arrest would be imminent. I asked them if they were eligible for the scheme or not and whether there was fraud at their end. They confirmed that they were eligible and the fraud lay in the forged counter-signature from the concerned line ministry. I suggested that instead of asking for anticipatory bail they should apply to the line ministry saying that they were otherwise eligible and apply for a fresh counter-signature. This we followed up with an order of the Calcutta High Court that the ministry deal with the representation and give its order within 30 days. We made the representation to the Ministry of Finance that we thought was the line ministry concerned but were told that the ministry concerned was the Ministry of Environment and Forests. So we did a similar thing with the ministry along with the court order asking them to deal with the matter in 30 days and with another order to the excise and customs authorities to complete the hearing of reassessment but not to pass on the order without leave of the court'.

The Ministry of Environment and Forests did not adjudicate on the representation because the matter was under CBI investigation that was still incomplete. In the process though, the directors of Balrampur did not have to take anticipatory bail. Meanwhile, the person who got the fake counter-signature guaranteed was nabbed by the CBI and put behind bars. Also, of the companies being investigated, some 19 companies had paid the additional excise customs demand but this company did not have to pay.

The third-generation partners had lived up to the commitment of understanding the client's problem and providing the appropriate solution. It was a matter of trust reinforced. The firm and its people both bolster the 'Khaitan' image. Says Ajay Bhargava: 'Each of us has had a great learning experience in terms of the variety of work and opportunity to independently deal with clients and handle their cases. The firm is unique in this regard'. For Ajay, partnership in 2004 was a life-changing event. 'From an intern to a partner was a dream come true and could only happen because of the vision of the firm'.

Roopa Sheth Mitra adds: 'My experience spanning 30 years with KCo has been fulfilling and varied and a great learning; there were opportunities galore. I was offered an opportunity to start the Bangalore office in 1993 with Rajiv and thereafter the Mumbai office in 2000 with Haigreve and Rabindra along with my husband to act as counsel for the firm but had to decline due to family commitments. Dealing with practically all branches of law would have been well-nigh impossible elsewhere. I have seen the firm evolve over these years as one of the finest, fittest and modern players in the much diversified business today'.

Yet, for all its modern management the firm never let the 'family feeling' get diluted, for Pinto Khaitan introduced the 'kcofamily' email ID, reinforcing the old-world values that the firm was first a family. These values have been inculcated in the youngsters by examples set by senior colleagues and will hopefully be transmitted to the future entrants because these are the values that have made KCo the 'best institution in the legal fraternity to work for now and in the coming years', says Ajay.

Old clients, brand new office

There are cases that drag on for decades and clients that stay on for centuries. One very staunch supporter of the Khaitans has been the Oberoi group that features in a case of considerable legal interest running for more than 10 years, which has not yet come to a conclusion. The Oberoi-owned East India Hotels had entered into an agreement with the Balaji group of hotels in Madras, which was to construct a five-star deluxe category hotel in Mount Road, Madras. EIH had also advanced more than Rs 15 crore to facilitate the construction under a technical services agreement under which EIH would have the exclusive rights to run, manage and operate the hotel and would, in turn, give the owner the right to use the Oberoi brand name, for which a royalty agreement was entered into.

'Balaji, which had taken loans from the Tourism Finance Corporation of India and Industrial Finance Corporation (secured creditors) to construct the hotel, defaulted and TFCI sold the nearly completed property to one Robust Hotels, which is a special purpose vehicle controlled by the Jhunjhunwalas, owners of the Hyatt brand in Mumbai apart

Value-added networking. Pinto Khaitan shows how

from others. EIH filed a suit that no other group save the Oberois could operate the hotel and secured a favourable judgment from the Madras High Court, which directed Robust and the Hyatt group to deposit the Rs 15 crore and interest with the court if they wanted to run the hotel under the Hyatt brand name. Failure to do so would lead to an injunction restraining the Robust group from operating the hotel under the Hyatt brand name. The matter is now pending adjudication in the Supreme Court', says Siddhartha. In a convoluted world of delayed resolution of cases, trust is important between client and firm; between firm and its counsel; between the judiciary and the advocates.

Says P.R.S. Oberoi: 'Our association with the firm, if memory serves, goes back to the 1940s. My father went to Calcutta in 1938 and must have asked for the best firm around and since then KCo have been our solicitors. My father was a close friend of Bhagwati Prasad Khaitan and M.L. Khaitan had been in our board for 25 years. Indeed, we must be amongst the firm's oldest clients and I have great regards for Mr Pinto Khaitan, whom we consult off and on but it is with Haigreve that we have been working closely these days. We have never been a litigating company. We went to the firm for corporate advice: they advised us on all our amalgamations, acquisitions, our brand protection and recently on our very successful rights issue. The most important quality that comes to my mind is that they are very quick with their response'.

Not every relationship dates back to generations though. Indeed, every year brings in new kinds of assignments. In 2003, KCo handled a public-private partnership project, advising the government of Punjab and Punjab Information and Communications Ltd on a joint-venture project with Quark Holding, US. Says Sharad Vaid: 'This was for setting up an IT township at Mohali on 2,000 acres under the IT Park Policy within the Industrial Policy of the Government of Punjab and the Industrial Park Scheme, 2002, of the Government of India. I assisted in finalizing documentation for it but more importantly, this paved the way for several disinvestment projects coming to KCo from the Punjab and other state governments'. Clients come from different industries and different sectors, state and private.

Amongst the most satisfying ones from both the client's and the firm's side has been the relationship with Siemens. Mr Ajai Jain, who heads legal affairs at Siemens, says that he has known the company for only three years, from the time he joined Siemens. Earlier he had encountered the firm in an arbitration in which Khaitans were representing the other side. 'We were so impressed with Haigreve that we decided to go with KCo for the new assignment. Today, it is like a partner to us on a day-to-day basis. All their offices are involved with us and we are working on two JVs with the firm. Our group companies, like Osram, too, use KCo's services and we are very pleased with Messrs Kulkarni, Haigreve, Chakrapani,

Sangvi, Arindam Ghosh, Daksha Baxi and Aniket from Calcutta, amongst the others whom we interact with.

'To summarize, our relationship has started very well; good services and reasonable fees. Indeed, it has been especially wonderful because it has never made fees an issue, though money is not a problem with us. KCo is on a contract with us and there was a very tricky problem and it helped us out but never talked of money because of the additional work that its partners put in. If ever there is an emergency, Khaitan is the first name that comes to us. The big issues aside, there are so many opinions, Fera matters – our parent company came up with an open offer – and Arindam and Joy handled it with great competence. We have worked together on so many matters: corporate restructuring, property related matters, litigations, securities law…', says Mr. Jain

Every office comes up with challenging assignments. Recalls Sharad Vaid: 'An interesting assignment came our way in 2005 over the purchase of the Rozagaon sugar unit of Dhampur Sugar by Balrampur Chini Mills Ltd. Mr Vivek Saraogi gave this work to the firm that Pinto Khaitan wanted Sharad Vaid to handle. Assisting him was Sudish Sharma in this matter where the deadlines were rather deadly. We had to work very hard on this assignment, drafting the business transfer agreement, escrow agreement, operating agreement, supplementary agreements, sale deed, personal guarantee and such others while also conducting the negotiations. It went off so well that not only did Mr Vivek Saraogi complement us but even Dhampur Sugar Mills was impressed enough to start giving us work thereafter', says Sharad Vaid. Indeed, the firm is also getting to be an expert in the capital market activity, handling Ansal Properties and Infrastructure's Qualified Institutional Placement for Rs 680 crores in 2006. 'We received the assignment for advising, assisting and guiding API but successful completion meant a number of other assignments from them', says Sharad Vaid.

Whoever says trust is a scarce commodity? Over the years, KCo and its counsel have been the recipients of enormous trust. Trust was established within the community when the family settled all its debts and then through exemplary service to clients. This time it was for the courts to demonstrate faith in its counsel. The matter was around a POS terminal or a 'Point of Sale' terminal that had both hardware and software, which was the product Dhruv Khaitan's Venture Infotek Global Private Limited was dealing in. VIGPL was in the business of facilitating processing of payments for debit and credit cards and provided POS terminals. In the case in question, VIGPL took the position that POS terminals are 'computers' and hence eligible for higher rate of tax depreciation (60 per cent). The tax authorities and the Income Tax Appellate Tribunal rejected the claim and the matter ultimately reached the Mumbai High Court.

Recalls Sanjay Sanghvi, 'KCo undertook detailed examination of the client's stand that POS terminals are indeed "Computers" as defined under Information Technology Act and advised them to file and appeal in the high court. We briefed senior counsel, Mr Soli Dastur, and represented the client, along with the senior counsel in high court'.

The question of law for the high court, framed for admission and subsequent adjudication was 'whether POS terminals are computers and accordingly can they claim depreciation at the rate of 60 per cent'. The majesty of the court and faith in the practitioners of law were established in two sentences. The court asked: 'Mr Dastur, what is your view, are POS terminals "computers"?' Mr Dastur replied: 'Yes, Your Lordships'. The court said: 'Appeal admitted!'

That is the case for trust in a land where it seems to have lost its way in a large measure.

MUMBAI
LEGAL

*My experience with KCo has been very happy; they are old-world solicitors that you do not get to see in these days of fast work, fast life and poor results. My association with them, of course, predates the Mumbai office and what impressed me about them was their meticulous eye for detail and the complete dedication to work, which is an object lesson for any firm of solicitors. I may not remember all the details of the many matters that I have done for the firm but I do know that it has been a pleasure to be briefed by it.* — **Iqbal M. Chagla**

Once again, it was the best of times; it was the worst of times, though there was nothing Dickensian about it. The global financial system had all but collapsed. Globalized India was able to keep its head high, thanks to the support that it was receiving from 'Bharat' (as the not so glitzy India is referred to). Bhagwati Prasad Khaitan's grandson had produced quite a consummate performance with the office in Mumbai that he had been asked to head. From a 'nobody' firm, in a matter of 10 years, it was everywhere: cutting international deals, securing landmark judgments, playing in the securities space, advising top Indian corporates comprehensively on a range of tricky issues, winning the battle for talent from law colleges and from the practising legal community, as its burgeoning legal strength outgrew office space with pleasing rapidity.

Says Haigreve: 'Dhruv Khaitan was amongst our first clients and he was planning a restructuring of his business. We helped him with that. I remember doing his transaction and then sending him a bill. He gave us a cheque for double the amount. More importantly, I learnt so much from him about paying attention to detail. He goes into the minutest

Hitting the bullseye: KCo goes to No.1, Indiabulls Centre. Pinto Khaitan and Ravi Kulkarni cut the ribbon to inaugurate the new Bombay office

planning and has also been such a fantastic client'. There were other Calcutta contacts chipping in too. 'Raghu Modi was selling his factory land in Mumbai and we handled the work. We got a lot of support from Harsh and Sanjeev Goenka. Apart from other things, they gave us their guest house to live in. There was also the massive help that we received by way of initial investment that came from Y.H. Dalmia and Umang Kejriwal, who lent us money to buy office space: Meher Chamber. All the work that our firm had done for them was more than amply rewarded. The Elpro group of the Dabriwala family too is constantly doing things and we have done a lot of work for them', says Haigreve.

Metal Box was yet another Calcutta contact from the opposition that came aboard. Recalls Mr Vinod Krishna: 'Metal Box became a client in Mumbai over property transactions and related issues, both in, and at times, outside of Mumbai'. In such transactions the buyer and seller are often at cross purposes. 'We often found that as our advocates, KCo was adept at dealing with and convincing the advocates of the opposite party; which often raised varied issues, which were offshoots of the inherent complexities facing the company. We found that Mr Haigreve Khaitan had a knack for addressing these apprehensions. This quality, coupled with his commercial acumen, the firm's impeccable reputation and an innovative approach to

## Making Mumbai happen

Mumbai just had to happen. *The American Lawyer* (April 2011) reports the birth of KCo in India's commercial capital: 'Two young Calcutta-based lawyers were travelling from their hometown to Mumbai almost on a fortnightly basis… that was till one of the clients politely asked for the address of the firm's Mumbai office. There was none!' Says Rabindra Jhunjhunwala: 'We were spending a lot of time in Mumbai and we were about to bank a big mandate but when the client asked where our Mumbai office was, we lost it'. The message was loud and clear.

solving issues, is what distinguishes KCo amongst legal firms. Besides, Sudip Mullick and Savita Singh, partners, are immaculate in their documentation and careful about addressing all aspects of the transaction in detail so as to avoid the matter later resulting in disputes and litigation'. For Metal Box, the surety of payments coming as per schedule was important as any defaults would adversely affect the company. 'KCo has almost always ensured successful consummation of the transactions where it has represented us', says Mr Krishna. What would have delighted Haigreve's grandfather is his next comment: 'We had inhibitions in that the services of such an established firm would be at a premium but we found in dealing with them that they often played a pivotal role in enhancing the transactibility and, at times, even the value of the transaction. Their attitude is always distinguished as befitting an old, professional firm. KCo was getting well set in Mumbai, family values and all'.

Meher Chamber, where it all began

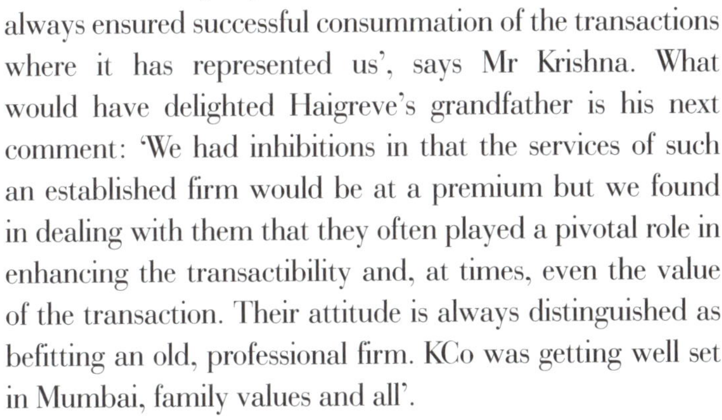

A key cog in the Mumbai wheel was Nilanjan Ghosh. 'When HK chose to move to Mumbai, I volunteered to move with him and the core team of HK, Prabhay Khaitan, Rabindra Jhunjhunwala and Sudip Mullick. It turned out to be a very good move professionally. Without a close circle of family and friends, I spent most of the time in office, that was really small to begin with, and found responsibilities coming my way. I was a law graduate by then. In 2003-04, there was a change in the Wildlife Protection Act that required all the rich and famous people to disclose their ivory, shahtoosh and leather possessions in a particular format. We started helping a few known business families in their disclosure and follow-up action. Suddenly there was a deluge of work in this matter and the firm got an opportunity to deal with the business community, which gave us a great deal of credibility'.

Meanwhile, the legal background and the administrative experience shaped out a specific job profile for Nilanjan. The partners believed that the firm needed a coordinating person and that is how Nilanjan evolved, 'learning from Mr Haigreve Khaitan every day; from his humility and the hard work on the one hand and from Mr Rabindra Jhunjhunwala on the other, picking up the art of communication and branding one of the many others from him as the firm and the Mumbai office evolved to a position amongst the top legal firms in the country. I am proud to be a small part of this amazing 100-year journey!'

Haigreve attributes the success to the initial group working and staying together, bonding. 'It was all about teamwork and all the support of our people... I only front-end it and get the credit. I received outstanding support every hour of the day; on days when not a single lawyer was available in Mumbai, we provided the services that our clients demanded of us. All the time, we were growing together; first the three of us came, followed by Tushna (who had earlier trained with me in Calcutta), who joined us from another firm. Then Sudip arrived. We came to work and went back together and gradually settled down. We knew that we had to get the best talent and gave partnerships to attract it as

The Mumbai partners
Top row (L–R): Dinesh Kumar Agrawal, Zakir Merchant, Aakash Choubey, Bhavik Narsana, Abhishek Sharma, Kalpana Unadkat, Joy Jacob, Vibhava Sawant, Ketan Kothari, Devidas Banerji, Nishant Singh

Bottom row (L–R): Shishir Mehta, Chakrapani Misra, Murali Neelakantan, Vaishali Sharma, Haigreve Khaitan, Ravi Kulkarni, Savita Singh, Rabindra Jhunjhunwala, Jose Madan, Arindam Ghosh

## Calcutta connection; Mumbai deals

'It was Prabhay, the great grandson of Durga Prasad Khaitan, who pushed for the Mumbai office, backed by P.L. Agarwal, Suman and Rajiv Khaitan too', says Haigreve. 'Rajiv had earlier started the computerization of the office in 1988 under my father and we got our first 286. Those were early days with computers in Calcutta and we were the first to do everything: from electronic typing to air-conditioning and computerization of accounts. There was much worry about the electricity bill if we went in for air-conditioning but we did all that. I did not intend coming to Mumbai. Prabhay, Saket and Rabindra were to come and I was to devote some time to Mumbai. Then Saket dropped out to do his MBA and I had to spend more time for the move to Mumbai…even then I did not realize that I would shift here. It was still more of Prabhay's and Saket's vision that Mumbai would be such a big opportunity and it was the Calcutta clients and contacts that were of great help'.

a part of the strategy. We got Ravi Kulkarni and Nikhilesh. Once they came on board, the perception that we were a Calcutta-based firm changed and it was easier to attract the best minds not only from India but from global firms, and we constantly pursue talent'.

Challenging cases with newer dimensions came its way; custom appeared from non-family sources, handled by non-family recruits. Tushna Thapliyal, amongst the first Mumbai recruits, handled the very interesting case of SMIFS Capital Markets vs the Securities and Exchange Board of India (Sebi). The Sebi had imposed a Rs 3-crore penalty on SMIFS Capital Markets for failure to make disclosures under Regulation 7 of the Sebi (Substantial Acquisition of Shares and Takeovers) Regulations, 1997. 'The order was successfully challenged and the firm got the penalty reduced to Rs 10,000', says Tushna Thapliyal.

The SMIFS matter was significant because it set the precedent for how the Securities Apellate Tribunal (SAT) views minor/procedural violations of this nature and also determined what an 'appropriate' penalty could be for such violations. In this case there was a huge penalty imposed for a minor violation. 'Our counsel was called away from the courtroom just before court started but the Sebi order was so out of line that I did not need to make any detailed oral arguments. I read out the order and explained the nature of the violation (not filing disclosure under the takeover regulations) and the chairperson did the rest, sternly telling Sebi where it had erred', recalls Trushna. There was the equally interesting case of the indirect acquisition of Seamec by Technip SA and Coflexip of France. The matter that went up to the Supreme Court was about when the actual change of control over Seamec took place – in April 2000 or July 2001 – because that would have a substantive impact on the price of the share. Says Tushna: 'The initial challenge to the open offer came from various shareholders over the date of making the open offer. KCo advised one of the shareholders, Mr Umesh Kumar Mehta. The main contention was that the acquisition took place in April 2000, when the offer price would have been Rs 238 per share. The acquirers, however, contended that a change of control only took place in July 2001 and the offer price was accordingly calculated at that time as Rs 43 per share'. The Seamec case's significance lay in its requiring the Indian courts and the Sebi to examine when change of control actually took place applying a foreign law, in this case the French company law.

The KCo ladies: Tushna, second from the left, was the first to come aboard in Mumbai

'The Sebi rejected the shareholder's contentions and held that change of control took place in July 2001. However, the Securities Appellate Tribunal reversed the Sebi decision and found favour with the shareholder's contention. On appeal by the acquirers, a full bench of the Supreme Court rejected the shareholder's contentions and held that change of control took place in July 2001. KCo, New Delhi, appeared for shareholder Mr Umesh Kumar Mehta, who was respondent before

## Bullish on Mumbai

'We have changed the face of the firm since we started the Mumbai office; literally, there is a sea change in the way people look at us', says Rabindra. 'This changed further after we moved to Indiabulls; we captured the attention of the legal world. We also opened up the partnership and did not hesitate to get people from outside. We bet big on people and premises at a time when the world was in the doldrums and globally there was uncertainty amidst the financial crisis. Yet that was when we chose to move out of 11,000 square feet space to 35,000 square feet and spend several crores on doing the place up. Today, anyone coming into the office is wowed by it and I can say that we are the best appointed facility amongst the law firms in India'.

the Supreme Court', recalls Tushna. It was one of the earlier cases where an indirect acquisition taking place under the Sebi Takeover Code was challenged by the shareholders of the Indian target company. 'It was also an example of activism in India by shareholders of a public listed company', says Tushna. 'This was essentially a Delhi experience and a fairly complex case challenging an offer price in which our Delhi office was involved at the Supreme Court level'.

As cases were competently dealt with, with expertise coming from various Khaitan offices in the country, word got around that there was this young firm that was worth a try and once it was given a try, KCo, Mumbai, knew how to keep the client happy. More importantly, it learnt how to keep the entire team happy yet honest. 'Even while modernizing, we retained the firm's values: how we take care of our people; and we continue to be a people-oriented firm. We do not take in people who we know will leave. We worry about people leaving. We want to retain people...Anybody can walk into a senior's room for advice but have the independence to do what he/she thinks is correct, though within our value systems. Law is important but it is equally important to tell the client what to do and what not to do', says Rabindra. Indeed, Gauri Rasgotra, KCo partner from Delhi, echoes these sentiments: 'The firm's culture of delegation, autonomy and unfailing support has always energized me. The policy was well laid out: "No matter what tomorrow brings, we will be there for you"'. These philosophies worked from Calcutta to Delhi; from Bangalore to Mumbai; from Meher Chamber to Construction House, as the Mumbai team had to move to accommodate its growing ranks. Even that was not enough.

A bigger, better and plusher accommodation was needed in keeping with the growth of business and the image of the firm. Yet there was the looming spectre of the global recession and to move or not to move was the question. It was a tense day at KCo, Mumbai. While the firm was bullish over its prospects, the whole world was in a bear hug. The partners were called to vote on the proposal to move to Indiabulls. 'I did not see sense in moving. I had grave reservations around the financial crisis and the market uncertainties that had dimmed prospects all around', says Rabindra. Yet no one else in the firm shared Rabindra's sense of foreboding; they all thought that it was a great idea. 'I was wrong and everyone else was right; and I am the happiest person to have been proved wrong because the move changed the game for the firm. The young and the restless have optimism unbounded'.

## Impressing the opponents

'What seemed to have worked very well for us is how the opposition was impressed with us when we represented one party. We got picked up by the other side when we did well in a matter. In the Blackstone deal, we were acting for the Hinduja family, then selling Gokuldas exports. Blackstone, a private equity firm on the other side, loved our work and gave us their own work', says Haigreve.

'The next move that worked wonders for us is the move into Indiabulls; it was the next big game-changer. The market saw that we could move into such a huge space at a time when the chips were down with the global meltdown, and our office enhanced our credibility'.

## The Kulkarni factor

'Ravi Kulkarni's joining KCo in 2005 changed the perspective of it being a family firm: the message was very positive', says Rabindra. 'The next game-changer was the advent of lawyers from foreign law firms: Murali, Kalpana, Bharat... This was a conscious decision to get out of the existing mould and give the firm an international character. There was also much work to be done to raise our profile from near zero to being top of the line with global rating agencies. I worked very hard on the rankings and today we are on every ranker's top of the league table and have won numerous awards. A lot of effort has gone into doing this and we actively changed perception from the time the Mumbai office was opened. I am sure this made a big difference when the laterals joined, they saw the firm as different from the other family-run firms'.

The Indiabulls space was 'a 30,000-square foot floor plate! Puran Kumar Associates, who have been the architects from day one in Mumbai, started to work on the design and planning. They took three months to do the place up, while taking on board the views of our senior management', recalls Chakrapani Misra. Shifting a 10-year-old organization, more so a law firm with 150 people, required precise teamwork and advance planning. We are lucky to have some of the most dedicated and active members in the administration team that made the transition really smooth. There was a client event on November 11, 2009, to showcase the new office. The compliments and encouragement received from all more than made up for the efforts'.

Indeed, the reason that senior counsel, Janak Dwarkadas, thought KCo was a young firm stemmed from his being 'one of the privileged invitees at the opening ceremony of its Mumbai office at Lower Parel a few years ago. It is located in a modern steel and glass structure and done up in as contemporary a style as any of the most young and emerging corporate offices one can imagine. A far cry from the old, musty, dusty and file-laden solicitor offices that one might associate a hundred-year-old firm of lawyers', he says. The firm impressed the old and the young. Amitabh

Sharma (formerly JSA), partner at Mumbai, whose practice areas are infrastructure, energy and natural resources, was literally allured into joining by Haigreve at a short meeting at Four Seasons.

'There is a charisma about the man and the energy that has helped him do wonders with the firm. Also, KCo has taken many partners, all excellent people, who have taken the outside world by surprise. This, supported by the good work that has been done in recent times, has meant a literal reincarnation of the firm that is now amongst the top three firms in the country. It has character and integrity and each of us holds integrity very close to his heart. The 100th year has augured well for us in terms of reach, potential and visibility. It has, indeed, taken us a hundred notches higher. The firm has the right mix and balance, is culturally very strong, is rooted in the ground and is not a "wannabe firm". It is very modern and yet, unlike a new firm, is deeply steeped in ethos', says Amitabh.

Amitabh's focus is M&A, acquisition and divestment, and he was working on the Leighton Holdings deal, which was selling 35 per cent of its stake in its Indian operations to the Welspun group, when he met Haigreve. 'I remember

## Kulkarni for Khaitans

'There was a lot of reinforcing feedback from Akanksha, who had joined KCo from our firm and I was gradually veering around to considering the offer from them very seriously. There was one big question though and people wondered how I, with my Little experience, would be able to work with a family-run Marwari firm but I decided to take the plunge anyway and promised Haigreve that I would give my full attention for three years. That my clients agreed to support me was a great confidence booster for me. I also wanted to have my own team move in with me and around six of my colleagues joined the firm with me. My children were entirely supportive of the move. So I served my three-month notice period and even tried to get a merger of Little with KCo but my senior partner refused to have anything to do with such a move. So I chose to join the Khaitans', says Ravi Kulkarni.

telling the lady that I was working with that I was planning a move and she actually came and checked out the firm and asked me to go ahead. Another client from Switzerland also checked out KCo for me and gave me a thumbs up for the move, while also promising to move, with me', recalls Amitabh.

Winning over Kulkarni. Ravi Kulkarni with R.N. Jhunjhunwala

Many a partner has been charmed into KCo's fold by Haigreve. Jose Madan's joining the firm in 2003 was quite unexpected for him. 'When I met Haigreve Khaitan on Saturday, July 30, 2003, along with two other Intellectual Property (IP) colleagues of mine, I already had an appointment letter from another law firm that I was supposed to join from Monday, August 1, 2003. Instead, I decided to join the IP Practice of Khaitan from August 1, 2003', says Madan, leaving one in no doubt about the unobtrusive persuasion that must have taken place during the meeting. 'Since then I have been a witness to the phenomenal and enviable growth the firm has been making in terms of work, strength and brand image, courtesy the dynamic leadership of Haigreve and the hard work, commitment and dedication of all the members of the firm. The work culture and work atmosphere here are exemplary. Working in IP against the backdrop of a full-service law firm has been quite challenging and exciting as compared to working in a boutique IP law firm. It has been a very interesting and rewarding journey for me', says Jose Madan

Ravi Kulkarni had been in the profession for 40 years, since 1970, from even before Haigreve was born, as he likes to say. 'I was with Little & Company as its administrating partner when the question of moving to Khaitan's first arose. In the days of yore, legal work in Mumbai involved straightforward litigation, conveyancing and standard corporate work. I had occasion to interact with KCo in a matter featuring an

## Rating from E*TRADE: excellent!

As the firm explores the frontiers of law in a liberalized India and a globalized world, it continues to secure landmark rulings. E*TRADE Finance Corporation, a US-based and SEC-listed large financial services group, had a subsidiary in Mauritius: E*TRADE Mauritius Limited. E*TRADE purchased shares of a listed company in India. In early 2008, E*TRADE sold the shares of the Indian company to another Mauritian company and realized huge capital gains, says Sanjay Sanghvi. Under the India-Mauritius Tax Treaty, capital gains realized by a resident of Mauritius from sale of shares of an Indian company are not taxable in India. E*TRADE being a resident of India and holding a valid 'Tax Residency Certificate' issued by the Mauritius Revenue Authority, claimed exemption from capital gains tax in India under the tax treaty. It approached Indian tax authorities for a nil rate withholding tax certificate to receive the sale price of shares without any tax deduction in India. The tax authorities chose to disagree with the position and denied the benefit of capital gains tax exemption in India and directed the payer (buyer of shares) to deduct 20 per cent tax from the sale price payable to E*TRADE.

E*TRADE filed a writ petition in Mumbai High Court challenging the order directing 20 per cent TDS. The High Court directed E*TRADE to approach the Director of Income-tax (international taxation) for a revision of the certificate and asked the Mauritian buyer company to deposit the tax amount in the court until the matter was decided by the director in his revision order. The DIT passed a revision order upholding the action of the tax authorities and appropriated the amount deposited with the high court towards tax liability.

KCo then advised E*TRADE to approach advance rulings authority for a binding advance ruling to determine the chargeability of capital gains to tax in India under the India-Mauritius Tax Treaty. The advice was on merits and KCo prepared a strong legal case, strategized on the matter, consulted Mr S.E. Dastur and represented the client along with Mr Dastur before the ARA. Recalls Sanjay: 'The tax department tried its best to convince the ARA that E*TRADE should not be granted the benefit of the tax treaty but could not counter the convincing documentary evidence of E*TRADE being the owner of shares of the Indian company, and drew support from the Supreme Court ruling in the Azadi Bachao Andolan matter'. Mr Dastur was, of course, in his element, and the ARA ruled in favour of E*TRADE that capital gains were exempt from tax in India. Post such a favourable ruling, the tax team of Khaitan also got the tax assessment completed in record time and got the refund of TDS with interest.

While the clients were extremely delighted with the firm, this positive advance ruling giving the benefit of India-Mauritius Tax Treaty also helped in clearing the clouds over applicability of this treaty at the ground level. Prior to this ruling, the Mumbai tax department, by and large, did not grant the benefit of this treaty to Mauritius residents. 'Our favourable advance ruling set a good precedent and boosted the confidence of foreign investors who invested in India from Mauritius and provided much-needed certainty about their tax position in India. As the firm explores the frontiers of law in a liberalized India and a globalized world, it continues to flourish. In the context of cross border taxation, this E*TRADE advance ruling was a landmark one', says Sanjay.

international client in a rather tricky matter and Mr R.K. Choudhury represented the firm. I was very impressed by the way he conducted himself and found the entire experience very pleasant. He gave me every support in the matter and treated me with great courtesy. That was in the 1980s'. When the time came for this Little's person to consider the Khaitan offer, past courtesies played their part.

Several years later, India was liberalized and the legal scene changed. There was much more by way of capital market work, much more international interest in the country and some of Kulkarni's international clients started talking about KCo and Haigreve. 'I was asked if I had seen Haigreve in action. It was also around this period that some of my juniors started looking at Khaitans. One actually joined the firm and she kept in touch with me. I was a little concerned about her joining a non-descript Calcutta outfit, giving up Little & Company. The feedback that I got from her, however, was very good. This was also the time that our own firm was coming under pressure from the new kids on the block and I had realized that Little needed to change but it was not happening fast enough', recalls Kulkarni. Meanwhile, Amarchand had made great strides and Little was in for a rude shock when Behram Vakil put in his papers and joined Zia Modi in 2001. Then Ajay Behl joined them and the firm was called CZB. Other colleagues also began to form their own companies and yet others got jobs as in-house counsel for corporates. The law school had started in Bangalore; there was a new way of teaching law and there was a new crop of lawyers coming into the scene with a modern approach to the profession.

Recalls Kulkarni: 'The colleagues who had stayed on at Little started saying that we were not doing cutting-edge legal work and their sense of restlessness rubbed off on to me as well because there was a lot of interesting and new work happening: power projects, international capital,

Time for Haigreve vision

capital market and financial services and, personally, age was going against me. I was 59, going on 60, and found new firms overtaking us. I knew that old firms with little more than heritage would fall by the wayside unless things were dramatically changed. I was in this frame of mind when a headhunter called me up. While I would have refused to take such a call even a few days ago, I found myself taking the conversation forward and saying that I would talk to him provided he gave me the name of the firm that he was seeking to recruit for.

'He came back with the name: KCo. Some of my junior colleagues were also talking to the firm and I was strongly urged to talk to Haigreve. So we did meet one day and I was impressed with his vision. He said he was recruiting people and there was instant chemistry between us; everything about the meeting was very positive. Haigreve kept the dialogue alive and met me in my office a couple of times. He wanted me to meet his father, and my meeting with Pinto, at the Golden Dragon at the Taj, clicked too. I also met Padam'. The magic had begun to work. Indeed, the magic worked in more ways than one.

Wherever there was a Khaitan, there was action. In the Mumbai High Court, Mr Iqbal Chagla found himself disconcertingly surrounded by people even during lunch hours. The busy counsel liked a peaceful meal; so why where people crowding him? There was young Nandini Khaitan, daughter of Padam Khaitan, quite a sparkling law graduate, who was plying the table with the most delectable home-made puchkas (better known as paani puri or golgappas in Mumbai). The senior counsel, who was otherwise fond of the firm for its eye for detail, says: 'My association became stronger with all the paani puri that Nandini would get for us...they were delicious and when they arrived during lunchtime, everyone would make a beeline for the table till Nandini put her foot down. Then

It may be slow and seeking to catch up but Calcutta is still home.

she would send paani puri to my home after that'.

Yet another senior counsel, Janak Dwarkadas, recounts: 'I was not aware of KCo's existence as a leading law firm from Calcutta for the past many decades'. He thinks of it as a young firm, especially because of Nandini. In the course of being briefed by the firm, she captivated hearts and minds. 'Having learnt of my fondness for "sondesh" from Calcutta, she never missed an opportunity to order a box of these delicious sweets every time either she or anyone else was coming from Calcutta. Besides being a very warm and caring personality, Nandini is extremely hardworking and a shrewd lawyer. She is always well prepared and would master her brief. I suppose she has inherited these talents from her father, Padam Khaitan. It was indeed a pleasure to get to know and to work with her'.

Delicious though the round savouries were, the relationship had to transcend them: there were cases to be fought and won; some of them were around food. Says I.M. Chagla: 'I recall the good fight that we had over Nandos; a case handled by Chakrapani'. Recalls Chakrapani: 'Our client was an international fast food chain, Nandos Inc. of South Africa, which

## Heart-wrench, yet homecoming

It was a heart-wrenching experience for Kulkarni to move out of his spacious Little's office and into what was little more than a work station. 'There was also a disturbing situation at home with my children choosing to opt for career changes themselves exactly at that point of time, but I received exceptional emotional and professional support from the entire office here, which helped me tide over a very difficult period. As far as KCo was concerned, my moving here was an absolute game-changer for the firm. Apart from anything else, the entire Mahindra account moved with me and that turned things around for the firm in some ways. We got big capital market deals from the ICICI Bank's dual listing work; Reliance Petroleum's listing, sale of the Thomson TV tube business to Videocon... Merrill Lynch acquisition of Hemendra Kothari's stake in DSP Merrill Lynch. These big deals started placing us on a different league and we became the leading firm for capital market deals in Mumbai'.

was planning to enter India. While the client was still at the planning stage, it received a Mumbai High Court Order restraining it from using the trademark Nandos. This order was passed ex-parte on the application of one Balkrishna Hatcheries of Bangalore that sold frozen meat and chicken under the brand name "Nandu's" and insisted that Nandos could not enter India because the name was too close to Nandu's'.

'Nandos approached us for representing them in the court and we moved the High Court to have the order vacated. Mr Iqbal Chagla and Mr Darius Khambata were our counsel and we urged the court to examine the registration of Balkrishna's brand rather than focus on whether the names were similar. Balkrishna's registration was for dealing in frozen meat and chicken and we submitted to the court that we were not into frozen meat but sold cooked food in a restaurant. The legal point was whether registration of a trademark could be stretched under Section 29(4) of the Trade Marks Act 1999 to include similar goods while

## The sound of music

'In 2008, we were approached by our long standing clients, Sa Re Ga Ma, to represent them against Nassir Hussain Productions Ltd, in a dispute which seemed like the worst nightmare come true for a party in the midst of negotiations', recalls Chakrapani.

Discussions for executing an agreement for distribution of royalty were on between the parties and drafts were being exchanged when suddenly the talks broke down. One minute the parties were discussing commercials across the table and the next minute, in a complete volte face, NHP had invoked arbitration relying on some yet-to-be-executed draft agreement. Simultaneously, NHP made an application to the high court for injuncting Sa Re Ga Ma from dealing with the subject matter of dispute till the disposal of arbitration proceedings.

'Though harried but yet unfazed, we, led by senior counsel Mr J. Dwarkadas, prepared our defense and were able to prove to the court that there was no question of any arbitration being initiated as the agreement had not been concluded. We successfully convinced the court that the drafts exchanged between the parties were for discussion purposes and hence could not be construed as final agreement', says Chakrapani.

deciding on the infringement of a registered trademark. Upon hearing both the parties, the Court inter ália decided that it could not, and Nandos was set for business in India; even senior counsel were taking note of the firm', Chakrapani says.

Inaugurating the Indiabulls office in style. At the reception (R-L) are C.K. Dhanuka, Haigreve Khaitan, Mr Anthony Good, Chairman of Cox & Kings and Pinto Khaitan

'From what one hears, KCo is making it big in the field of transactional law and Haigreve Khaitan is taking it well ahead', says Mr Rohit Kapadia, senior counsel. He has done several interesting cases with the firm, one featuring two feuding Shah brothers where KCo secured a fair deal for its client. The two Shah brothers, C.D. (elder) and H.D. Shah (younger) were essentially in the realty business and in 1993, H.D. Shah opted out on the basis of an MOU to have mutually acceptable settlement. It involved the senior Shah paying Rs 20 crore to the younger brother. When the commitment was not honoured, C.D. Shah and family filed a suit in the Mumbai High Court for enforcement of the MOU and the matter was transferred to arbitration in 2002, being a family dispute, with the late Justice V.D. Tulzapurkar appointed as arbitrator. Parties filed their statements of claim and written statements.

Says H.K. Sudhakara of KCo: 'The respondents raised every possible defence, such as the MOU not being registered, the claim becoming time-barred and one of the respondents not having signed the MOU, amongst others. Issues were framed. Affidavits in evidence were filed but Justice Tulzapurkar passed away sometime in 2003 and the H.D. Shah family approached the high court for appointment of a new arbitrator. Justice D.R. Dhanuka, who was appointed by the high court, heard the matter and passed an award in favour of the H.D. Shah group'. The award was Rs 19.40 crore (balance payable under the MOU) plus simple interest of six per cent per annum from the date of the

MOU. As far as the unregistered MOU and claim time issues were concerned, Justice Dhanuka held that those defences were not available in a family dispute. This was based on the Singhania judgment. 'The interesting part of this arbitration was that, every possible application was taken out by the parties under the Arbitration and Conciliation Act and the arbitration went on for nearly 10 years and one would expect the C.D. Shah group to file appeal under Section 34', says Sudhakara. This matter was handled by Mr Rohit Kapadia, who also handled the Severn Trent Water Purification matter, which had interesting points of law as well.

More importantly, the firm had the right people to handle difficult cases and acquired in-house expertise even for non-legal areas of emerging requirements to help itself deliver well-rounded, perfectly competent service. Thus came about the invitation to Daksha Baxi, who heads the direct tax practice. Says Daksha: 'While KCo solicitors were extremely well versed with tax laws, Haigreve and others realized that like other areas of law, tax was fast becoming a specialized area, especially with increasing cross-border transactions and application of the principles of international taxation. They brought me in as a specialist in direct taxation within the firm'. Generally, direct taxation is looked after by chartered accountants. One could ask why a law firm wanted this specialization in-house. The simple answer is that taxation is today integral to international deals and firms consider it essential to have this expertise. 'When I was approached by Haigreve more than four years ago, I thought it was a fantastic opportunity. I was impressed with his vision that I found to be looking to the future; not too many law firms were looking at a direct tax practice but Haigreve said that the firm could do well with my support'.

Daksha's brief was taxation as a support for transactions and to establish it as an independent core practice area. 'I

## For a billion-dollar deal

Apax Partners is a $40-billion advisory firm, a pure play fund, engaged in long-term equity in five sectors (technology and telecom, retail and consumer, media, healthcare and financial and business services), headquartered in London. 'We set up in India four years ago with a seven people team and wished to continue with a global strategy that worked for us: focus on our sectors and work on large deals, not less than $500 million. A lot of our competitors in India were, of course, focusing on smaller deals but we had a long hard think and said that it would not make sense to have a different India strategy. We had a single partnership and fund structure and did not want to be different in India …so we chose to focus on $200 million to $500 million deals. There were no obvious deals in the offing; they would have to be created; they would have to be complex and it meant that we would need to be creative and the deals would need nurturing. Proprietary transactions were the obvious target and we would, therefore, have to be opportunistic', says Shashank Singh, Apax Partners.

'In terms of partnerships with legal firms, we wanted a firm that would be sensitive to our model. Several deals would not fructify. The idea was to partner with a firm that would not demand a lot by way of broken deal fees but be happy with good fees for successful deals. When we came in, we did try to forge some partnerships on this principle that did not quite work out. There was a real struggle for people's time and we would he handed over to the associates with little partner time given. We bounced from firm to firm and were dissatisfied till we came across Haigreve (in an unusual way) and started work on Patni ($1.22 billion acquisition of Patni Computer by US-based iGate) last October. We met and gave him the engagement from Apax to structure the deal in which we were funding iGate (a US Nasdaq listed company) and were backing them to go after Patni. We had our own set of advisers and we were doing diligence; investing ourselves and getting iGate to invest in Patni, which meant that Apax was doing due diligence on both iGate and Patni. We had met Phaneesh Murthy (earlier with Infosys) for a different deal that did not pan out but told him that iGate could be interested in an underperforming Patni.

'We found that KCo and Haigreve, personally, knew what they were doing: they had fantastic knowledge of the securities space and M&A law and we asked both iGate and Patni to use Haigreve as their counsel. What impressed us is that both Haigreve and Rabindra put in a lot of personal time. It was end December and they would be in our office at all hours of the day or night. Again, in the negotiations they took a very principled stand… It so turned out that one of the counterparties was Ashok Wadha from Ambit with whom Haigreve had a personal equation. Ashok tried to push for certain things as accepted market standards and Haigreve, to his great credit, did not accept it. Indeed, he pushed Ashok far more than we would have. That is what convinced me about his integrity… This was a highly successful, landmark transaction that we closed in May, 2011'.

have found no legal-accounting dichotomy because one is considering comprehensive documentation that has a substantive role for taxation. Besides, there is need for independent taxation advice not only for Indian clients but international clients as well who need advice on a broad front–on the new types of transactions involving carbon credits, financial services, the electronic commerce space and a host of emerging issues that need to be examined for characterization of income, thereby identifying its source and taxability in crossborder scenarios. This opens up tremendous opportunity for us. I joined on June 1, 2007, and, with the support of the firm and hard work, we have more or less met our targets even as we have built up a team with more partners that we are still ramping up'. Amongst others that Daksha handled was the E*TRADE matter with Sanjay Sanghvi.

Not only are new professionals coming in; generational contacts are renewing their relationships. The grandsons of Bhagwati Babu and his friend Sankardas Banerji were coming together in the 21st century. Says Devidas Banerji: 'After completing my law, I was working with Clifford Chance in England, one of the magic circle firms in London. In early 2007, I moved to their Singapore office to be closer to India. It was in Singapore that I first met Haigreve. Our families have known each other for three generations. My

## 'Retreat' to move forward

We started a 'retreat' for the Mumbai office as an annual get-together from 2006 at a nearby resort to which we also invited some of partners from other offices. There were about 35 participants in 2006 as the concept caught on and became an activity, which all the participants look forward to throughout the year. In 2007, the retreat moved to Goa; to Pondicherry in 2008, to Udaipur in 2010 and moved back to Calcutta in 2011, to celebrate the centenary of the firm. ITC Sonar, Calcutta, had more than 300 participants from all KCo offices, in a grand function, befitting the great occasion. It was indeed a proud moment for all of us when all the senior partners shared the stage and cut the Centenary Cake on 11.11.11! —*Nilanjan Ghose*

## The special KCo fabric

'My engagement with KCo has largely been with Haigreve yet I can see that the firm has a special fabric; a character that permeates through the organization. That is not applicable for most firms where one needs to develop relations of trust with certain individuals. For a professional services company, this fabric is very important because it makes for a consistency of characteristics that is a stabilizing influence even as it provides a sense of security to its clients' — *Gaurav Deepak, Avendus*

grandfather Sankardas Banerji and BP had worked together and I had heard of Pinto Khaitan from my father Shibadas Banerji. After I met Haigreve and had the occasion to see the Mumbai office, I started to form an opinion about the firm, that built on my initial comfort levels with the firm whose reputation I was familiar with, having known of it from Calcutta. What made the difference was that I found the firm to be at par with international firms in terms of working atmosphere and work ethic. It was a great atmosphere because there were like-minded, dynamic people around and the firm was progressive and on the upward trajectory. It was obviously a big move for me but both Mr Pinto Khaitan and Haigreve provided me with the necessary comfort levels and I felt happy with the confidence that they inspired'.

'Let me tell you something about Haigreve; he was 34 when I met him. For someone of his age, he is a person that you come across once in a generation', says Ravi Kulkarni. 'He has exceptional qualities as a lawyer, as a professional, as a human being, and is extremely humble. Only exceptional people can be humble because they know that they have everything in them. This is why he has achieved what he has in Mumbai over the past 10 years. Being a Khaitan may have helped but, even if he had not been a Khaitan, he would have led the firm to the kind of eminence that he has in the past 10 years. He has done this almost single-handedly. I feel extremely happy and proud of Haigreve's vision.

Pinto has, of course, been supportive and the guiding spirit'.

It is not just insiders who say BP's grandson is special. So do clients: 'Innovations on a job come in the manner one structures a deal and connects the dots. Sometimes I need Haigreve to figure things out under multiple heads and he has to consider the problem in its totality: this is the law, this is what you want and this is how you can put it together', says Gaurav Deepak of Avendus. Haigreve has the ability 'to simplify the problem and make the deal less messy. That is very important in our business. He also has a sense of the various issues that are of concern to us but what I honestly find most comforting about him is his ability to keep trust, be the nice human being that he is and innovate. Essentially, this means producing value beyond what one would normally achieve. Such people do not come in one package. Counselling the client is OK, developing trust over a period is good, increasing comfort levels is fine but channelizing discussions from various quarters towards a common goal and getting people to rally around that and making things happen is special', says Gaurav.

Devidas co-heads the banking and finance department, which is a new practice for the firm, and says: 'Having come here has been very satisfying from the work perspective and the response from clients has been very encouraging because within a short span of time, we have developed a strong reputation with some strong clients, including international

## The Marwari factor

Was being a Marwari firm ever a disadvantage? Says Haigreve: 'Not really, Mumbai is very cosmopolitan; people are not interested in the community you belong to but the work that you do. The community gave us access to such a wealth of clients and I found only advantages in being a member of this business community; the entire community supported us! Also, the fees were fantastic in Mumbai and often ran into tens of lakhs and we have been able to charge over a crore on several occasions; in one matter, we got more than Rs 5 crore for one deal'.

## PowerDesk

It was important to make full use of technology every step of the way and the Mumbai office engaged in the twin strategy of firm development initiatives and technology initiatives, especially to introduce software for recording timesheets and storing files. Dhruv Khaitan introduced them to the Pune-based software company, Uberall Solutions, and the two partnered over the years to develop software in-house for the most sophisticated of KCo needs. 'We named our software PowerDesk ,that literally runs the firm today; controlling information from the time an inquiry comes in to entering timesheets, preparing bills, accounting, all administrative functions, HR activities, communication related activities and much more'. The work does not stop as new modules of client relationship management or the knowledge portal are being worked on. 'All our offices are live on PowerDesk and getting the benefit of the hard work put in by the full team headed by Haigreve Khaitan, Tina Gosar our CFO and, of course, the Uberall team. All management reports are available at the press of a button in terms of productivity, work-in-progress, marketing reports and many more', says Nilanjan.

banks like Deutsche, DBS, HSBC and Standard Chartered and domestic banks such as Axis Bank, Bank of India and HDFC. Our speciality is in structuring banking deals on the lines of international practice, and this practice will grow. In the next few years, not only in terms of my practice, we see ourselves amongst the top-most legal firms in the country that will inspire other successful people to come back. A lot of people have returned to India from international practices because of the atmosphere and ethics here. KCo is definitely not run like a family-run firm, as one might have thought and which may have caused some initial reservation that was soon dispelled.' Indeed, the firm has actively sought to improve its credibility with the emerging legal talent.

'In our early years, when we went for campus recruitments, we would get the second or third-day slots, after everyone had recruited the best of the lot. We focused on getting good students for internships and showcased what we are; we consciously improved our profile with the law schools and today when we go for recruitments to the different National Law Schools, we are given the first slot on day one', says Rabindra.

Amongst the many people who have contributed to the phenomenal Mumbai growth is N.R. Kulkarni, former client, who also joined the firm to shore up its administration. 'KCo has had an amazing business growth at the Mumbai office. When it came to Mumbai it did two things: organizational planning and business planning; and divided the work into teams. The firm has a long-term strategic plan and

## Comfort zone

Kushagra Bajaj, present-generation business leader from amongst the old family connections, currently joint managing director, Bajaj Hindustan, says: 'My association with the firm is more of a personal one with Haigreve. If he is not there when I need him, I am not comfortable. While, indeed, our relationship goes all the way back to his father, it is his calm and composed nature and the firmness with which he articulates his understanding about what the client needs and the clarity in his mind about what the law says that provides one with the sense of comfort. I got to appreciate his calibre when we planned an acquisition once and found that he was leaving for Germany. I requested him to cancel the trip because we wanted to conclude the deal in three or four days. He did so and we interacted very closely then, working round-the-clock. What struck me was his interpretation of the takeover code that was very clear from day one; he logically and calmly convinced everyone that what he was saying was right, while the others wanted to stretch the law.

'The main point was that those being acquired wanted the money upfront and to hand over the shares to us. The law required us to make an open offer during which the shares would not get registered in our names. Technically, the Sebi has the authority to strike down a takeover, which was what Haigreve was pointing out. The others insisted that the Sebi had never invoked such authority or struck down a done deal and reversed a transaction and thus the issue of a sale reversal was a theoretical one in nature. Haigreve cautioned everyone about the rules of the game, especially when the sums involved were so large. Arguably, there were no such instances historically but the possibility of crores of rupees getting stuck because of a statutory issue was real. Haigreve single-handedly convinced everyone that the funds should be put in escrow to ensure that our risks were minimal. He wanted the law to be followed in letter and spirit and, being conservative by nature, I felt comfort in his position. I felt secure because he knew what we needed, the law, and did not want us to get carried away by our enthusiasm and keenness for the acquisition to go through. Eventually, it did not because the sellers were impatient but I am happy that we were correctly counselled and that our solicitor got everyone on our team on the same page'.

an operating plan for the year. It develops a list of strategic initiatives for the year, which is an important part of the plan to maintain its competitive position. In order to get commitment from partners, it gives them ownership of the various initiatives. Some of the successful ones are IT, training and knowledge management. For training, it has excellent facilities at a hall named Paathshala. The dining hall is called Eatopia and there is the pervading air of congeniality', he says.

The clients are impressed! Rahul Raisurana, Standard Chartered Private Equity Advisory (India) Private Ltd (R) and Samrat Zaveri, MD, Trendsmith (India) Ltd, share a happy moment with Haigreve and Ravi Kulkarni

Says Sudip Mullik, who helped set up the Mumbai firm from scratch: 'When we came to Mumbai, we had no choice but to specialize and I did the donkey's work in terms of conveyancing and litigation. We never had the concept of individual realizations. In Mumbai, the firm is divided into teams, the firm does well if the group does well and if the overall pie gets bigger, everyone gets more even if one's share in the total income is smaller'.

If Mumbai has meant money; it has also meant Bollywood; especially with a client like Sa Re Ga Ma. Only sometimes the melody has been off key. Chakrapani recalls a Wednesday evening when he was hit with the news that the movie, *Anjaana Anjaani*, to be released on Friday, would have a suit filed against its release. 'We were not representing the producer or the person with the grievance but acting for the music company that had sold a 40-second clip of a song to the producer of *Anjaana Anjaani*'. It was this 40-second clip that became the bone of contention and could have led to a restraint on the release of the Ranbir Kapoor-Priyanka Chopra starrer.

The plaintiff was the producer of yesteryear blockbusters, B. Subhash, who had assigned all music rights of the film *Disco Dancer* (of 'I am a disco dancer' fame) to Sa Re Ga Ma in perpetuity. In turn, Sa Re Ga Ma assigned rights to use a 40-second clip of 'I am a disco dancer' to Nadiadwala for use in *Anjaana Anjaani*. On the eve of the release of the movie, Subhash approached the Bombay High Court contending that he had not given the rights and that Nadiadwala had no business using his song in the movie. 'We had this difficult task of protecting the new producer, ensuring that the movie got released on Friday, without even being a party to the proceedings. Led by Mr Dwarkadas, we moved the court overnight and filed a parallel suit in the Bombay High Court asking for orders that we had a right to give away the clipping. Both our matters were heard on the same day and we were able to get the movie released as scheduled'.

For all the successes, there could hardly be a more self-effacing leader than Haigreve. He makes no bones about the fact that the success achieved by the Mumbai Khaitans 'owes itself to support that it received from both within the firm and outside; right from my grandfather and father'. He insists for ample measure: 'I do believe that I got accepted because of the "family" and that made things easy. A lot of clients came or started coming because of the family connection; because I was Pinto Khaitan's son'.

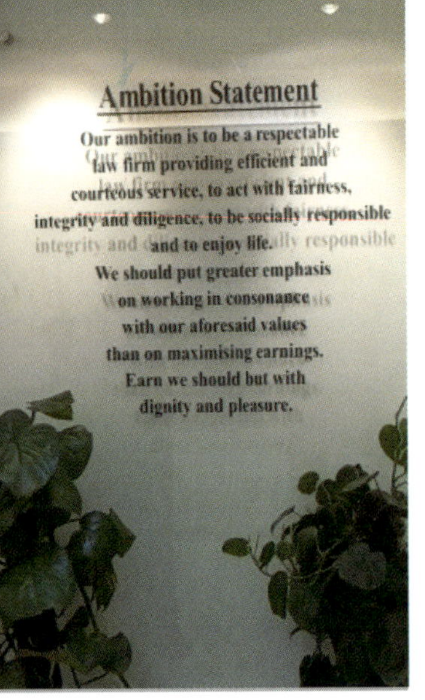


Ambition laced with ethics

Counters Kushagra Bajaj: 'Admittedly, I was introduced to Haigreve by Pinto Chachaji but we are not professionally associated because our fathers knew each other. The rapport between us has been built because of professional reasons and because of the comfort levels we have with each other. When we floated Bajaj Corp, I wanted him on my board but he was already on the boards of 15 other companies. I refused to take no for an answer and Haigreve quit one board to join ours.

'Today, Haigreve knows more about our businesses than possibly I do because he knows every little detail. At least 99 per cent of what we do on the corporate side involves him in some form or the other. It could be through an opinion or a second opinion even in areas that he says are not his forte. Our firms interact at the level of domain specialists but

## Progress Report

Bacchu Pal wraps up the firm's progress over the years: 'KCo has grown in the last three decades. First, they established an office in Delhi, then in Bangalore in 1993 and in Mumbai in 2001. I firmly believe that all these expansions and success was due to the policy of delegation adopted earlier and the efficiency of almost all the lawyers, solicitors or otherwise working as KCo. From time to time the firm had to be reconstituted as some severed their relationships but KCo withstood the exits. By and large the credit goes to Mr Pradip Kumar Khaitan, an astute legal consultant, capable of turning on his charm in critical situations. I am yet to hear anything adverse regarding his capability and integrity from anyone. His dynamism and the ability to carry his colleagues explain why the firm is considered as one of the most efficient law firms of the country. The sincerity and industry of Mr R.K. Choudhury, Purushottam Lal Agarwal, RNJ and Nand Gopal Khaitan have played their respective parts in the success. Two youngsters need special mention: Haigreve Khaitan and Rabindra Nath Jhunjhunwalla have, by their efficiency and intelligence, solidly entrenched the firm in Mumbai. In Calcutta, Arvind Jhunjhunwalla and Roopa Sheth work hard and keep abreast with the changing times, which are throwing up new challenges in the adverse industrial scene in West Bengal. Everyone that I have the good fortune to know is working as a team to ensure that KCo retains its position as a reliable institution in the eyes of its clientele as well as counsel who have worked with them'.

when it comes to finalizing anything, I need him to give it a once over even if he is not the specialist concerned'.

Other clients add to this perspective. 'It is very difficult to find someone like Haigreve. Hard work and intelligence are hygiene factors; so is trust. It is the strong sense of innovation that singles him out. He can help create value out of commercial innovation, which is the firm's forte that is not restricted to just law. I have also seen him carry people from both sides of a deal even the occasional obstinate person. Haigreve, a normally cool person, is capable of using his temper to good effect, and has once got a particularly difficult party to stop messing around with us. Over the years that we have known him, our transactions have increased and KCo is our internal counsel; when we raised money we used the firm. I have seen him on our side or on the opposing side – buying companies – and helping companies raise money and selling', says Gaurav Deepak.

What about foreign clients? It may or may not be easy for a foreign company entering India. Some do it with elan; some do it haltingly. Wolfgang Fobo, Regional Director, Asia/Pacific, Maurer Söhne, Munich, Germany, did so 'feeling as secure as a baby in its mother's arms' and is not miserly about expressing his satisfaction. Negotiating the acquisition of majority stake in a company needed a local scout who knew exactly how to navigate through a legal labyrinth that a foreigner may be confronted with. Says Rabindra Jhunjhunwala who handled the acquisition of 68 per cent of Sanfield India's stake from its promoters by Transtec Investment GmbH. 'Sanfield (India) Limited is a leading Indian construction company involved in design, engineering and manufacturing of high performance construction-related products, and repair and rehabilitation of bridges. The deal was concluded in January 2010 and KCo advised Transtec and its German legal counsel on all aspects of the transaction'.

The transaction was considered one of its kind in the bearings and expansion joints manufacturing industry, especially where a foreign company was keen to make inroads in a predominantly domestic market. Serving the Germans was never going to be easy but, as Rabindra says: 'I think, we did well and in the end have made great friends. They will think of us if they ever need lawyers in India'. Wolfgang Fobo, who represented the Germans, says: 'Even after the

## Dedicated professionalism

In the course of my association with KCo, I have also had the opportunity to work with Haigreive Khaitan, Chakrapani and other members of the Mumbai legal team. Each one of them, under the able leadership and guidance of my friend Ravi Kulkarni, has conducted himself with dedication and professionalism, which has taken KCo to the heights of success that it enjoys today even after a century of its birth.

— *Janak Dwarakadas*

A 100 years celebrated in style

deal was concluded over a handshake, one needed a legal expert to convert the negotiations into an agreement and do so in an environment in which the foreigner feels secure'. For him Khaitan delivered every inch of the way with its legal advice and documentation of the takeover issues, while advising the client on the 'minefields to be avoided, the safe payment terms for the execution date and of clauses in the contract that had to be formulated for protecting us'.

It has been a decade now. Has the young team made mistakes? 'Yes', says Rabindra. 'We have made mistakes. We have erred on the side of caution and have always ended up taking up less office space, because we were not sure that we would outgrow our space so quickly. We underestimated our potential', he says taking a hard look at the vast Mumbai office, teeming with people and a flurry of activity. The look says it all: there is growth in the air and the firm is rebranding itself for the next century: through an intensely worked out exercise to look within and portray itself as a dynamic 21st-century global player.

# THE CENTURION Takes a Bow

*We remain proud of our history and look resolutely at the future, heralding the wave of institutionalization of the legal profession in India. We want to be able to fall back on a hundred years of experience without fighting shy of reinvention. This firm bears a family name today; but, it is one of the most professionally organized firms in India.*

**— Haigreve Khaitan**

Everybody wants to be a KCo; certainly if the name is Khaitan and the man is an advocate. The firm had become a heritage brand and Gopal Mookherjee found himself defending brand KCo in a trademark case in which another person from Rajasthan got a Khaitan & Company registered as a services entity. 'I successfully defended the KCo (solicitors) in that trademark case, the plaint and the pleadings of which provide interesting material on the background and character of the firm. The applications provide details of its registered associations with international bodies and their application for registration of their trademark'. Clearly this was an attempt to trade upon and benefit from the reputation and goodwill of the heritage firm amounted to 'passing off' and marked an infringement of the firm's registered trademark, 'within the meaning of the Trade Marks Act, 1999', recalls Gopal Mookherjee.

Just as the brand Khaitan had to be defended, so did the legitimate demonstration of allegiance to the Indian flag by an Indian demand to be legally permitted. Gauri Rasgotra recalls the famous flag case in which Mr Naveen Jindal, now a member of Parliament and leading industrialist, wanted to establish the right of all citizens in India to fly the national flag, which was restricted by the Flag Code of India. 'After an arduous legal struggle in the Supreme Court from 1999 to January 2004, the apex court did grant to every Indian the right to fly the national flag in a respectful manner

Facing page: Cutting the centenary cake: R.N. Jhunjhunwala, N.G Khaitan, Ravi Kulkarni, P.L. Agarwal, Padam Khaitan and Rajiv Khaitan

in 2004. Mr Abhishek Singhvi, leading advocate, also a member of Parliament today, argued this case on behalf of our client who kept his spirits up despite the ups and downs of the case. It was also a brave judgment by the court and it is a matter of some satisfaction that we were able to take the issue to its logical conclusion by obtaining an order that enshrines the right to fly the flag. Among the most fascinating aspects of the case was the extensive research we were forced to do on the issue of freedom of expression in other countries on the rights of their citizens to fly their national flag and judgments of their courts in this regard', says Gauri.

Not surprisingly, KCo Delhi impressed senior counsel with its sincerity and indeed 'helped immensely in the detailed and complex arguments in precedent- establishing cases like the Singhania's case (2006), which rooted strongly the special status and special equity of family settlements; the CESC electricity case, which laid down the boundaries of the jurisdiction of state electricity regulatory commissions; and the contemporaneous, ongoing Satyam tax case, involving elucidation of the approach of tax authorities to successor entities where the predecessor had indulged in rapacious exploitation of the company', says Mr Abhishek Manu Singhvi.

Even the self-effacing P.L. Agarwal says: 'KCo has been involved in developing innovative models for creating securities to secure long-term finance from ICICI Limited when consortium lending was started by it, requiring the creation of security by depositing title deeds in favour of one of the consortium members, which was also accepted on behalf of other lenders. This mode of creating security was successfully followed and adopted by financial institutions and banks as valid and enforceable security'. Even the government can be moved by the characteristic Khaitan approach and, of course, courts can be persuaded by its effective strategies as Hemant Kanoria appreciated during the Dishergarh Power

## Padam vs Padam

It was quite a Kramer vs Kramer situation. Mr Padam Khaitan received a strange call from Mr Madhusudan Dalmia himself; his son-in-law's father. 'Why was his sambandhi suing him?' The normally unflappable solicitor was flummoxed. An equally incredulous Padam Khaitan asked: 'Why would I even dream of it?' Mr Dalmia, however, had the legal papers served on him by KCo! The mystery soon unfolded itself: a Jaipur-based lawyer, also a Padam Kumar Khaitan, who had started a firm by the name of Khaitan & Company, had sent the legal notice to Mr Dalmia and KCo, solicitors, found itself defending its nearly 100 year reputation through a case that Gopal Mukherjee handled. C.S. No. 23 of 2008 in the High Court at Calcutta, Ordinary Original Civil Jurisdiction featuring KCo vs Padam Khaitan. That set off another round of confusion and, once again, Padam Khaitan's telephone would not stop ringing. 'Was he taking on his own family firm?'

The defendant was injuncted from infringing the registered trademarks of KCo as well as passing off or attempting to pass off his business and services as the original KCo and ensure the destruction of all letterheads or visiting cards and business papers that may have been created using the KCo brand name. All's well that ends well as relations between the-laws ended in a big laugh while the encroacher realized that it did not pay to cross the real Khaitan.

Even Justice Sanjib Banerjee, presiding over the interlocutory court when the injunction petition was taken up for hearing, was confused into thinking that Mr Padam Khaitan was indeed in dispute with his family firm and had to be disabused of the notion. Once the confusion was cleared there was hardly any need for an argument before the court that granted ex-parte ad-interim injunction against the defendant.

takeover. 'The sunrise areas of legal practice in India will be in mergers and acquisitions, private equity, investments, competition law and such others. I am sure that KCo has developed its skills to capture the large emerging opportunities. Indian companies are going overseas now: opening offices and starting businesses and they need legal advice; there are international contracts and agreements to be made. These are the areas in which one expects the firm to be expanding'.

Meanwhile, not everything has been smooth sailing. Indeed, the more things change the more they remain the same. Liberalization had set the country free of many things but had not yet eliminated some of the ministerial baggage even in the more progressive ministries. The Texmaco case of the eighties that KCo has been involved with is a testimony to that. The Indian Railways, as one knows, outsources the assembly of its rolling stock. Sometimes, it provides the iron and steel, wheel sets, axles, bogies and couplers to the assemblers, who are often required to do no more than job work, albeit of a sophisticated nature. Texmaco, one such wagon maker, found itself stuck with an excise demand on the entire value of the wagon though its work was limited to assembling the product with parts provided by the Railways; the payment too was only for the value-addition that Texmaco provided and understandably did not include the value of the free-supply parts that were given to it.

The excise department was, however, stubbornly holding on to its demand that Texmaco pay up on the value of the final product. There were two issues here: to determine the assessable value of the wagon that Texmaco was supplying, which was owned by the Railways and, therefore, the correct assessable excise duty (which was none of Texmaco's concerns), which the Railways would have to pay. It was a matter between the finance and the railway ministries with an intermediary order supplier needlessly being implicated.

This was another case that C.M. Ghorawat handled. When the litigation reached the division bench of the Calcutta High Court, KCo counsel, Mr R.N. Bajoria, persuaded the judges to direct the two ministries, railways and finance, to sort out

## Aloft the banner

'With Gauri Rasgotra and her team, I have had occasion to do several landmark matters. I joked with the then (later Chief) Justice Khare that he had carried the flag case with him over several years and several adjournments from Court 6 to Court 1. We worked diligently with the entire Khaitan team on detailed written submissions with comprehensive global comparisons and the Supreme Court suo motu reproduced them in their entirety in its journal section. The judgment has been hailed as path breaking'.

*—Abhishek Manu Singhvi, M. P.*

## The ASPIRE equation

Piyush and Dhruv Khaitan, grandsons of Debi Prasad, have encapsulated the qualities that one looks for in a legal firm in an acronym, 'Aspire' that they find in abundance in KCo. The alphabets stand for accessibility, which is a major problem with other lawyers; strategic approach: the firm is never content with providing proforma, legally-correct advice but dovetailing it with the client's strategic needs; proactivity: one can be reactive, respond to situations or the brief or be proactive and go beyond the brief, anticipate issues and identify workable solutions; integrity: to be completely forthright about the ethical and practical sides of any situation so that the client knows where it stands; result orientation: to not just give theoretical advice but produce results and, finally, enjoyment: to stimulate a working culture replete with light-heartedness and laughter, so that the participants are not drowned in solemnity or tension. We like working with KCo because the people who work with us have demonstrated these features and in no small measure!'

the matter of the entire demand being raised on Texmaco. Good sense prevailed and the two ministries sorted out all the pending disputes, while Texmaco was exonerated of all the demands. Did matters rest there? Not quite; around 2011, Texmaco found itself facing another demand of interest under Section 11A of the Central Excise Act, arising out of delay in payment of duty by Texmaco to the excise authorities upon resolution of the earlier dispute.

Once again matters went to the Calcutta High Court that, in a judgment delivered on June 29, 2011, accepted Texmaco's submissions that any liability to pay interest arises only when the liability is crystallized or determined. In this case, Texmaco paid the moment it was determined. A division bench of Mr Justice Bhaskar Bhattacharya and Dr Sambuddha Chakrabarty quashed the huge demand on account of interest under Section 11A of the Central Excise Act, 1944.

Not just the government, the private sector too came up with cases that one can look back on with amusement. One featured burnt hearts over *Namastey London*! Aniket Agarwal, son of P.L. Agarwal recalls that case, which had all the ingredients of a masala movie. It was in 2009, when Mr Vipul Amrutlal Shah of Blockbuster Movie Entertainers and producer and director of several successful box office Hindi films had a problem. A Bengali film, *Poran Jai Jolia Re* (Heart on Fire), released in West Bengal, was substantially a copy and remake of a hugely popular Hindi film *Namastey London*, produced and directed by him. He came to KCo Calcutta, with the problem that was handled by Aniket Agarwal, along with Anshumala Bansal and Rusha Saha. Says Aniket: 'Hitherto, in India, a very narrow meaning had been ascribed to the word "copy" in the context of copyright infringement of a cinematographic film. It had been interpreted by some judgments to mean a carbon copy or replica in whole or part of the original'. KCo put

## Restructuring solutions

KCo continues to contribute significantly to advances in law facilitating corporate restructuring. The merger of group companies of Areva was a case in point. Says Aniket Agarwal: 'The addition of authorized share capital of the amalgamating companies to the authorized share capital of the amalgamated company as part of the merger was approved by the court without payment of any additional filing fee on the footing that such fee had already been paid by the amalgamating companies'. There was also the 'reorganization and reduction of capital as part of single window proceedings and clearance for sanction of mergers/demergers (Shrishti Infrastructure Development Corporation Limited); arrangements between corporates entailing transfer of undertakings for a combination of shares and cash consideration flowing to the transferor company itself (Tata Global Beverages Limited); and such like'.

Recognizing that all forms of corporate restructuring through court have their root in a fundamental economic need and event, the firm's approach has 'been to provide not only effective but timely solutions meeting the requirements of its clients. Achieving quick closure of the process and indeed expediting the same much before the usual mandated periods, in accordance with special needs of clients, has been the constant endeavour of the firm. Thus, for example, in the case of corporate restructuring of GKW and Graphite (both listed entities), the firm was able to achieve closure of process within a record time of 45 days, much to the delight of the clients. The firm continues to provide unique corporate restructuring solutions in these spheres', explains Aniket.

up a formidable team of Mr S.N. Mookherjee, Mr Ranjan Bachawat, Mr Ratnanko Banerjee, Mr Rudraman Bhattacharya, Mr Sayan Roy Chowdhury and Mr Subhasish Sengupta to address the uphill task, 'a challenge that the team took up with great gusto'. It meant pouring over numerous decisions and the facts, day after day and night after night, and, finally, filing a suit and application for interim relief in the Calcutta High Court.

It began in 1911; football was its fever pitch then. Football still excites the KCo boys

The interlocutory application was moved before the interlocutory court seeking ad interim order of injunction against exhibition and exploitation of the Bengali film. The application was heard for days and the court viewed both the films and found that the Bengali film was a substantial copy of the Hindi one and passed an interim order of injunction on August 10, 2009. The matter was carried in appeal and also heard at length by the division bench that considered the material and arguments and, by an order and judgment dated September 1, 2009, affirmed the decision of the court below, confirming the order of injunction. This was a very significant decision in the context of copyright law and was one of the very few instances where such an injunction had been granted against a cinematographic film, especially when the film had been released and exhibited in the theatres for a number of days. 'The court, inter alia, applied the tests laid down in the decision of the Supreme Court in the case of R. G. Anand vs Deluxe Films Ltd reported in AIR 1978 SC 1613 and the ratio of the Australian decision in the case of Seccola vs Universal City Studios reported in 46 ALR 189 and held that where there was a similarity in a film taken as a whole with another film there was infringement of copyright. The court understood the word "copy" in a wider sense'. The landmark judgment made the burning of midnight oil for a month well worth the while and 'ultimately the defendants settled the matter by admitting and acknowledging the intellectual property rights of the plaintiff and paying him an agreed amount for a retrospective license to use such rights', says Aniket.

Over the seven years that Nikhilesh Panchal has been with the firm, from April 2005, there has never been a dull movement. KCo and the legal world were going through a transition and the profession was transforming itself and adopting international practices in those days. 'The nature of assignments, the size of the transaction, the client and his expectations, just about everything was changing', while this heritage firm, with its roots at Calcutta, known for its tranquil ways, was moving into the hurly-burly of things. The welcome at the Ballard Estate office was fond; the colours on its wall were striking, the people were courteous and the first presentation welcoming. 'There was no looking back', says Nikhilesh.

The warmth of the welcome was supplemented by the challenge of the assignments that became addictive. 'Fulfilment for me was completing each of the challenging assignments; growth came with each fulfilment'. There were numerous mergers and acquisitions as those of Mil Pharm in the UK and Pharmacin in the Netherlands for Aurobindo Pharma; acquisition of Punjab Tractor by M&M and Kinetic's two wheeler business for Mahindra Two Wheelers; structuring and acquiring forging plants at Germany and UK for Mahindra Forging; doing

What Sudarshan Birla has to say...

**It is not often that one comes across such a distinguished history, which still continues to establish new landmarks, even after a full century. In keeping with tradition, the children of most major Partners of the Firm have since also joined the profession and are doing brilliantly well. The Firm - as it should - has always maintained a very high level of integrity and legal wisdom. There is a great emphasis on client relationships.**

**I extend my heartiest congratulations and best wishes to all the present Partners and participants of the Firm and express my highest regard and respect for the Seniors who are no more with us.**

**(S.K. Birla)**

## Continuous competence

Throughout his long association with KCo, Abhishek Manu Singhvi has found the firm to be 'extremely efficient and organized with multi-layered teams dealing with diverse aspects of procedural and substantive lawyering. I realized the strong bond of trust that it had developed with the top bosses and owners of the corporations that it represented, Marwaris and non-Marwaris alike. It was a bond developed painstakingly over generations'.

In Delhi, Sanjeev Kumar and his team have interacted with Mr Singhvi on several cases, especially relating to mining and environmental law, including those involving companies like Visa and Lafarge. 'Haigreve, Rabindra and their colleagues have assisted me in important corporate cases at Cochin while Pinto Khaitan, one of the sharpest legal minds with an intensely practical approach, has spent considerable time in high profile and complex cases like Birla-Lodha and diverse other corporate battles'.

There is hardly any Khaitan partner or associate, past or present, who has not worked with Mr Singhvi, 'except maybe a very small number of people from Calcutta. Apart from the names mentioned earlier, I can recollect Padam Khaitan (well prepared and conscientious), Krishna Kumar, Ashutosh Patra, Umesh and OP, Sanjay Khaitan, Suman, Praveen Kumar, Ajay and Vanita Bhargava, Rajiv Khaitan and many others who cannot find mention only because of constraints of space', he says.

the first Bank QIP for the Bank of India; East Asiatic Company's acquisition of the global brand, Farex; the acquisition of Gear Business by Mahindra Sar, a joint venture company, of which the Mahindras acquired the entire stake; the CDR of EPC Industries, the subsequent investment by the turnaround fund Schroder and bringing it out of the Board for Industrial and Financial Reconstruction's purview.

There was equally exciting work on the capital market front that Nikhilesh recalls: the Gammon IPO; the Mundra Port and SEZ Limited IPO; the Adani Power Limited IPO; the Idea Cellular IPO; the IPOs of Mahindra like that of Tech Mahindra, Mahindra & Mahindra Financial Services Limited and Mahindra Holidays; the Indiabulls Business Trust listing on Singapore Stock Exchange; the Cox & King Limited's IPO; the JSW Steel IPO; move KSK's listing from AIM market to the London Stock Exchange's Main Board;

the second largest rights issue of Central Bank of India; and the recent rights issue of Bajaj Hindustan Limited.

Says Nikhilesh: 'Besides, there is interesting advisory work relating to settlements amongst the Blue River Fund shareholders; structuring of online and wealth management group business for Edelweiss; the setting up of overseas subsidiary and step-down subsidiaries of Edelweiss Capital Limited; the structuring of promoter's shareholding of Godawari Power Co. Limited through a scheme of arrangement, amongst others. The interesting part of the work is the total commitment of the associates and colleagues in ensuring that each assignment is successfully completed. Nothing can be more inspiring for anyone than when colleagues provide tireless support with a never-say-no attitude and help one move into a transaction swiftly and accomplish timely turnarounds consistently'.

Each day comes with a new challenge and a new experience, at all the KCo offices. Amongst the more interesting

## Always by the side

'KCo has been an integral part of the group for the quality of the service that it provides. It is always available and always on your side', says Harsh Goenka. 'KCo lawyers bring such a breadth of knowledge in various areas of legal as well as commercial advice. I particularly recall a negotiation when they were more enthusiastic about the deal that we were pursuing than we were. The firm has always tried to find solutions to problems, be they around income tax or corporate law or structuring within the group. It has given us sane and practical advice. Legal firms trend to be aggressive and litigious. KCo has been legalistic but conciliatory... seeking to find solutions rather than focusing on problems. My experience with the firm is exemplary: not only do I, personally, get quality service, even our middle-level managers get it.

'What helps in our dealings is that the firm knows the history of each company in the group and while briefing it, we do not have to start from scratch; we can come straight to the point. KCo, actually, knows most of the nooks and corners of our office. Indeed, when we need to examine our own history and the people concerned have left, we ask the firm and it provides the necessary records because as lawyers, the documentation with them has been better'.

merger-demerger through court schemes in 2010 was a scheme of arrangement involving merger, demerger and restructuring of the Infotel telecom group of Punjab. 'Post-restructuring, it is being used by the Mukesh Ambani group for a fresh entry of Reliance Industries into the telecom sector. This transaction involved intricate financial restructuring, a complicated scheme that was most challenging and exciting', says Sharad Vaid. There was more excitement in advising the new management of Mahindra Satyam, following the Satyam scam, which has been amongst the most interesting matter that Gauri Rasgotra from KCo, Delhi, handled.

The case involved advising the beleaguered firm on a wide range of issues relating to corporate laws and income tax arising from the largest corporate fraud in India. 'It was an interesting and fulfilling experience. What made it worthwhile was the professionalism and dedication of the people that we worked for on this matter along with the uniqueness and topical interest of the issues involved these made working a pleasure', Gauri says. Apart from the advisory work, the matter also involved income tax issues, which went before the Supreme Court, which involved resolving inexplicable tax assessments from the department on fictitious, fraudulent income and sales that never existed. 'The matter was ably argued in court by Harish Salve and Abhishek Singhvi. Indeed if the income as assessed by the tax authorities existed, there would be no reason for Ramalinga Raju to be in jail! It has been wonderful working with S. Durgashanker (former CFO) and his team from Mahindra Satyam in this matter in which we were assisted enormously by Mr Ravi Kulkarni from Mumbai'.

Such cases came KCo's way probably because the firm has been at the forefront of corporate restructuring matters. Indeed, the firm has been known to handle restructuring requiring approval of the high court under the Companies Act with great distinction. It has advised and acted for several leadings corporate houses in Calcutta and other cities across a wide range of businesses by enabling various types of mergers, demergers and other arrangements. These include reverse mergers where holding companies (such as Techno Electric & Engineering Company Limited) were merged with their subsidiaries (Super Wind Project Limited) with the resulting company retaining the name of the holding company (Techno Electric); bifurcation-cum-consolidation between various entities (Dhunseri Tea & Industries Limited, South Asian Petrochem Limited and Dhunseri Investments Limited); de-subsidization by distribution of investment in shares in subsidiary to shareholders of the holding company (Pressman Group); repayment of capital in kind (Bata Properties limited); Pan India Mergers/Demergers involving entities and jurisdictions situated in various states (Philips group companies in Calcutta, Bangalore and Mumbai and Areva T&D group companies in Calcutta, Madras and New Delhi); amongst others, says Aniket Agarwal.

Amongst the most sensitive and complex cases handled by KCo in recent times is the Lafarge case, which has laid down

A centenary is time for fun: Pinto Khaitan at the firm Olympics

## Complex questions; competent response

A merger of two listed companies looked simple enough; both companies were owned by Siemens, Germany. Yet it turned out to be quite complex with labour issues, corporate laws violation issues, stamp duty issues and a property law related issues. Says Ajai Jain: 'The good part is that when we approach KCo, we had advice readily available on each issue. Once again, there was no question of payments for extra work. We had to complete the merger and the firm went the extra mile for us, made several trips to Ahmedabad, worked with another firm and handled a rather serious corporate law violation matter. The response time was very good and we achieved the target within the time agreed upon'. The companies were Siemens Healthcare Diagnostics Limited with Siemens limited, both listed entities and the merger was completed on March 2011.

important principles in environmental law and become a leading case in the field. The client was Lafarge Umiam Mining Private Ltd, a 100 per cent subsidiary of Lafarge Surma Cement Ltd, a Bangladeshi company. This is a joint venture between Lafarge SA, France and Cemento Molins, Spain. Lafarge Surma Cement of Bangladesh established a plant at Chhatak, Bangladesh, with a captive limestone mine at Nongtrai village, Meghalaya, which was leased to Lafarge Surma's 100 per cent subsidiary, Lafarge Umiam Mining Private Ltd. The cement plant in Bangladesh was totally dependent for its limestone supply on the Meghalaya mine to be supplied from the Indian state to Chhatak in Bangladesh through a conveyor belt.

The project commenced after comfort letters were exchanged between the governments of India and Bangladesh supporting the project. However, Lafarge Umiam Mining was directed to stop mining on the premise that forest clearance under Section 2 of the Forest (Conservation) Act, 1980, had not been obtained by Lafarge. 'It was stated that the area lies in the midst of a dense forest and no mining should be allowed to be carried on without first obtaining forest clearance', says Sanjeev.

'There were also allegations of fraud and deliberate concealment of facts levelled against Lafarge and it was in this backdrop that Lafarge filed a petition before the Supreme Court seeking a direction to the Ministry of Environment and Forest to grant forest clearance to Lafarge. The case entailed many intricate issues such as international relations between India and Bangladesh, environment vis-à-vis development, environmental clearance, forest clearance and mining in a tropical, moist, deciduous forest. Environment being one of the important facets of Article 21 of the Constitution of India, principles of inter-generational equity, doc-

## 'PG or not to PG'

St Xavier's had been granted autonomy but was that to hang like an albatross round its neck? BCom graduates from the college were suddenly confronted by the Calcutta University refusing to treat them at par with other colleges affiliated to it in 2009 for its post graduate courses. Some affected students filed a writ application under Article 226 of the Constitution of India before the Calcutta High Court seeking appropriate direction on the Calcutta University to treat them at par. St Xavier's College (Autonomous) was made proforma respondent and no relief was claimed against it. The high court directed the respondents to file the affidavit-in-opposition and the petitioning students to file their affidavit-in-reply and fixed a date for hearing. The college was in a fix: it wanted its students to be treated at par but could not openly support them in the court because, despite being autonomous, it had plenty of dealings with the Calcutta University. Moreover, the Pro Vice-Chancellor of the university was a member of the St Xavier's governing body. KCo was asked for advice and RNJ, who attended an emergency meeting of the college governing council, convened specially for this single agenda, advised the college to file an affidavit as required by the court but not to describe it as an affidavit-in-opposition or affidavit-in-support. Instead, he wanted the facts and documents to be placed for consideration of the court; to assist it to arrive at a just decision. This advice was followed and the court considered facts and documents that would be deemed to be beyond the access of the students and which the university could not disclose in affidavit. The court allowed the writ application and directed the university to admit them treating them at par. The college was spared the embarrassment; the students were spared the discrimination for all times. The university changed its rules to treat St Xavier's at par, thanks to smart some use of the legal system.

trine of proportionality, sustainable development and precautionary principle ex post facto clearance were involved. After detailed arguments, the apex court delivered the judgment and final order on July 6, 2011, in two parts.

The bench comprised the Chief Justice, Mr S.H. Kapadia, Mr Justice Aftab Alam and Mr Justice K.S. Panicker Radhakrishnan, with the judgment authored by the Chief Justice. More importantly, the court said that the guidelines issued by it would operate in all future cases of environmental and forest clearances till a regulatory mechanism was in place. The MoEF was directed to file a compliance report on the implementation of these guidelines within six months. 'This is a landmark judgment in the context of environment and mining, especially for projects involving use of forest land for non-forest purposes. The judgment dwells deep into many areas that were hitherto untouched by any judicial interpretation. We were led by Mr Fali Nariman, with Mr Mukul Rohatgi, Mr Abhishek Manu Singhvi and Mr Jayant Bhushan also represented us', says Sanjeev.

The Mumbai office exudes the same spirit of commitment and confidence. Mr M.L. Bhakta, who has observed the firm at close quarters, says: 'After the establishment of the Mumbai office of Khaitan, Kanga has interacted with Khaitan in a large number of matters, some relating to high property value and all, I repeat all, were happily concluded. Personally, I see a bright future for the young third-generation solicitor, Haigreve Khaitan. He is following the footsteps of his illustrious father in becoming one of the finest commercial lawyers in Mumbai. He has built a good team in Mumbai and, within a short span of time the Mumbai office of Khaitan has built substantial goodwill and reputation'. It is in the fitness of things that Khaitan has recently been named as one of Asia's fastest-growing law firms by *Asia Law Business*, a leading law magazine published from Hong Kong. All the while it retains its homely qualities, quite distinct from the dog-eat-dog attitude prevalent in many modern firms.

Says Ravi Kulkarni: 'Thus after I joined the firm, on the one hand, work started flowing, both Indian and international and, on the other, the firm literally anchored me through a difficult period, even as I gave my everything to the firm. We moved into Construction House at Ballard Estate and soon started outgrowing whatever space that we had taken. Today, even the current premises are inadequate for us. After three years of relentless efforts, I felt somewhat tired and asked Haigreve if he would let me go. I was told by Sudip Mullik that I could only leave in a coffin. However, since then I have not been totally hands on but have served as a mentor and senior partner'.

A tribute to the land of its birth

'When the Mumbai office opened, I came closer to the firm. Haigreve came to look for office space and we helped him. Indeed, he stayed at our guest house. In a manner of speaking, we feel that the Mumbai office started from our home and it fills me with great pride today to see the firm at Indiabulls Centre. It is like being in an investment bank in London in its heydays and I was amazed by the energy levels there and the buzz around that office. This is quite in contrast to established law firms in Mumbai that normally represent loads of files and cobwebs and renovation that never happened', says Harsh Goenka. Also, there were a lot of very bright youngsters working with the firm.

Bhavik Narsana joined KCo in April 2006 and walked into a non-stressed-out environment that must have been quite unique for a law firm. 'This was difficult to believe but it is true even today. I could notice people very calm and relaxed and enjoying their work. I felt at ease from the very first day itself'. Bhavik had a limited exposure to corporate law practice and proceeded to quickly learn

## Lafarge wins

The court allowed the Lafarge petition and dismissed that filed by one Shella Action Committee challenging the environmental clearance and the Stage 1 Forest Clearance granted to Lafarge, inter-alia on the following grounds:

- Invoking doctrine of proportionality, principles of sustainable development, inter-generational equity and the polluter pays principle in favour of Lafarge in facts and circumstances of case;
- The inputs provided by the local village Durbar of Nongtrai and the participation of the local people in the decision-making process;
- Invoking the need to maintain balance between environment and economic sustainability. It was held that the MoEF had taken requisite care to protect the environment. Under the circumstances, the stage-I forest clearance and the revised environmental clearances granted to Lafarge were upheld.

On the basis of these findings, the court found no reason to interfere with the decision of the MoEF granting site clearance, environmental clearance and stage-I forest clearance to Lafarge. The court also issued guidelines that would operate in all future cases of environmental and forest clearances till a regulatory mechanism was in place. The MoEF was directed to file a compliance report on the implementation of these guidelines within six months.

almost all his corporate law practice, courtesy the numerous cases that he got involved with. 'KCo was growing and there was a lot of work which gave a lot of exposure to its associates. In fact, once seniors got confidence, associates were given a free hand to handle the matters. At a very early stage I was given an opportunity to negotiate definitive transaction documents, which gave me a lot of confidence'. These set the stage for the young lawyer to manage a lot of work on his own, something 'that was a very important for my career', says Bhavik.

'I was trained by the best possible combination of individual lawyers, Haigreve and Rabindra. Amongst the many other things, Haigreve taught me to be practical, quick and commercial in my approach to matters, while Rabindra trained me to be more organized and have an eye for detail'. This is the essence of the training that has shaped him as a corporate lawyer as he successfully negotiated with Amarchand as lawyers for Warburg Pincus as the counterparty. 'That was the first time I was required to negotiate a matter independently. The meeting went on for a continuous 30 hours. By the end, I had learned a lot but, more importantly, I received a lot of praise from the clients, which was most satisfying'. Indeed, the firm continues to amaze him with its nimble-footedness, innovativeness and its ability to adapt to changing economic and market scenarios that helps it sus-

## Centenary recapitulations

'As we grew, we made a conscious effort to professionalize the firm. We are a cosmopolitan lot. Of course, what matters is quality and not size. Looking to the future, I feel so far our competition did not take us seriously. Now they will and will not be always fair. We must remember that a client will come to us because he needs us and not because we need him. We will have to serve the client with superior service on competitive terms. We have to deliver what he wants', said Pinto Khaitan at the Calcutta retreat on the occasion of the 100th birthday of the firm. He drew attention to an IIM professor saying that 100-year-old firms displayed some common qualities, determination and humility are two of them. 'We cannot afford to be arrogant or insensitive. A client looks for a solution and our guidance on what he should do. Very few clients are interested in an erudite discussion of the legal provisions and case law. Even in the past, our success has been because we could advise the client well in time (often on the phone) on what he needs to do and this advice stood the test of time. With laws getting more and more complex, we have to specialize. Earlier one person did everything. Today, most transactions require lawyers from different fields to collaborate. We have to be up to speed in every way. We have to put ourselves in our clients' shoes. We have to gear ourselves up for real competition'.

There was also the vast horizon ahead of a globalizing India. 'There will also be opportunity for law firms beyond India. As firms grow, they will be managed by professional managers. Firms may become incorporated entities, inviting investors like other ventures, as is happening overseas. All this will happen only when our political leaders see the wisdom of allowing Indians to become world achievers and do not get bogged down with the risks associated with it.

'We do not live in a perfect world. We have to make the best of the situation. We have to be ready for constant change. Networking and strong relationships with clients will go a long way in our progress'.

tain and improve its position in the legal market.

Similar experiences visited new arrivals at the Delhi office too that continued to strengthen itself, taking in new talent and inducting bright young people with global exposure that has made it a vibrant place to be in, while improving the quality of corporate and litigation work significantly. 'The induction of Bharat Anand as a partner in Delhi office in early 2009 has made a big difference in the working style in Delhi; it has instilled a sense of urgency in achieving greater heights, attracting international clients like Harley Davidson, Blackstone, Siemens and leading Indian corporates, even as we retain old clients', says Sharad. It has also attracted exciting talent.

How did Bharat Anand, who read law at Cambridge and worked at Freshfields, a 'magic-circle' firm in London, choose to come aboard KCo in 2009? Essentially, Bharat developed a healthy respect for the firm over interactions with it from the other side while at Freshfields. Ever since, KCo has provided excitement and adventure in his life on the one hand and a fascinating workspace on the other. 'The bottom line is that KCo is very fertile ground for a cross section of local and international talent to combine and seek professional fulfilment in an enabling environment'. Excitement came to the fore in April 2009, when Bharat got a phone call from Anoop Prakash, CEO, Harley Davidson, India.

His first requirement was total confidentiality around the prospective assignment because it was a project that would make quite a few motorbike aficionado hearts go aflutter if they got to know about it. For KCo it was a matter of donning its 'can-do' hat and getting to work. Anoop wanted the firm to help it import a dozen 800-plus cc bikes in India for it to be able to launch the vehicle in the country, while ensuring that the matter was kept 100 per cent under wraps, even while securing all necessary clearances and ensuring that there would be no last-minute hold-up by the customs. Everything had to be done in a fortnight: not a mean thing to accomplish in India. Says Bharat: 'The critical driver was to actually make it happen; not to get it stuck in customs for this was a publicity-backed event and yet had to have all the surprise element'. The event was a great success and Harley has since expanded its distribution network in India amidst growing popularity with its fans. It is not the bike that provided the best of adventures though, nor the heaviest of weathers.

Here were Bharat Anand and Aditya Jajodia of Assam Company flying to Toronto for a major mine acquisition when all aircraft over the Atlantic were grounded. The two men of business from India had flown into the Icelandic volcanic ash crisis and were forced to take a detour. It meant going to Toronto via Greece, making it after a gruelling 24-hour travel and just about in time for the meeting. This was in April 2010 and Bharat recalls: 'There was just time for a shower' but the good news was that it turned out to be a very successful outing for Assam Company.

Says Bharat: 'Every deal has its high! Recent exciting experiences include negotiating the sale of Andhra Paper Mills to the $30-billion International Paper. We were against a formidable and experienced team, at least four or five times our size!'. Size does not matter; mind power does as more partners realized as they joined KCo. The clients agree. Says Amit Mehta of the L.N. Bangur group: 'It is always a great experience to work with KCo. What I am telling you is not something that I would say lightly: had it not been for their help, we would not have been able to stitch together a deal lauded by the market as a landmark and game-changing deal in the pulp and paper industry'.

Daksha with N R Kulkarni and Pinto Khaitan at the KCo Retreat

The L.N. Bangur family sold its stake in AP Paper for about $300 million to International Paper, the world's largest pulp and paper company, with a $25 billion turnover. 'For us, KCo was not just a law firm, giving opinions on matters

## Justice V.N. Khare, Former Chief Justice, Calcutta High Court

A 100 years is a great event in the life of a firm of solicitors for no institution can survive and flourish for so long without excellent standards and values and KCo certainly fits into the category of institutions with abiding values. It is not just that the firm has come thus far with an excellent reputation, it has in the process contributed some outstanding luminaries to the legal world. Judges, jurists and lawyers have worked with this firm. In the process, it has served the interests of law, of society, brought justice to those who deserved it and brought an awareness of law to those who were unaware. Even today, I do interact with members of the firm in the course of the some arbitration that I handle and I find them to be meritorious, hardworking, honest and straightforward. Certainly the firm has a bright future.

of law and preparing the legal documents. Haigreve Khaitan was one of the members of the core team of just three people, Bharat from the Delhi office, Bhavik and Daksha, along with the rest of the KCo team, who helped us swing the $300 million deal'. Clearly, this is one client that looks forward to a continuing relationship with KCo. 'It is a formidable one and shall set new benchmarks', says Amit. Sreyash Bangur hits the nail on the head when he talks of the 'hassle-free' relationship between firm and client: 'In the two years of our association, the only email that I have exchanged with Haigreveji is about the centenary celebrations!'

Supported by old colleagues and new, old clients and new; KCo continues to move ahead. Representing Hari Shankar Singhania before the Supreme Court in relation to the appointment of an arbitrator under the Arbitration Act, 1940, was like strengthening historical ties. The disputes related to the distribution of immovable assets of the Singhania family. 'When the client came to us, he had already lost in two courts and was apprehensively exploring the possibility of moving the last court of appeal', says Gauri. 'I worked with Mr Pinto Khaitan on this matter and, after a careful study of the issues, we convinced the client that the judges of the court believed in equity and looking at such a long and tortuous litigation between the families, may be induced to grant appropriate relief. We briefed Abhishek Singhvi and Parag Tripathi in this matter. A lot of hard work went into this and, after much research and written on several points of arguments, the court indeed gave a favourable order to our client'.

Old principles and modern management have served the firm well and 'today we need to take the next big decision on whether we should remain an independent firm and compete with global firms or join hands with a like-minded global law firm. Clearly the focus has to be the world even as the world comes to India. Just as Kumar Mangalam Birla has become an Indian MNC, or the Tatas, with footprints across the world, we too need to have a global presence. So far there is no Indian firm in the legal space that has gone in for a global presence. Globally though, there are so many mergers amongst legal firms, there are transatlantic mergers... These do not necessarily mean loss of independence; they actually mean a sort of networking under a common brand name and thus what obtains is not necessarily one global firm,' says Pinto Khaitan. How tough has the going been despite the wealth of talent in the firm and its unparalleled knowledge heritage?

Says Mr Pinto Khaitan: 'The problem is that things change slowly in India. Mindsets are hard to change. We have archaic laws, archaic judicial systems; we have people ignoring the law and the law enforcers not enforcing them. We do not even allow law firms to advertise to the extent that the Bar Council advised us to close down our website because it was deemed a transgression to have one.

'Yet the big four consulting firms with multidisciplinary practices, including legal practices, are allowed to have websites and talk about themselves. The law changes slowly in India and no one is interested in understanding the need to change to allow Indian law firms to spread their wings

Celebrating the centenary in style. Haigreve Khaitan, Pinto Khaitan, R.N. Jhunjhunwala, Ravi Kulkarni, P.L. Agarwal, N.G. Khaitan, O.P. Agarwal and Padam Khaitan

globally. Truly speaking, India seems like an obstacle race and one has to learn how to run it to succeed'.

Times are a changing. As the former Chief Justice of India, Mr P.N. Bhagwati, says: 'There was a time when a lawyer was regarded as a family friend. He commanded respect. At present the public image of lawyers is far from satisfactory. They are regarded as fortune seekers rather than persons engaged in service to the society. In short, the profession of law has become a money-making racket, forgetting its obligation to the society. Of late, lawyers seem to operate on the law of demand and supply of law. Commercialism has overtaken the profession by and large. Lawyers have forgotten their social obligation; that they are the guardians of noble ideals and tradition and obligation to serve people of the country who are suffering from want and deprivation who have no means or capacity to obtain their legal rights'.

Where does he place KCo? 'The point is that the senior partners of KCo have not indulged in frivolous litigation. On the contrary, they have always followed the dicta of Abraham Lincoln who told the lawyers of his time: "Discourage litigation, persuade your neighbours to compromise whenever you can, point out to them how the nominal winner is often the real loser-in fees, expenses and waste of time"', says Mr P.N. Bhagwati.

Consider KCo from the perspective of Apax Partners, which is amongst the world's largest and best-established private equity firms: 'We greatly appreciated the work and we have hopefully found the partner that we can work with. KCo is working on our other deals (having concluded the billion-dollar iGate-Patni deal, amongst the largest in the Indian IT space) too. Essentially, the firm has an excellent reputation, especially around securities law and is creative around structures, which is the core of the matter. It is easy for lawyers to say no on the basis of a routine perusal of the law. Good M&A lawyers find ways to break new grounds as the business expands. KCo thus has a great attitude and a great approach to work. A service provider needs to provide the service and that is the important orientation that the firm has. All round, the team has impressed me: Haigreve, Rabindra, Akash (who got promoted to partner after the deal) and, generally, everyone helped and today you are looking at a satisfied client', says Shashank Singh. There is much more excitement that lies ahead.

Says Kushagra Bajaj: 'I have seen the firm grow under Haigreve from Ballard Pier to Indiabulls; adding more people and costs and being successful. He has been rewarded but you do not get rewards if you do not take risks. I am happy that he came to Mumbai, which is where corporate India exists... not coming here would have made things difficult for the firm'.

## Inspiration from within

This institution will run on systemic excellence but it will remain transparent. We combine the old with the new, we maximize earnings but with dignity and pleasure. We work hard to enjoy life. I see us as an amalgam of these and every other contradiction that brings out the very best in us. We shall move from strength to strength because of the unflinching will to excel that has carried us so far.

— *Haigreve Khaitan*

In terms of headline grabbers, it still has the first client of a hundred years ago. KCo is representing the Birla family in the matter relating to the will of Priyamvada Devi Birla. The proceedings before the Supreme Court in the criminal matter and the five trusts created by M.P. Birla and Priyamvada Birla has been another rewarding experience for its advocates. Says Gauri: 'The estate of Birlas was valued at Rs 5,000 crores (around $1.1 billion). This was another very high-profile litigation in which I was lucky to be involved and which resulted in working with two eminent lawyers. We briefed Ram Jethmalani and Mahesh Jethmalani in this criminal matter, which went in favour of the Birlas. I worked closely with N.G. Khaitan on this matter'. However, there was nothing like sealing a billion-dollar deal for a firm that earned Rs 3 as its first fee a hundred years ago; nor perhaps something as heady as settling a Rs 1,400 crore deal for a client in international negotiations.

November 11 seems to do exciting things for KCo. It seemed to be normal enough meeting with a French client, Seenk, in 2009, which was planning to take over a small company and getting into the design school space. Then the magic began to happen over several rounds of meeting at 1IB, when the client and firm took to each other. As design experts, the Seenk team took a keen interest in the way the firm worked, the way it had appointed its office, its stationery, various branding material and made an important observation: 'You have so much history and are a top-class law firm but somehow your existing branding does not do justice to what the firm stands for; it does not adequately represent the firm'.

This got Rabindra going. He had been passionate about standardization and had worked on the KCo branding, bringing about changes over time. 'Our black-and-white logo was added to the email signature, stationery across all offices was standardized and, after moving to Mumbai, the stationery was redesigned across offices. For the first time our logo was placed at the firm's reception; we started focusing on branding and introduced colour into the logo, the KCo stationery and pitching material. Blue looked good to us and we used that consistently; we were showcasing the brand as other professional companies did; presenting it not only by its services but also by a unified, firm, wide visual style, its brand, colour, stationery and pitching material, printed matter and the like'.

Yet it needed the Seenk comment to prompt some thinking on re-branding. The centenary, a year-and-a-half away, would provide the perfect launch pad. Everyone got excited and set firm goals of coming up with something that would establish it as a strong brand name in the industry with a unique and distinguished visual identity to set it apart from the other leading firms in the country. The look had to be international and exude a standard at par with the best in the world while maintaining the proud-to-be-Indian image. 'We were willing to let go of the traditional concepts and embrace the modern, through a new look and feel, new forms and colour', says Rabindra. The business development team, along with Aakash, Ashish, Nilanjan, worked tirelessly along with Seenk to capture all the elements and deliver a very sophisticated and world class product. 'The new Khaitan logotype is the emblem which represents the brand, we have taken the route based on continuity, keeping the logo more conservative with a shape but making it more contemporary and stylized. It reflects the values that the firm advocates. Here is a 100-year-old firm with a lot of history and yet vibrant and modern'.

Says Seenk: 'The designer's speciality is his ability to understand his client. However, an interesting inversion takes place when the designer becomes his client's client. This becomes an ideal situation for developing one's objectivity'. When Seenk first saw KCo's visual identity, as expressed in its email signature, it was a bit concerned that its only option would be to go in for an 'evolution'. On the one hand it was impressed by the brand's professionalism, its rigour and modernity and, on the other, it found the logo rather old-fashioned and lacking in punch. It was, however, confident enough about its relationship with KCo to be able to speak its mind.

Even so, the initial designs proposed were conservative; it was as though we were putting continuity before real change. 'In the end, we realized that expressing a veritable ambition, modernity and creativity could only be achieved through evolution. We began by rotating the diamond through 180° and saw it as an open, rather than as a closed structure. A ribbon, which ran around the diamond offered the twin notions of human endeavour and of a service sector company. This interlacing ribbon further distanced the identity from its previous hegemonic stature, static and self-sufficient. Rather, human solidarity, talent, competence and complementarity all began to surface in the identity, giving expression to a strength comprising intelligence and tranquility', says Seenk.

Intelligence and tranqulity: these seem to be the abiding images of the Khaitan approach to things – complex or simple, more often the former. Dealing with complexities of the law, of the mind, of emotions and egos. Who better than Phaneesh Murthy to talk about these qualities as he encountered them during the iGate takeover of Patni? 'As I look back, we were doing very complex transaction: not only was a smaller firm buying a bigger one – it was a leveraged buyout in which a public company was buying another public company with primary and secondary listings in the market – there were serious emotional issues on the part of the sellers. I think we were looking for a firm that understood all the issues involved in terms of cross-border debt and capital markets and also, in many ways, advise us on handling the emotional

aspects. Khaitan was able to help us through the emotional roller coaster of this journey thanks to its unique understanding of the Indian culture.

'Important though that was, there was also, very specifically, the understanding of and networking within the industry that enabled the firm to feed us with intelligence from time to time that was a bonus. Most importantly, what I really admired was the extreme business focus to law that the firm brought to the table that made a phenomenal difference to the deal'.

Getting set for a double century. Pinto Khaitan sets the vision

How would Haigrieve deal with Phaneesh's qualms? 'Haigreve's typical language to me was: "Phaneesh, tell me what you want and I will figure out the right process to achieve it without taking any risks". That to my mind was the real thing. Yet there were also very important aspects around the firm's knowledge of the details, of some of the quirky features of the takeover code in India that helped us a great deal'. Essentially, Naren Patni had requested that certain monies be paid to him on certain accounts – small amounts in the overall scheme of things – but Haigreve refused to let iGate pay because he knew that any amount paid would be construed as part of the overall consideration and then have to be a part of the offer to all shareholders. 'Through his intricate knowledge of the code, he genuinely protected us in areas we did not even know that we needed protection. Here the firm served less as a legal partner and more as a business partner', says Phaneesh.

Even more was the firm's commitment to the deal in terms of time. 'It was available to us 24x7, which was particularly important because we were doing the deal, across multiple locations. I was in California for the large part; the sellers were also partly in India and partly in the US and had lawyers both in India and the US. Yet we managed to wrap it all up in four months from start to finish because of the amazing commitment of the partners. It is so easy to shake your hand over a deal. The devil is in the detail but they turned out everything so quickly, ensuring that we stayed true to our focus and that the other party too stayed true to the focus. In this the firm went beyond the call of duty. In this it was quite phenomenal'.

To repeat a phrase from Phaneesh: 'Tell me what you want and I will figure out the right process to achieve it without taking any risks. That is the essence of the Khaitan mental lexicon as far as its clients are concerned. That is the management focus that it brings to issues; that is the bullseye that it seeks to hit with its legal strategies. Most importantly, that is the commitment that it made to itself a hundred years ago: November 11, 1911. That is not just a date that astrologers might find of import or others dismiss as just a number. It is a date when the sons of Naurangrai Khaitan made their tryst with destiny; at Calcutta's revered Kali temple. What pledge did Debi Prasad make to the mighty goddess that day one does not quite know. The 'prasad', a hundred years down the line, is quite divine; the pledge redeemed a hundred times over.